MENDING *the* MOON

TOR BOOKS BY SUSAN PALWICK

Flying in Place
The Necessary Beggar
Shelter
Mending the Moon

MENDING
the MOON

SUSAN PALWICK

A TOM DOHERTY ASSOCIATES BOOK
NEW YORK

MENDING THE MOON

Edited by Patrick Nielsen Hayden

A Tor Book
Published by Tom Doherty Associates, LLC
175 Fifth Avenue
New York, NY 10010

www.tor-forge.com

Tor® is a registered trademark of Tom Doherty Associates, LLC.

Library of Congress Cataloging-in-Publication Data

Palwick, Susan.
    Mending the moon / Susan Palwick.—First edition.
        p. cm.
    "A Tom Doherty Associates book."
    ISBN 978-0-7653-2758-1 (hardcover)
    ISBN 978-1-4299-8715-8 (e-book)
    1. Murder victims—Fiction.   2. Suicide victims—Fiction.   3. Mothers and sons—Fiction.   4. Friends—Fiction.   I. Title.
PS3566.A554M46 2013
813'.6—dc23

                                                        2012043362

Tor books may be purchased for educational, business, or promotional use. For information on bulk purchases, please contact Macmillan Corporate and Premium Sales Department at 1-800-221-7945 extension 5442 or write specialmarkets@macmillan.com.

First Edition: May 2013

Printed in the United States of America

0 9 8 7 6 5 4 3 2 1

For Jim Winn

PART ONE

1

*M*elinda Soto, four years old, looks out her bedroom window and sees the full moon, orange and bulbous, rising over the Washoe Valley. Melinda has seen the moon before, has listened to her parents explaining why it waxes and wanes, but she has never noticed the pits and shadows on its surface. In her picture books, as in the pictures she draws herself—at school and at home, in bold marker or wavering pencil or the waxy smudge of crayon— the moon is always purely white, as spotless and serene as a newly peeled egg.

Now she rests her arms on the windowsill, breathing the wildness of sagebrush and frowning up at the orange circle marred with dark blotches. "Mama!" she calls, and a little while later her mother, smelling of soap and sweat from mopping the kitchen floor, comes up behind her with a hug. Melinda could have gone to find her mother, indeed half expects to be scolded for not doing so, for interrupting kitchen tasks, but she's afraid to lose sight of the moon, as if only her gaze keeps it safe.

"What is it, baby?"

"The moon's dirty. Look. There are spots on it."

She can feel her mother's smile, a warmth at her back. "That's how it always looks. You just never noticed before."

"Can you wash it?" Melinda wonders if Mama could mop the moon, the way she mops the floors.

"No." Mama laughs. "I can't wash it. No one can wash it. It's too far away. And anyway, those aren't stains. They're holes. Craters where things crashed into the moon. Rocks. Big rocks that move through outer space."

"People throw *rocks* at the moon?" Melinda is both astonished and indignant. Why would anyone want to hurt the moon, and how could anyone throw a rock that far?

"No. People don't throw them. They're rocks that fly through outer space. They're called asteroids. A long time ago, some of them crashed into the moon, and now it has craters. Like when your ball bounces in the dirt, and it leaves a little scooped-out place."

"But you can fill the dirt back in."

"Here you can, yes. But not up there."

"The moon doesn't look right," Melinda says, her words definite and her fingers clenched on the windowsill. "I want to fix it."

"You can't, honey. That's the way it is. You can't get there to fill the dirt back in. It's too far away for mending."

Melinda resists the urge to suck her thumb, a habit she has only recently broken. Sucking her thumb would mean she was a baby again, and surely only a big girl can mend the moon. She likes the word "mend"—her mother's word, a grown-up word—likes how the m sounds in mend and moon and Mama blend into mmmm-mmm, into the sound for happiness, or for someone thinking, or for cleaning. Mop. But the more she stares at the pockmarked moon, the more the shadows look like bruises, like the painful places on her knees and elbows when she falls. "I want to anyway. I'm going to. Will you help me?"

Mama kisses her head. "As soon as you tell me how, I'll help you with all my heart. Let's get into bed now, all right? Sleep tight, Melinda. Sweet dreams."

Melinda never finds a way to mend the moon, but decades later, all her friends will know the story of how she promised herself that she would when she was a child. It is, she often says, her origin story.

Sixty years later, in a dormitory at the University of Nevada, Reno, Jeremy Soto wakes up on the floor of his room. He has a headache, and his face is glued to the latest issue of *Comrade Cosmos* by a trail of drool.

He groans, rolls over, and looks at the clock. He remembers groggily that he fell asleep after lunch, thanks to spending too long in the CC chat room last night. Now it's five o'clock, and his English class starts in half an hour, and he hasn't even finished reading the book, which has to be the most boring thing ever written. *Cranford.* A book about lonely old women: no wonder Very Bitchy assigned it.

He gets up and makes his way to his backpack, a journey of three feet that requires him to sidestep two piles of textbooks, three dirty socks, and an empty pizza box that's several days old. He isn't even sure which of the books and socks are his and which are his roommate's. On the way, he glances at the mirror over his bureau. His hair looks like stuffing coming out of a torn couch, and the trail of drool shines faintly white against his dark skin.

Pathetic. "This round to the Emperor of Entropy," he mutters.

He rummages in his backpack and finds his copy of *Cranford.* He's been using a crumpled copy of the class syllabus as a bookmark, which at least makes it easy to figure out how much more reading he has to do.

He checks the syllabus, checks his place in the book—he's forty pages behind *last* week's assignment—and checks the clock. Twenty minutes to class. This is not going to work.

The logical approach would be to skip class, but VB has a strict attendance policy. He's already used up his three allowed absences. Any more will hurt his grade, which isn't exactly great to begin with. He could always hide in the back of the room and hope VB won't call on him, but since she's one of his mother's best friends, that's dicey, too.

He speed-flips through *Cranford,* wondering again why he signed up for this section. What was he thinking? That Very Bitchy would go easy on him because she's known him since he was three? They've never liked each other. Mom still tells the story of how he bit VB the first time she babysat and tried to get him to eat spinach.

Cranford. Literary spinach, with a hefty dose of beets. His friends in other 101 sections are reading, like, two-page essays and newspaper columns. Very Bitchy has them reading fucking endless British novels about old ladies.

And Mom's coming home from Mexico tomorrow. He's already gotten her postcard; she sends one every trip. One to him, one to VB, one to Aunt Rosemary. Rosie's not really his aunt, but she's Mom's other best friend, even if she and VB don't get along much better than he and VB do.

Mom prides herself on finding the perfect postcard for each person. Jeremy's shows sea turtles swimming past coral, probably because he had a series of pet turtles when he was a kid, although they kept dying. Lame, Mom.

Her neat, tiny script covers the other side.

Sitting at sunny poolside. Great food here: you'd love it. Just met guy your age, Percy, who likes CC too. He was impressed that I'd read some issues. His mom won't go near it. I told him I couldn't talk about the discussion boards; that's your territory. Snorkeled with turtles like ones in pic. Miss you. Be good. Love, Mom

When she's back home, she'll call him to have lunch, and maybe he'll be able to get out of it for a few days, but eventually, he'll have to face her. She'll ask him about English, and he'll tell her it's going fine, because he can't tell her that one of her best friends is the worst professor on the planet. And she'll ask him what he wants to major in and he'll have to say that he doesn't know yet, except that he knows he doesn't want to major in English.

And she'll ask him how Spanish is going—or worse, try to speak it with him—and he'll have to tell her it's going even worse than English. He didn't have to take Spanish at all; he had four years in high school and managed to pass, barely. But when he was signing up for classes, Mom insisted that he take a Spanish conversation and culture class, so he wouldn't lose his roots.

His roots are Guatemalan, not Spanish or Mexican. He told her that. He even tried telling her that if she wants him to study his roots, he should be learning K'iché, not Spanish. That promptly sent her to the Internet to find somebody at UNR who taught K'iché, which promptly sent *him* into a speech about how he doesn't care about his roots; *she's* the one who cares about his roots, and if she cares so much, why doesn't *she* learn K'iché? Why can't she let him be an American? Isn't that why she brought him here?

And she said that it was important for him to learn about where he came from, and he said fine, and did just enough research to figure out that if your birth parents were Mayans who spoke K'iché and were probably slaughtered by Spanish-speaking troops funded by the CIA, English and Spanish are the *last* languages you'd want to study.

And she said, yes, she could see his point, but English was required in college, and Spanish was really useful.

How can she complain that they never talk?

And why'd he cave in to the pressure, anyway? He's the one taking the classes, and he doesn't need Spanish to graduate. Next semester he'll only take things he either has to take or wants to take. It's his life. He has to stop letting Mom control him.

He looks at the clock again. Fifteen minutes until class, and it takes ten to get there. Crap. Think, Jeremy. Panic is not your friend. Panic is the ally of entropy. That's what Comrade Cosmos always says, and he's right. There's more than enough entropy in the room right now anyway, with the socks and pizza box. Jeremy really has to clean up. He's good about picking up after himself at home, where he has Mom to nag him—although she's a fine one to talk, with her rocks and books and lists scattered all over the house—but here, everything winds up in heaps on the floor. Entropy.

In his psych class, which is required but much more interesting than Spanish, the prof talks about internal and external loci of control, how people with external loci are less mature than the others. Mom, Jeremy's pretty sure, would completely agree.

Maybe he should have lived at home this semester after all, like she wanted him to. But that would be caving again, and the dorm really is more fun, and if he didn't live on campus, he'd have even more trouble getting to class on time.

Ten minutes to *Cranford*. Time to go. He hears Mom's voice in his head: *Get a move on, kiddo. Time's a wasting.*

He crams the novel back into his backpack, shoves on his shoes, and does a quick visual scan for his cell phone. He can't find it. All right, never mind: VB takes a very dim view of phones in class anyway. But just as he's shrugging into his jacket and getting ready to sprint across campus, he hears the theme music from the latest CC movie, the triumphant "March of Order Restored."

That's his phone.

The music's coming from under one of the pizza boxes. Cursing, Jeremy shoves the box aside with his foot and scoops up the ringing phone. If it's somebody important, he'll answer it on his way to class.

Unknown Caller. Probably a telemarketer. Jeremy sighs as he

turns off the light and leaves the room. He'll have to remember to put the phone on silent before he walks into class.

"Hello? Yes, this is Jeremy. Who's this?"

*f*ive minutes to class. Earlier in her career, Veronique would have gotten there at 5:15, as soon as the previous class left. These days, she gives herself thirty seconds to walk down the hall to the classroom. The less time she has to spend teaching, the better. All she wants to do is retire.

She can't retire. The house isn't paid for, and she can't pay the mortgage on her retirement income, and she can't sell, not in this market. When she and Sarabeth bought the house, she was a newly tenured associate professor. She believed that one day she'd make full professor, a promotion that carried with it a ten percent raise and a corresponding bump in retirement income. She and Sarabeth had two salaries. They'd be able to retire, maybe even a little early, and enjoy some well-earned leisure.

But Sarabeth found another lover and walked out, and seven years into Veronique's tenure, the chair of the department told her gently that she wasn't promotable. Once, she would have been. Once, associate professors had been promoted to full simply for doing more of the things they'd done to get tenure. This was no longer true. Veronique, the chair said, choosing his words very carefully, was a valued member of the department, but didn't have enough of a national profile to be promoted.

In short, she wasn't famous enough.

To be fair, Veronique had expected something like this when she walked into his office, since even then she was bored with what she'd done to earn tenure. She'd written her doctoral dissertation on narratives of female flight in nineteenth-century protest literature, women running away from home to seek better lives. As an assistant professor, she'd published a string of scholarly articles on writers like Stowe, Gaskell, and Eliot. But around the time when Sarabeth ran away, literary criticism had started to seem like a use-less exercise, intellectual masturbation. Veronique found herself much more interested in how people who didn't have the luxury of running away created homes where they were. She didn't think they used footnotes.

Even then, she knew her boredom with the profession was her problem, not the department's. Her feeling trapped in a job she'd come to hate was her problem, not the department's. The fact that she lacked the courage to run, or even walk, away from tenure was her problem, not the department's.

The conversation stung anyway, and it hurts more now than it did then. These days, Veronique doubts that anyone considers her a valued member of the department. They're waiting for her to retire. A young, hungry lecturer could teach her courses for a fraction of her salary, and would undoubtedly be more popular with students.

Four minutes to class: time to go. Her tote bag holds *Cranford*, the folder of graded reading responses she'll hand back today, a bottle of water, her keys—there've been thefts on campus, so she keeps her office locked—and a list of discussion points, although she knows she'll wind up doing most of the talking.

She reminds herself, as she always does before class, that there are good students in this section. Amy Castillon: smart young woman, hardworking and perceptive. And then there's that boy, the shy one in the corner—Charles?—whose in-class writing exer-cises are more polished than most of the finished essays she gets from the others.

And then, God help her, there's Jeremy, who seems unable to fasten the Velcro tabs on his sneakers without his mother's help. Why did he sign up for her section? He's not a good student. The only text he cares about is that blasted comic book, and he isn't es-pecially articulate even on that subject. Dealing with him tactfully is a nightmare; avoiding Melinda's unspoken questions is even worse.

Three minutes to showtime. Veronique scans her office and

sees nothing else she needs to bring. All right. She puts her tote bag over her arm, so she'll have a hand free to open her office door, and grabs the cane she uses when her arthritis acts up. It's been raining all day, last week's glorious Indian-summer weather replaced by biting autumn gloom. Saturday's Halloween. She hopes her students don't expect candy, which some colleagues hand out this time of year. Her knee hurts.

Limping into class, only ten seconds late, she takes a quick survey of the seats. A scattering of students, huddled into jackets and sweaters, sit slumped in their usual places. One child wears flip-flops; her toes look faintly blue around their sparkly pink nail polish. A Vegas native, and not the sharpest mind in the room. By the time she figures out how to dress for the weather up here, she'll be ready to graduate.

Only Amy's sitting up straight, and even she seems more subdued than usual. "Hi, Professor Bellamy."

Veronique nods a greeting, too oppressed by the apathy in the room to speak. Eleven out of twenty students, and no Jeremy. He's always late, even without the excuse of bad weather. Veronique doesn't understand why rain or snow slows kids down, even the ones who don't have to drive to campus, but it's a consistent pattern.

She looks unhappily at the clock. Time to start. More students will drag themselves in, probably, but it's not fair to the ones who got here on time for her to stall. She clears her throat. "Please open your books to—"

She senses movement at the door and turns to see who it is. Jeremy, face haggard, phone clamped to his ear, rushes to her desk and thrusts the phone at her. He's shaking. "This has to be a joke. This can't—this can't be happening. You talk to him."

"What? Talk to whom? Jeremy, this is—"

"Please," he says, and she realizes in horror that he's crying. The other students, more awake now, stir and stare—this is the most interesting thing that's happened all semester—as Jeremy presses the phone into her hand. "Please, talk to him."

* * *

*Y*ou're on until nine?" the charge nurse asks. "We just called the family. They'll be here soon. I'll let them know a chaplain's here in case they want to talk to you."

"Thank you," says Rosemary Watkins. "I'll go make sure the consult room's unlocked." The ER's family consult room has comfortable furniture in soothing colors, but very strange lighting. There's no wall switch, and to turn on the floor lamp, you have to step on a button that invariably gets shoved underneath a chair. On top of that, the bulb keeps burning out.

The room's intended as a place where families can absorb bad news in privacy and something resembling comfort; making them sit in the dark is a little too grimly fitting. And it's hard to keep the room stocked with tissues.

The consult room's outside the ER proper, in an adjoining hallway. Ordinarily, Rosemary would grab a tissue box from an empty room on her way out of the ER, but there aren't any empty rooms tonight. She can make out the voices of at least three howling children, two male drunks engaged in a shouting contest—a pair of security guards speeds past, power-walking toward that room— and a female patient yelling for someone to bring her pain meds *now* goddammit *now* I need a shot *now* where are you fuckers?

Her friends wonder why she volunteers in such a noisy, dirty, chaotic place. "I'm not saying you have OCD," Melinda told her once, "but you do tend to have meltdowns if your outfits aren't perfectly coordinated."

And Veronique, acerbic as always, added, "You can't walk into Melinda's house without trying to dust all her books and geodes, and you can't walk into mine without offering to sweep up stray bits of cat food in the kitchen, but you spend four hours a week in an ER?"

But that's why she does it. If she can bring even a little bit of order to this place, offer even a temporary oasis, maybe one or two patients will feel better. And, anyway, the upheaval here comforts her; her own life seems serene by contrast. Most of the time, she feels competent at the hospital.

She's not clergy, of course. The hospital trains laypeople to minister to patients, with the most difficult cases reserved for the staff chaplains. But she's been doing this for seven years now, and at least some of the ER staff routinely ask her to visit patients, or to talk to distraught relatives, or to bless their own hands.

Heading for the hallway, Rosemary dodges left around a portable X-ray machine and right around a gangly teenaged boy on crutches hobbling toward the restroom. The crowd of medical staff around the code room, closest to the ER entrance, has dispersed; there's nothing more to do there. Rosemary glances into the room, but sees only a drawn curtain. Beyond the curtain, she knows, is the body of a thirty-five-year-old woman, brain-dead from an aneurysm, being kept alive on a ventilator. When the family arrives, the doctor will ask what they want to do next and gently bring up the subject of organ donation. And then Rosemary will do whatever she can to help.

She skirts a family—mother and father, each carrying a screaming twin infant—being escorted into the ER by a registration clerk, and finally manages to escape into the hallway. Fifteen feet to her left, she sees the open door of the consult room, a dim glow spilling out into the corridor. She won't have to call security to have the room opened, then. Good. She walks down the hallway and glances inside. Not one but two boxes of tissues, one on each table. Thank God for small favors.

Rosemary stands there, debating her next move. It's seven o'clock. She's been here for two hours, on her feet the entire time. Ordinarily she'd take a break now, but she knows that if she sits down, if she allows herself to be alone, she'll think about her first visit of the evening. She spent forty minutes with an eighty-year-old woman with a broken hip, who clung to Rosemary's arm and keened, "There's no one here! I'll die alone. No one cares about me! I used to have people. They're all gone! No one's here."

"I'm here, Lisa. You're not alone. My name's Rosemary, and I'm here with you." But Lisa kept howling. She howled while Rosemary sang a lullaby. She howled while Rosemary, in desperation, recited the Our Father. Chaplains aren't supposed to pray with patients who haven't requested it, but many elderly dementia patients respond to the familiar words of the Lord's Prayer.

Lisa didn't. Rosemary couldn't even sit down: Lisa had one hand clamped around Rosemary's fingers and the other around her wrist, and between the bedrail and the angles of their respective arms, standing was the only option.

At last a surgical nurse in blue gown, cap, and booties came to take Lisa to surgery, and gently pried her fingers from Rosemary's arm. "Okay, Lisa, time to let go now, all right? I'm going to take you upstairs. We're going to fix your hip. You have to let go of this nice lady's arm, sweetheart."

The whole time, Lisa continued her keening. "There's no one here! No one cares! No one loves me! Why won't anyone come help me? Why isn't anyone here?"

Rosemary should have taken a break after that visit, gotten a cup of coffee or escaped into the chapel for a while. Instead, she washed her hands at the sink in Lisa's room, trying to scrub the feel of those frantic fingers from her skin, and moved on to the next patient, and then the next, and the next. Those were brief, pleasant visits: a few prayers for healing, a few casual conversations about pets and gardening. None were what she needed. She kept looking for someone who knew she was there. And then the charge nurse waved her over and told her about the aneurysm.

She needs to eat; she's already slightly shaky, and dealing with the family will require energy and concentration. She has to be present to them. She can't do this one on autopilot. During a quieter shift, she could ask the charge nurse to page her in the cafeteria when the family showed up, but right now, things are too hectic. It's not a good time for a volunteer to try to ask anybody for anything.

Rosemary stands paralyzed in the corridor. She knows this is a ridiculous stalemate. She wouldn't have any trouble deciding what to do if she weren't so tired, and being so tired is a major red flag that she needs to take a break and refuel.

But if she takes a break, she'll think about Lisa again. No: she has to keep busy. So she stops for a long slurp at a water fountain and goes back into the ER, bracing herself against the barrage of noise and activity. She hears the static of the department's PA system clicking on, and then, improbably, her own name being announced from the nursing station.

"Rosemary, call on 57. Chaplain Rosemary, pick up line 57."

She squints, thinking she's misheard—who could be calling her here, and why?—and then feels a sudden surge of panic. Walter. Something's happened to Walter.

This makes no sense, since no one at Walter's nursing home would call the ER to find her. They'd call her cell, which she keeps on silent at the hospital and checks regularly. But she's reaching for the nearest hall phone even as she works this out. "Hello, this is Rosemary. May I help you?"

Seven hundred and fifty miles away, Anna Clark settles down in front of the evening news with a glass of white wine and her knitting. It's raining, typical Seattle weather, but she doesn't mind. She likes being surrounded by water; it's one reason she and William bought the house on Mercer Island. Living on the island makes her feel calm, self-contained, protected by moats.

She is, of necessity, a highly social person. She organizes openings at her husband's art gallery: ordering food and flowers, schmoozing with artists and patrons. She's on the board of the private school where their son attended K–12, and she's in a knitting group run by one of the other Blake School board members. But she also finds too much social contact exhausting and treasures her time alone.

She's knitting an ornate lace shawl with outrageously high-end yarn—a qiviut-cashmere blend she ordered from a musk-ox farm in Canada—and she has to concentrate on the minute stitches. The tray table on her lap holds Barbara Walker's *Treasury of Knitting Patterns,* open to page 204, Frost Flowers, a twenty-four-row repeat in a multiple of thirty-four stitches plus two. Walker assures her readers that this is actually a simple lace, quickly learned after the knitter has gone once through the pattern, but Anna's only on row fourteen. If she decides she likes the pattern, she'll photocopy it and return the book to its shelf. If she doesn't, she'll rip what she's done and start again with another pattern.

William isn't home; he's working late, getting ready for a show at the gallery. He took the dog with him into the city. Percy's not home, either. He doesn't like being surrounded by water unless it comes with a lot of sunshine, and he's fled to Mexico for two weeks to escape the onset of autumn. William's parents had extra time-share points. The resort's American-owned: by a Seattle company, in fact, one that's made a big deal about how good their security is, since so many Americans have been killed down there. Percy went down by himself, which seems a little odd for a kid his age, but Anna knows he'll meet people. Most of his friends are working or in school, and can't take the time. He decided to take a year off between college and starting his MBA, to give himself more time to study for the GMAT, so of course he wound up back home, in his old room with its garish comic posters and high school lacrosse trophies. Anna had hoped he'd redecorate—the colors in that room give her a headache—but he's kept it the way it is. Well, of course. It's only for a year.

She'll be glad when he's in school again. Miranda Tobin, another parent on the Blake School board, always asks about him. "And how's dear Percy? Still back with you and Bill?" Miranda's son Tobias—Toby Tobin, what a terrible name to give your child!—was one of Percy's lacrosse teammates at Blake. Percy thought Toby was an ass; Anna thinks the same of Miranda. It must be a dominant gene. Toby's in his first year at Harvard Medical School, a fact Miranda trots out at every opportunity. "He can't decide between neurosurgery and urology," she told everyone last week. "They both pay well, but the hours are better in urology."

After interactions like that, an evening alone in the house is healing balm. The house feels very peaceful like this, the drone of the TV and the steady pattering of raindrops the only sounds. Anna focuses on her knitting pattern: yo, p2 tog, p2, yo, p2 tog, k2, p1, yo, p4, p2 tog, p4, p2 tog-b, p4, yo, p1, k2, p2, yo, p2 tog, p2, repeat. The length of the repeat is dizzying, and it's easy to get lost. Lace knitting is a precision sport. She can't fudge if she makes a mistake, and ripping the fine, fuzzy qiviut is a challenge in itself.

She works her way through the pattern, paying absent attention to the television—weather, sports, traffic, the usual state budget woes—and looks up only when she hears the front door open. William calls out a muffled "hello"; Anna hears Bartholomew's toenails clicking across the floor before he nuzzles her arm in greeting and lies down next to her chair, 120 pounds of Irish Wolfhound hitting the carpet with a thump. He yawns, hugely, essence of dog breath and wet dog wafting over her. Her nose wrinkles.

"You're home early."

William comes into the living room, rubbing his hands together for warmth, and bends to kiss the top of her head. "The setup was easier than I thought. Three of Kip's friends helped."

"Do you think the show will go well?"

William shrugs. "We'll see. The work's not to my taste, but a lot of people like it. Have you eaten?"

"Soup and salad. I can heat up that leftover quiche if you're hungry."

"I'll do it. Don't get up." He goes into the kitchen, Bart raising a head to sniff in his direction before flopping down again, and

Anna hears the dull thud of the fridge door closing, the soft hum of the microwave.

"On second thought," she calls, "I'll have a piece too."

"Okay."

She's folded up her knitting and is about to turn off the TV when something catches her attention. "Mexico," the announcer says, and Anna looks up to see a somber anchorwoman. "An American tourist has been found brutally murdered in the Castillo del Sol resort in Cabo San Lucas. The resort owners, Seattle hospitality magnates David and Delores Strucking, have issued a statement—"

Percy. Anna's chest constricts, and for a moment the TV's drowned out by the white noise in her head. She forces herself to focus, hears, "The woman's body"—a woman, good, no, not good, of course not good, but at least it's not Percy, and Anna breathes more easily again—"was discovered by housekeeping staff. Her name is being withheld pending notification of the family. We'll be sure to keep you updated on this story as it develops."

Panic pricks Anna's throat. "Will? William! Come here! Something horrible has happened. We have to fly Percy home."

2

Comrade Cosmos was born during the humid summer of 2002 in Princeton, New Jersey, when a group of Information Systems majors, sharing a rented house and bored with the usual rules of beer pong, invented a new challenge. The winners of each match would have to invent a superhero; the losers would have to create that superhero's nemesis. Later, the boyfriend of one of the participants said, "It was kind of like their version of the *Villa Diodati*." The boyfriend was an English major, and while his professors might not have ranked Comrade Cosmos and the Emperor of Entropy with Mary Shelley's Frankenstein, the comparison was apt in at least one way. Just as several stories came from that famous summer of 1816 on the shores of Lake Geneva, so a number of hero-and-villain pairs were born of the 2002 beer-pong rules. In both cases, however, only one narrative went on to capture the imagination of the wider culture.

Desi Santamaria and her friend Peter Phillips were the winners who came up with Comrade Cosmos, Champion of Order. CC lore has it that the hero was largely a response to the fact that this particular round of beer pong had knocked eight full cups of beer to the floor. However improbable that number may be, we know for a fact that the losers, Jacob Morganthau and Honoree McKenzie, responded by creating the Emperor of Entropy, Curator of Chaos.

These characters might have been as fully forgotten as the others invented that summer, save for a fortuitous combination of talents. Desi had a flair for graphic art and had been devouring DC and Marvel comics since she could read. Jacob, who'd almost majored in English himself, wasn't half bad with a storyline. Peter was a canny marketer, and Honoree, even more than the others, excelled at Web design and publishing.

Thus an empire was born.

It started small, of course, with a modest Web-comic. Comrade Cosmos—muscles bulging beneath skintight blue and gold spandex, teeth and hair perfectly straight and aligned—answered the summons of a small-town mayor whose tiny community of Oblivion, Nebraska, had been destroyed by a windstorm. The panels showed wreckage everywhere: car parts strewn across the high school football field, pet goldfish and small mammals impaled on the branches of trees, bras and jock straps hanging from the steeple of the First Presbyterian Church of Oblivion, and a black, yawning pit where the local fire station had once stood. Sobbing citizens wandered the streets, searching for their fenders, their hamsters, their underwear.

"This was no ordinary storm," the mayor told Comrade Cosmos.

"Like unto a tornado it was, and yet not so, for it was one wild wind everywhere with no focus or funnel." These words were gummed, spat, and sputtered by an old man whose dentures had been blown clean out of his mouth, and whose pigtailed granddaughter had to translate for him.

"Our fire station was brick and metal and had stood against many fierce winds," the fire chief told CC, "and yet this one demolished it."

"No," proclaimed Comrade Cosmos, "it was clearly no ordinary storm! It is most evidently the work of that dastardly coward, that vilest villain, the Emperor of Entropy!"

At these words, the Emperor himself appeared: a swirling darkness in human shape, his eyes glowing red coals, exploded galaxies flowing through the emptiness he occupied. One of the distinctive features of the CCverse, from the beginning, was that invoking EE—naming him, speaking of him, sometimes even just thinking of him—summoned him instantly, for this most dangerous of genii is inherently everywhere, omnipresent, lurking in the very fabric of creation. Comrade Cosmos, in contrast, has always been merely a frail human, although initially one with bulging muscles clad in spandex.

"You have perceived aright," boasted the Emperor, flinging his arms of shadow wide to encompass the devastation of Oblivion. "This is my work, the play of an instant, a mere eyeblink and flick of my finger. How shall you withstand me, puny superhero? It would take you years to undo even a microfraction of the chaos I have caused. Admit your frailty, and despair!"

"Never," said Comrade Cosmos, and turned to bow to the assembled townspeople, who had gathered to gape at this confrontation. "Good folk, our enemy is only one, but we are many. He can wreck entire towns with the flick of a finger, but he has only ten fingers, and we have thousands, if we summon friends and family and even strangers to help us. No repair is wasted, here or anywhere. Whenever you hammer a nail or sew on a button or feed a hungry child, whenever you chop wood or carry water, whenever you plant a garden or pave a road, you work to defeat our enemy. Together, we can repair the world. Let us begin!"

The townspeople responded to this stirring speech with tears of joy and cheers of assent, and promptly started the work of rebuilding the town. No one shirked. All helped with happy hearts: bricklayers, grandmothers, doctors, schoolchildren, the mayor himself pouring concrete. Comrade Cosmos dug and hauled and hammered and painted with the rest of them, and in due course—as EE stood in the background, shooting off the tiny stars that meant he was fuming—Cosmos gestured expansively over a neat, sparkling town square and announced, "Oblivion is restored!"

Wordplay has always been a feature of the CCverse. The cultural critics who study Comrade Cosmos, noting that its language and images are a derivative stew drawn from Tolkien, the King James Bible, Shakespeare, Milton, and *Buffy the Vampire Slayer*—to name only the most prominent sources—observe that it survived, and then thrived, by keying into cultural anxieties. CC was born of the fear and grief following September 11, 2001; the yawning pit where the Oblivion fire station once stood clearly recalls Ground Zero, and the destruction of Oblivion echoes the scale and sense-lessness of the terrorist attacks.

Literary naysayers, and there are many, claim that the storylines are simplistic and the characters cardboard, although even they ad-mit that this has become less true in recent years. Staunch Ameri-can nationalists maintain that CC is clearly communist: his title is Comrade, and he encourages and empowers collective action. A variety of liberal Christian clergy—the type who read graphic nov-els as carefully as they do the Bible—maintain instead that "CC" stands for Corpus Christi, the Body of Christ, and that the super-hero empowers his followers to do God's work in the world. They see in the Oblivion storyline, and many others, strong parallels to the Book of Acts.

Other clergy, often less liberal, contest this by pointing out that the wind and fire EE brings with him are the external, physical manifestations of the Holy Spirit who descends on the disciples at Pentecost, and that EE's omnipresence echoes that of God Him-self. The CCverse is a howl of rage at a God who permits horror, and portrays a fractured universe in which the Son himself—for even these readers agree that CC is Christ—must work to heal the excesses of his father. According to this interpretation, *CC* rewrites *Paradise Lost* as a war, not between God and His fallen angels, but between the persons of the Trinity itself, and thus reinscribes chaos and destruction even as it claims to work against them.

Secular observers point out, more mildly, that "EE" stands not only for the Emperor of Entropy but for Electrical Engineering, while "CC" could be Closed Circuit or Cheat Code or Cyber-Crime. The computerist school of CC criticism reads the series as an entirely tongue-in-cheek comment on debates within the computing community, one that pokes fun at how the field attempts to organize ones and zeros, the very stuff of entropy, into meaningful language.

Santamaria, Phillips, Morganthau, and McKenzie don't comment on any of this. They simply rake in the proceeds from their creation and its spin-offs, from the graphic novels, MMO games, feature films, T-shirts, and action figures the CCverse has generated in such profusion. "The meaning resides with the reader," Morganthau responds briskly whenever anyone asks for a definitive interpretation. "We all have our own ways of creating order. What do *you* think it means?"

Certainly the multiplicity of meanings holds the keys to *CC*'s success. Were the central conflict not such a blank slate, it would simply be a good-versus-evil superhero story, however skillfully rendered by the artists, writers, actors, directors, game designers, and other creative professionals who now preside over the CCverse. The huge, and hugely improbable, success of the franchise depends precisely upon the indeterminacy of interpretation. For seven years now, we have found in *CC* what we want to find, or fear to find, or need to find. We find support for our cynical despair and for our idealistic dreams, for our horror and our hope, for existential dismissal of human effort and fervent faith in its efficacy. *CC* means all things to all people.

And thus CC fandom, even more than usual for such franchises, is split between people who cheer for the putative hero and those who side with the avowed villain. Readers who ally themselves with Comrade Cosmos staunchly defend order, idealism, and community, and condemn their entropy-besotted counterparts as adolescent poseurs. The Minions of the Emperor, as EE followers label themselves, deride Comrades as naive children who are afraid of reality and have never faced up to the second law of thermodynamics. Comrades respond that they're fully aware of the second law of thermodynamics, thank you, which is exactly why they put their energy into trying to keep the world working. They further point out that Minions themselves consume vast amounts of energy in the form of the donuts they devour at their club meetings— donuts being the Emperor's favorite food, as they symbolize the void at the center of creation—and that if any given Minion expended the resulting calories in oh, say, community service, rather than ranting about nihilism, that Minion would realize that entropy can indeed be reversed.

To this, Minions only snicker. They pride themselves on taking the long view. As they munch their donuts, they vie to see who can make the longest list of ways for that year's Comrade Corps project to fail.

Comrades, true to their communal nature, choose a new service project each year. In October, Comrades around the world propose projects. In November, a round of early Internet voting whittles the list down to ten or twenty, and in December, a final vote decides the mandate for the coming year. Projects have included planting trees, knitting hats and scarves for the homeless, visiting nursing homes, making weekly verbal amends for wrongs, and fostering stray animals.

Minions find all of this funny beyond belief, and say that it sounds like a cross between the Cub Scouts and an AA meeting. Every February, on Valentine's Day, the Minions publish (again on the Internet, naturally) a compilation of lists about how that year's project will fail. The list for the tree-planting year included fire, drought, flood, gypsy moths, longhorn beetles, elm bark beetles, tent caterpillars, and loggers, among many other threats. The list for the knitting year included moths; dropped stitches; fiber allergies; Comrades unable to master knitting at all; and wool short-ages resulting from wolves, coyotes, feral sheepdogs, and bloat, foot rot, and scrapie, along with a host of other ovine illnesses.

Indeed, a certain number of Comrades were unable to learn to knit, and had to be offered alternatives. Some managed to learn to crochet, sew, or embroider. Others made themselves useful untangling snarled yarn or holding skeins as knitters wound them into balls. Still others opted out of needlecraft entirely, retreating to the honorable fallback position of tending and watering the trees planted the previous year.

Direct sabotage of Comrade projects, however, is considered profoundly bad form, running counter to the entire Minion ethos. In one famous case, a Minion was accused of sneaking into an animal shelter in Ann Arbor, Michigan, and releasing a group of kittens due to be fostered by Comrades. The local Minion cohort released a statement vehemently denying responsibility. "We would never do this. The whole point of our philosophy is to do nothing, to wait for Entropy to undo all things. Helping Entropy along would be a denial of the truth that Entropy doesn't need us: Entropy will conquer quite nicely without any effort on our part. Furthermore, a number of us are very fond of cats, who are fine models of Doing Nothing themselves."

The Ann Arbor Minions were so offended by the charges that they became Comrades for a day and helped the shelter staff search for the missing kittens, all of whom were recovered safely. The next day, a PETA splinter group claimed responsibility in a somewhat incoherent manifesto maintaining that domesticating any animal was an act of coercion.

There is no law in CC fandom against switching sides, often more than once, although this usually takes place at the individual level, rather than collectively. An ability to empathize with the opponent's perspective is considered a strength among Comrades, and Minions understand that everyone goes soft once in a while and needs a dose of wishful thinking. Indeed, Comrade-Minion marriages are quite common, and at least as long-lasting as any other kind, and Minion parents insist as firmly on picked-up rooms and acceptable grades as Comrades do.

The WISS ("Why I Switched Sides") essay has been a commonplace in fan writing since a famous piece published by Desi Santamaria on Salon.com in 2005. Santamaria, a staunch Comrade, wrote movingly about a breast-cancer scare that temporarily sent her spinning into the clutches of the Emperor, only to have the love and support of family, friends, and fans—including no small number of Minions—pull her back.

Medical crises and conditions are WISS commonplaces. More than a few Minions, for instance, have described how going on antidepressants transformed them into Comrades, and some now believe that an emphasis on Entropy is itself a symptom of disordered neurotransmitters. Other predictable staples of the WISS essay are divorce, natural disaster, and war, on the Comrade-to-Minion side, and childbirth, natural beauty, and humanitarian outpourings, on the other. "Why the Chinese Earthquake Made Me a Minion" essays are matched by "Why Seeing Yosemite for the First Time Made Me a Comrade."

A fluctuating number of fans identify as Equilibrists and maintain one foot in each camp. They plant trees, but pore over the numerous threats to woodland ecosystems as they gloomily devour their donuts. They apologize to people they have offended, but mock those same people when safely in Minion territory. They foster strays, but write editorials decrying no-kill shelters as economically impractical. This group prides itself on being balanced. The balancing act is very hard work, however, and sooner or later, almost all Equilibrists topple to one side or the other, either temporarily or for the long haul.

What the CCverse provides all its followers, regardless of ideological lens, is an affirmation of reality. *Comrade Cosmos* may be a comic book, but it is anything but escapist. Within its pages, as in the world, shit happens, everywhere, all the time. Tragedy is un-avoidable. To name, invoke, or even think of entropy is to summon it. Our worlds can be ripped apart, drop-kicked, and shattered, in an instant. We know these things will happen to us. *CC* suggests that when they do, we can survive them.

3

*W*here were you when you heard the news?

Throughout his life, Jeremy has listened to high school teachers, college professors, and his friends' parents discuss this question. Where were you when you heard that Pearl Harbor had been bombed, that JFK had been shot, that the Twin Towers had fallen? Most people's lives contain at least one such historic moment, a freeze frame they recall in vivid detail and can relive at will, and sometimes all unwilling.

Two days ago, most of the people sitting in Rosemary's living room right now would have said that their moment was 9/11. Jeremy remembers 9/11, but only as a blur of drawn adult faces and incomprehensible images on the television, which his mother quickly turned off and lugged into the garage. He remembers the event, but it was mediated through other people's reactions. It was theirs, not his.

His moment has now arrived: a personal cataclysm, not a national one, but every bit as shattering. He knows that for the rest of his life, he will remember exactly what it felt like to rush through the rain to his English 101 class while a Spanish-accented voice on his cell phone informed him, both urgently and haltingly, that his mother was dead.

Because they've now all talked about it, he knows what the others will remember, too. VB will remember learning of Melinda's death from that same voice when Jeremy pressed his cell phone on her in class. Mother Hen—Henrietta Alphonse-Smith, the priest at Mom and Aunt Rosie's church—will remember being called away from a late supper of salad, grilled cheese, and cream of broccoli soup to answer a call from Veronique, voice stuttering and breaking. Rosemary will remember Hen's strained, quiet words on the other end of the line in the ER. "Rosie, I have terrible news." Tom Duquesne, Melinda's attorney and a fellow parishioner at St. Phil's, will remember answering his phone to hear Rosemary sobbing on the other end.

"Can't be," Jeremy says now. He's sitting on Rosemary's couch clutching a glass of water he hasn't been able to drink. The water shakes and shivers in his hands. He watches the dancing ripple, as broken and refracted as he feels. He can't think, can't form coherent sentences. Language has broken.

Someone, maybe Mother Hen, has put a sweater around his shoulders. He hates being in this house because it reminds him of Uncle Walter, who no longer knows that Jeremy is his godson or that Aunt Rosie is his wife. Being in his own house—Mom's house, filled with Mom's stuff—would be worse. "Can't be. It's someone else."

This has to be a mistake.

Tom clears his throat. He's a tall, skinny man, slightly stooped, his remaining hair gray. He wears glasses and cardigans. He's always reminded Jeremy a little of Mr. Rogers. Right now, he's paler than Jeremy has ever seen him. "No. Jeremy, I'm sorry. It's not a mistake. I called the local police, and then I talked to people at the American consulate. Your mother's dead."

No no no. "Someone else," Jeremy says doggedly. Has to be.

Tom's voice is distorted, too slow. "They have positive ID from her passport, and she was in her own room." Tom's voice breaks completely now.

VB stands up and starts pacing, but then she starts limping, so she sits down again. Once, Jeremy would have found this funny, although he'd have known better than to say so to anyone. VB shakes her head. "Someone broke into Melinda's room and didn't take her passport? What kind of robber is that?"

Tom clears his throat again and takes a breath Jeremy can hear even from across the room. "It wasn't a robbery. The police don't think any of her belongings are missing." He looks away from all of them, out Rosemary's living room window. "This is—it's horrible, but you're going to hear it on the news and people are going to be talking about it, so you need to hear it from me first." He looks at Jeremy. "Do you want me to tell you privately? We can go in another room."

Five minutes ago, Jeremy was so numb that he didn't think he'd ever feel anything again, but now dread constricts his chest. "No. Not alone." Hen comes to sit on the couch next to him. She reaches out her hand, but he ignores it. He's using all of his energy to stay still, to stay sitting. "What?"

"All right." Another breath. "She was raped and stabbed. The police think there was only one assailant."

Where were you when you heard the news?

When Jeremy can think clearly again—when his thoughts have stopped scattering like small, terrified animals—he will realize that there are levels to this question, that cataclysm arrives in waves. Where were you when you heard that she was dead? Where were you when you heard that she'd been raped and stabbed?

All sound is muffled now, although no one else has spoken. Rosemary's hand has gone to her mouth. VB isn't sitting where she was just a minute ago. Jeremy hears a rasping noise, grinding gears on a car. VB's retching into a wastebasket.

There's a weight on his shoulder. Hen's hand. "Jeremy?" He blinks, shakes his head. He can't speak.

"I'm so very sorry." That's Tom. Jeremy sees his cheeks shining in the light. The light from the closest end table, and something else is shining there. A paperweight. There's a flower in it.

He picked out the paperweight for Aunt Rosie's birthday, a long time ago. He was little. Too short to see the tabletop where the paperweights were. Mom picked each one up and knelt down to show it to him. "How about this, Jer? Do you like this one?" Two flowers, pink and yellow. "Which one do you like better?"

Something moves jerkily across his vision. VB, going back to her seat.

"Do they know who did it?" That's Hen. Her hand isn't on Jeremy's shoulder anymore. Her hands are clenched in her lap. They look more like fists. She sees him looking at her hands and they relax, unfold, press flat against the blue of her skirt.

"No. Not yet. But the police said there's a lot of DNA evidence."

"Oh, God," Rosemary says. VB gags again, just once. Jeremy doesn't yet realize consciously what this means, but Hen reaches for something on the floor. His glass. He dropped his glass. There's water all over Aunt Rosie's nice carpet.

A Christmas party here when he was seven or eight, with the special punch Jeremy loved, cranberry juice with ginger ale and cloves. He felt so grown up drinking it. Mommy said the punch would stain. He was very careful, but he still spilled some. Mom, frowning and disappointed. Aunt Rosie, reassuring him.

"I'll wipe it up," Hen says. "Jeremy, I'll get it."

*r*aped? Rosemary feels herself recoiling, shrinking into the couch, her mind slamming shut. And Jeremy hearing this, oh God, and he's dropped his glass.

Hen gets paper towels, wipes up the water, and goes into the kitchen to throw the wet towels away. I should have done that,

Rosemary thinks. It's my house. But she can't move. No one speaks until Hen gets back and sits down again.

A pause. Utter silence, into which Hen says, "Let us pray."

Too late, Rosemary thinks. Too late. But she bows her head and tries to listen to the prayer.

Usually she loves Hen's prayers, but she can only make out snatches of this one. We don't know why. Pain and anger. Sin of vengeance. Thank you for Melinda's life. Help her friends and family. Jeremy. Heal. Comfort. Bless. Amen.

Amen, echo Tom and Jeremy: even Jeremy, sitting dazed and blank on the couch. Veronique doesn't respond to the prayer, but she wouldn't. Rosemary doesn't because she still can't. How many times has she prayed like this with patients and families? She would have prayed this way with the family of the aneurysm patient, if she hadn't gotten the phone call first. Would her prayer have sounded as empty to them as this one sounds to her? She feels herself checking for her usual sense of God's presence, her soul a tongue searching for a missing tooth. She finds only a hole the size of a galaxy.

Voices, discussing. Jeremy doesn't want to go back to the dorm tonight, doesn't want to go back to the house. He'll stay in Hen's guest room; Hen calls her husband Ed to instruct him to make up the bed. When she gets home, she'll activate the parish phone tree used in emergencies, which before now have never been more serious than a service canceled because of snow.

Tom, Hen, and Veronique talk logistics. Melinda would want to be cremated, but should that happen in Mexico, or the States? Less expensive to have her cremated there if no one objects, but does Jeremy—or anyone else—need to see the body for closure? Will the body be fit to be seen? Won't someone have to go down to Mexico to make arrangements? And if the police catch Melinda's murderer and there's a trial, what then? Would she have wanted them to be there? Would there be any reason for them to be there?

"She didn't believe in the death penalty," Jeremy says. It's the first thing he's said since hearing how Melinda died. Rosemary's heart twists. Does Jeremy agree with his mother's position now, if he ever did?

Does Rosemary?

Tom shakes his head. "Mexico doesn't have the death penalty. They won't even extradite Americans who might face it for American crimes."

"We could go down there and kill him ourselves," Veronique says, and hearing the rage in her voice, Rosemary thinks she just might be capable of it.

Tom grunts. "Tempting, but hardly advisable. I don't think life in a Mexican prison is any fun. We need time to absorb this. We need sleep. We're all in shock. We can figure out next steps tomorrow."

Tom and Hen leave, flanking Jeremy. Veronique goes into the kitchen and comes back out with a cup of tea that Rosemary didn't ask for and doesn't want. "You need to stay hydrated," she says, putting it clumsily on the table next to Rosemary's chair. Some tea has slopped into the saucer. Rosemary hates that.

Veronique and Rosemary have never been close, not as close as either of them was to Melinda. Vera's trying to do the right thing. Rosemary knows that.

Rosemary stays in her chair, paralyzed. She wants Walter. If Walter were here, he'd know what to do.

There's nothing to do. She knows that.

The phone rings. It's Beth Adams from church, shocked and horrified, needing to talk, but Rosemary can't talk. She can't be a chaplain right now. Melinda was her best friend.

She hangs up. The phone rings again. She ignores the call and turns the ringer off. No more. No more tonight. No.

Veronique, hovering, trying to help but inept at it, and she needs help herself now; Rosemary knows that. She's grieving too. Rosemary drinks the tea—herbal, peppermint—and lets Vera, lead her upstairs, lets Vera wait while she undresses and puts on a nightgown, lets Vera tuck her into bed like a child.

What time is it? Early, too early. The clock on her bureau says it's only nine o'clock. It feels like three in the morning. It feels like a different year than the one she lived in this morning.

Veronique sees her looking at the clock. "Do you want the alarm set?"

"No. Thank you. I doubt I'll sleep much, anyway." A small, distant part of her brain knows that giving Veronique ways to be useful is the most healing thing she can do.

Rosemary herself can't be useful. Even if she knew a way to be useful, she couldn't manage it, and there's nothing.

Veronique leaves. Rosemary closes her eyes, trying to block out the day, but instead she sees a bruised face, teeth missing, one eye swollen shut, a swathe of blond hair torn out, blood from a shoulder abrasion seeping onto a "Hello, Kitty!" T-shirt.

What was her name? Rosemary doesn't remember, but she remembers the face and the story: the pretty young woman, attacked and abandoned in a downtown parking garage, who made her way to the hospital only to learn that she couldn't be treated. Not here. Only one hospital in town was authorized to do rape exams.

Rosemary remembers a nurse ranting about the situation. "It's horrible! They have to have someone specially trained, so they've decided to keep one ER staffed with those people twenty-four/seven. But I know how to do rape exams! I'd be happy to be on call just for that! How can they put this poor girl through that?"

Rosemary came home and told Walter about it. They didn't know he was sick yet, although in retrospect the signs were there. Greater reliance on Post-it notes. More trouble with names. But that evening, Walter seemed completely himself. He listened to her story about the rape victim, and then he put his arms around her and hugged, rocking.

Melinda had helped Rosemary move Walter into the nursing home: had stood with Rosemary while they loaded him into the ambulance, had helped Rosemary unpack Walter's things in the bleak pale room. And afterward, back here, Melinda had put her arms around Rosemary and hugged, rocking.

Shivering in her bed, Rosemary hugs herself. There's no one else left to do it.

When Jeremy is eight or nine, Melinda reads *Charlotte's Web* to him, one chapter each night before bed. He can read, but he'd rather listen, and she treasures the connection the ritual provides. She thinks he does, too. She delights in the rhythms of E. B. White's language, the sheer joy of reading his prose aloud. She never smells cut grass without remembering White's description of the barn, which "smelled of the perspiration of tired horses and the wonderful sweet breath of patient cows." Jeremy doesn't care about poetics, but he's enthralled by Charlotte's determined quest to save Wilbur.

Melinda's read the book so often that she hardly needs to look at the pages. The edition she holds now, its pages foxed and wrinkled and spotted with miscellaneous stains, is the one she read during her own childhood, the title almost worn away on the cover and binding. Melinda was seven when White's classic was published, nine when her parents gave it to her for Christmas. She spent months reading the book to the end and then turning back to the first page. Like Jeremy, she loved Charlotte's quest, as improbable as mending the moon.

Of course she and Jeremy both cry when Charlotte says goodbye to Wilbur. Melinda thinks that anyone who can read the book without tears must lack a soul. "No one was with her when she died." As well as she knows the story, Melinda's voice cracks on that line, at the image of the deserted fairgrounds and the small gray spider, all alone.

And then the happy ending back at the farm, Charlotte's descendants thriving and adopting Wilbur, although none of them "ever quite took her place in his heart." Melinda knows the last chapter is necessary, but it never moves her as deeply as Charlotte's death.

After Melinda has read the last sentence, Jeremy starts to suck his thumb—a habit he mostly broke a long time ago, but still slips into when he's sad—and says, "Mommy, you're never going to die, are you?"

Melinda takes a deep breath, savoring the fragrances of fresh sheets and wool blankets and newly-bathed boy. She's known this topic would come up sometime. "Everybody dies, Jeremy. But most people don't die until they're very, very old. I hope I won't die for a very long time."

He was two and a half when she adopted him; he still dimly remembers the long plane trip from Guatemala. She's always told him the truth about his adoption. Now he says, "Did my first mommy die?"

"I don't know, sweetie. All I know is that she was very poor, and she wanted you to have a better, safer home than she could give you, so she gave you to the people who gave you to me. I don't know what happened to her after that."

In fact, Jeremy was found wandering in the rubble of a wrecked village, and his parents are almost certainly dead. But she won't tell him that, not yet.

"Maybe she died, and you're Wilbur. 'Cept you didn't carry me in your mouth." He giggles, but then grows pensive again. "Charlotte would have been happy that Wilbur took care of her babies after she died. So they'd be okay."

"Yes, that's right."

"And my first mommy wanted somebody to take care of me."

"That's right. So you'd be okay."

He reaches for her hand, his thumb moist against hers, but wrinkles his nose and looks away to show that the gesture belongs to some other, younger Jeremy. "If you die, who'll take care of me?"

"Our friends. Aunt Rosemary and Uncle Walter and Aunt

Veronique. But I don't think I'll die for a very long time, Jeremy. People live a lot longer than spiders do."

He lets go of her hand, the thumb returning to his mouth. Around it, he says, "Katy killed a spider at school the other day. It wasn't hurting anybody."

"A lot of people are scared of spiders."

"The teacher said some spiders hurt people, but this spider wasn't one of those kinds. It was just building a web, but it wasn't writing anything. I guess it wasn't as smart as Charlotte."

"I've never seen a spider as smart as Charlotte."

"I was sad when Katy killed the spider. But the teacher said that if it was a bad spider, then we'd have to kill it, so it wouldn't hurt anybody. Would a bad spider's mommy be sorry if it died?"

"All mothers are sorry when their babies die. Jeremy, are you afraid you're bad?"

"I'm talking about the *spider*. What if the bad spider's mommy was dead, like Charlotte? Then she couldn't be sad. But even if it's a bad spider, how do you know if its mommy is alive? Or if it has babies?"

"You don't," Melinda says, stroking his soft dark hair. "But Jeremy, everything alive is someone's baby. And all parents, whether they're still alive or not, want their babies to live."

A week later, during an informal get-together at Rosemary and Walter's, Jeremy finds a house spider in the bathroom and sternly forbids anyone to kill it. Walter deftly transfers the creature to a piece of paper and takes it outside, as Rosemary and Melinda praise Jeremy for his compassion. Jeremy stays outside with the spider to make sure it's safe.

When Walter comes back inside, Melinda tells her friends about the bedtime conversation. Walter and Rosemary have already promised to take care of Jeremy if anything ever happens to her. She had a new will drawn up when she adopted him, naming them his guardians in the event of her death.

But of course that's just a precaution. None of them believe that anything like that will ever happen. By the time Melinda dies, surely Jeremy will be an adult with a family of his own.

Veronique splits a can of cat food between two bowls. She's shaking so badly that she can hardly handle the fork. But the cats have to eat, and they can't open the cans by themselves.

She almost asked Rosemary if she could stay there, crash in the guest bedroom, because she didn't trust herself to drive. But she'd driven to Rosie's, so of course she could drive back home. And the cats have to eat.

Has it really only been a few hours since she learned about Melinda?

Sillybeth and Nepotuk wind between her ankles, howling as mournfully as if they've never been fed in the history of the world. If she isn't careful, they'll trip her. All she needs now is a broken hip.

She uses the fork to mash and mix up the portions of cat food; the metal tines scrape loudly against the bottom of the stainless steel bowls. The noise sounds like a scream. Veronique wants to scream. She can feel the scream inside her, building like a sneeze.

But she'd scare the cats. They're innocent; none of this is their fault. No fair to take it out on them.

Melinda was innocent.

Melinda was one of the most cheerful people Veronique ever met, and one of the kindest, and someone who could have smart conversations about books, which was how Veronique met her, at a reading group Melinda facilitated at the library where she worked as a reference librarian. Melinda was younger than Veronique. She shouldn't have died first, and she shouldn't have died that way. No one should die that way.

Except the bastard who did this. There is no death too vile or painful for him, and Veronique would gladly administer it with her own hands, which are still shaking as the fork screams against the metal and her rage screams inside her belly.

She realizes that she's been stirring the cat food for minutes. She picks up the bowls and walks crabwise, stepping carefully around the cats, to the shoe tray where she always puts their food. Her hands are clenched so hard on the bowls that they hurt.

She knew even before Jeremy reminded them that Melinda didn't believe in the death penalty; she knows that Rosemary doesn't, either, and certainly Hen wouldn't. Religious reasons. But Veronique's not religious. Her parents weren't perfect, but at least they steered clear of institutionalized superstition. Rosemary was raised in the church, and Veronique understands habit. She was always more mystified by Melinda's reasons, since Melinda only began attending church as an adult.

She'd just started, in fact, when she and Veronique met. "Oh, I've been going to St. Phil's, but it's still mostly cultural anthropology. Fascinating, though, and there's really good preaching there. Very literate. I think you'd enjoy it."

Veronique thought not. She learned later that Melinda had helped Rosemary find an obscure article about first-century liturgy, and that Rosemary had invited Melinda to her church, and Melinda had accepted out of curiosity. Six months or so after Veronique met her, Melinda was long past the cultural-anthropology stage, and had gone native. She wasn't pushy about it, though, so Veronique could stay friends with her. It was like learning that a sane, intelligent adult you admired liked to chew bubblegum or play hopscotch or make dress-up clothing for stuffed animals: incomprehensible, and a little embarrassing, but as long as the person didn't insist that you partake of this bizarre hobby as well, friendly relations could be maintained.

She has to admit that the woman priest handled things well tonight; Veronique didn't even find her prayer too offensive. But she supposes priests have a lot of practice at helping people through horror. How they reconcile that with their fairy tale about a loving God, Veronique can't imagine.

The cats now have their heads safely ensconced in their food bowls. Veronique escapes to the living room and sits on the couch, but quickly finds herself back on her feet. When she sits still, she starts to think about what happened to Melinda, and then she feels sick. She doesn't want to throw up again. She hates throwing up.

She has to relax somehow, or she's going to be up all night. She doesn't keep alcohol in the house, having had some bad run-ins with it when she was younger. She could listen to music, but that's not enough. She needs something completely involving. She needs to read. Books have been her refuge since early childhood, a bulwark against the painful, messy world.

But she can't read. Not now. She wonders how long it will be before even the sight of a book won't remind her unbearably of Melinda.

*a*nna's on the computer in the den, checking flights. One way from Cabo to Seattle, leaving tomorrow. William's pacing with the cordless: every minute or so, regularly as a metronome, she sees him passing the den doorway, first one way and then the other. "It's going right to voice mail," he calls in to her.

"Leave voice mail, then." She's amazed at how reasonable the flights are: $272 even for the next day, and it's not a bad itinerary. She clicks on a flight leaving Cabo about five and getting into Sea-Tac about ten. Alaska Air, by way of San Francisco. Not bad at all. She books it; Expedia has her credit card on file.

William crosses the doorway again.

She gets up, calves and back taut with tension, and walks into the living room. "Honey, give me the phone. I'll leave him voice mail with the itinerary."

"You bought the ticket already?" He squints at her. "Shouldn't we check with him first?"

"No. I bought the ticket. He's coming home."

William cracks his knuckles, a tic he displays only under extreme stress. "What if he doesn't want to? He isn't a child anymore."

"He's my child," Anna says, realizing with annoyance that her voice has grown shrill, "and he's coming home." She's gone into Warrior Mother mode. Her son is in a dangerous place; she's doing what she has to do to bring him back to the safety of the house, to get him back on the right side of the moat. She'll bring him home and raise the drawbridge: Percy will never again vacation anyplace where someone has been murdered.

She's completely aware that this is irrational, that this policy would keep him from going on any trips at all. At the moment, she doesn't care.

William gives her the phone, but folds his hands over hers to keep her from using it. She senses him calming himself, knows that he's picked up on her bubbling hysteria and realized that he has to be the sensible one. They've always been a good team that way, able to balance each other. "Anna, he's fine. He'll be fine. I'm sure there isn't a maniac with a machete running around the resort. The woman who died probably knew the person who killed her, or it was a drug deal gone bad or something. Percy isn't a target."

She knows he's right. At the moment, she doesn't care. Castillo del Sol was supposed to be safe. She pulls her hands from his, extracting the cordless at the same time, and hits the redial button.

"Hi, this is Percy. You know what to do."

Voice fraying, she leaves him the flight information, along with instructions to call home the minute he gets the message. "Dad and I love you. We need to know you're okay. Bye."

She hangs up, redials. Same thing. She doesn't leave a message this time.

She wants to throw the phone across the room.

"Why," she asks her husband, "does he have his phone off?"

William sits down now, sagging into an armchair. Bart, banished to his spot in front of the fireplace because he kept trying to follow his pacing master, bolts over and nuzzles William's knee for reassurance. "Damned if I know. Maybe he's trying to be responsible and avoid international rates?"

Anna almost laughs. "That would be a first." Percy has gifts, but being sensible about money isn't one of them. "He has to know we're worried about him. He should have called us. This doesn't make sense." Now she's the one pacing.

"Give me the phone. I'll call the resort." She does; he does, but after a minute he puts the phone down with a grimace. "All circuits busy. I'm sure every friend and relative of everyone staying there is as worried as we are."

"Oh, God." Anna flings herself into the chair next to his. Bart trots over to nudge her hand; she tolerates this and then pats him, knowing that he's picked up on the emotions of his humans and needs reassurance. Poor thing. She can't imagine not being able to speak.

Bart licks her arm and goes back to William. A minute later, he comes back to Anna.

Now the dog's the one pacing.

"Let me take him for a walk," William says, standing up. "He obviously needs to burn off some energy. So do I."

Anna bites back her annoyance. "And what am I supposed to do?"

William rubs his eyes. "You could always come with us." She knows that he knows she won't. She hates walking the dog. She's never walked the dog. She feeds the dog and makes sure he has chew toys and cleans up after him inside the house—mopping up fur, slobber, masticated bits of chew toy—but outside, he's William's and Percy's.

As much as she enjoyed being alone before, she doesn't think she could stand it now. "Please don't leave right now, William. What if he calls? He'll want to talk to you. I need you here. Please."

"All right. All right." He sits down again. "So what do we do instead?"

"I have no idea." Bart's come to her again, and, huge as he is, has crawled halfway into her lap. Aren't Irish Wolfhounds supposed to be calm?

William stands up. "Anna, I can't stand this. I need to move. We can both go: I'll forward the house phone to my cell." But just as he's crossing the room to the dog's leash, hanging on a hook by the door—it's a measure of Bart's loyalty or neurosis that he doesn't remove himself from Anna's lap at this signal for Walk— the phone rings. It's much closer to Anna, but William gets to it first, because she's weighed down by the dog.

"Percy! Oh, thank God." Anna hears the relief in William's voice, feels joy washing over her like a drug. "Are you all right? Where are you?"

She watches William's face, sees him frown. "Okay. Okay, then. Right. See you soon." He ends the call and says quietly, "He's at the airport."

"And you didn't tell him about the flight? He must be there trying to book a ticket! William, honestly! Call him back and tell him—"

"Not the airport at Cabo." William's voice is oddly flat, and he's still frowning. "He's at Sea-Tac already. He called to see if we can pick him up."

4

*A*ll superheroes need origin stories, tales that explain what has set them apart: Spider-Man's radioactive arachnid bite, Superman's extraterrestrial birth, Batman's childhood trauma. Whether their special powers are a function of magic, metabolism, or machinery, there is always a foundational myth.

This is, of course, equally true of most supervillains. Consider the Joker and his chemical bath.

When Santamaria, Phillips, Morganthau, and McKenzie—the CC Four, as they are universally known—realized that their creation was a success and would be staying around for a while, they knew they had to decide where Comrade Cosmos had come from. He was an unusual superhero, strictly speaking not a superhero at all, since he had no special powers save an unusual gift for inspiring and organizing people. Furthermore, his nemesis was not a twisted sociopath, but the personification of a thermodynamic principle.

The CC Four went on a creative retreat, backpacking along the Pacific Rim Trail in Oregon one Labor Day weekend and hashing out Cosmos's backstory over their evening campfires. They decided that since his gifts were entirely human, their origins should be, too. The key to his personality, they decided, was his family.

Over the course of the weekend, they determined that CC's father, Charlie Cosmos, had earned his PhD in Rhetoric and Composition, writing his doctoral dissertation on the persuasive rhetoric of bumper stickers before leaving the academy to become a union organizer. While he was still in graduate school he met his wife, the beautiful physicist and Tai Chi master Anelda Villon, whose lucrative research career underwrote Charlie's passion for organizing daycare workers, burger flippers in fast-food joints, and carwash employees.

CC had a happy childhood. From Charlie, he acquired an abiding respect for the collective power of seemingly insignificant people, along with a knack for turning phrases. From Anelda, he learned the power of science and the importance of balance, of equilibrium, of yin and yang.

When CC was five, his little sister Vanessa was born. When he was eight, Vanessa had her first seizure. Over the course of the next five years, although Vanessa received excellent medical care and enormous love from her family, her epilepsy left her increasingly impaired. Before her first seizure, she had been a bright child, hyperverbal and affectionate. By the time she was ten, she no longer spoke, no longer recognized or responded to her own name.

This tragedy had a profound effect on the Cosmos clan. Anelda, distracted on her drive to work by an NPR story about epilepsy research, skidded on some garbage that had spilled onto the street during a freak windstorm, and was killed in the ensuing accident. Charlie, heartbroken, had a massive stroke triggered by the stress of his losses. He lived, but wound up in a wheelchair, the right side of his body essentially nonfunctional.

By the time CC was eighteen, his mother was dead and he was responsible for the care of two invalids, a task made easier by the continuing revenue from Anelda's scientific patents. He has always insisted on caring for them at home, albeit with a great deal of help from aides and therapists.

CC's loved ones were felled by disorder: the electrical storm in the brain, the coffee grounds and tire-slicing broken bottle scattered over the street, the weakened artery rupturing and unable to channel blood cells in their proper course. There was no one he could blame for these horrors, no vengeance he could exact. His enemy was simply the propensity of matter to fall apart.

The evening he fully realized this—after an exhausting day of dealing with insurance companies, durable-medical-equipment firms, his sister's constant drooling, and his father's incontinence—he paced and wept in his mother's old study, mourning all that had befallen him. "Curse you, Entropy!" he groaned in his grief, and at that moment, EE appeared, all shadow and stardust and howling darkness, cackling in the immemorial style of more embodied supervillains.

EE appeared when CC named him. Anyone who has studied the power of names in myth and folklore will recognize the motif. CC himself has never told anyone his first name. He withholds it in solidarity with Vanessa, who no longer knows her name, and with Charlie, who remembers his name but can no longer speak. Charlie and Vanessa's caregivers call him Mr. Cosmos. Communities devastated by sudden disaster or slowly accumulating chaos call him Comrade.

Rumors about Cosmos's name, and about what will or might happen should it ever be revealed—the end of this universe, the birth of a new one, the long-awaited advent of peace on Earth— are rife in fan communities. The CC Four will neither confirm nor deny these speculations.

Eating their baked beans and gorp around the glow of fading embers that Labor Day weekend, the Four fretted about the history they had just given their hero. Was it too dark? Would it irrevocably alter the tone of what had, until now, been a fairly tongue-in-cheek series? Would they be sued by disabilities advocates or lambasted by the American Stroke Association?

Even as they obsessed over PR issues, however, they knew in their bones that the history they had invented, or chosen or discovered, was the right one. It made sense. It felt true. It grounded CC, gave him more weight and depth and focus.

As a consequence, the series indeed darkened, but it also became even more popular than it had been before. It spoke to anyone who had ever struggled against chaos, whether in the form of hurricane debris or medical catastrophe or spilled coffee grounds. That is to say, it spoke to nearly all of us.

Along with origin stories, all superheroes also need buddies, sidekicks, or love interests. For most of them, the challenge is to find the one person with whom they can share their secret identity, often while leading a complicated double life: trying to hide the secret from the rest of the world while protecting the one to whom it has been revealed.

Comrade Cosmos has the opposite problem. While his first name is indeed a secret, everyone knows who he is and what he does. If he goes to the grocery store in jeans and a T-shirt to buy milk, the cashier will recognize him. Because he is a superhero of and for the people, even more than most superheroes are, he has never disguised himself. Since his archenemy is a principle of thermodynamics, he has never had to hide for fear of reprisals.

At the beginning of the series, he wore the standard spandex tights-and-cape combo so beloved of his ilk, but the CC Four quickly realized that the outfit simply wasn't practical for their character. In issue 12, he developed a spandex allergy and boxed up his suit for storage in the attic. He's shown as being relieved by this development, since he's always preferred natural fibers. A thought bubble above his head reads, "Heroes are what they do, not what they wear." Later, he will confess to his diary that he only wore the "silly suit" in the first place because he wasn't sure he could be a superhero without a cape. Before he had internalized his work and his reasons for doing it, he needed that external badge of authority. Now he doesn't.

His neighbors in the tiny Topeka suburb of Keyhole, Kansas—a location he chose for its geographical centrality and low cost of living—know who he is, although they do not know his first name. The health-care aides, therapists, doctors, and insurance-company employees with whom he so constantly deals know that they are negotiating hours, treatment plans, and reimbursements with a hero. His home phone number is listed—Cosmos, C.—although his cell number isn't, and he has the transparent e-mail address of comrade.cosmos@gmail.com.

Obviously, this creates some boundary issues. His phone rings at all hours with pleas for assistance. Strangers knock on his door to ask for help for themselves, their families, their communities. Although his mother's patents have made him as wealthy as Bruce Wayne, he is constantly turning down inappropriate gifts: offers from grateful beneficiaries of his services to pay his mortgage, free wheelchair vans, even bags of groceries that appear mysteriously on his doorstep. He doggedly diverts these resources to places that need them more than he does: food banks, struggling community hospitals and nursing homes, young married couples with young children trying to keep their homes in the midst of layoffs and foreclosures.

He also routinely turns down offers of lucrative endorsements. The purveyors of products and services as diverse as housing developments, closet-organizer systems, and air-traffic-control software eagerly clamor to use his name. "We are champions of order," the CEO of a company selling high-tech litter boxes once told him, "protecting the floors and noses of our customers from unwanted intrusion by cat waste, and we believe we are doing your work."

"Good," said Cosmos, who—even more emphatically than he shed his spandex suit—has long since shed the pseudo-Shakespearian diction of the first webzine. "Wonderful. That's great, really. Keep doing my work. But, you know, everybody should be champions of order, or at least part of the anti-Entropy resistance—that's what I do, bub, try to make everybody else a champion of order—and I don't need the money, and I just don't want my picture on a litter box. I don't even like cats, much, although maybe it's just because I've never lived with any. Sorry."

In the frame, he looks drawn, exhausted, with rumpled hair and bags under his eyes. In this issue, he has just had to fire his sister's home health-care aide, a minor imp of Entropy who tried to steal her medication for black-market resale. The agency has not yet sent a replacement, and so Cosmos has had to handle all of her care himself. He hasn't gotten much sleep. He's a little snappish.

Several issues later, Cosmos discovers that the litter box company has been using his name and likeness anyway. An attorney contacts him to find out if he wants to sue. He refuses. He's not a brand. He won't copyright his name or visage.

"But then anyone will be able to claim that they're doing your work!" the attorney protests.

"Well, if they are, good for them. I *want* everybody to be doing my work. If everybody were doing my work, I wouldn't have to do so much of it, and neither would the other people who are doing it but aren't getting enough help. If everybody were doing my work, we'd all be less burned out, you know?"

"Harummph!" snorts the attorney. "So if imitators sprang up claiming to be you, stealing your identity, that wouldn't bother you?"

"Stealing my identity? If they're stealing my Social Security number or Google password, sure, it bothers me. But imitators? I *want* people to imitate me. Have you been paying attention at *all*? *Any* of you? Imitating me is the entire *point*. I want more imitators than Elvis. I won't be happy until I have so many imitators that even *I* can't tell who I am anymore. Beware of non-imitations! Say, are you allergic to spandex?"

"Pardon?"

"I have a present for you," Cosmos says, and sends him the box with the tights and cape in it. When the attorney calls to thank him, he tells Cosmos the ensemble doesn't fit. "Sure it does," Cosmos says wearily. "It fits everybody. Try again. Just keep trying: you'll see."

This sequence offers obvious opportunity for Christian exegesis, and clergy leapt on it, pointing out the correspondences between Cosmos's rhetoric and Jesus' love-your-neighbor commandment, identifying the attorney with the rich young lawyer in the Gospels. Jesus, like Cosmos, had to struggle to escape the needy multitudes and find time and space for himself.

But clergy—and therapists, teachers, health-care providers, social workers, and emergency personnel—relate to Cosmos quite aside from any theological subtext. They identify with his efforts to lead his own life in the midst of constant, urgent demands from others. They empathize with the fact that he can't go to dinner parties without the other guests telling him how chaos has struck their own lives, just as doctors can't attend social events without being treated to catalogs of symptoms. They feel in their own bones the pressure he faces, the fact that he always has to be on his best behavior, because he represents more than himself. If Cosmos disappoints or betrays his constituency, they will lose faith not just in him, but in everything he stands for.

Helping professionals know from firsthand experience what a prison such expectations can be. They know the burden of fiduciary trust. And thus many of them, early in the life of the franchise, became as concerned about Cosmos as if he were flesh and blood, a friend or family member. Scores of them wrote letters to the CC Four, fretting about Cosmos's reluctance to ask for help with his own difficulties, cataloging his symptoms of stress, demanding that he get an unlisted number and disconnect his doorbell. "Give him a vacation!" more than one reader insisted. "He can't delegate any more than he does, because his entire mission's about delegation, but he needs a break from delegating. He needs to go on a trip where he isn't responsible for anybody but himself and doesn't have to worry about anything. That would be hard, of course, because of Charlie and Vanessa. But if you can't give him a vacation, for heaven's sake, can't you give the poor guy a friend? Somebody who knows his first name? Somebody he can hang with when he wants to drink beer and let his hair down?"

Thus Roger Cadwallader was born.

Roger is a librarian, another Champion of Order. He runs the Keyhole Community Library almost single-handedly, since most of the rest of the staff has been laid off in one or another budget emergency. Roger and Cosmos met when Cosmos went to the library to borrow some audiobooks for his father. Cosmos watched Roger, middle-aged and balding and spreading at the waist, explain the Dewey Decimal System to a visiting third-grade class. He could tell from Roger's smile and nod that Roger knew who he was. He was deeply grateful that Roger didn't say, "Hey, kids, look who's here! It's Comrade Cosmos!"

Roger treated Cosmos like any other patron. After they became friends, Cosmos learned about Roger's struggles to keep the library open, to maintain the funding he needs to acquire materials. He learned that Roger is a widower who nursed his wife through cancer, and is thus as intimately familiar with health-care snarls and insurance companies as Cosmos himself. He discovered that when his nerves are jangled, going to the library after hours to help Roger reshelve books—unasked, simply as an act of companionship—is just what he needs to regain his balance.

Roger does not know, and probably will never know, Cosmos's first name. Cosmos still has a listed phone number and a working doorbell. But now Cosmos also has a friend and sidekick, and often, in the deep silence of the library at night, after everything has been returned to its rightful place and the integrity of the Dewey Decimal System has been upheld, he and Roger sit behind the reference desk and share a beer.

5

*t*he windshield wipers emit a steady squeak as Anna, William, and Percy drive back from the airport. The car's a Lexus, and it's last year's model. It shouldn't make infuriating noises. Anna makes a mental note to call the dealer tomorrow.

Her earlier panic and determination have dissolved into exhaustion and badly jangled nerves; from William's white knuckles on the steering wheel, she guesses he feels the same. Percy huddles in the backseat. He's hugging his backpack; his small duffel bag sits next to him. When Anna spotted him waiting for them at the curb, he looked as impossibly huge-eyed as a child. He hugged her more fiercely than he has in years.

"You're all right. You're safe," she told him. "Oh, Percy, it must have been horrible."

"Yeah." He shivered. He didn't seem to want to meet her eyes; he was probably steeling himself for a barrage of questions. "Can I get into the car now? It's cold here, after Mexico."

"So," Anna says now, risking one question at least, "do you feel like talking about it?"

"Not yet," William says firmly. "Not while I'm driving, please. Save that for home. Tell us about the vacation part. There must have been some fun, too. You were there five days before—"

"Yeah," says Percy. "Well, you know, I swam every day. I went snorkeling, and I saw fish, but there are more in Hawai'i, and the water's clearer and warmer. But I saw sea lions and manta rays; that was pretty cool. And there were whales and dolphins. And the market there's awesome, Mom, you'd love it, it's right around the harbor with all the cruise boats and tour boats and stuff, all kinds of jewelry and pottery." Even over the windshield wipers, she hears him swallow. "I was going to buy you something, but I was waiting until the last day, and then—"

"Percy," she says. "For God's sake. You're home and you're all right. That's more precious to me than any souvenir."

"Your mother bought you something," William says. "A plane ticket. For tomorrow. Only then it turned out you were already on the plane."

Anna feels her jaw clenching. Is he going to give her grief about the two hundred seventy dollars? Under the circumstances, that's spare change. "I'll try to cancel it," she snaps. "I don't even remember if it's a refundable ticket. It probably isn't, but if I call—"

"I'm sorry," Percy says. "I'll pay you back, Mom. I should have called you to say I was coming home, but it all happened so quickly."

"Honey, it's okay." William, eyebrows raised, shoots her a glance. Percy's never, ever, offered to reimburse them for anything before. Anna shrugs, mouths "shock." People act oddly in crises.

"You hungry?" William asks, changing the subject. "We can stop to eat. There isn't much in the house."

"Nah, I ate at the airport. I want to go home."

No one says anything for the rest of the drive. When they get into the house, Bart trots up with a joyous bark to greet Percy, whose face brightens into a smile when he sees the dog. Bart jumps up, putting his paws on Percy's shoulders, and licks Percy's face.

"Bart," William says, snapping his fingers, "down. Come on, Perse—you know better than to let him do that."

"This once," Anna says, "I think we can forgive it."

"No bad habits. If he did that to my mother, she'd collapse under the weight."

"He doesn't like your mother. He ignores her. Percy's his person."

But Bart, obedient, is down on all fours again. Percy looks like he's about to cry. His eyes are red; his fingers tap a jittering rhythm against his thighs. "Sweetheart," Anna says, "sit down. Let me make you some soup, anyway."

"Not hungry, Mom." But he sits on the couch, and seems to calm a little when the dog's head is pillowed in his lap.

"All right," William says. "Now. Now, tell us about it."

Percy looks down at the dog's ears. He starts running them through his fingers, but stops when Bart pulls away with a soft whimper of displeasure. "I—this morning I got up and went to the pool, but there were all these police outside one of the rooms, and then somebody said there'd been a murder, and I just—I wanted to come home. A bunch of us did. We all got a van to the airport and booked flights."

"What did people at the resort say about the murder?" William's leaning forward, eyes narrowed. Sometimes Anna thinks he should have been a lawyer, not an art dealer. Does he have to probe? Right now, this minute, when Percy hasn't even been home for an hour? Can't he just let Percy say whatever he needs to say?

"Well, nobody knew much. Some lady, stabbed in her room, they said, and somebody said the place had been ransacked, robbed, but it was all rumors. I mean, the police weren't saying anything, which meant the resort people weren't, either." He hugs himself, shivering; his foot's beating a tattoo against the carpet. "I don't want to think about it. I want to go to bed now."

"All right," William says, but he's frowning again, and Anna wonders how in the world Percy's going to sleep, with all that nervous energy. This isn't like him; he's usually a fairly calm kid. "We know you must be tired after the flight. It's good to have you home, Perse."

Anna follows him into his room, garish posters be damned. She wants to sit with him while he falls asleep, the way she did when he was small, wants to stand guard over him to keep the monsters at bay. But he turns to her, face slack with exhaustion, holding his hands up as if to ward her off. "Mom. Do you mind?"

Stung, she steps back. The boy who hugged her so fiercely at the airport has vanished. "I—"

"I know you're glad I'm back. I'm glad I'm back. But I'd like some privacy."

Anna tries to smile. "All right. Will you let the dog stay in here, though?"

To her relief, Percy nods. "Yeah. I'd like him to. I missed him."

Anna sticks her head into the hallway and calls Bart, who lopes joyously toward the summons. Bart's ancestors hunted wolves, and Anna feels a primitive relief in the assurance that the animal will protect her child.

She finds William in the study, peering at the computer. He's still frowning. When he hears her walk into the room, he looks up. The frown dissolves, but his face remains grave. "Anna, I'm reading the news stories. AP, Reuters. They say no description of the killing has been released to the public: that cop thing of using the details to weed out suspects and false confessions."

Percy's home. That's all that counts. She shakes her head. "So?"

"Sit down." William pushes the extra desk chair toward her. She sits. "According to the news stories, one of the housekeepers found the body and called the front office, who called the police, but they kept the whole thing very quiet precisely because they didn't want the other guests to panic."

Anna rubs her eyes. She's very tired. She feels like she should know what this means, but her mind veers away when she tries to consider it. "Yes, and? William, I'm sorry, but can you cut to the chase? I don't know where you're going with this."

William gives her a long, level look. His voice is strained, on the verge of cracking. "The guests weren't told what had happened until a few hours before it made the news. None of them knew anything until then; the cops came in plainclothes. A guest interviewed at the resort said it just seemed like a normal day, with people hanging out by the pool and eating in the restaurant. They specifically asked that no one leave until the police had interviewed everyone."

Now Anna's frowning. The angles of the room seem to be bending, and she has to blink to make them straight again. She doesn't want to understand this. She doesn't want to know what he's trying to tell her. "But Percy said—"

"Yes. Exactly." William shakes his head. He looks older than he did two hours ago. "By the time the news went public, he was already on the plane. He had to be. The timing doesn't work otherwise."

Melinda's life as a mother begins with a thirteen-hour flight home to Reno from Guatemala City. Jeremy, who's two and a half but looks younger, who's unused to motion and pressure changes, cramped space and strange adults holding him, howls almost the entire way, earning glares from other passengers. Melinda and Walter try to quiet him with food, with toys, with songs and games. He won't nap, and Melinda refuses to give him anything to help him sleep, although she's heard of other parents doing so on planes.

Long past both exhaustion and tears, she tries to cradle her new son, whispering into his hair, "I love you, I love you, I love you." She's intensely grateful that Walter came with her. What would she have done without him to handle paperwork, bribes, luggage, and maps?

Everyone they've encountered on the trip—except the officials directly involved in the adoption, who know the true story—have mistaken Walter and Melinda for a couple. It's a logical mistake, and it's no one else's business that Melinda decided to adopt as a single parent, so she and Walter don't correct the well-meaning fellow passengers who congratulate them on the adoption.

Jeremy has brown skin and dark black hair. Melinda's hair is ash-blond, already graying, and Walter's a redhead. It's obvious that Jeremy's adopted. Melinda has thought about this, about the problems Jeremy will face because he looks different—Reno is still in many ways a small town—but has decided that life in an orphanage would be much worse.

They have to change planes in Dallas; that flight's delayed, and the wait turns into a new species of hell. Jeremy lies on his back, kicks his heels, and screams himself purple. But finally a flight attendant produces a finger puppet from somewhere and sings a lullaby in Spanish, and he quiets. Spanish isn't really his mother tongue; K'iché is. But Spanish is what he heard at the orphanage.

Melinda—shamefully, she now realizes—knows only one Spanish song, the hymn *"Santo, Santo, Santo, Mi Corazón,"* which the overwhelmingly white congregation at St. Phil's sings every few weeks. She and Walter take turns singing it to Jeremy, until at last he sleeps.

They sleep, too, on that second flight, and wake on landing. Rosemary and Tom, beaming, are waiting at the gate with a new stroller. Veronique's there, too, not beaming—Melinda wouldn't recognize her if she were—but bearing a shopping bag of toys and clothing. Everyone admires Jeremy, coos at him, touches his soft skin. Melinda's grateful that he continues to sleep soundly through all this, worn out from his previous tantrums.

The other four come into the house, help get Jeremy settled in his crib—soon enough he'll need a big-boy bed—and praise his loveliness. "You're home," Rosemary says. "The hard part's over."

"Oh, no," Melinda says, looking at her sleeping child. So small. He's been stunted until now, like most of the orphanage kids. But she paid for an American-trained doctor down there to evaluate him, and he's basically healthy. He'll grow, and she'll help him grow, and she'll grow, too. "The hard part's just started."

*j*eremy awakens to the sound of birdsong. When he opens his eyes, he sees sunlight streaming through a window, and he thinks the sunlight should make him happy, because it was raining yesterday, but the window's in the wrong place. This isn't his dorm room, and it's not the house. Where is he?

And then he remembers where he is, and why.

He wishes he could go back to sleep, but he knows he won't be able to. He's alert now, awake. Too awake: tense. He slept well. This is a better bed than any he usually sleeps in: expensive sheets, just the right kind of pillow, a fine firm mattress. And everything smells like fabric softener.

The smell of clean laundry has always been the scent of safety for him. But now it brings a vertiginous rush of memory, and he understands quite clearly that everything he sees and hears and smells and tastes from now on, for longer than he wants to imagine, and maybe for the rest of his life, will plunge him into Mom-movies.

His mother, sorting the laundry, letting him fold the easy stuff, the towels and dishcloths. How old was he then? Six? Eight? *If you're really good, I'll teach you to iron.*

Mom, waving a red fabric napkin like a bullfighter's cape. Using a pair of socks as hand puppets and challenging him to match the other pairs in under a minute, while her two hands delivered an NBC sports–style commentary. Right hand wagging, fingers and thumb opening and closing like a talking mouth: "Will he find the other argyle? He only has ten seconds left, Joe! Can he do it?"

And now the left hand: "Yes! Yes, Cindy-Lou, he used his eagle eyes to find the other argyle inside the arm of that shirt! Here he goes! He's putting them together! He's matching heel to heel!"

Back to the right: "And yes, he's done it! Look at that, Joe! He matched all the socks in *under a minute*! Jeremy Soto is once again the champion sock-matcher!"

Mom doing the laundry, every week, several times a week. Putting clean, soft jeans, neatly folded, on his closet shelf, even when he was fighting with her, being shitty to her, neglecting his own chores. Yard work. Taking out the garbage.

They had such stupid fights about taking out the garbage.

They had fights about how much time he spent reading *CC* instead of doing homework. They had fights about going to church camp. They had fights about the fact that he was adopted.

He'll always remember Mom, and he will never remember his birth mother, never know anything about her. All he knows, from the Internet and the library, is the chaos of the country he came from.

Why couldn't Mom vacation in the States? She could have gone to San Francisco, Sedona, Palm Springs. If she'd stayed here, she'd have been safe. Safer.

Is he being a racist now? He doesn't know. He doesn't care.

He forces himself to sit up, to swing his feet out of bed and onto the floor. He has to get up. He can't lie in Hen's guest room and cry all day.

Get a move on, kiddo. Time's a wasting. Mom's voice, in his head.

He grabs the small duffel bag on the dresser—Hen stopped by the dorm last night so he could pick up some clothing—and pulls on jeans and a shirt. Then he shuffles into shoes and follows the smell of food downstairs.

Lasagna. He smells lasagna. Mom always made lasagna, because it was his favorite food.

He hears voices before he rounds the corner into the dining room. Very Bitchy. She's the last person he wants to see. He knows he should thank her for taking the phone last night, for canceling class and driving him to Aunt Rosie's, but all he feels right now is despair and rage. None of it should have happened. He shouldn't have to be in a position to have to thank VB. He shouldn't have had to wake up in a strange room, shouldn't have to be wondering if someone else's lasagna will be as good as his mother's.

Hen, VB, and Rosemary are sitting around the table. They look up as he enters. VB and Aunt Rosie say, "Good morning," nearly in unison, too obviously trying to sound cheerful.

"Jeremy." Hen isn't trying to sound cheerful. "How are you? Did you get any sleep?"

"I slept fine," he says, and sits down. The table's huge, meant to seat eight or ten, too large for the room. Behind Jeremy is a cabinet with glass doors showing piles of teacups and little statues and stuff. Fragile stuff, all pink and blue. If he moves, he'll break something. If he breathes, he'll break something.

"Are you hungry?" Hen says. "Everybody from church has been bringing food, because I told them you're staying with me and they don't know what else to do. We have enough lasagna to feed the five thousand."

"I guess I could eat." Much as he loves lasagna, he prefers cereal right after waking up. But he's a guest, and has to take what he's given.

His rage grows, flaring in his gut. His whole life, he's been a guest.

Rosemary heaps his pink-and-blue plate, and Hen brings him a glass of milk. He looks down at the food. Mom made him lasagna every birthday. One year when he was little and into fossils, she cooked metal dinosaur charms into the lasagna, as if the meat and noodles were geologic layers. "Chew carefully, kids!"

His eyes are wet. He doesn't want them to be. He stabs his fork into the food and winces as the metal skids off the bottom of the plate. No dinosaurs here: it's just Hen's china. He has to be careful. He can't scratch the priest's precious plates, even though he longs to break everything on the table, everything in the cabinet, everything in the house.

He can't eat this. He puts his fork down.

"Tom's going down to Mexico to get your mom," Hen says.

"Do you want to go? I need to ask now, because he's leaving in a few hours."

The smell of the food's making him sick. "Why would I want to do that? He's not 'getting my mom.' She's not alive anymore. He's getting what's left of her."

"Right," Hen says. She sounds very calm. "Jeremy, do you want to see her body, or is it okay with you if she's cremated there? You can take your time with that one. Tom won't have to make that call for a day or two."

"I don't have to take my time." He picks up his fork again. He has to try to eat. How can he eat? "I don't want to see her dead. I don't want to see what happened to her. Let them burn her."

"Think about it," Hen says. "Tom will let us know when we need to decide."

"I've decided." He can't eat, not right now. He suddenly yearns to go jogging, to run forever, to burn all the fury out of his system. With each step, he'll picture stomping on the face and balls of the bastard who did this. He'll punch the air and imagine connecting with flesh, blood, and bone.

He pushes away from the table, stands up. "Not hungry. Sorry."

"That's fine," Hen says. "We're going to sit in the living room and start working on your mom's service. Will you join us?"

"Yeah. Sure." His fury flames and flares. "While we're at it, are we having a service for my other mother? The one murdered in Guatemala?"

He's only saying it to let out his rage, to make them feel guilty. He researched Guatemala because Mom expected him to. If he's anything, he's American. But Hen, for once, looks at a loss. VB and Rosie rustle, suck in air, cough. "Do you want us to?" Rosemary says at last. "We'll certainly pray for her."

"Great. Terrific." Jeremy brushes past the treacherous cabinet into the living room and plunks himself down on the couch, hard. The others stand now, too, and follow him. "You gonna pray for everybody else murdered or disappeared down there? In the genocide? All two hundred thousand of them?" He realizes he's punching the couch with each word.

Good. That feels good, even though he's being a complete hypocrite. He doesn't care about politics. He never has. Mom wanted him to be some kind of radical, but all he wanted to do was read *CC,* and he's a hypocrite about that, too, because he's not even a good Comrade. He's just a fan.

But he's on a roll, so he keeps punching. "You gonna pray for all the victims of all those other genocides, Germany and Cambodia and fucking Armenia, and Darfur and Sierra Leone and probably a dozen other places I don't even know about?"

"Yes," Hen says. "We are."

"Yeah, good. That'll really help." He switches arms. Keep hitting, even though it hurts. "That'll keep all those people from being dead, won't it? It'll stop people from killing each other, because that always works. Right."

"Prayer," says Hen, "reminds us to do other things. I believe that prayer helps by itself, but the other things certainly do. Helping with money and food, with medical supplies, with aid to relief organizations—"

"Not to mention military aid," Jeremy said. Relief organizations: please. Fucking Comrade Hen. Even if Jeremy ever had been a good Comrade, he couldn't be one now. Not anymore, not after this. Time to write a WISS essay. Jeremy will be a Minion for the rest of his life, eating donuts and lasagna.

He can't sit anymore. The punching isn't enough. He gets up and moves restlessly around the room, hating himself for his charade but unable to stop. "The U.S. underwrote the Guatemalan civil war. They supported the government because they were afraid of communism, even though the government was butchering Mayans. The U.S. knew what was going on, but they kept providing training and weapons and money. Just like we funded fucking Al Qaeda."

"Couldn't agree more," Very Bitchy says, giving him an odd look, and Hen nods.

Rosemary's frowning. She would be. Walter was military before he went to law school, and they're Republicans. Somehow Mom still stayed friends with them. "Rosie and I just don't discuss politics," she told him once.

Tough luck. He glares at Rosemary, says, "Oh, you think it doesn't matter? You think this is a wonderful country of freedom and liberty, and I should be grateful, right?"

Rosemary coughs. "Well, actually—"

"Well, actually, it kind of sucks that the country that took me in is also the one that helped kill my real mother." All three of them wince, but he goes on. He doesn't care whose feelings he hurts, and he realizes in a giddy rush that he isn't faking anymore. "Yeah, I know, Mom was my real mother because she took care of me, and if she hadn't I'd be in an orphanage and I wouldn't be able to talk or walk, boo-hoo, you probably wish right now that I couldn't talk, right?"

"No." All of them speak in unison.

Which means yes. He doesn't care. "The day Mom told me about the war in Guatemala? The day she told me my real mother had been killed by the fucking Guatemalan army with weapons from the U.S.? They destroyed six hundred and twenty-six Mayan villages. They cut open the wombs of pregnant women and cut babies in half. 'Course she didn't tell me those parts. I had to do research. Had to find out on my own." He glares at Very Bitchy. "You think I'm stupid. You think I don't know how to do research, but I do." Even if it was just to get Mom off my back.

VB gazes coolly back. "Yes, you certainly do, Jeremy. So do I. The genocide was in the early eighties. You were born in 1990, and your mother adopted you in 1993."

"Yeah, 1990." Library facts he doesn't even know he remembers march out of his mouth. "The year the army massacred thirteen people, including kids, in Santiago Atitlan. And 1993? That's when the UN peace talks were suspended because they weren't working. There'd been civil war that whole time, remember?"

Very Bitchy's sitting up straighter now. She gives him one of her thin smiles and starts to say something, but Henrietta interrupts her with a cough. "That must have been very hard," Hen says quietly. "Learning about your birth mother."

"Hard? Hard for Mom, or me?"

"Both of you."

"Yeah, sure." He jabs the air with both fists, one-two. VB and Aunt Rosie shrink back. Hen simply watches him. "I don't know if it was hard for her, because right afterwards she gave me this speech about how God is great and loving and we have to do good deeds to try to fix the world, like anything could fix my real mother being dead."

He looks at them, these white white women, with their white skin even whiter now because they're all paler than usual. His fault. Aunt Rosie's started to cry. His fault. He doesn't care. He's tired of being the only brown person. Not in Reno, certainly, but in Mom's circles. He's tired of being Mom's token. "My real mother. The one who looked like me. The one who took care of me and loved me until she got her head blown off, or maybe she was raped by some army bastard and didn't love me. Or maybe she was raped and loved me anyway. I figure those are the three most likely options. Or maybe somebody else took care of me, but I know *somebody* loved me, because I was still alive. And whatever happened, it ends with heads being blown off, and you're going to talk to me about God and love?"

They stare at him. "This is entirely healthy and very understandable," Hen says. "Of course you're angry. So are we."

"Great. That makes me feel so much better." He sits down again, in a free chair this time, and starts clenching and unclenching his hands to try to get them to unknot.

"Jeremy," Aunt Rosie says. "Your mother loved—"

"Me. I know. And all of you love me, and all your husbands or whatever love me, too. Walter was great, really, a great guy, when he still knew his own name. Tom's a great guy." He looks at Hen.

"Ed's a great guy. But none of them look like me, and they aren't my dad. Even if my dad was a rapist."

"No," Aunt Rosie says. She hasn't reacted to the Walter barb. Not visibly, anyway. "They aren't. Would you rather have stayed in the orphanage?" Her voice is very gentle.

"No." Exhaustion sweeps over him. " 'Course not."

Very Bitchy is still peering at him. "Jeremy, what would Comrade Cosmos do?"

"What?" Jeremy squints at her. VB, deigning to talk about Comrade Cosmos? Either she's on drugs or Jeremy's much more pathetic than he sounds even to himself. "How the hell do I know? He's just a story. A comic book, remember?"

Very Bitchy nods. Hen's frowning, and Rosemary looks as startled as Jeremy feels. "Yes, I know. But he's the story you live your life by, and you just outlined a series of stories about what might have happened to the people who raised you. Stories are important." She sits forward on her chair. "Well?"

"I have no idea. What could he do? What could anybody do? He restores order. He makes things right again. But entropy's won, down there. It's too broken to fix."

"Nothing's too broken to fix," Hen says.

He stands up, shaky, breathing hard. "Mom is. And I don't see your God doing anything about it, and a comic book can't, either." He swallows, throat raw, and says, "I have to get outside. Have to walk. You—all of you, make your plans. I'll tell you if I want to change anything when I get back."

They murmur assent, and he escapes to the front door. Here's his jacket, hanging with Hen and Ed's stuff. Here are his hat and gloves in the pocket. Here's the doorknob.

And then he's out, away, into a gloriously golden autumn day. Run. Run it out. Run forever.

* * *

*t*hat was smart," Hen says. "Asking him about Comrade Cosmos."

"Thank you." Veronique despises comic books, the dumbing down of narrative, but they're what speaks to Jeremy. And she thinks that she doesn't despise them as much, right now, as she despises any Judeo-Christian god who could allow this to happen to Melinda.

Rosemary and the priest are trying to be kind, including her in the funeral planning the same way Melinda always included her in social events, picnics and Scrabble nights and the Alaska cruise. She knows it's good of them. She doesn't care. Her knee still hurts, even though it's not raining anymore. Her head throbs. Her chest aches. She envy's Jeremy's ability—his license—simply to leave. He's Melinda's son. He can do whatever he wants right now, short of damage to property or people.

She plans to cancel her classes next week. She'll call in sick. She has plenty of sick time, and she might as well use it. Given how rotten she feels right now, it's not even a stretch.

Only relatives get bereavement leave; it doesn't matter that Melinda was her best friend. These days, Veronique and Sarabeth could register as domestic partners, if Sarabeth were still around, but there's nothing similar for platonic friends so close they might as well be family.

Part of her knows that her department would understand, even if there's no formal paperwork for the situation. But she'd rather nurse her resentment.

"We need to pick out hymns," Hen says quietly. "Can you tell me which were Melinda's favorites?"

"The old ones," Rosemary says. "'Simple Gifts.' Shape-note hymns. She liked Taizé, too."

"Good. That's a good start. Thank you, Rosie."

Veronique shakes her head. "I'm sorry. I couldn't do this even if I knew Melinda's taste in church music. I can't think about pretty little songs right now. I should go home. I'm not a church-goer. You two can plan the service."

The priest nods. "If you need to go home, we'll understand. But what do you want to talk about?"

Veronique glares at her. What does this woman *think* she wants to talk about? What other topic is there, right now? "I know Melinda didn't believe in the death penalty. I know you probably don't, either. But right now, if I could get my hands on the guy who did this—"

"I know," Rosemary says. "Me, too."

"Me three," says the priest, but she's as unruffled as ever, and Veronique's stomach feels like a cauldron. Honor complexity, she always tells her students, and they never do, but she has to. "Except that before I came over here, I browsed the Net a bit. Read the news stories, which didn't say much. No one heard anything, even though the rooms on either side of hers were occupied."

Rosemary shivers. "Weird."

"That's one word for it. No leads, but the police are collecting DNA samples from staff and guests, yada yada. So then I looked at the reader comments: equal parts 'what a terrible tragedy' and racist rants about how Mexicans just love to murder American tourists, and those made me furious, too. So if I want to kill the killer and I want to kill the idiots spewing bigoted filth, what does that make me?"

"Human," says the priest. "Are they using her name yet?"

"No."

The priest nods. "I think that has to wait until Tom's identified the body. Even though there's really no doubt."

Veronique can't imagine having to identify the body. Someone should go with Tom, just for moral support, but she certainly won't do it. She should go home. She should leave. Why does she keep talking?

But she keeps talking. "I keep thinking about Melinda's book group at the library. I was there once when some woman asked why Melinda wouldn't let us read murder mysteries. She could have been one of my students: 'Why do we have to read all these serious books?' Idiot. And Melinda said, 'I don't want to read about people dying horribly, especially in books that *aren't* supposed to be serious.' She said, 'Those books turn senseless, violent death into a puzzle with a neat solution: once you've caught the murderer, the puzzle's solved, and the world's safe again.' She said that was fundamentally dishonest."

Rosemary laughs; the priest raises an eyebrow. "She said all that? To a library patron?"

"She did." If you can't imagine her doing that, lady priest, you didn't know her very well. "The woman walked out, of course. But here we are, in a murder mystery. I *hate* murder mysteries. I hate this. Melinda would have hated it."

"We all hate it," the priest says gently. She looks at her watch. "But planning Melinda's service is the best thing we can do right now. It's necessary, and it's constructive. And I'm sorry, but I have to leave in fifteen minutes. I promised to keep the church doors open this afternoon. A lot of people will want to talk. I'm glad Sunday's All Souls. That's one small blessing."

And I, Veronique thinks, am sick of talking, and think the word "blessing" is obscene in this setting. She stands. "I have to leave now. I'm sorry. You have my number if there's anything specific I can do."

As she walks down the priest's driveway to her car, she wonders if she's just running away. Women in flight. But she can't flee this. No matter where she goes, she can't unknow what has happened. If she could, she would.

*r*osemary drives home in a haze of pain and grief. This is even worse than Walter's diagnosis and decline: for all its horrors, Alzheimer's is an illness, a natural process. What happened to Melinda—

She can't even think what to call it, how to describe it. Her brain freezes at the mere attempt.

She remembers the last time she saw Melinda, at church the

Sunday before she left for Mexico. She'd been happy, glad that Jeremy was surviving his first semester of college, glad that she was taking a long overdue solo vacation.

It was an utterly normal Sunday morning: no omens, no premonitions, no gathering thunderclouds. Walter's condition had at least produced clues, growing evidence that something was wrong, that worse was coming. There had been time to adjust, to prepare.

Walter. Should she tell him about Melinda? Can he understand? Will he remember Melinda?

Will he remember Rosemary?

Can she even bear to visit him?

She weighs options as she drives. Melinda's name hasn't been made public yet, but it will be soon, within the next few days. There are televisions all over the nursing home, and while Rosemary doubts that the staff often puts on the news—especially in the Alzheimer's wing—this is a local story, one that might even interrupt other programming. And people will be talking about it. Can she trust that Walter won't see or hear anything, or that if he does, he won't have one of his sudden, increasingly rare flashes of recognition and understand his loss?

She can't take the gamble, can't risk his finding out when she isn't with him. She has to try to tell him.

Melinda's one of their oldest friends. Walter and Rosemary knew her before Veronique did, before anyone at church did; they were the ones who invited her to St. Phil's.

Walter has more memories of Melinda than anyone else Rosemary knows. Even if Rosemary decides not to tell him that Melinda's dead, maybe she can somehow spark those memories. Maybe, if even only for a few minutes, she can take both of them back to a happier time.

And so, instead of going home, she goes to the nursing home for the first time in weeks. It's early afternoon, and Golden Meadows has a rehab wing, which means that many of its denizens still get visitors. Right now, the bright halls bustle: aides, doctors, relatives with flowers, children bringing crayoned artwork to their grandparents. Residents sit in the corridors in their wheelchairs, aimless but smiling, able to respond to a passing stranger's "Hello" or "Good morning."

At night, the visitors leave, and the halls darken. The wheelchairs and their occupants gather around the nursing station, carried by time and gravity, like leaves collecting in a drain. The residents moan; sometimes they scream or sob, reaching out clawlike, beseeching hands to anyone walking by.

During the day, the facility seems clean, almost antiseptic. At night, it smells faintly of urine and feces, interlaced with the astringent scent of bleach and the mostly unappetizing aromas from dinner trays.

Rosemary hates the nursing home at night.

Even at 1 P.M. on a brilliantly sunny day, she's shaking as she walks into the facility. She realizes, with shame, that she worries what the staff will say about her, the wife who no longer visits, who's abandoned her husband.

Maybe they won't judge her. Maybe they'll understand. The day Walter was admitted, an aide told Rosemary, "It's so hard, with Alzheimer's. They stop knowing you, and it gets too painful to visit." Even at the time, she recognized this as a kindness: a stranger giving her permission to let go, to leave Walter's husk behind.

Guilt grips her anyway. She remembers a presentation on grief during her chaplaincy training. Guilt's a universal response to loss, the teacher said. Everyone feels it. What you need to tell mourners is that if they didn't feel guilty about whatever's tearing them apart right now, they'd feel guilty about something else.

Rosemary walks to Walter's room without looking right or left, without meeting the eyes of staff or other visitors or the helpless creatures in their wheelchairs. Later, she'll go to the nursing station and alert someone there about the Melinda situation, but right now she needs to see Walter, before she loses her nerve. She wonders if he'll look different: thinner, grayer. But there's been no dramatic change in his condition. They'd have called her if there had been.

When she enters his room, an attendant's helping him out of his wheelchair and back into bed. She can see only his scrawny neck and large ears, the random tufts of gray hair he's kept despite swathes of baldness, his stooped shoulders under the blue-and-white cotton pajamas she bought on sale at Macy's last summer. Walter has always insisted on 100% cotton pajamas. From the bunching of the bottoms around his waist, she can tell he's wearing Depends under them.

No one has seen her yet. She stands and watches his tottering rise from the wheelchair, his slow-motion crash-landing in bed, the fussing of the aide who tucks him in. "There you go, Walter. Do you want me to raise or lower the bed? Do you need another pillow? What's that, sweetheart?" Rosemary didn't hear him say anything. "Do you want the TV on?"

Oh, God. Not the TV. Please, not the TV. Not unless it's cartoons or old movies, with the news locked out.

Aching, Rosemary tries to look at Walter as if he's a stranger. If he were a patient in the ER, someone she'd never met, what would she see? An old man, frail, being helped by someone kind. An old man who's safe despite disability and disintegration. She isn't watching a tragedy. She's watching an act of compassion.

But she can't get that distance. He's Walter. They've spent over half their lives together.

Perhaps she's made a noise, because now one bony finger points at the door. The aide turns to follow it. "Why, look, Walter! You have a visitor!"

Rosemary has never met this aide before. How long has the woman been working here? What will she think of the wife who's only appeared now for the first time?

"I'm Rosemary. Walter's wife."

"Walter! Your wife's here!" The aide beams, introduces herself with some Filipina name that speeds by in a blur and that Rosemary's too embarrassed to ask for again, and then says, "Walter just had a nice lunch. Didn't you, Walter? You had ham and mashed potatoes. You had a good appetite today."

"That's wonderful," Rosemary says weakly. Ham. He's always loved ham. She used to love making it for him. She blinks back tears and says, "Thank you for taking care of him."

She expects the aide to retort, *Someone has to.* But instead the woman only says cheerfully, "It's my pleasure. I'll leave you two alone now, so you can have your visit. Let me know if you need anything." Short and bustling, she looks Rosemary in the eyes as she passes, and smiles, and squeezes Rosemary's arm. It's okay, the touch seems to say. It's okay that you haven't been here. He didn't miss you, and the rest of us understand. And you're here now.

Rosemary walks to the bed now, sits on the chair placed there should Walter feel like sitting up, or should anyone come to see him. "Walter? It's Rosie. Do you remember me?"

"Hello," he says, and holds his hand out for her to shake. Throat aching, she does. "It's nice to meet you." His voice is soft, tentative, as if he hasn't used it in a while. "Do you live here?"

She swallows. "No. I live in the house where you used to live. I'm your wife. Do you remember living with me?" She speaks gently, as she'd speak to an ER patient, a stranger.

His gaze clouds now, and his hand goes to his mouth in a gesture she knows, a signal of social embarrassment. It's what he's always done after a faux pas: mangling a client's name, forgetting an appointment, neglecting to ask after a neighbor's sick child.

His body still remembers, even if his mind doesn't.

And she's made him feel bad: stupid, stupid. Of course he doesn't know her. It's obvious that he doesn't. Why did she even ask? "It's all right," she says. "Shall I tell you a story?" When Walter was a little boy, he loved hearing his mother tell him stories.

Later, he loved the radio. He's always enjoyed listening more than reading.

He smiles uncertainly, but nods. "Why, sure. That would be fine."

"All right. I'm going to tell you a story you knew once, to see if you still know it. But if you don't, it's all right. It's not a test." He looks anxious again; he picks up a corner of his sheet and frets it between thumb and forefinger. She shouldn't have said that.

Squeezing his hand, to calm herself as much as him, she takes a breath. "Once upon a time, there was a little boy who loved listening to stories. When he grew into a young man, he went to the theater one night, and he met a young woman who loved stories, too. They fell in love, and they got married."

"What did he look like?" Walter asks.

"He looked like you," Rosemary says steadily, "and the young woman looked like me, a long time ago. Have you heard this story before?"

"Noooo." He draws the word out thoughtfully, frowning.

"Well, that's all right. I'll tell you some more. The young man and the young woman got married, and they were very happy, except that they couldn't have children. But they had each other. They loved each other very much, and they loved their friends. One of their friends was named Melinda. She'd never found anyone to marry, but she decided she wanted a child anyway. She learned that there was a little boy in a faraway country called Guatemala. His parents were dead, and she decided she'd be his new mommy. So she got on an airplane to go get him."

Walter's gaze has wandered away; he's looking out the window. Rosemary can't tell if he's heard her or not.

"Melinda didn't go to Guatemala by herself," she says, taking a deep breath. "The young man—well, he wasn't so young anymore—the husband of the couple, he went with her. To help her, and to keep her company. His wife stayed home. Walter? Do you remember this story?"

At his name, he turns to look at her again, eyes cloudy. His hand goes to his mouth.

Rosemary swallows. "You were the young man, Walter. You got on the airplane with our friend Melinda. You went to Guatemala to help her get her son. Do you remember any of this?"

His hand travels up from his mouth to scratch his ear. "Jeremy?" he says.

"Yes!" Rosemary feels a surge of hope. "Yes, Jeremy! Melinda's son. Our godson. The two of you went to Guatemala to get him! Do you remember?"

"He cried." Walter shivers and hugs himself. "He kept crying, poor little boy. He didn't know where he was. Too many strangers." Walter's weeping now himself, slow tears dripping down his furrowed cheeks, and Rosemary, stricken, knows that Walter is on a plane full of strangers, headed from a life he cannot recall to a destination he cannot imagine.

She won't tell him about Melinda. She can't. It would be too cruel, after everything else he's lost. If he ever remembers Melinda, let him remember her alive.

6

*a*nd what of Cosmos's love life? He's had various relationships over the run of the franchise. The most serious was with a nurse named Zeldine, whose work with pediatric AIDS patients he admired as much as she admired his own humanitarian efforts. They dated for a full year, but ultimately—as is so often true in real-life relationships—the very factors that pulled them together also pushed them apart. The more time they spent together, the more they felt they were neglecting their constituencies. Plans for romantic dinners, movie nights, or weekends away were invariably interrupted by crises. When they did manage to sneak off to get some alone time, they often discovered chaos waiting for them when they returned.

At last Zeldine told Cosmos that they could no longer be together. "Each of us is already in a relationship. Our truest bond, even though it's a negative one, is with the Emperor himself. That relationship began when we were born. It will end only when we die."

"*Everyone's* in that relationship," Cosmos said, weeping. He'd been thinking of proposing. He'd been looking at rings.

He moved in to try to embrace Zeldine, but she held him at arms' length, although her own eyes were brimming over. "Yes, my love. Everyone is. But you and I have the misfortune to recognize it. We have, in effect, already forsaken all others."

Cosmos's breakup with Zeldine forced him to realize that his wistful fantasies of marriage and family were probably impossible. Charlie and Vanessa are a full-time job in themselves; so's the work of being Comrade Number One. Just as some clergy take a vow of celibacy so they'll have more platonic love to bestow on the entire world, so Cosmos must husband his energies to care for a family much larger and more various than any nuclear grouping of parents and children.

Because he is human, sometimes he becomes bitter about this.

Because his fans are human, they don't accept it. Cosmos fanfic—as robust and varied as any devoted to *Buffy, Lord of the Rings,* or *Harry Potter*—features as a prominent subcategory the "how to date Cosmos" story, known as Cosmos Cosmo.

Even within the series proper, Cosmos is an object of erotic fascination, and occasional obsession, for both women and men. He has received countless propositions and proposals, and has had to invoke several restraining orders. He and Roger sometimes pretend to be a gay couple to discourage would-be suitors, both Cosmos's and Roger's, since it turns out that a middle-aged librarian can pack an inappropriately erotic punch for a certain kind of geeky adolescent, especially one who has a Giles fixation from over-immersion in the Buffyverse.

There is also, as any scholar of fanfic would expect, a thriving community of slash writers. Cosmos is most often paired with Roger, for obvious reasons; while readers are given no evidence that the Cosmos/Roger relationship is anything but platonic, fan writers seize on these charades and turn them into the real thing. But fanfic Cosmos has also had dalliances with the Emperor himself—as physically impossible as that would actually be—and, since many slash writers cross fandoms, with Harry, Dumbledore, Giles, Xander, Frodo, Legolas, and Gollum.

Zeldine, meanwhile, has hooked up with Anelda (although this required a time-travel subplot), Hermione, and Galadriel, among others. More than one fanfic scholar has observed wryly that all this madcap dalliance is in itself a species of chaos, and that the Emperor blesses it. Fan writers don't care. They make their own order.

Repeatedly asked whether Cosmos will ever get to settle down and be happy, the CC Four have said only that they don't believe this is possible while he's still caring for Charlie and Vanessa. Afterward, who knows?

The more thoughtful observers of the CCverse, both fannish and academic, tend to agree that he will probably never marry or settle into a fulfilling relationship. Cosmos has had the misfortune, or the grace, to face the void too steadily and too young. Like certain combat veterans, like many survivors of the disasters he has helped mend, he can never return fully to the sunlight, although he delights in it and is its champion.

And there is surely more pain to come. The loss of Vanessa and Charlie, while inevitable, will undo Cosmos. In that darkness, only the Emperor will be visible, waiting at the end of all things, final partner and eternal companion.

7

a week and a day after the lunch at Hen's house, Veronique sits in the family pew, at the front of the church, at Melinda's funeral. Because the building gives her hives and she wants to be able to make a quick escape, she sits on the aisle. Jeremy's next to her, with Rosemary sandwiched between him and Tom.

Veronique wears a black suit she bought for this wretched occasion. She already owned black pumps. Walking in them, even the short distance from the car into church, made her remember why she never wears heels anymore. Her knee throbs.

She hates being here. She hates being at Melinda's funeral. She hates being stuffed into the suit. She hates being in a church. Melinda used to invite her to come, citing research claiming that people who are part of faith communities live longer, happier lives than those who aren't.

"It's science!" Melinda said, laughing.

"It's social science," said Veronique, "which means it's pseudoscience."

She understands perfectly well that churches can be good support systems. But even were she a parishioner here, the keystone of that support would now be gone.

Behind her, she hears a vast rustling punctuated by sobs. The small sanctuary is standing-room only, packed with parishioners, people from other local churches, library staff and patrons, Melinda's neighbors, members of the adoptive-parent group she attended for several years, and curiosity seekers who've been following the story.

Hen requested no recording equipment, but Veronique suspects that some of the strangers are reporters, or regular people sneaking in cameras to sell pictures to the news. Cell phones all have cameras, anyway. Veronique loathes all of this. She's suffocating, and not just because the sanctuary's unbearably hot. She's sick of platitudes, of good behavior, of pious lies.

None are the priest's fault. Even Veronique recognizes her short sermon as a model of rhetorical tact, gracefully balancing mourning and hope, rage and redemption: honoring anger and grief while stressing the need for compassion. Before offering the mike to anyone who wishes to speak, she asks everyone to take a moment of silence to pray for Melinda's murderer. "This is what Melinda would have done, and difficult as it may be, it is what our faith requires of us."

Maybe it's what Melinda would have done, but Veronique couldn't do it even if she were the praying type. She wonders how many people here can. She's glad she can't see anyone else's face. She keeps remembering Tom's account of identifying the body. He came to Rosemary's house straight from the airport; Veronique was there organizing the photographs to be displayed at the service. Tom walked in without ringing the bell and asked for scotch, straight up, which he drank straight down. The fury on his face didn't abate much after he emptied his glass.

"Horrible. I'll never forget it, and I won't go into details, because neither of you needs those pictures in your head. Thank

God Jeremy wasn't there. Thank God he was okay with cremating her. No one should have had to look at that body. I shouldn't have: they'd already identified her from dental records." He raised the empty glass, looked at it, and put it down again with a sharp sigh, waving off Rosemary's offer. "No. No more. I probably shouldn't have had that much. All I can say is that the *animal* who killed her—"

He stopped, pale. "No. I'll stop now. That's enough."

Melinda was cremated after he identified her, and he brought home the ashes. Veronique can't imagine that trip. She doesn't want to, and yet she finds herself compulsively trying. How can Tom tolerate his memories of the journey? How could he stand to carry that burden? Veronique knows from her parents' deaths what a shockingly small space a cremated body occupies, and how unexpectedly heavy it is.

Melinda's urn sits on a pedestal in front of the altar. "So the service will have a focal point," Rosemary said. It's gray marble, understated and tasteful. Jeremy chose it. He asked that some of his mother's ashes be put in the columbarium, with the rest to be divided between her garden and the Nevada desert, the vast expanses she'd loved. To Veronique, this seems the decision of someone older and wiser than the Jeremy she's known. She's heard that some events can make you grow up overnight. If that's true, surely this is one of them.

And now the priest's asking them to pray for the animal who killed Melinda. Veronique wonders how many prayers run along the lines of, "Lord, please deliver this bastard to the police so they can fry him in boiling oil. Let him die in agony and burn in hell."

After that little exercise, the open mike is a relief. All kinds of people get up to talk. Some tell funny or moving stories about Melinda, but few are good storytellers, and Veronique finds her attention wandering. She tries to count clichés, but loses count after ten variations on: "It seems impossible that this little urn in front of us could hold anyone as beloved and huge-spirited as Melinda."

The woman currently at the mike is meandering on about how Melinda taught her how to garden. She's in the middle of a complicated and heartfelt story about zucchini, but her voice is soft, and she isn't speaking into the mike properly. Veronique wonders how many people can actually hear her.

The priest stands to the left of the altar, ready to comfort anyone who breaks down or tactfully cut off anyone who rambles. People have been coming up to talk for half an hour now. There's still a line, but Veronique hopes the priest won't let many more speak. According to the bulletin, they still have to do the bread and wine bit, and depending on how many in the crowd participate, rather than staying in their seats to watch the quaint tribal rituals of practicing Christians, that could take a while. Veronique and Sarabeth once attended a wedding where the communion part of the service dragged on for forty-five minutes.

Veronique opens her purse, extracts a notepad and pen, and scribbles a note to Rosemary, which she passes across Jeremy.

How long will communion take? Are we here all day?

Not all day. Relax. 4 communion teams, 2f 2 b. I'm serving chalice.

Things should go quickly, then. Good. Somewhat relieved, Veronique leans back and tries to pay attention to zucchini lady, but she's stepping down from the mike. The priest steps forward. "Thank you all for these wonderful remembrances. I can see that many other people wish to speak, but I'd ask—"

"Lemme talk!" A figure pushes its way from the back of the church, through the crowd standing behind the pews. A man, sloppily dressed and clearly drunk. "I gotta talk."

"Sir," the priest says, "I'm sure Melinda's family and friends would like to hear your thoughts—"

"Oh, really?" mutters Veronique. Next to her, Jeremy groans.

"—but we need to move on, so if you can wait until—"

"Can't wait," the man says, and grabs the mike.

Here we go, Veronique thinks. The nutcases are coming out of the woodwork. Tom stands up and signals to the priest. Nine fingers, one, one: Call the police? The priest shakes her head: wait.

The man at the mike is oblivious to all this. "This is so sad," he slurs. "Sad and horrible. I knew her: nice lady. She helped me look stuff up. Sure can't pray for the shithead who killed her, though." Veronique hears coughing, a few muffled gasps, some strangled laughter. Well, at least he isn't being pious or polite. Good for him.

But then he says, "Now, I'm no racist," and Veronique's heart sinks, and sure enough he's off on a meandering rant against Mexicans, "all those illegals and dope dealers who just love to kill Americans. We should just close the borders. And Melinda's family, you should sue Mexico. The whole damn government. Start a class-action suit. All the other people who've had family killed down there can join in."

The priest steps up to interrupt him, but he waves her away with a glare and clutches the microphone. Tom's on his cell phone. Veronique wonders why she didn't see police cars in front of the church, but surely it won't take them long to arrive.

The drunk's voice has risen. "Close the borders! All those illegals making too many babies, living off our welfare—"

Not if they're undocumented, they aren't. Veronique sighs. Another failure of critical thinking.

"—raping our women. No more killing Americans! We gotta—"

Rosemary stands up, turns to face the congregation, and, in a surprisingly strong voice, starts singing. "In Christ there is no East or West."

Now the priest chimes in, cuing the organist. "In him no South or North."

Self-righteous idiots. The churchgoers are no better informed than the heckler, even if they're more politically correct. Haven't these people heard of the Crusades? But now others who know the hymn join the swell. "But one great fellowship of love throughout the whole wide earth."

Right. One great fellowship of love. Melinda died of love? Do believers even *think* about what they sing?

Throughout the sanctuary, though, there's a great scrambling for hymnals and flipping of pages; by the end of the next verse, almost everyone in the church is singing. "Join hands disciples of the faith, whate'er your race may be! Who serves my Father as his child is surely kin to me."

As if no other faiths even exist. Typical arrogant Christian colonialist crap.

Veronique, seething, wants to spit, to scream. How could Melinda stand this place? Melinda had a brain.

At least the voices have drowned out Drunk Guy. If they hadn't, the organ would have. The organist—Veronique remembers Melinda telling her that he's a gay botanist—pulls out all the stops, playing the hymn with crashing bass notes and long vibratos, like an especially dramatic version of Bach's Toccata and Fugue in D Minor.

By the time the cops get there, Drunk Guy's already leaving under his own power, covering his ears. When the narthex doors have closed behind him, a cheer goes up from the pews. Veronique sits mute, stony and furious. She can't join either party here. Nobody's offering viable options. All she can do is sit, shaken and shaking.

The priest's been in a huddle with one of the police officers. Now she comes up to the lectern and taps on the mike, waiting patiently for everyone to settle down. "I'd like to acknowledge Rosemary Watkins for instigating that fine piece of nonviolent resistance."

Laughter and applause fill the sanctuary. Veronique doesn't applaud. Will Rosemary notice or care? Does Veronique care if Rosemary notices or cares?

When the crowd has quieted again, the priest goes on. "We all need to pray for the man who just left, just as we pray for Melinda's murderer." There are mutters of disagreement—maybe some of these people are coming to their senses—but the priest says calmly, "God welcomes everyone. Our visitor doesn't know that, but we do. If he'd stayed, I'd have invited him to communion, just as I invite every single one of you to communion. Jesus fed Judas at the Last Supper, even though he knew Judas had betrayed him. There's a place for all of us at God's table."

Veronique, to her mortification, feels her eyes tearing up. Such a pretty promise, but no church in the world has ever kept it. If only it were true! She's ached for that kind of welcome her entire life, and never found it. For a moment, she almost can't blame people who come here, lured by the promise. But the promise is empty, a two-millennium tradition of snake oil and confidence men.

When her vision clears, she sees the police officer standing next to the priest, who says quietly, "There's an announcement. Because the service has already been disrupted, I thought you should all hear this. Then we'll return to our regularly scheduled programming. Officer Zebrowski?"

The cop, holding his hat to his chest, takes the mike and nods out at the crowd. "I'm so sorry for everyone's loss. From everything I've heard, she was a great lady." He clears his throat; his voice is soft and somber. "So, ah, while all of you have been honoring her in here, there's been news out there. We believe we know who killed Melinda."

*l*ater, among all the tears and questions, the fury and horror, Anna will find some small shred of comfort in knowing that her son wasn't a criminal mastermind. If he'd been smarter, he'd have stayed at the resort and bluffed his way through the police questioning, although the DNA would have damned him anyway. If he'd been smarter, he wouldn't have told his parents a story that contradicted the news sources. If he'd been smarter, he'd have fled somewhere no one would have thought to look for him, instead of coming home.

None of that would have made the horror any easier, but it would have meant that he was conniving, calculating, coldly maneuvering for his own survival. It would have meant that she'd raised a monster without knowing it. This way, she can keep viewing what happened as a momentary, incomprehensible lapse.

Anna will never understand what happened, or why. Other resort guests interviewed in the newspaper will say Percy was drunk the night he killed Melinda. She knows that alcohol is a disinhibitor, that it enables violent behavior.

But Percy has never been violent. She has never seen him violent, cannot even imagine him hurting anyone. He was never a bully in school. In her long search for answers—a search that will stretch on sporadically for years—she'll meet people who saw him drunk at one time or another, at high school parties or in college, and none will say they were ever afraid of him. She'll talk to women he dated, who were never afraid of him.

There are no explanations. There are only facts. There is only chronology.

Here is the chronology:

The morning after Percy's return home, Friday morning, Anna and William both wake up early. "I'm going to talk to him," William says, putting on his robe, and Anna puts on her own robe and slippers and pads after him out of the bedroom, because William's so intense and she thinks it will be easier for Percy if she's there, too, to soften the conversation.

Percy, who always sleeps until noon if he doesn't have to be at school or work, isn't in the house. The dog isn't in the house. The dog's leash isn't on its hook. Ergo, Percy is walking the dog.

It's still raining, and although Percy likes walking the dog and has always been good about it, he normally comes back quickly in bad weather. This time, though, he doesn't come back for an hour. When he finally shows up, it's with a big bag of coffee and pastries—croissants, muffins, bagels—from the local Starbucks.

By the time he gets back, the Mexican police have called, and William has put them off with a polite promise that Percy will call them back when he gets home, and William has called the family attorney, Carl Schacht, who has arrived at the house with his own Starbucks coffee, and the three of them are sitting waiting when Percy walks in.

"Do you have anything you need to tell us?" Carl asks gently, and Percy gives the three of them a dumbfounded look and shakes his head.

"Why did you come home early?" Carl asks gently, and Percy says he panicked. He was scared. He wanted to come home. That's all.

It makes sense. Anna, listening, believes it, believes that Carl believes it, even though by then she and William have worried and fretted the thing to bits, even though dread pools in Anna's gut and weighs every step she takes, even though even Bart has begun to act oddly, impossibly anxious.

Carl gives William the number of a colleague, a good criminal attorney. "Just in case," he says. "I hope to God you won't need this."

Friday afternoon, the FBI calls. The Cabo police contacted the attaché in Mexico City, who has formally requested FBI assistance.

Friday evening, the FBI visits. They ask for a DNA sample: strictly routine, they're collecting DNA samples from everyone who was at the resort then, and of course there's nothing to worry about if he had nothing to do with the crime.

Percy begins to cry. They ask why he left the resort when everyone was asked to stay, and he says he panicked. He was scared. He wanted to come home. That's all.

This time, Anna doesn't believe him. This time, the words sound too rehearsed, although the tears clearly aren't.

"Percy," William says, "give them a sample."

Anna will remember how Percy looked at his father and then at her, pleading, and she will think later that this is when she knew, knew for sure even though she wouldn't let herself know, because why would he balk if he were innocent?

He gives them the sample, a cheek swab. How could he not give it?

"How long," William asks, clearing his throat, "will the test take?"

Five to ten days, the agents say. Strictly routine. If you think of anything we need to know, call us. They give Percy their card. They leave.

Anna and William go to bed. When they wake up the next morning, Saturday, Percy and the dog are out. It's still raining. Percy comes back more quickly this time, without Starbucks.

Life becomes an echo of normal again, except that Percy wakes up unusually early every day. When he's not home, Anna pores over news stories about Melinda Soto. She learns that Melinda was a librarian who led book groups and loved to garden and had a son, just a little younger than Percy, adopted from Guatemala. She learns that Melinda was active in her church, was an avid amateur geologist and astronomer, volunteered at the local food bank. She stares at photographs of Melinda, an angular woman with long blond hair, graying at the roots, and many laugh lines. In the photos she's wearing jeans, fleece, hand-knit sweaters. She looks like a Seattleite, a liberal tree-hugger, someone who could be one of their neighbors.

William doesn't want to know anything about Melinda. He buries himself in work. When Percy's home, he doesn't want to know anything about Melinda, either, and the expression of panic and anguish that contorts his face whenever Anna even mentions Melinda's name only deepens Anna's dread and certainty.

Later, Anna will wonder why Percy didn't flee. She will go back over those days as carefully as a detective combing a crime scene, looking for shreds of evidence. She will remember small kindnesses on Percy's part, an uncharacteristic "I love you" as she got into the car one day. She will remember that he didn't work on his B-school essay, which had obsessed him before he left for Mexico. She will remember that he spent hours lying on the living room floor, his head pillowed on Bart's stomach, and that several times she caught him standing in the center of a room or hallway, staring into space.

She will ask herself what she could, or should, have known, and what she could, or should, have done.

The Saturday morning of Melinda Soto's funeral, a week and a day after Percy's return home, Anna wakes up at dawn. For once, it isn't raining. She rises, careful not to wake William, and goes into the kitchen to make coffee. She wonders if she will catch Percy still at home, for once.

Percy isn't in the house. Bart isn't in the house. The leash is off its hook.

Anna, with a sigh, pours her coffee and sits down in the kitchen to wait for him. This will be a longer walk, since the weather's better.

When William wakes up an hour later, Percy isn't back.

An hour after that, he still isn't back.

At lunchtime, he isn't back.

At one o'clock, a young woman who introduces herself as Karen rings their doorbell. Karen has a long braid and a flowered backpack, and Bart is with her. The dog was tied to a tree at Clarke Beach, Karen says. The dog was howling. I saw him there and then a few hours later he was still there, and I thought something was wrong. This is the right address on the tags, right? This is your dog?

At five o'clock, the police will find Percy's body in the water, pockets weighted with stones.

There is no note. There are no explanations. But the DNA is a match, and Melinda Soto's murder is officially solved.

An American. Another American. Dear Lord, how is Jeremy going to deal with this? For his sake, Rosemary wishes the murderer had been any other nationality: Mexican, Swedish, Canadian. But she can't make it so by wishing.

Crouched in her pew, she weeps: for Melinda, for the monster who killed Melinda and has now, according to Officer Zebrowski, killed himself, for the monster's family and friends—she can't imagine what they must be going through—and for Walter, who is mixed in with all her tears. Whatever else she cries for now, she also cries for him.

She knows that if she let herself, she could cry for days. But she has a job to do, one that has always steadied her. And so when the time comes for communion, she dries her tears, puts aside her grief, and carefully carries the chalice to her station at the rear of the sanctuary. Glen Arbuthnot, a priest from another parish, is serving the bread.

For all the bickering and petty politics and other nonsense that happens in every parish, Rosemary has always seen the church as a refuge, as a ship sheltering its passengers from the storms outside, taking on any castaway willing to grab the life buoys tossed from the deck. She can't count how often she's heard the cliché comparing the Episcopal Church to a stool with three legs: Scripture, Tradition, and Reason. It's a boring metaphor. Stools aren't very dynamic. They don't go anywhere.

Ships go on voyages. They navigate storms and reefs, witness dawns and sunsets and schools of leaping dolphins. They seek safe harbors, but always set out into the wide, wild world again, for what use is a ship that only stays at dock? They hail other vessels, exchange news, help crews who need supplies or directions. They rove and rescue.

Tradition is the body of the boat. Scripture is its sails, a patchwork of translations and commentaries. Reason is the captain at the wheel, guiding the tiller; Christ is the compass. Of course the boat is a sailboat, not a motorboat, for it has to travel where the Spirit blows. But without reason at the helm, it will founder.

Of all the planks forming the hull and decks, the sacraments are the most enduring and important, whatever sandings and new coats of paint or varnish they receive over the years. Rosemary has watched Prayer Books come and go, has listened to debates over the merits of Rite I versus Rite II, has endured contemporary services featuring kazoos and bongo drums. But Communion is constant: the Body and Blood, the gift of inclusion, the food for the journey.

She smells the bread now, and smiles. Other parishes serve wafers, which Hen calls "fish food," but St. Phil's prides itself on real bread, homemade by parishioners. The wine is homemade, too, and packs more than the usual punch. Rosemary hopes no one expected grape juice.

A surprising number of people come to her station; many are strangers. Maybe Hen's speech about universal welcome found some takers. "Here is the Blood of Christ, the cup of salvation." Rosemary loves saying the phrase, loves looking people in the eyes while they either drink from the chalice or dip their bread into it. She tries to see each of them as Christ. Usually it works.

There are, of course, the standard technical difficulties. Some people won't take the chalice themselves, which means that Rosemary has to raise it to their mouths and tip it. Other people intinct but then lose half their bread in the wine, which becomes a sea of bobbing purple crumbs. Hen keeps a spoon at the altar to fish breadcrumbs out of the chalice, but that's yards away. And because this is a funeral, most of the women wear lipstick, which leaves smudges on the rim of the chalice. Chalice bearers carry linen napkins—the technical name is a purificator, but to Rosemary that sounds too much like a futuristic food processor—and are trained to serve, wipe the rim, rotate the chalice a few degrees, and serve again. But today the napkin isn't cutting it. She needs steel wool.

The experience doesn't feel very sacred.

Nor do most of the faces in front of her reflect the gentle vulnerability she usually sees. Sunday communion is an unhurried affair, and Rosemary can usually exchange eye contact and smiles with the people she serves, who often squeeze her hand or whisper "thank you" after their Amen. She loves serving people she loves.

This is more like serving at McDonald's. Her fingers are sore from scrubbing away lipstick, and she desperately needs more wine on top of the breadcrumbs. She sees a deacon circulating to the stations with a pitcher, refilling chalices, but Rosemary's station is last. The line of people in front of her seems distracted and impatient. They don't look at her when they take the wine. Some take it like medicine, or punishment. Too few say Amen.

Two women in line are talking, a hissed conversation. Rosemary can only make out a few words. "Glad he's dead, the bastard . . . kill him myself." She glances at Glen, whose face is stony. A moment later, his expression softens again as he serves the next person in line.

"This is the Body of Christ, the Bread of Heaven."

The whisperers creep forward, their conversation more audible now. "That drunk was on the right track," one of them says. "Jeremy should sue the parents. Civil damages. Get something, anyway."

Al Antonuccio, who's on the vestry, is in front of them in line. He and Rosemary exchange a glance, and then he turns to the woman behind him. "Excuse me, ladies, but Eucharist is a sacred occasion even when it's not happening at a funeral. Would you mind saving your conversation for later?"

They glower at him, but stop talking. Al steps forward, receives the bread from Glen, and then intincts in Rosemary's chalice. The first woman is receiving the bread. As Al moves away from the communion station, her friend mutters to his back, "Fuck you."

The first woman, standing in front of Rosemary now, stifles a laugh. She's probably one of the people who laughed at the intruder, too. Rosemary gapes, frozen, almost too shocked to be angry. The woman looks at her, shrugs, dips her bread in the chalice before Rosemary has gathered her wits enough to say anything, and strolls away.

Ms. Fuck You is standing in front of Glen, who frowns down at her. Rosemary watches, fascinated. Will he refuse to serve her?

She's heard clergy discuss the matter. Is there ever a situation when it's appropriate for a priest to withhold the sacrament? Most of the priests she knows—a liberal lot, to be sure—take Hen's approach to the subject. Jesus fed Judas; therefore we feed everyone.

Rosemary heard a story once about a priest in the south, during the 1960s, who one Sunday refused to serve any parishioners who belonged to the local all-white country club. He did it only once, to make a point, and returned to serving everyone the following Sunday. Rosemary has always wondered if any of his parishioners left the country club as a result, or if they only said nasty things about him when they gathered for golf or tennis. He was lucky his vestry didn't fire him.

She watches Glen and Ms. Fuck You. You have to serve her, Glen. Hen said so: this isn't your parish. And anyway, if you don't, MFU won't understand. She'll think it's because she cursed, and not because she was nasty or litigious or vengeful or immature or whatever your reasons are, and they might be something else entirely, except I'm pretty sure that the f-word isn't one of them. If you don't serve her, she's not going to get it. It will be wasted protest. And she's presumably a mourner, although I've never seen her before and have no idea how she knew Melinda. Library, probably.

Glen has evidently been chugging along on the same train of thought, or one on parallel tracks, because he emits a barely audible sigh and holds out a piece of bread. "This is the Body of Christ, the Bread of Heaven."

Ms. Fuck You takes it, and intincts, and goes to rejoin her friend. Rosemary can't tell from watching her if she feels any remorse or not.

*j*eremy can't wait to get out of the sanctuary. Half an hour ago, he would have said it was actually kind of fun to listen to people talk about Mom during the service, especially when he knew her side of the story. She was incredibly annoyed by the woman with the zucchini, and he'd heard her making off-color jokes with VB on the phone. "I think she keeps them in her underwear drawer. She's obsessed with size."

But the minute the cop made his announcement, all Jeremy wanted to do was race into the parish hall, or outside, and check the news on his iPhone. Percy Clark, the cop said. Another guest at the resort. Positive DNA match, and now he's drowned himself.

Percy Clark? Is this the Percy Mom talked to at the pool, the CC fan? Postcard Percy? It can't be the same guy, can it? But how many people named Percy could have been at the resort?

He wants to check his phone; he sees plenty of other people checking theirs. He wants to call the cops and get the full story. He wants to hit something. But instead he's trapped next to Hen in the back of the sanctuary, receiving condolences.

He's tired and hungry and hot, and he really needs to drink something and sit down, and he doesn't know most of these people. Nobody knows what to say. He doesn't know which are worse: the ones who look mournful, wring his hand, and whimper, "I'm so sorry for your loss," or the ones who didn't get up to the mike and want to tell him long stories about his mother, or the ones—all men—who punch his arm and say, "Hey! The bastard's dead! Fantastic!" as if their favorite football team has just taken home a trophy.

Percy's dead. We win. But oh, wait: Mom's still dead, too, isn't she?

Tie.

And then there are the people who presume to tell him what Mom would have wanted. "Your mother would want you to be strong." "Your mother would want you to put all this behind you and have a good life." "Your mother would want you to continue her legacy."

Whatever the people in front of him say or do, Jeremy says only, "Thank you for coming," which is universally useful and easy to remember. What he really wants to say, especially to the last group, is, "You don't have a clue what my mother would want. My mother would want me to have a drink of water right now. My mother would want me to have some privacy. My mother would want anybody who hasn't known her for at least twenty years to shut up."

He's lost count of how many people have said, "If there's anything I can do for you, please let me know." His jacket pockets are stuffed with business cards and slips of paper with scribbled telephone numbers. He plans to throw all of them away, and maybe to burn the suit, as soon as he's safely out of here.

"Yes, there is something you can do for me. Leave me alone." But he can't say that, much less scream it at the top of his lungs.

Finally it's over. Hen touches his arm. "You okay?"

Jeremy glares at her. "What do you think?" Then he's out, into the blessedly cool narthex, at the tail of a line of people filing into the parish hall. They're walking past the Mom Memorial tables Aunt Rosie and VB arranged: photos, some of her favorite rocks and houseplants, the library newsletters she edited.

Jeremy can't deal with this anymore. He's been doing his duty for hours now. He needs a break. He ducks out the narthex door and heads toward the thick shrubs along one side of the parking lot. There's a gap leading to an empty field. When he still came to church, the Sunday school kids played out there a lot, and the field was a great place to hide Easter eggs.

He's bigger than he was the last time he did this, and his suit snags on a branch as he pushes his way through. But then he's in the field, hidden from anyone looking out the parish hall windows. He's safe.

It's chilly out here, despite the sunshine. Shivering, Jeremy sits down on the grass and pulls his knees to his chest. His need to Google Percy has suddenly dissolved. Percy's not going anywhere. Percy will keep.

He doesn't want to know anything about Percy. He wants Percy never to have existed. If Percy had never been born, there would be two fewer dead bodies in the world right now.

It's quiet and peaceful out here. Jeremy sits and watches the clouds, watches the birds, plays idly with bits of dirt. He's just start-ing to get truly cold when Tom's head pokes through the gap in the hedge. "Hey, you."

"Hey."

"How you holding up?" Jeremy shrugs, and Tom eases the rest of himself through the makeshift gate. "Yeah. Me, too."

Tom plunks himself down next to Jeremy. They sit there with-out speaking for maybe ten minutes, until Tom's phone rings. He sighs and answers it. "Hi, Hen. Yes, I found him. We're in the field. Has the crowd thinned out?" A grunt. "Really. Okay, I'll tell him."

Tom flips the phone closed and sticks it back in his pocket. "Hen says most of the strangers are gone. It's just us Philistines." This is an old parish joke. "So some folks are cleaning up, and Hen's getting ready to leave, too, but she says there's something she thinks you should see in her office."

"'Kay," Jeremy says, hunching his shoulders. His knees are stiff from sitting for so long; Tom has to help him up, even though Tom's older than he is. They work their way through the hedge again, Jeremy's suit snagging in two different places this time—the suit's definitely ruined now, but that may be the best thing that's happened all day—and plod back across the parking lot to the church.

When they get back inside, Jeremy realizes how cold he was out there. The warmth inside enfolds him like a blanket, and he feels himself relaxing.

The building's mostly empty again. The sexton's collecting dis-carded bulletins in the sanctuary, and waves. Jeremy nods and turns to walk down the hall to Hen's office. He hears a few voices from the parish hall, the familiar *chunk-clunk* of chairs being stacked for storage, the whir of a vacuum cleaner.

Hen's office is cozy and cluttered, the desk a continent of ever-shifting piles of paper, the walls decorated with icons and framed greeting cards and a large quilt of a Celtic cross, a gift from Hen's last parish when she came to St. Phil's. She gestures to a chair, and Jeremy sits. "Sorry I left," he says. "I guess I should have stayed to be nice to everybody."

She shakes her head. "Nope. No shoulds, not for you, not today. You held up in that receiving line better than a lot of people would have. Your priority right now is taking care of yourself, Jeremy."

He looks down at his knees. He feels obscurely ashamed. "Well, okay. Thanks."

"But should you feel like writing some thank-you notes"—she pauses, and he looks up to find her grinning, so he'll know the "should" is a joke—"here are the cards from people who sent flowers."

He feels a stab of annoyance, infuriating as a mosquito bite. "I don't want flowers. I asked for donations to Doctors Without Borders. Mom gave them money every month."

"I know. But some people always send flowers anyway." She holds up a small pile of cards. "If you don't want to deal with these, Rosie and I can. But, you know, I grew up on Emily Post, and she insists that the principal mourner hand-write thank-you notes. She says it's a way to do something useful and connect yourself to the world again. And I think there's something to that."

Jeremy scowls. "I thought you said there were no shoulds."

"There aren't. It's just a suggestion. When my mother died, I actually found writing the notes helpful."

Jeremy blinks. It's never occurred to him that Hen had parents, although of course she must have. "Can you keep them for me? For, like, a week or something? And I'll think about it?"

"Sure," Hen says, and tucks the cards into a small manila envelope and sticks it to her overflowing bulletin board. "But there's one you need to see, Jer. You absolutely don't need to respond to it if you don't want to. It came with this." She nods at a tiny pine tree in a fancy ceramic pot next to her desk. Jeremy just assumed it was part of her office decor, a new addition he hadn't seen yet. A miniature Christmas tree for the rector's office.

He squints at it. "Someone sent me a Christmas tree?"

"Evergreen," Hen says. "Always green, always alive. It's a symbol of eternal life and of hope, which is why they got used for Christmas trees in the first place." She pushes another card, larger than the others, across the desk. "You should read this."

Jeremy picks it up, reads the delicate script.

Dear Jeremy, and all of Melinda's friends:
You don't know me, but my son Percy was staying at Castillo del Sol when Melinda was killed. I am so terribly sorry. I read that she loved to garden. Please plant this tree somewhere in her honor.
   With deepest sympathy, Anna Clark, Mercer Island, Washington

Jeremy blinks and rereads the note. He shakes his head to try to keep his brain from scrambling. It doesn't work. "I don't—I—"

"The card came yesterday," Hen says, "inside a larger envelope with a note on the outside, explaining that the card went with a plant that would be delivered today. I guess she really wanted to write the card herself, instead of having the florist do it."

Jeremy's still shaking his head. "I don't—Clark. *Clark*? This is from Percy's *mother*?"

"Sure looks like it," Hen says gently. "She must have sent it before Percy died."

Jeremy's skull is buzzing, as if someone's hit it with a tuning fork. "So she sends me a tree because her son killed Mom? What the hell?" He doesn't even care that he's cursing in a church. "Of all the nerve—"

"Jeremy," Hen says, and her voice is firmer now, "she may not have known yet. She must have sent it before the DNA results came in. When she sent the tree, she may have had no idea that her son was the murderer."

"I have no clue what to do with this," Jeremy says.

"I don't expect you to. Neither do I. But the others are pro forma expressions of sympathy. This one isn't. It requires more thought, that's all."

"Fuck," Jeremy says. Hen doesn't even raise an eyebrow. "What am I supposed to do? Send them a cactus to plant for Percy?"

"No. Not unless you want to." She stands up. "Come on. I'm tired, and you must be exhausted. Let's go back to the house. The tree will be fine here in the office, for the time being."

"Good," Jeremy says. "Keep it. Use it for firewood." He hands her the card. "Keep that, too."

PART TWO

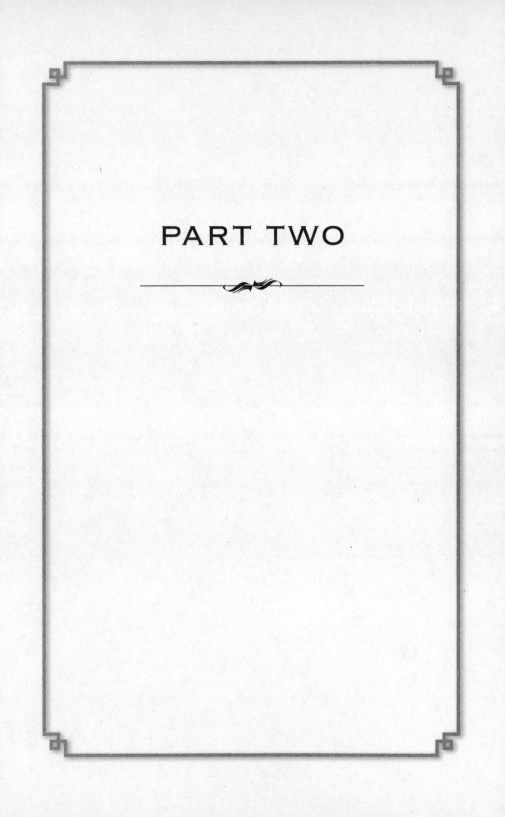

8

a week after Percy's death, a thank-you note arrives from Reno. It's on church stationery, handwritten like Anna's own note.

Dear Anna,

I am writing on behalf of Jeremy and all of us who loved Melinda to thank you for the lovely sapling. Sending it was an extraordinarily thoughtful gesture. We have not planted it yet, but certainly will when we feel led to the right location. Please know that it will be loved and cared for.

I can't imagine what you must be feeling now. Whatever our children have done, we love them, and this is the worst loss any parent can face. My heart breaks for you, and I hope your friends and family are supporting you. May the God of mercy and compassion enfold you and help you find healing.

In sorrow, The Rev. Dr. Henrietta Alphonse-Smith, Rector, St. Philip's Episcopal Church.

Anna, who has slogged out through the ever-present rain to get the mail on the day the note arrives, never shows it to William. William doesn't know about the tree. She paid for it with her own credit card, not one of the ones they use jointly. She doesn't know where the impulse to keep it secret comes from. She can't think clearly about anything right now. She wonders if she'll ever think clearly again.

She can't even remember when she decided to send the tree, or why. That was before Percy died, before Karen showed up at their door with Bart, and everything before that moment has faded, become impossibly distant. The world has fractured.

Anna has become a dumb animal. She sleeps, eats, and relieves herself. She weeps. She finds herself walking in circles, finds herself in rooms she doesn't remember entering and doesn't know why she entered.

She has not gone into Percy's room. The police searched it, seized his journal and computer, impounded the luggage he took to Mexico to examine it for forensic evidence. She can't imagine why they have to do this. They know he killed Melinda Soto. What else do they need? And yet another part of her hopes they find some answer, some reason, so she'll have one, too.

In any case, she has not yet been able to bring herself to go back into his room. William, meanwhile, seems barely able even to remain in the house. He vanishes for hours. Not to work, Anna knows—he's closed the gallery for a month "due to family emergency"—and he comes home every night, at least, but he won't tell her where he's gone. Maybe he doesn't know. Maybe he doesn't remember. He gets in the car every morning and drives away, and when Anna checks the odometer she sees that he's clocked hundreds of miles. She thinks he simply drives, the way she simply wanders the house.

William isn't home when the note comes. Anna tucks it into the zippered pocket of her Gore-Tex jacket. By the time William does get home, she's in bed: not asleep, exactly, because sleep is difficult if not impossible now, but in that gray twilight where it is easier to pretend to be asleep than to open her eyes, to speak, to ask him where he's been.

The next morning, William—eerily like Percy—is already gone when Anna gets up. She makes herself coffee and tries to eat some toast, which might as well be cardboard. Then she puts on sweats and her Gore-Tex slicker and walks the dog.

William, who adored Bart when Percy was still alive, will have nothing to do with him now, won't even touch him. Of course, he also won't touch Anna. Anna walks the dog because Bart has to be walked, and out of some obscure feeling that it isn't fair to punish the animal for the complete collapse that has befallen the family. Bart can't possibly understand any of this—neither can Anna, and she has what she's always been told is a first-rate primate brain—and he's dependent on his human keepers. William and Percy promised to take care of him when they brought him home as a puppy. Percy can't keep that promise anymore. William, for whatever reason, won't.

Anna's the only one left. And the dog's demands are simple: food, water, exercise, affection. The first three, Anna can provide. The fourth is harder. Bart's size and smell, the sheer dogginess of him, have always oppressed her, although she knows that as dogs go, he's unusually calm and well behaved. Bereft of the men, he fastens himself to her, follows her everywhere, rests his enormous head in her lap and looks up at her with liquid brown eyes.

There are times when she finds this unbearable, when she wants to shove him away, give him away, sell him, kill him, tie him up outside in the rain, take him into the city and abandon him. Several times, she's been on the verge of calling their vet, or the Humane Society.

But she doesn't. Percy loved this dog. Her last memory of Percy is of watching him nap with Bart. And Bart is the last of them who saw Percy alive.

Sometimes at night, Bart begins to howl, and William mutters and pulls his pillow over his head, and Anna gets up, fuming and cursing, determined to be rid of the dog by morning. But then she remembers what Karen said, and she pictures Percy wading into the water. She can all too clearly see Bart howling after him, straining against his leash, watching Percy disappear. He kept howling, Karen said.

And Anna, throat thick with tears each time she imagines this—Anna who wants to howl, too, and sometimes does—gets up and goes to the dog and strokes him, her sobs mingling with his whimpers, until he calms. Sometimes she talks to him the way she'd talk to Percy if he were here, if he were still alive. "Why did you do it? I know you did, they tell me you did, and the way you acted makes me believe that, but I don't understand. *Why*, Percy? What happened?"

Whatever happened, it was some terrible aberration. It was not Percy. Her private theory is that someone drugged one of the beers he drank that night. The police have shown her the tab from the hotel bar. He only had four beers: not enough to get terribly drunk, much less psychotic, and so she thinks someone put something in his drink and he reacted terribly to it. She thinks the drug made him a monster. She thinks that when it wore off, Percy couldn't live with himself, couldn't even bear the idea of confessing to his parents.

She knows that she will never know if this is true. She has a hazy sense that the drugs that might have this effect don't last in the body long. She doesn't research the issue; she doesn't want to learn that she's wrong and have this fragile explanation shattered. She's glad that Percy's body was cremated, although she hasn't had the strength to go pick up his ashes. His remains are past any possible testing. She can maintain her theory in whatever now passes for peace.

William identified the body. She couldn't, although already she feels guilty for sparing herself that one last glimpse of the child she bore. She feared that the sight of Percy's bloated and discolored corpse would, like acid, erase all other memories.

She and William have not talked about a funeral. She and William have barely spoken. The house phone rings and both of them ignore it. The doorbell rings and both of them ignore it.

She knows that William has spoken to his parents, knows that they want to fly out from Boston. She's told William she can't handle that right now, can't deal with them. She knows they're family, but she's always found them suffocating. William knows that.

William's clients have sent tactfully minimalist condolence cards. Several times, this first week post-Percy, Anna has opened the door to find offerings on their doorstep. A roast chicken from their next-door neighbor. Flowers from Karen, with a scribbled note on pink paper dotted with tear stains.

I read about it in the paper. I can't believe I'm the one who brought your dog back. I'm so sorry.

Flowers, notes, food. Anna and William eat the food, when they remember to eat and can stand to eat, but the flowers die, and Anna opens the notes haphazardly, letting them pile up and then ripping through five or ten of them until she can't stand it anymore. There aren't that many, anyway.

Whatever small gestures the outside world has made, they are encased in silence. Right now, that's what Anna wants. Carl, she knows, has gone to some effort to minimize media coverage, although some shots of Percy from Stanford have wound up in the papers and on the Internet. She can't bear to read the reader comments on the news stories.

She wonders if the people who loved Melinda Soto feel encased in silence.

Anna has never had a great many friends—she has many acquaintances, but otherwise centered herself on William and Percy—and those she has, some old friends from college and a couple who used to live in the neighborhood but moved away, are scattered across the country. She probably has e-mail from them, or maybe some of the messages from the unanswered calls are from them, and she will appreciate their thoughts when she has the time and energy to deal with them. Right now, she doesn't and can't.

Her moat has been breached, terribly. She's trying to raise the drawbridges again.

She's glad she isn't working now. Before Percy was born, and sporadically thereafter, she did freelance writing and consulting work for nonprofits. But between the gallery and the money she inherited from her parents, she didn't really need to work. She stayed busy caring for her husband and son, keeping her house, knitting and reading and traveling. She has never felt bored or lonely. She has led a simple, quiet life, and has loved it, and if the quiet now seems more suffocating than soothing, well, she suspects she would feel that way whatever she'd spent her time doing. At least she knows how to enjoy her own company, how to treasure silence.

The morning after the note arrives from Reno, Anna walks the dog, as usual. When she gets back to the house, there's a strange car in the driveway.

Anna, still half a block away, stops, nerves taut. The car's a blue Prius. She doesn't know anyone who drives a blue Prius. If the car were a police car, she'd keep walking, hoping that maybe the police have brought Percy's ashes home. But she doesn't know who this is, can't imagine who it might be.

Bart, next to her, looks up inquiringly. "I don't know," she says. "Sit, Bart."

Bart sits. It's impossible to own any dog as large as an Irish Wolfhound without investing in a great many obedience classes, and Bart is exquisitely trained.

Anna stands squinting at the blue Prius. Is anyone inside? If she moved a few feet closer to the house, she'd be able to tell if someone's at the door, but she feels paralyzed. And then she sees someone emerging from behind the car, someone waving and calling out to her. "Anna! There you are!"

An elderly woman wearing a garish orange and green plaid coat, her slight frame topped with a frizzy mass of snow-white hair. William's mother.

*t*wo weeks after the funeral, Jeremy moves back into the house. He doesn't feel right staying at Hen's anymore, although she and Ed say he can stay as long as he likes. He doesn't want to go back to the dorm, either; he might not want that even if he had any interest in returning to school.

VB helped him get in touch with the proper people on campus, who expedited his withdrawal with a full refund. It usually wouldn't be a full refund; there usually wouldn't be any refund, this late in the semester. But the proper people mouth platitudes about Extraordinary Circumstances, and pull strings, and give him his money back. Or Mom's money. It was hers; now it's his. Like the house, and everything inside it.

Technically, it's not quite his yet. Technically, it's in trust until he's twenty-one. Tom's the trustee. Tom's also taking care of the bills until Jeremy can, as Tom puts it, "get your feet back under you." Jeremy supposes moving back into the house is part of getting back on his feet, but he doesn't feel very steady.

Tom and Hen and Ed and Rosie and VB all offer to come with him, the first time he goes back to the house. He doesn't want anyone else there, though. So Tom picks him up at the dorm, packs all his stuff into a station wagon, and helps him unload it onto the front porch. "You sure you don't want me to stay?"

"I'm sure."

"I can sit in the car, just stay to make sure—"

"Tom, I'm okay, okay? I just— I need to do this by myself. I'd be more comfortable if you left." He knows it may take him a while to get through the front door. He doesn't want Tom watching. He doesn't want to feel eyes at his back. He's glad the front door is hidden from the sidewalk by a huge juniper bush, but he still doesn't want Tom in the driveway.

"You have my cell number?"

"Of course." *Just go already.* "I'll call you if I need to, I promise."

"All right." Tom turns and gets back into the car. He sits in the front seat, watching Jeremy through the windshield, until Jeremy makes waving motions. Go. Shoo. Get out of here. Then, finally, he starts the car, and pulls out of the driveway, and drives away.

Jeremy feels his knees go weak. There's a garden bench on the front porch, mostly covered by boxes now, but he moves a few of them and sits down. He takes a deep breath, smelling juniper, watching the quail in the yard. Then he gets up again.

In the end, it takes him only the normal amount of time to get through the front door, because he suddenly has to pee. He tries not to look at anything as he hurries to the bathroom, tries not to smell anything—Mom's lavender sachets, the dusty smell of all the books in the house—tries not to hear the silence. Usually she'd call out as soon as she heard the front door open. "Hey, Jer! Welcome home!"

That used to drive him nuts. She'd welcome him home if he'd just walked down the hill for potato chips, if he'd just come in from raking or mowing the lawn, if he'd gone out to get the mail. Anytime he crossed that threshold, however briefly he'd been gone, she yelled her cheerful greeting. He used to wonder what drugs she was on.

Now he'd give anything to hear her voice.

He's determined to empty his bladder without crying. He manages that, blessedly—a small three-minute victory—but as he turns to wash his hands, he's ambushed by the soap dish, an ugly clay slab with a long-necked head and four round blobby legs: a dinosaur. He made it for Mom for Mother's Day when he was, like, five or something. When he was into dinosaurs and fossils. It's painted a muddy purple, with one streaking green eye, and he's begged her a thousand times to toss the fucking thing, for God's sake, but she won't. Wouldn't.

"It's your house now," Hen told him when he was still at hers. "Make it your house, Jeremy. Don't turn it into a Melinda Museum. It's all right for you to change things. I know you probably won't want to do that right away, but remember that you can redo the place the way you want to when you're ready."

Shortly after she said that, it occurred to him that he would now, at last, be able to get rid of the hideous dinosaur soap dish. He'd imagined hurling it against a wall and watching it explode into dust and shards; he'd even pictured what a pain in the butt it would be to sweep up all the pieces.

But now he can't touch it. He can't even use the soap it holds, a girly handcrafted artisanal lavender-and-oatmeal bar from someplace in California. Mom was probably the last person who touched this bar of soap. Some of her molecules may still be clinging to it. He can't wash them away.

So he goes into the kitchen, where he knows there's ordinary hand soap in a dispenser at the sink, and washes his hands there. The kitchen's a Mom-mine: the café curtains she made hanging in the window, rocks she collected lined up on the windowsill, an avocado pit, suspended by toothpicks and sprouting roots, in a glass of water. The glass is almost empty. Jeremy refills it. At some point someone will have to plant the pit—that's clearly what Mom wanted to do—but he doesn't know how or where. He'll give it to Aunt Rosie. She'll know.

He should send it to Seattle.

The baby Christmas tree is still in Hen's office. Hen says she wrote a thank-you note, but that it would be fine if he wrote one, too. He has no intention of doing this anytime soon, if ever.

Jeremy opens the fridge, as empty as it always is when Mom's on a trip—at least he won't have to worry about whether to discard or memorialize her leftovers—and checks the shopping list held to the door with a magnet. "Quinoa, sprouts, tofu, yogurt, blueberries, granola, bananas, soy milk, coffee, artichokes." He snorts.

Rabbit-Mom, with her grains and greens. The only tastes he shares with her here are the fruit and coffee. He tears the list from the pad, ready to crumple it, and then stops.

She wrote this list.

Stupid, Jeremy. What are you going to do, bronze the thing?

But he can no more throw it away than he could shatter the hideous soap dish. With a sigh, he folds the note and shoves it into a junk drawer overflowing with miscellaneous debris. Speaking of which, time to bring the boxes in from the porch.

That keeps him busy for twenty minutes, good physical work, undemanding and satisfying. He stacks the boxes neatly in the front hall and then, feeling a little more cheerful, dons a backpack full of clothing and picks up a similarly stuffed suitcase. He knows his clothing will go in his room. This is an easy task.

Going up the stairs, he hears the familiar creak on the sixth and tenth steps, remembers countless weekend mornings when, as he lay in bed, that squeaking warned him that Mom was coming upstairs to rouse him for breakfast. *Time's a wasting.*

His eyes are wet again. His bedroom, at least, should be safe. His bedroom's full of him, not Mom. But when he shoulders his way through the door, he sees, neatly folded on his narrow single bed, a small pile of laundry.

Of course. He came over two weeks before Mom's trip to do laundry, but he got pulled into a discussion on the CC boards and never got around to it, so he left it here. He figured he'd do it when Mom got back from Mexico, and he had enough other clothing in the dorm, so it wasn't crucial.

Mom did it for him.

Aching, he looks around the room and suddenly hates it. It's too small, too cramped with bookshelves and boxes of *CC* issues, too childish. There are still plastic dinosaurs sitting on a shelf, and there isn't even room for a real desk in here. That's one reason he wanted to live in the dorm, because he felt like he'd outgrown this room. Mom offered him the guest room or the attic, but moving everything was too complicated when he was getting ready to start college at the same time. He told her he'd move over the summer, but privately he believed that he'd never live in this house again, that he'd move into an apartment at the end of the academic year, maybe a frat house or something, and after college he'd get the hell out of Reno and go someplace where he wouldn't feel so self-conscious, someplace more diverse. San Francisco. Seattle. He knew he'd have to share living space for a long time, but at least he wouldn't be sharing it with her.

Now he'd give anything to be sharing it with her.

He wishes he could leave Reno now, but how would he pay for it? The thing's impossible, and anyway he has a hazy sense that it's important to stick around for a while, to let his insides settle as much as they ever will.

He can move within the house itself, though, switch things up at least that much.

Mom herself naturally had the nicest bedroom in the house—she'd lived here for years before he showed up, after all—and Jeremy realizes that if he wants to, he can move in there. That room has windows on two sides, a big walk-in closet, even a little verandah. From the windows, you can see trees and mountains, and Mom hung a finch feeder from the eaves, so the birds congregate there, bright spots of yellow and orange and red. "Flying flowers even in winter," she called them once.

It's a great room. It has space for everything Jeremy will want. He stands in his old bedroom, dreaming. He'll leave the finch feeders there. He'll get a cat—he and Mom had a cat once and both adored it, but it died when he was a junior in high school, and Mom decided not to get another one because she wanted to travel and he'd be going to college soon—and he and the cat can sit in Mom's rocking chair, the one her grandfather made for her grandmother, and watch the flying flowers, and sunlight will dapple the floor and the breeze coming in through the windows will smell like sagebrush and juniper.

This is a summer fantasy, he realizes. He's thinking about the future. He's thinking about a life without Mom. Grief and guilt swamp him again. Too soon, too soon.

*r*osemary, aching, pulls into Melinda's driveway. No: not Melinda's driveway anymore. It's Jeremy's driveway now.

Veronique, next to her, unbuckles her seat belt. "Before I forget, what do you want me to bring to Thanksgiving?" The holiday's next week. None of them feel remotely festive, but gathering for the holiday is better than being alone. Veronique has been included for years, because Melinda wanted her to be; Rosemary has inherited her now.

I want you to take away the two empty chairs, Rosemary thinks grimly. She and Walter have always hosted, fed Melinda and Jeremy and Veronique and sometimes a few stragglers from church. Walter's empty place would have been hard enough, this year. Now she'll have to deal with Melinda's, too.

"Salad," she says. "Salad or a side, whatever you prefer. Just let me know."

"I'll do my usual, then, that salad with cranberries and walnuts."

"That's great. Thanks."

Veronique, hand on the car door, looks over at her. "You know, if you're going to get out, you'll have to take off your seat belt."

"Right," Rosemary says, pulling the buckle. "I knew that. I just—I'm not sure I'm ready for this."

"Of course not. How could we be? But Jeremy thinks he is, and we promised to help him. Come on: you can't expect a nineteen-year-old kid to know what to do with his mother's shoes and clothing."

"I guess not."

"Dibs on that jacket she got in Montana. The boiled-wool one with the southwestern design and the concho buttons. If it fits me. Rosemary, get out of the car."

She does, finally. Vera waits next to the car until Rosemary crosses in front of it to stand on the front walk, and then she comes up behind Rosemary, on her right, and nudges her slightly. "Good. You're out of the car. Now walk."

Vera the sheepdog. Rosemary complies. Waiting won't make this any easier.

Jeremy calls, "Come in," when they ring the bell. They find him waiting in the kitchen. He's made tea and laid out a plate of cookies, Pepperidge Farm Mint Milano, on one of Melinda's good plates. When he sees them, he offers up a passable imitation of a smile. "Thanks for coming. It's nice of you."

He looks terrible: drawn, too thin, his warm brown skin an ashen gray, as if he hasn't slept in days. Rosemary moves in to hug him; he smells slightly sour.

How do you tell a murdered friend's bereaved son that he needs to take a shower?

You don't.

Rosemary steps back, away from him, and opens her mouth to ask him how he is, but Jeremy says, "Don't ask me how I am, okay? For one thing, I don't know. For another, well, what is there to say?"

"Good," Veronique says briskly. "Thank you. I wasn't going to ask, because I assume you're about how we are, which is lousy, but I didn't want you to think I was being rude. Or uncaring."

"It's good of you to come," he says again. They're all standing around the table. He nods at it. "Please have some tea, because otherwise it will just get cold, and I won't drink it, and that would have driven Mom nuts. If you don't want the cookies, though, I'll eat them. I was going to bake, but I bailed instead. That would have driven Mom nuts, too."

Rosemary feels herself relaxing. He still has his sense of humor. Good.

They sit, nibble cookies, sip tea. Veronique asks if he's thought about when he'll come back to school, and he shrugs. A year or two, he says, when he figures out what he wants to do. He bends his head, shoves his cookie around his plate with one finger. "Mom tried to get me to take some time off after high school. She said I was too unfocused. Pretty ironic I'm doing it now, huh?" His voice is thick.

"It's a good idea," Rosemary says weakly.

Veronique chews her cookie, swallows, takes a long slurp of tea, and puts her mug back on the table with a decisive thunk. "I think we've reached the end of the small talk. The tea and cookies were good, Jeremy. Shall we tackle your mother's room now?"

Rosemary follows the other two up the stairs; Vera evidently doesn't feel the need to herd her this time. Melinda's room is painted in shades of green and lavender; Jeremy's piled a stack of broken-down storage boxes in the middle of the floor, with packing tape and scissors next to them. Such a pretty room. Rosemary looks around at the framed dried flowers, the cross-stitch sampler Melinda got at a yard sale—she always claimed she was hopeless at any needlework herself, although she admired it—the collection of baskets and ceramic boxes on top of the bureau.

Veronique's looking around, too. She wipes a tear from her cheek, as briskly as she always does everything, and says, "You're going to repaint when you move in here, I assume? More macho colors?"

"I dunno. I haven't gotten that far. Whatever I do, we need to deal with her clothing and stuff, right?"

Rosemary realizes she's shaking. She feels almost nauseous. She can't stand the idea of disassembling the room. She hasn't been able to pack up Walter's things, either, except for what he needs in the nursing home. If she keeps everything the way it is, she can pretend he's coming home.

If only they could leave this room alone. If only Melinda were coming home. But this is what Jeremy wants to do, and Veronique's right. They promised to help him.

It will get easier, Rosemary tells herself. Once we're doing the work, once everything's packed up and the room's dismantled, it won't be so hard. All right. Time to dive in.

She picks up a box. "Where do you want me to start, Jeremy? Closet, or drawers?"

Veronique nods approvingly. "You take one. I'll take the other."

"You could flip a coin," Jeremy says.

"No." Veronique shakes her head. "I'll take the dresser. It's likely to be more straightforward. And Rosie's the one with the fashion sense, so she should take the closet. But mind you put that jacket aside for me, if you find it."

They split up. Rosemary's calmer now that she has a clearly defined task. The closet will probably be more work than the bureau— it's a large walk-in with two tiers of hanging clothing, plus boxes, and it's stuffed—but Vera can help when she's done discarding underthings no one else will want.

Rosemary has always loved clothing, and while she and Melinda never had terribly similar tastes—Melinda's ran to Birkenstocks and hemp, and what skirts she wore were long, baggy, and embroidered— Rosie still expects to enjoy the process of packing up the garments for use by someone else. She'll drive them to Goodwill, or call the local women's shelter to see if they can be used there; she can even bring some to the hospital, since with winter coming, there will be more homeless patients in the ER who need warm garments. There are fewer female patients in this category than male, and anyway the ER staff doesn't like to keep too much around—their compassion is tempered by prudent caution against becoming known on the streets as a source of free loot—but Rosemary can stow some sweaters and jackets in a storage room and let a few of the staff know they're there.

She believes that such recycling, like Holy Communion, transforms loss and brokenness into food. But even as she tells herself this, she has a sudden, unwanted memory of an article she read about a Holocaust survivor. The woman's job was to sort the piles of shoes and clothing left behind by inmates heading into the infamous showers of Auschwitz. She stole items she thought her friends in the barracks could use, and she survived the work by concentrating entirely on how she was helping her friends. She didn't, couldn't, allow herself to think about where the items came from.

Rosemary wants to think only about all the people this clothing will help, but she doesn't know if she'll be able to keep herself from thinking about Melinda. Does she even want to?

She's always pitied the Holocaust survivor, scorning the woman's delusion. Now she finds herself admiring the discipline involved in maintaining it.

You said you'd help. You promised. She steps into the closet, turns to reach for the nearest item, and finds herself grasping a fuzzy purple cardigan covered with beaded flowers. The thing's hideous, but Melinda loved it. She found it in a thrift store in Philadelphia when she was there for an ALA conference, and shipped her find home even though it was high summer at the time and she wouldn't be able to wear the sweater for months. Every year, she delighted in the first day cold enough for her to wear it. Over the years, she bought turtlenecks and earrings, and even a pair of purple suede boots, specifically to match it.

This can't go to strangers. It just can't. Rosemary wouldn't be caught dead in it, though. She takes it carefully off its hanger and carries it out of the closet, back into the bedroom proper, where she expects to find Jeremy and Vera busily at work.

Jeremy's sitting on the bed next to a half-packed box of tchotchkes, cradling a glass bottle. Hand-blown, from the looks of it: swirling brown ridges. "She got this in Guatemala when she went down there to meet me the first time," he says. "There was some snag and she had to wait an extra day to meet me and she was really antsy, so she went shopping to distract herself, even though adopting me was costing a fortune and the last thing she needed was to spend more money. But she found this in a little shop and it was cheap, and she loved the shape and the color, so she bought it, and then she went back to her hotel room and sat on her bed holding it on her lap, just like this." He shakes his head. "She kept rubbing the bottle, because she liked how the glass felt, and then the phone rang and it was the adoption people telling her that everything was going ahead, that she could come meet me. She called this her magic bottle. She said she rubbed it and I came out, like a genie."

Rosemary's heard the story, but she's never seen the bottle. She didn't know Melinda still had it. Jeremy looks up at her and says, "If I keep rubbing it, do you suppose I'll get Mom back?"

He's trying to be funny again. It's not working. Rosemary retreats into chaplain mode. What would she tell the son of a dead patient at the hospital?

"No, but you'll get your memories of her back. You can keep that, you know. You don't have to pack everything." She holds up the sweater and turns to Vera. "One of us has to keep this. I'll never wear it. Will you?"

"Oh, Lord. That old thing." Vera sighs and puts a stack of bras into a trash bag. "I guess I'll wear it, if no one else will, but I can't wear it at home because the cats will either shred it or shed all over it, or both. I could keep it in my office, I guess. Maybe even wear it to teach. Would that wake everybody up, Jeremy?"

He shrugs, rocking the glass bottle, and Vera sighs again. "All right, kids. Here's my show-and-tell item." She waves a flowing blue scarf, billowing silk, like a piece of parachute. "Remember this?"

"Of course," Rosemary says. "Her strip-of-sky scarf." If Melinda wore the sweater on cold days when she delighted in the change of seasons, she wore the blue scarf during gloomy weather—rare enough in Nevada, the sunniest and driest state in the country— when she needed to remind herself what good weather looked like.

"I'll wear the hairy grape sweater if you'll wear this," Veronique says.

Rosemary prefers her scarves a bit more understated, but she can see herself wearing this. She can't see herself wearing the hairy grape. "Deal."

"Did you find my boiled-wool jacket?"

"No. Not yet. This is as far as I got."

Vera snorts. "We aren't being very efficient, are we? I think we should get Ed and Tom to do this. We could supervise them—watch from across the room and tell them what to keep and what to toss—but they wouldn't get bogged down in memories of why Melinda wore whatever, and where it came from, and what she said about it."

Rosemary walks to the bed and sits down next to Jeremy, the old mattress sagging under the double weight. Melinda really should have been sleeping on a better bed. "I don't think efficiency's the point. You know, this feels like liturgy. It should be liturgy. We have house blessings, after all."

"We do?" Veronique asks. "You do? I've never heard of that."

"It's in the *Book of Occasional Services*. There's a gorgeous one in the New Zealand prayer book, too. Anyway, there are house blessings, and there's a service for the deconsecration of a church, and some clergy are doing divorce liturgies now, which makes sense."

Veronique looks skeptical. "How would it work? What would you call it? The Goodwill Liturgy?"

Jeremy lets out a sharp bark. "That's pretty good, Prof Bellamy."

"It's not bad." Rosemary hugs the hairy grape. She closes her eyes so she can think better. "Mmmm . . . A service for the Blessing of Belongings, maybe? Anyway, a lot of people would show up to help, kind of like a barn-raising, and whenever they found something with a story attached, they'd go ring a bell in the middle of the room—or maybe they'd all have their own little bells—and that would be the signal for everyone else to stop so the person who just rang the bell could tell the story about whatever they just found."

Jeremy groans. "That would take forever."

"Maybe. It would take a while, sure. It would take as long as it needed to take, and people could come and go. It would be open-ended. It would be a way to get the packing-up done and honor the memories of the community and support the mourners."

"I dunno, Aunt Rosie. The open mike at the funeral was bad

enough. And I don't think I'd want everybody from church crammed into Mom's bedroom, you know?"

"Not everyone would come. It would be a self-selecting group."

Jeremy snorts. "Yakking women. No offense."

"Interesting idea," Veronique says, "but I take our young man's point. How would you limit how long each person spoke? Would there be priests in the house, too? What would they be doing? Would the family have a way of kicking everyone out when they'd had enough?"

Rosemary shakes her head. "I don't know. This just occurred to me." She looks down at the hairy grape, runs her fingers carefully over the delicate beaded flowers. "Okay, how about you ring the bell and then you only have a minute to tell the story? To keep the process moving so the packing actually gets done?"

Vera purses her lips. "Maybe. It needs work."

"I know," Rosemary says, but even as she folds the hairy grape and puts it on the bed, even as she stands up and gets ready to renew her battle with the closet, the idea plucks at her. She'll have to talk to Hen about it. She turns to Jeremy and holds her hands out for the bottle. "Let me put that in the other room for you, okay? Where it will be safe? And then we can get back to the packing?"

"Here," he says, and shoves it at her.

She takes it. The glass is warm from his hands. "Do you want to stop? It's okay if you aren't ready yet."

"I'm ready," he says. "At least I think I am. I want the room to be cleared out, you know. I just don't want to go through the process of doing it. But I don't want other people to do it for me, either. So I guess I just have to hang tough." He sighs. "I know she'd want me to move into the room, to enjoy it. It makes me feel like The Bird Who Cleans the World, that's all."

When Jeremy is still very small, four or five, Melinda reads to him from a slim volume of Mayan fables called *The Bird Who Cleans the World*. The author, Mayan himself, explains that his mother told him these stories when he was a child. They're mostly animal stories, moral fables and creation myths.

Melinda originally plans to read Jeremy one story a night; at that rate, the book will get them through a month of bedtimes. But she rejects some of the tales because they're too sad, or too baldly about the horrible fates meeting disobedient children, and Jeremy seems uninterested in many of the others.

He responds to only two of the tales. One describes a huge flood that covers the earth, leaving only one house standing on a mountaintop. Inside the house, animals of every species take refuge. When the waters begin to recede, a buzzard is sent out to survey how much land has been uncovered, and in the bird's greed and hunger it eats the bodies of the dead animals that it finds, and ever after is cursed, or blessed, with the task of cleaning the world by eating carrion and corpses, the reeking and rotting.

"We heard that story in Sunday school," Jeremy says. " 'Cept it didn't talk about the buzzword."

"Buzzard, honey." Where did he get the word "buzzword"? Or has she, trying to interpret his childish speech, transformed his syllables into a word she knew? "It's not quite the same story. It's a little different."

"The aminals are in a house, not a boat."

"Animals, honey. Yes, that's right."

"And in Sunday school it's a pretty white bird that flies out. It comes back with a flower."

"An olive branch, to show that things are alive. That's right."

Jeremy sucks his thumb thoughtfully for a moment, and then says, "This one doesn't have a rainbow."

"No."

"So it could rain again. God didn't promise to be good."

She smiles. Yes, come to think of it, the rainbow *is* God's promise to be good, even if people aren't. "Well, this story doesn't talk about God. It doesn't say why the flood happened."

"So maybe nobody was bad? It just rained for no reason?"

"Maybe. We don't know."

"The dead animals weren't bad?"

"We don't know if they were. The story's not really about them. It's about the b— the buzzard." She almost said "big bird," but doesn't want him to get the scavenger in this tale confused with the friendly yellow creature on *Sesame Street*.

"He was bad." Jeremy frowns now, clearly concentrating very hard. "Because he ate the dead animals?"

"No. Because he didn't fly right back to the house, the way he was supposed to."

"So he was punished. He had to eat dead things. But he *liked* eating dead things."

"Yes, he did. And he was doing a good thing by eating them. He was cleaning the world. But the other animals didn't want to be around him, because he smelled bad. So he had to be lonely."

He looks utterly perplexed, and Melinda reaches out to smooth the soft bangs off his forehead, realizing belatedly that the seemingly simple tale has led them into thickets of ambiguity that many adults would find bewildering. Terrible things happen for no reason, and only the lucky survive. The buzzard is bad for doing something good, and he's punished by being forced to keep doing what he wants to do, but in isolation. The bird that cleans the world is held in contempt, shunned, rather than honored. She thinks of a line from the Psalms: "The stone that the builders rejected has become the cornerstone." Isaiah's suffering servant, and Christ's agonizing crucifixion after his friends abandon him.

This is dark stuff, grown-up stuff. She wonders, as Jeremy resumes sucking his thumb and drifts off to sleep—at this stage he'll wake again if he feels her weight lift from the mattress, so she'll sit a while longer—if the fable was composed before or after the Mayans were exposed to Catholicism. Liberation theology. This is the worldview of a people who've seen too much suffering and death, as far from the complacent triumphalism of right-wing American

Protestantism as you can get. No easy answers here, no assured salvation, no rainbows: just paradox and the stench of corpses.

The next night she reads him another fable, one she's chosen for its simplicity and happy ending. A cricket disturbs the rest of some jaguars who dislike his singing, but he and a rabbit, his friend and ally, defeat the jaguars by gathering gourds of wasps, which chase the predators away by stinging them.

Jeremy likes the story, and asks for it again the next night. It has Christian subtexts, too: the last shall be first, the smallest shall be greatest. Jeremy doesn't understand that part yet, of course. He only knows that the cricket and the rabbit, for all their tininess, are smart, and that their quick thinking keeps them safe.

A week or two later, Veronique and Rosemary come over for Scrabble. After the game, Melinda shows them the book. "You know, for anybody who survived the civil war, that second story must have seemed like a joke. No wasps defeated the army when it overran the Mayan villages. The little guys lost."

Veronique looks up from the illustration she's been studying. "Your little guy won. And this author, Victor Montejo"—she raps the book with her knuckles—"it says he wrote another book about watching a village being destroyed. But he included the wasp story anyway."

"I still like the buzzard one better. But it's hard."

Rosemary grimaces. "Yup. No meaning in disaster: only in the work you do afterwards, even if no one says thank you."

*b*one-weary, Veronique puts the shopping bag from Melinda's house on her own bed. She and Rosemary just packed this bag, and now she has to unpack it again. Why does so much of life seem like useless repetition, like an utterly random reordering of insignificant bits of matter and energy? Move a sweater here, move it there. Teach the same classes to different generations of students who all begin to blur into one dully staring face. Grade new stacks of papers, which all begin to blur into one dull essay, distinguished only by increasing numbers of sentence-level errors.

She really needs to retire.

She really can't retire.

She really needs to put away the things in the bag, or they'll become another burden, another weight on her shoulders.

At least they aren't in a mystery story anymore. They know who killed Melinda. In a mystery novel, that would be a happy ending.

Veronique isn't happy. She doubts anyone else is, either.

She reaches into the bag and pulls out the hairy grape, which in her current enervated state feels as heavy as a full-length mink coat. She has to hang this in the closet, at least, although she'll only take it out again the next time she goes to campus, so she can put it in her office. But she needs to put it away now so the cats won't have their way with it.

She's closed her bedroom door to keep them out, and they're wailing and mewling outside, butting the door with their heads. *You never feed us. You have never fed us. Not once in the last thousand years have you fed us.*

She feeds them twice a day, fed them just before coming upstairs. They've already forgotten this, or abandoned the offering as unacceptable. Rummaging in her closet for a hanger while the cats mourn outside, Veronique thinks it might be nice to be a cat, for whom each opening of a cat food can is unprecedented cause for rejoicing, rather than the same damn thing all over again.

The hairy grape is safely stowed. Next? Veronique peers into the bag—how can she already have forgotten what it contains?—and spots a woven basket. She didn't really want this, but Jeremy insisted she take some of the items cluttering Melinda's nightstand and windowsills and bureau, and the basket's innocuous enough. She'll find some use for it.

Inside the basket is a small white box holding a pair of earrings, silver with opal and lapis inlay. These, Veronique genuinely likes. Melinda had lovely taste in jewelry.

And below that, a scarf: not the billowing blue thing Rosemary took, but red chenille, a spot of brightness. It glowed like a ruby when Veronique came across it in Melinda's bottom dresser drawer, and the color lifted her heart for a moment even as her fingers treasured the soft fabric. For those reasons, she claimed the scarf. She rarely wears scarves, but she'll wear this one.

She hauls herself upright and walks to her own dresser, across the room. The scarf goes in the top drawer, next to neatly folded socks. The earrings go in her small jewelry box. That leaves the basket. Indecisive, she holds it in both hands. She doesn't know where to put it. She can't think of a spot in the house where it will look right, and anyway, the cats are as likely to claw and chew this as they are to savage the hairy grape. Finally she goes back to the closet and stands on tiptoe to deposit the basket on an upper shelf.

There. The rearranging's done. Melinda's possessions have been integrated with Veronique's.

The bedroom door shakes, and Veronique opens it. The cats erupt inside, crying and winding themselves around her ankles, distraught and bereft. *You never love us. You have never loved us. Not once in the last thousand years have you loved us.*

She bends to pat them, her knee screaming almost as loudly as they are, and then speaks aloud. "Cats, we're going downstairs now. I'm going to sit on the couch. You can join me, but you have to let me get downstairs without tripping me."

She accomplishes this by gripping the bannister with both hands, a maneuver she knows would look ridiculous were anyone else here to see her. For the first time in a long time, she permits herself a stab of self-pity that no one is.

Chocolate. Just one square, medicinal. That's what she needs. She keeps a bar of Trader Joe's 72% cacao in the kitchen for just such emergencies.

Settled on the couch with one cat in her lap and the other curled next to her, the chocolate on a napkin on the side table, Veronique looks around her living room: clean uncluttered lines, clean uncluttered surfaces, Danish modern and Georgia O'Keefe. It occurs to her, as she takes the first nibble of chocolate and one of the cats begins to purr, that Melinda's possessions are indeed a collection of stories: belongings as books, as a library accessible only to a select clique of readers. She, Rosie, and Jeremy know the story of the brown bottle. To the rest of the world, it's just a piece of glass.

Veronique looks around her living room again. There's a large set of bookcases along one wall, holding volumes readable by anyone who speaks English. What other stories are here? When she dies, who will come to divvy up her belongings, and what tales will they tell?

She bought the furniture at various stores, the O'Keefe prints online. Aside from the literal books, the place is as devoid of narrative as the showrooms where she bought the furniture. She might as well be sitting in a doctor's waiting room or an airline departure gate.

Despite the warmth of the small mammal stretched across her lap, despite her satisfying sugar buzz, Veronique feels a sudden chill. She finds herself longing for the heft and comfort of the hairy grape.

9

*f*rom the beginning, the toll of time has been an important consideration in the CCverse. In other superhero franchises, the characters have long histories, but once they have reached adulthood, they tend not to age. The CC Four decided early on that this would not be the case for Cosmos and his loved ones. He and the people around him get older at the rate of "one second per second," as MacKenzie likes to say. They age in real time. In time, they will die.

In the first issue, Cosmos was twenty-three. Now he's thirty. His thirtieth birthday was the occasion for a special double issue, a huge party in which all the people he'd helped arrived by the hundreds—nay, by the thousands—to cheer him on and wish him well. The party filled the Keyhole football stadium, overflowed onto the streets, and lasted for days, a combination of Mardi Gras, the Fourth of July, and Bilbo Baggins's eleventy-first birthday party.

Naturally, the Emperor was there, too, a constellation-studded darkness looming over the crowd. "Carpe diem, indeed," he intoned. "Party while ye may, for in the end, I will win, whatever you do. I always win. Mine is the last face you will see."

"Tell me something I don't know," said Cosmos, wearing a garish Hawaiian shirt. He was a little tipsy on his third beer. "And what of you, esteemed opponent? How old are you?"

"I am as old as the universe, puny mortal. I will live as long as time itself. When all you have done and all you have loved are dust, when their descendants to the fiftieth generation are dust, I will still move throughout the galaxies. I dwell in eternity, and my garb is creation, and—"

"And you're damnably long-winded," Cosmos said with a hiccup, taking another swig of beer. "Let me rephrase the question. When's your birthday, O Emperor?"

"I was born when the first molecules—"

"Oh, pshaw," Cosmos said, and belched. "Nobody knows when that is, do they?" He grabbed a microphone connected to the stadium's PA system. "Hey, everybody! The Emperor doesn't know when his birthday is!"

A huge "awwwww" of feigned sympathy filled the stadium.

"He's never had a birthday cake!"

"Awwwwww!"

"And if he did, he wouldn't invite anybody to share it!"

"Booooo!"

"He outlives everybody, like a vampire, so he's afraid to get close to them! The Emperor doesn't have any friends, only Minions!"

"Awwwwww!"

Cosmos waved his beer bottle over his head, burped again, and said into the microphone, "I'm feeling generous, Emperor, so I'll give you a present. From now on, my birthday's yours, too. We can eat cake together. You're always welcome to my party."

"I am always present, mortal, welcome or not. I am always with you. I—"

"Yeah," said Cosmos, "but now you're invited." The thought balloon above his head read, *Like a vampire.*

"That makes no difference, mortal."

"Sure it does. It means that I'm not clinging to time I can't keep, that I'm not fetishizing my lost youth, that I accept the inevitability of aging and death. The difference between us, Emperor, is that my Comrades love me. Your Minions only fear you, or acquiesce to you, or think it's amusing to adopt nihilistic stances. That's why you've never had a birthday cake. Nihilists don't bake."

"My Minions accept the inevitability—"

"Your Minions are boring," Cosmos said, "and they need to get lives while they still can. Sure, we'll all be dust before long, except lonely old you, watching everybody crumble. Why hurry the process? Hey, everybody, let's sing 'Happy Birthday' to the Emperor!"

So the crowd sang, and cheered, and the Emperor tried to harummph and cackle but instead only loomed, looking nonplussed and decidedly annoyed. For form's sake, he created a blast of chaos that blew bottles and balloons and bunting, frosting and ribbons and ice-cream bowls, all over Keyhole, but Cosmos led the assembled masses in an impromptu reggae version of "I've Been Working on the Railroad," and they got the mess cleaned up in no time.

Many commentaries on this issue point out that Cosmos's offer to share a birthday with EE is, in fact, simply another illustration of his promise to respect his own mortality. We all share birthdays with EE: he has not one birthday, but an infinite number. His birthday is every moment, for in every moment something is born, and at that moment begins to die.

And so it has become the custom of the CCverse to invite EE to all birthday and anniversary celebrations, to explicitly acknowledge his presence. He is there every year, wearing a party hat, when CC cuts his cake and when Roger has his annual bowling birthday bash. He sits in the corner when Cosmos feeds his sister Vanessa the lemon ice she loves on her own birthday, and when he and his

father watch *Star Trek* reruns on Charlie's birthday. He is the ac-
knowledged guest of honor every year on Anelda's birthday, which
the family observes by putting flowers on her grave in the Keyhole
Memorial Cemetery and by lighting a candle at home.

Issue number 76 narrated the poignant story of a woman who,
although she called herself a Comrade, refused to invite EE to her
son's birthday party. The spindly boy was three but looked much
younger, a pincushion of IVs, as thickly festooned with lines as a
ship's rigging. He had just been diagnosed with leukemia. "He
can't die," she said, bringing presents and candy to little Johnny's
hospital room even though, wretchedly ill from chemotherapy, he
couldn't enjoy any of it. "I won't let him. I won't acknowledge
death. My child will, *must*, outlive me."

When Johnny grew worse, she kidnapped him from the hospital, removing the needles from his arms and carrying him the ten
blocks to Cosmos's doorway. The doorbell interrupted Vanessa
and Charlie's dinner, and Cosmos, spoon of baby food in hand,
discovered the sobbing mother and her limp child on his front
porch. "Please," she said. "Please, you have to save him."

"I can't. If the doctors can't, I can't either. That isn't how it
works."

"Save him!"

"I wish I could. I'm so sorry."

"I'll do anything, anything, just name your price—"

"I'd do anything, too," Cosmos said sadly, "if there were anything to do."

"He hates the hospital. He hates the needles."

"Let him die at home, then." And Cosmos brought them inside and sat them down and called Zeldine, with whom he's still
on good terms, to arrange home hospice care, which he knew
would include grief support for the mother.

"It's his birthday! How can I plan his death on his birthday?"

"You aren't planning his death," Cosmos said, placing his hand
gently on Johnny's bald head. "You're planning the rest of his life.

Spend it with him. Let him decide what it should look like. The hospice people will help you."

The mother, wild-eyed, said, "This is unbearable."

"Yes."

"How will I survive it?"

"By breathing. By eating. Let your body tell you what it needs to survive." And Cosmos and the mother wept together, while the child slept and while the Emperor, the darkness at one end of the room, stretched out his arms to embrace them all.

Cosmos's hair is a little thinner than it was when we first met him, a little grayer. Although he is still young, his face is more lined and his eyes more troubled. In his bedroom he keeps a copy of *The Velveteen Rabbit*, which Anelda read to him when he was a little boy. Sometimes he reads it to himself. Sometimes he reads it to Vanessa and Charlie. What the story means to him is that wearing out—feeling threadbare, exhausted, done in—is proof of having been greatly cherished.

The book itself is falling apart, but he won't replace it. His mother's hands held it once.

10

Jeremy wakes up on New Year's Day feeling about two tons lighter than he did yesterday. January, finally. The holidays are over. Thank God. Mom's birthday is in March, and that's going to be horrible, but he has a few months before then. A reprieve.

He rolls and stretches. As his Christmas gift to himself, he bought a good queen-sized mattress, although it's just sitting on the floor because he couldn't be bothered buying a box spring and frame for it. He doesn't understand why those things are so expensive.

He's in Mom's room now; he's using her bureau, because it's bigger than his, and he couldn't bring himself to touch the paint job because he remembers how she agonized over the colors and then went through all the hassle of putting down dropsheets and using brushes and getting paint in her hair. She was so proud of the results. He made fun of the green and purple then, and he's still not crazy about them, but doesn't hate them, either. They're pale. Subdued, but a bit too dark to be pastel, so they don't look too girly, whatever VB said. After a while, you don't even notice them. He can live with this color scheme, even if it clashes with his posters.

He's moved in his old desk—a door on top of two small filing cabinets—and his bookshelves, with all his *CC* issues and books and action figures neatly arranged, for once. Jeremy knows it won't stay neat for long, but still, Mom would be proud, even if she never managed to tame her own clutter. For that matter, CC would be proud. Maybe Jeremy's not entirely a Minion yet.

He could have put his desk and shelves in Mom's study instead, and maybe someday he will, but he hasn't been able to tackle the study yet. That was Mom's haven—her sanctum sanctorum, Aunt Rosie called it—and right now, moving the furniture around would feel like killing Mom all over again. He doesn't even know for sure what's in there. One of his New Year's resolutions is to find out, to start going through her files, anyway.

He's glad Mom always gave Tom copies of her really important papers, the will and whatnot. That's spared him having to tackle the files before now.

His other New Year's resolution is to get a job. Maybe at the local comic store, Symbolia, if they're hiring. Maybe even at the library. Or maybe he can work in the UNR bookstore, if they have openings. He doesn't know if anybody has openings, the way the economy's crumped, and it's not like he has any particular skills. But he knows his *CC*, which could make him useful at Symbolia— although a lot of people know their *CC*, which is what makes it *CC*—and he figures he has an in at the library because of Mom, although he doesn't know if he could stand working there and having to deal with people talking about her, or not talking about her, or wanting to talk about her but not doing it for fear of hurting his feelings, and tiptoeing around him instead, or talking in whispers behind his back. Too much like seventh grade. Too much like the funeral. Too much like the interminable, horrible fucking holidays.

Thanksgiving was tolerable, barely. He went to Aunt Rosie's

house, the way he and Mom always had, and even though the two empty chairs—Mom's and Uncle Walter's—gaped at everybody through the whole meal, he got through it by focusing on his plate and eating. He likes to eat, and Aunt Rosie's a good cook, and he would have had to eat that day anyway. And Thanksgiving's just about food: no gifts or trees or carols.

Of course, it's also about gratitude, or it's supposed to be. The toughest moment at Thanksgiving was when Aunt Rosie very quietly asked people to name what they were grateful for, "even though it's been a really hard year." There followed a bunch of high-minded, noble statements about being grateful for community and healing and yada yada yada, and Jeremy knew that when the obnoxious exercise got to him, he should say he was grateful for everybody who's helped him. But he couldn't. He still can't. If the world were working right, he wouldn't need their help. He doesn't want to need their help. Their help hurts.

So instead, looking at his plate, he said, "I'm grateful for good food," and dug in before Aunt Rosie even said grace. Rude, he knew. Very opinionated. But nobody scolded him. They were cutting him slack because of Mom. Jeremy figures that if people are going to cut you slack, you might as well use it.

The next morning, opening his fridge to see all the leftovers Aunt Rosie had sent home with him, he felt mildly ashamed. Not enough to call and apologize, though.

Christmas was much worse than Thanksgiving. For one thing, there was all the crap that went along with it, commercials and lights and reminders everywhere you turned, so you couldn't ignore it even if you wanted to. And it had been Mom's favorite holiday, and she'd thrown a Christmas party every year, and he sure as hell wasn't going to do that, but should he decorate? Get a tree? What would he put under it? Should he go to church on Christmas Eve, the way he and Mom always had? That was the one service all year he liked. Pretty candles. Nice music, and everybody got to sing, plus it was at night so you didn't have to drag your ass out of bed at the crack of dawn and get yourself ready to be polite to a bunch of church ladies before your brain had even kicked in for the day.

He'd almost decided that he'd go to the service when Hen called to ask him about the Percy-plant. That fucking little tree. The Sunday school kids wanted to decorate it and use it in the Christmas pageant. Was that okay with Jeremy? Did he want it at the house instead?

No, he didn't want it at the house, and sure, the kids could use it. But he promptly decided that if the Percy-plant was gussied up for Christmas, no way was he going to church. He found himself hoping that the sapling would droop and die under the weight of Sunday school ornaments, like the pathetic tree in *A Charlie Brown Christmas.*

That was another thing. He and Mom had watched the Peanuts special every year, and why was he kidding himself even thinking about going to church? The minute the choir started singing "Hark, the Herald Angels Sing," he'd lose it. He and Mom had always sung along to that with the Peanuts gang at the end of the show.

In the end, he survived the month between Christmas and New Year's simply by putting his head down and barreling through. He did a lot of cooking for himself, splurging on good meat and expensive olive oil, losing himself in recipes and aromas. This is the best thing about being back home; he couldn't cook in the dorms. He watched movies, even had some friends over to watch with him—although they all scattered the second the movies were over, because they had no idea what to say to him about Mom—but he barely turned on the TV or radio, because he knew he'd be buried under Christmas commercials and jingle-bell kitsch, endless exhortations to shop. Instead of shopping, he got the last stuff out of his old room and cleaned like a demon.

On Christmas Day itself, he went to Rosie's house for brunch. Tom was there, too, and Hen and Ed, and VB. He didn't want to go, but he couldn't say no, and staying home would have been worse. Aunt Rosie had told him very firmly that he didn't have to give anyone gifts, but he would have felt crappy if he hadn't, since he had a strong feeling he'd be getting stuff. And it was a chance to give away more of Mom's things that he didn't want, anyway. They were nice things, or at any rate things she'd loved, and someone should have them.

So he gave Aunt Rosie a bunch of Mom's old flowery teacups, and she cried. She gave him a nice Lands' End down vest, one of Uncle Walter's, "because he can't use it in the nursing home, and he'd want you to have it."

He gave VB the *Little House on the Prairie* books Mom had read when she was a kid and had lugged around with her ever since, and VB cried. She gave him an Amazon.com gift card.

He gave Tom a bunch of Mom's books about geology, because Tom likes rocks, too, and Tom didn't cry but cleared his throat and coughed and stammered a bit and finally managed to say thank you, he'd enjoy these very much. Tom gave Jeremy a gift card to Emerald City, the café two miles from the house.

Jeremy gave Hen Mom's *Book of Common Prayer,* even though he supposed that Hen already had ten million of the things, and Hen cried, and then he gave Ed some of Mom's seed packets, because Ed's a gardener, too, and Ed didn't cry—thank God—and then Hen and Ed gave Jeremy a nice woolen hat and scarf, with a card saying that they hoped the gift would feel like a warm hug and remind him he was loved, and to his absolute humiliation, he cried, and everybody else cried too this time, even Ed, and it was by far the soggiest Christmas Jeremy had ever experienced, and he hated it.

And then, finally, they were done with presents, which was a little awkward because Jeremy didn't have anything for Uncle Walter.

He felt rotten about that, but he had no idea what the guy could use. Everybody told him not to feel bad: anything Walter needed, he already had. But Aunt Rosie cried.

Then they all stopped crying and ate, which was the only decent part of the day. Jeremy had baked some beer bread and made a cheese soufflé, and bread pudding for dessert. He hadn't had the energy to cook anything for Thanksgiving, so he tried to make up for it at Christmas. Everyone said how delicious his food was, and seemed to mean it, which made him as happy as anything could.

The week between Christmas and New Year's was a blur. He listened to a lot of music. He pigged out on a gift basket Mom's coworkers at the library had sent, which was really damned comradely of them, and even roused himself to write a thank-you note. He watched DVDs, including all three of the extended editions of *The Lord of the Rings,* which made an entire day vanish in a surfeit of clashing swords, hairy hobbit feet, and travel-brochure vistas of New Zealand. It was a perfect way to lose a day, but he could only do it once. The four *Comrade Cosmos* movies are the only ones he's ever been able to keep on infinite loop, but he saw the first one with Mom, and refused to see the second one with Mom, and got the DVDs of the last two from Mom, so he can't watch them right now without thinking about her even more than usual, which means he can't watch them. He wonders if he'll ever be able to watch them again.

Mom's a constant background buzz in his brain. White noise. TV static.

That week between holidays always felt like dead time even when Mom was alive. This year, it was torture.

And then New Year's Eve: a quiet dinner at VB's, old movies like *Bringing Up Baby* and *North by Northwest* until midnight, and then apple cider, because VB doesn't like champagne. Jeremy actually agrees with her on this, although he doesn't like the cider either. It's too sweet.

And now, finally, January. He gives one last stretch, rolls out of bed, and goes downstairs to make coffee. It's good French roast—none of that flavored crap Mom liked, hazelnut and peppermint and whatnot—and he has some German stollen from Aunt Rosie to eat with it. After his breakfast, he showers, throws on sweats, and steels himself to begin unearthing Mom's study.

He can't even remember the last time he was fully in the room. When they were both still living here, he'd often stop in the doorway to tell her whatever he needed to say—that he was going out, that he was back in, that he'd finished unloading the dishwasher—but he rarely crossed the threshold. There's only one chair in the room, a rolling office job Mom could scoot wherever she needed to go. Consciously or not, she designed the space to be perfect for her, but not to welcome anyone else.

He stands on the threshold now, bare toes clenched on the hardwood floor, and scans the room. Two windowed walls meet at right angles; Mom staked out the space because of the light. The windowsills are cluttered with rocks and paperweights and plants, mostly cacti, which is good because he hasn't been in here to water them. It's all pretty dusty, but it was dusty even when Mom was alive.

Her desk sits diagonally between the windows. She spent a fortune on that desk. It's a wooden rolltop with ornately carved legs, designed to look old, and Jeremy has always thought it would suit VB better than Mom. It's new, though, and has built-in file drawers and a slide-out keyboard shelf and openings for computer cables in the back. Whenever Jeremy's seen the surface of the desk, it's been a blizzard of papers and stickies and paper clips and Mom's ever-present rocks. Sometimes he thinks she went to library school because it forced her to be organized, but she always said that the beauty of the rolltop was that you could just close the lid on all that.

The lid's closed now. He wonders what he'll find underneath.

Every available bit of wall space has shelves piled with books. Some of the shelves are stand-alone units, often bought at yard sales; Mom always gloated over these, since, chronically short on bookshelves herself, she could never imagine why anyone else would sell them. The books are shelved two and three deep, with piles of more books teetering in front of them whenever there's enough space. There are lots of natural-science books, especially about botany and geology and astronomy. Lots of other nonfiction stuff, especially art and design and local history. There's a whole shelf of church books, a slew of C. S. Lewis and Bonhoeffer and Barbara Brown Taylor, although Mom kept her *Book of Common Prayer,* along with Laura Ingalls Wilder, in her bedroom, which is why Jeremy had those to give at Christmas. There's a fiction section: the Mitford series, the Narnia series, a really battered set of Oz books from when Mom was a kid, Kristin Lavransdatter, George Eliot. And there are at least four shelves of books about kids, about adoption, about Guatemala.

Jeremy knows he has to go through all of it, but he'll save those shelves for last.

In front of the desk, flanked by all those bookshelves, is a round table. Mom couldn't close the lid on this one, and it's heaped with stuff, papers stacked every which way, her checkbook on top of a pile of something that looks like bills—although Tom must have paid them, since the power hasn't been turned off—a bunch of maps and library books, mostly about Mexico. She must have been studying them before she left. Jeremy looks at the teetering pile and nearly despairs. Just cleaning off this table is going to be a nightmare.

All right. Start with the computer. Along with compulsively collecting rocks and books, Mom made constant to-do lists, usually discarded and replaced with new ones before she'd crossed off half the items, or even any of them. When Jeremy was younger, a perpetual drift of lists—lists on counters, on the fridge, taped to walls—was part of the landscape of the house. But about two years ago, Mom started keeping one master list on her computer. It covered everything but groceries; that list still lived on the fridge. If he can get some sense of what her priorities were, maybe he'll know where to start in here. If he's lucky, maybe her reminders to herself will be directions for him.

He takes a deep breath and steps into the room, talking himself through it. Over the threshold: good. Past the table of doom. Quick glance out the window at the dead garden—he has a narrow, fleeting sense that in a few months it will be green and growing again, but the vision vanishes too quickly to be called hope—and then turn to the rolltop desk. Fuss with Mom's chair, a super-adjustable mesh thing that looks like an alien exoskeleton, so it will be high enough and deep enough for you. Fix it so you can lean back if you need to, so you can recline and breathe, take a break from the desk to stare up at the ceiling.

Open the rolltop desk.

It sticks a little, and for a panicky moment Jeremy's afraid that she locked it and that he'll have to search for the key, a quest that could take years, but then, blessedly, it gives. The top rolls back with a clacking noise, like a stick dragged along an iron fence.

Rocks, stickies, books, papers, paper clips, rubber bands, index cards, file folders. Another map of Mexico. Pens and pencils and scissors and tape, a stapler, a hole punch. He doesn't know how all of this can even fit on the desktop, but it's about what he expected, with the computer monitor plunk in the middle of everything, surrounded by strata of crud. No wonder Mom loved looking at striped cliff faces so much.

He turns on the computer and waits for it to boot up, and then stares in dismay at the screen. "Shit." The computer's password-protected, and he has no idea what the password is. He doesn't know how many tries he has before the system shuts him out. He could look for it in Mom's files, but he doesn't think even Mom was naive enough to have a file labeled "Computer Password." If she wrote it down at all, it's probably scribbled on one of the bits of paper in the study. Jeremy could call Tom and ask if he knows it, but he decides to save that as a last resort. Today's a holiday.

He stares glumly at the blinking cursor. Okay. What would Mom pick as her password? He thinks for a minute, and then, on a whim, types his own name: Jeremy.

Logging in, the computer tells him, and then the homescreen appears.

Oh, Mom.

You aren't supposed to use anything as obvious as an only child's name as your password. Mom knew that. She'd done it anyway.

Sighing, he opens the "My Documents" folder and sorts by date. Sure enough, there's "Todolist.doc," right at the top. Jeremy opens it.

After Mexico: dentist, pick up dry-cleaning, make ALA res, oil change, finish Xmas shopping for J.

Finish. Which means she'd started. Yes, of course she had. As disorganized as she was about everything else, she started her Christmas shopping in January, because of the sales. Jeremy always left his until the last minute, but she was usually done in March. She wrapped stuff as she got it, which meant sometimes she didn't remember what she'd bought. One year he'd gotten two of the same CC action figure. He was surprised that this late in the year, she'd had any shopping left to do at all.

He realizes that somewhere in the house, she must have hidden wrapped presents for him. Of course she did. Why hasn't he thought about that until now? It never occurred to him. He thought about Peanuts and her party and the Christmas Eve service, but not the hidden presents? Why?

Because it hurts too much.

Jeremy sits in his mother's insectoid chair and hugs himself. Should he look for his gifts? Does he want to? They must be in here, in the study. Should he look now, or leave them hidden, a surprise to be discovered in the course of sorting through the monumental volume of crap in here?

But his eyes have already gone to the cabinet doors under one of the bookshelves, which used to be an entertainment unit. His presents have to be there. It's the only place in the room she could have hidden them.

*M*elinda sits cross-legged on the living room floor, wrapping one of Jeremy's Christmas gifts. It's September, and he's been living in the dorms for a month. As little as they've been talking lately, she desperately misses having him in the house.

She's been watching a popular-science program, BBC's biography of the planet. Last night she learned that the moon is slowly creeping away from the Earth, getting a centimeter farther away every year. This news fills Melinda with melancholy. The moon can't be mended, and it's slipping away, a scarred child trying to leave its parent. Jeremy's doing the same thing, although—given the state of the economy—a centimeter a year may be all he can manage.

Wrapping Christmas gifts comforts her. In a few months, he'll be home for winter break.

She never knows what to get him anymore, though. He's still into *Comrade Cosmos,* but his tastes have changed. For his birthday this year she got him a T-shirt that showed CC standing defiantly, holding up a hammer and nails, while EE loomed as a swirling mist behind him. She thought it was a great image, but Jeremy sneered at it. "Mom, that's Sally Honu's work, and she's a totally second-rate artist. Victor Evans and Erica James are so much better."

Clearly, she no longer has the chops to choose good gifts, although to be fair, he might have sneered at anything she gave him. "You can return it," she told him, unable to keep from snapping. "I kept the receipt." She felt both vindicated and ashamed when he blushed.

"Sorry. I'm sorry, Mom. It was nice of you to try. It's one of Honu's better panels, really."

He liked the chocolate she gave him, and he really enjoyed their meal at Fourth Street Bistro, an extravagance she allowed herself because it was his last birthday before he left for school. He savored the food, exclaimed over the seasoning, asked smart questions when the owner stopped by the table to see how they were enjoying their meal. He's never liked Melinda's cooking—with the notable exception of her lasagna, which she cooks for him but won't eat herself, since it contains meat—but it turns out that he loves nouvelle cuisine.

Today at Sundance Books she saw a cookbook from Tra Vigne, a swanky Northern Italian restaurant in Napa she and Rosemary and Walter went to once during a winery tour. She bought it for Jeremy and wrote on the inside cover, *Their food's a little like Fourth Street's; maybe you can learn to cook your own! Happy eating! Love, Mom.*

Jeremy's never been an academic superstar. He's certainly bright enough, but he's a classic underachiever, and she worries about him in college. He barely even got into UNR, which is a decent state school but no Harvard, and as desperate as he's been to get out of the house, he had no interest in applying anywhere else. The way Veronique slides around any discussion of how he's doing in her class is sufficient indication that Melinda's worry is well-founded. He enjoys cooking, though—he's always been happy to make breakfast or whip up batches of cookies for church coffee hour, even after he stopped going to church—and she hopes the cookbook may nudge him to think about being a chef, or at least pursuing the hobby more seriously.

She hopes it isn't too much of a nudge. She knows she has to be careful. He's so prickly these days, so resentful of any suggestion that she has an agenda for him. She doesn't know how much of this is normal growing pains and how much is his continuing issues with the adoption.

She reminds herself that he's an adolescent. If he didn't have issues with the adoption, he'd have issues with something else, and thank God his physical health has always been good. If there are any lingering developmental delays from the orphanage, Melinda can't detect them. He's an indifferent student, but so are lots of kids who didn't spend their first few years institutionalized in war-torn countries.

Sighing, she smooths the Christmas paper around the book and tapes it. Then she clambers to her feet and walks into her study. There's too much stuff on the floor right now for her to sit and wrap in here. She really needs to straighten up.

She always needs to straighten up.

Laughing at herself, she opens the cabinet under the shelves of geology books—this unit was one of her better yard-sale finds—and pulls out the shopping bag of Jeremy's gifts. She's wrapped them already, but she recognizes them by shape and size. More chocolate, a gourmet assortment of fair-trade dark ranging from 65% to 90% cacao. A red woolen pullover, since red has always been Jeremy's favorite color. The soundtrack of the Charlie Brown Christmas special. That one's a bit of a risk, since any day now she expects him to disdain their old tradition as childish, but the CD was on huge sale at Borders last January.

She puts the wrapped book in the bag and replaces it in the cabinet. Since he's not living at home, she probably doesn't have to be so careful about hiding stuff in here, but this way he can't stumble across anything on his rare visits, and she doesn't have to worry about reminding herself to hide the bag before he comes home on Christmas break.

She closes the cabinet, stands, and rocks back on her heels, stretching her lower back. There are still a few things she wants to get him, small stuff. Stocking stuffers, really: things she knows he'll use. Some of his favorite razors, socks, a pencil case since he's been keeping pens and pencils in a Ziploc bag in his backpack. And of course she'll bring something back from Mexico for him, probably a souvenir for right away and something a bit nicer for Christmas.

The holidays always go so fast. She's glad she's planned this

Mexico trip, though. Part of her current sadness, she knows, is the annual advent of shorter days, whatever the moon's doing. By October, sun and warm water will be just what she needs, a final taste of summer before winter kicks in.

Still in her bathrobe, hands wrapped around a mug of coffee, Veronique sits at her tiny kitchen table and stares balefully at her calendar. January 1. That means that the holidays are over. Tomorrow, she'll have to start prepping her spring classes. It's not like this will be a tremendous amount of work—she's teaching a Women & Lit class she's done a million times and a nineteenth-century British survey, one of her bread-and-butter courses—but just thinking about it makes her chest ache. In a little over two weeks, she'll be back in the classroom, dealing with a new crop of blunted brains.

Melinda always took her out to dinner on the first day of class. It happened by accident the first time; they'd been trying to find a time to have dinner, and that night just happened to work. Halfway through the meal, Veronique made some offhand comment about how nice this was, a little reward for making it through the first day of classes, and Melinda promptly said, "Well then, we'll have to make it a tradition."

And so they had, for what, seven or eight years now? The first day of classes, both spring and fall semester—and the one year Veronique was foolish enough to teach summer school, which left her feeling like she'd been flattened by an army tank—they invariably went out for Thai food. The tradition had become more important each year, as Veronique's boredom with teaching morphed into active hatred of it.

Classes start in two weeks. What's she going to do?

She's weeping now, furious at herself but still flummoxed by the question, which feels like a real and pressing problem. She could take herself out to dinner, but that would feel like an exercise in misery. The real problem is that she dreads returning to the classroom. Her courses this semester are essentially prepped, but that's because she's taught them so often that they bore her into somnolence.

She could get in her car tomorrow, drive to Canada, and vanish. Go AWOL. Who cares how cold it is this time of year? Maybe the weather would deter people from looking for her. She pictures herself leaping across ice floes to reach freedom, like Eliza in *Uncle Tom's Cabin.*

She seriously entertains this fantasy for a moment, picturing what she'd pack—which of her shoes would work best on ice floes?—and then discards it. She has to take care of the cats, who would not consider a road trip to Canada, with or without ice floes, a good time. Her knee's hardly up to leaping. And God knows that if she could afford to just pick up and leave her job, she would have done it years ago. No, that won't work.

She takes a long swallow of coffee, sweet and creamy. Her doctor's been on her for years now to cut down on sugar and cholesterol, but she's never planned to live forever and she needs her pleasures. Savoring her French roast, she forces herself to think about work. The 19c Brit syllabus is pretty much dictated by the department; not much leeway there. But Women & Lit's an open topic. She can teach it however she wants.

Since the middle of last semester, it's been advertised as Women & Work, a topic that allows her to teach everything from Stowe's *Uncle Tom's Cabin,* with its oppressed slave women toiling away under the lash, to Ehrenreich's *Nickel and Dimed,* with its oppressed Wal-Mart employees sorting endless piles of Jordache jeans. The topic resonates with the students, most of whom are working their way through school. For a long time, it was one of Veronique's more popular courses, which is why she keeps teaching it. But she's tired of it, as of so much else, and as she's grown more bored, so have the students. Time for a change.

All right, so what would be more interesting?

Women & Tourism.

Women & Murder.

Women & Abandonment.

Veronique feels encased in lead. What's she thinking? She can't prep a new course, with an entirely new set of books to be ordered, in two weeks. That's insane.

Women & Violence.

She blinks. Trendy. Relevant. Related, God knows, to Melinda, which means Veronique will have some emotional energy invested in the work. She can still use the Stowe, the first book on the syllabus, which will leave a month for the other books to come in, if she orders them in the next few days.

The students won't have signed up for this topic. On the other hand, Women & Lit satisfies both college and departmental requirements and always fills: she'll have students no matter what she teaches.

She pushes herself away from the breakfast table, already making lists as she heads upstairs to search her shelves, and the library database, for good fits. Stowe. Glaspell's "A Jury of Her Peers." *Beloved. Bastard Out of Carolina,* or *I Know Why the Caged Bird Sings.* Something by Kingsolver, who's always a hit with students.

That's a thin list, but it's a start, and she'll find others. Maybe she can do this. Maybe she can force herself through another semester.

*g*one, finally. Anna waves the detested rental car out of the driveway and goes inside to collapse onto the couch. William's parents have been in Seattle for a month and a half, from before Thanksgiving to now, New Year's Day. Even if she felt close to them, even if the visit hadn't come at such a hideous time, having them here for so long would have been a strain.

The one blessing is that they stayed in a hotel, not at the house. William spent a lot of time with them, which meant that Anna didn't have to, although it also meant she didn't see much of

William. But that was true even before his parents descended on Seattle.

She suspects she'll see even less of him now.

She knows they have to talk. She's afraid to talk to him, afraid of guilt and accusations and recriminations, most afraid of having to witness his pain, since her own is vast and unsupportable and inescapable, the air she breathes and the lungs she breathes it with. She can't face what happened yet. She can't face talking to William about any of it, having to witness his own grief. His only son, his boy. Percy.

She hasn't been able to face anyone else, either. Her New Year's resolution is to get back into the world again: to help William with Kip's postponed opening, to go back to her knitting group, to turn her energies back to the Blake board, which will be meeting in a few weeks.

Before Marjorie and David came, all of that would have seemed unbearable. Now it will be a relief.

Marjorie and David, of course, arrived with an agenda. Communication. Openness. Transparency. They wanted everyone to share feelings, to use the incomprehensible horror of what Percy did and how he died as an opportunity for personal growth. They wanted to help William and Anna through the holidays, which they knew could be meaningful even in grief, and they wanted to help plan Percy's funeral as a community celebration of life. They hadn't been especially close to their only grandson, mostly because they lived in Massachusetts, but in this case, that was a blessing, because it gave them clearer heads with which to supervise their son and his wife.

Anna didn't want to be supervised.

She found their ideas about growth and transparency and celebration obscene.

She knows they meant well. They always mean well. But they always mean well in such a high-handed, officious, controlling way that it makes her want to scream. The funeral is none of their business. They kept telling her and William that it was important to have a service for closure, but Anna isn't sure she wants closure, even if she should. How can you have closure on the death of your only child? How is that possible under any circumstances, let alone these? She's simply not up to the ordeal of a memorial service, especially one that includes any form of the word "celebration." She suspects William feels the same way, although they haven't discussed it directly. They've only discussed it through his parents.

In any case, the date's now fixed. Percy's memorial service will be on July 24, which would have been his twenty-third birthday. That's going to be a brutal day anyway: they might as well have the memorial then, and pack all the misery into as short a span as possible. At least it's a Saturday, the most convenient day for such an event.

Marjorie and David wouldn't leave Seattle until the date was set. They'll come back in July, for the service. Anna fervently hopes they won't stay another six weeks.

She's closed her eyes in sheer weariness, but she feels a wet nose nudging her hand, which rests on one knee. "Hello, Bart," she says without opening her eyes; a warm tongue licks her palm in response. She hears soft thumping now, the dog's tail beating a tattoo against the carpet.

"Don't get your hopes up. The days of nonstop walks are over." While Marjorie and David were here, she took Bart on three, four, five walks a day: to get away from them when they were in the house, and to relieve her stress through exercise when they and William were off somewhere without her. As much as she longed to be alone, she couldn't stand being in the house by herself; she kept finding herself listening for Percy's footsteps. So she'd fidget and pace and wind up taking the dog out, again. A few times, Bart even refused the leash, flopping down with his long head on his lanky paws. If you want to go out again, human, do it by yourself.

But David and Marjorie are gone, finally, and the weather's at its most wretched, and the dog will just have to cope with the old, two-walk-a-day regimen while Anna tries to resume her old life. She's pretty sure that no one in her knitting group or on the Blake board will want her to share her feelings about Percy. That's the up-side of the isolation she's felt: the common decency of privacy.

Marjorie and David kept pestering her about how she needed to find a support group. There are bereavement groups for suicide survivors, they told her, and she's sure that's true, but she doesn't think she could deal with a room full of other people's overwhelm-ing grief and anger, that maelstrom of sheer agony.

William, who knows her horror of touchy-feely group therapy, suggested a psychologist during one of their infrequent conversa-tions. He's seeing one himself. He's on medication now, and thinks it will help her—although to her he seems flat and foggy, blunted and blurred—but she doesn't need to talk to a shrink and she doesn't need to be on drugs. What she needs is to know that other people whose children have committed horrible crimes have sur-vived the experience, have made sense of it somehow and gone on with their lives.

That's the support group she really needs, but she doesn't think it exists. She can't find Mothers of Murderers Anonymous in the phone book. If Marjorie were in this situation, she'd start up a chapter herself, and probably organize a national charitable foun-dation of some sort into the bargain. But Anna isn't Marjorie. She never has been, never will be. William skipped the section in the manual explaining that men are supposed to marry women who remind them of their mothers.

In lieu of group therapy, she kept reading everything she could find about Melinda Soto. She read articles about the funeral, read the online archive of library newsletters Melinda edited, read the online guestbook set up by the library: note after note talking about how wonderful she was, how incomprehensible her death is.

Many of the notes express rage at Percy. Anna keeps reading them anyway. She understands the rage. She shares it.

So much pain, pain that overwhelms the words meant to express it.

The dog's still licking her hand. The sensation was soothing at first, but now it's as grating as if her hand were being raked over glass. Anna pulls away from Bart's slobber, gets up, and makes her way into the bathroom to clean the dog spit off her skin. Her hands yearn to knit; she craves the softness of yarn and the familiar, reassuring movements of the needles. She hasn't knit since Marjorie and David showed up. She knows the rhythm of the stitches will calm her, help her think more clearly again. Knitting is a promise that she can still function, still do useful work.

Her knitting bag's where she left it the night Melinda Soto was killed, half under an easy chair in the living room. She's heading back into the living room to collect it, to resume work on the Frost Flowers shawl, when the phone rings. She picks up in the kitchen, hoping it's not David and Marjorie saying that their flight's been delayed, or offering yet more ideas for the memorial service. Please, be anyone but them.

It's Miranda Tobin.

Watch what you wish for.

"Anna, *dear,* I'm just calling to find out how you and William are doing."

Anna doubts this very much, and she wouldn't know how to answer the question even if it were sincere. She and Miranda have never been close. She fumbles for words and comes up dry.

"Anna? Are you there?"

"Yes, I'm here. It's—a hard question to answer. I don't have words for it." Only the silent scream. "It was kind of you to call, Miranda."

If the call's really a compassionate gesture, Miranda will recognize this as dismissal and get off the phone. Of course she doesn't. "Toby and I were talking just last night about how *terrible* it all is. We just can't understand it."

"No one can understand it," Anna says. Her mouth tastes like blood, and her hand hurts from gripping the phone. If Percy had to kill someone, why couldn't he kill Miranda Tobin?

Anna recognizes this as humor too black to share with anyone, even William. Especially William. She clears her throat and says, "We're having the memorial service on July 24. It would have been Percy's birthday. It would be lovely to see you and Toby there."

"Oh, we'd *love* to come, but I'm afraid we'll be in Europe then. It's Toby's last free summer, really, because things will heat up so much in his second year at Harvard Med, so we thought we'd take the chance to see France and Italy."

I cannot, thinks Anna, believe that I'm having this conversation. She wonders if Miranda expects her to ask about the trip, or say that she hopes they have a wonderful time. "Well, I'm sorry you can't be there. It was really very kind of you to call, but—"

"Anna, dear, I'm sorry to be the one to have to tell you this, but, well, we had a board meeting last night—"

Ah. "I've taken a leave of absence from the board," Anna says, "although I'm thinking of coming back. Weren't you told?"

"Yes, of course, we all know that, and of course you would, you have to, I can't even *imagine* what this must be like for you, but Anna, *dear,* I thought you should know. There's talk about asking you to resign."

The room shifts slightly, and then settles. "Resign?" Anna says. "They're asking me? Or telling me?"

"Well, you know, because it's a school, and well, we want the public to focus on the *fine* young people who attend Blake."

And not on the rapist murderers, Anna thinks grimly. She can't even blame them, but she's shaking anyway. All the work she's put into that place, the hours of meetings and events and fundraisers and school functions, not to mention the tuition she and William paid for Percy's very *fine* education. "I understand completely," she says, trying to keep her voice under control. "I'm a PR liability. If it were Toby, I'm sure I'd have come to the same conclusion about you."

Miranda coughs, sounding a bit strangled, but then regains her dovelike tones. "I thought it was cruel, just to send a letter. I thought someone should tell you in person."

The hell you did, Anna thinks. You wanted to gloat. She's so angry she can barely form syllables. "Well, I have the message now. Thank you."

"I just didn't want you to be blindsided, Anna. When you get the letter."

This time it registers. A letter. They've written a letter? Already? Percy's only been dead six weeks. They couldn't have waited another few months? Or, if they couldn't wait, they couldn't send someone to tell her in person?

Miranda's still talking, but Anna can't make it out, doesn't want to. She hangs up.

She no longer has the slightest desire to knit. She entertains a brief fantasy about strangling Miranda Tobin with her yarn, and then dismisses it. She knows the Blake board made the decision they had to make, but the way they've done it still enrages her.

All right, she'll preempt them. She'll send out a letter of resignation before she can get their letter firing her.

Halfway down the hall to her study, she stops. No. She can't do that. Because Miranda will know the truth, and will tell everyone else, and then her own letter will merely look thin and desperate, as indeed it would be. There's no good way to handle the situation, but giving Miranda Tobin another reason to gloat would definitely be a bad one.

The silent scream bubbles into unspoken words. I wasn't a bad mother I wasn't I don't know why this happened but it's not my fault, it has to be but it can't be, how can it be my fault that my child did this thing I can't even bear to think about?

Anna feels a huge shudder pass through her body. She swallows. She's standing in front of Percy's bedroom.

It's not like this is unusual. She walks past this door too many times each day to count. She hasn't gone inside. She's told herself that she'll do that when she's ready. There's no hurry. Nothing inside is going anywhere.

She stands in the dark hallway, looking at Percy's doorknob. It's just a room, now. He's not in it. The police have returned what they took, six big boxes worth, which William lugged back into the room. They're still there, Anna supposes, sitting on the floor or the bed: pieces of Percy's life, torn out of context.

She can't bring Percy back. She can't undo what he did or comfort the people who loved Melinda Soto. She can't restore his good name at the school he attended from the ages of five to eighteen. But she can put his things back where he kept them, back where they belong. That tiny bit, she can make right.

She opens the door and turns on the overhead light. Someone—William? the cops?—lowered the blinds, making the room even gloomier than it would be anyway. Resolutely, stepping around boxes, Anna crosses to the windows and raises the slats, allowing such daylight as there is to filter into the room. Then she turns on Percy's desk lamp and bedside lamp.

There. It's a little more cheerful now. She takes a deep breath and looks around. He was a neat kid. Too neat? Should his neatness have alarmed her? His comic-book posters march across the walls, lined up with architectural precision, interrupted only by a Stanford pennant and his framed diplomas. On his desk, a small wooden one he's had ever since he started junior high school, his GMAT study book sits centered, flanked by a row of pencils, a calculator, an eraser. Ordinarily his computer would be on the desk, too, but it's not; she supposes it's in one of the boxes, since she knows the police took it. She doesn't believe they found anything interesting on it, although William talked to them in much more depth than she did. Surely William would have told her if anything had turned up, though. Even in his present state, he wouldn't have withheld any information that would explain any of this.

One narrow bookshelf is full of textbooks and a few beat-up

novels. The other bookcase, much larger, houses Percy's comic collection, each issue stored in a plastic slipcase, each year of issues boxed and labeled. William, who deals regularly with art collectors, says that many of them are more passionate about the act of collecting than about what they collect. Had they fastened on stamps or coins or bottle caps, they would be equally driven. Percy, says William, fastened on a comic book, which worked out well, because the comic book is popular and ubiquitous and inexpensive.

She walks to the closet and opens it. Button-down shirts and slacks hang neatly from the racks. There are a few ties, a collection of shoes in a rack on the door. The shelves are empty; she suspects she'll find whatever was there in the police boxes.

Percy's dresser, too, holds only what you'd expect. Socks, briefs, polo shirts, jeans, sweatpants. Everything looks rumpled, so the police must have searched it.

Her first cursory inspection completed, Anna looks around the room again. There's a small photo frame on the desk. Percy, thirteen or fourteen—no, he was fourteen then—his arms around puppy Bart, who licks his cheek as Percy laughs, eyes closed and face to the sun, oblivious to the camera. William took the photo.

How did this sunny, joyous kid turn into the person who killed Melinda Soto? What didn't Anna know about Percy?

Almost everything, she thinks. But couldn't any parent say the same? Couldn't she and William say the same of each other, especially now? Do any of us really know the people we love? Anna thinks bleakly that she probably understands Bart, that simple and reliably demonstrative creature, better than she does any of the people in her life.

It occurs to her that this is a reciprocal principle, that the people in her life also don't understand her, but she shoves that thought away. It will only lead to self-pity, which is entirely too imminent a threat right now anyway, now that her rage over the Blake mess has, at least for the moment, faded to a dull ache.

All right. What can she do now, after the fact, to deepen her knowledge of her son?

She looks around the room again. Those ghastly posters, rank upon rank of blinding primary colors and over-exaggerated gestures. The carefully preserved comic books. She's never understood this *Comrade Cosmos* phenomenon, which bores her almost literally to tears, but something about it meant a great deal to Percy.

All right. Every day, she will unpack one box—which should take an hour or two—and read as many of the comic books as she can stomach, starting at the beginning. The second process should keep her busy for a long time.

Wearing an Irish fisherman's cardigan Walter gave her for Christmas five years ago, Rosemary carefully pulls the last ornament off her tree. It's antique glass, opalescent and fragile, and belonged to Walter's grandmother. It's the first ornament to go on the tree and the last to come off, taking pride of place even over the treetop angel. She packs it carefully into a thickly padded box and sets it aside. She keeps it in her bedside drawer, fearing that catastrophe would befall it in the garage.

New Year's Day is always something of a relief, but always leaves her feeling desolate, too: the warmth of Christmas fled even though, according to the church calendar, the season lasts until Epiphany on January 6. January 1 is a dull dud of a holiday, a dead spot in the year designed to allow people to recover from hangovers. Since Rosemary doesn't have one, she simply winds up feeling tired and out of sorts.

She enjoyed New Year's Eve at Vera's; that's always a pleasant, civilized evening. She was glad, if surprised, that Jeremy joined them. She'd thought he'd want to be with his friends, but he'd merely explained with a shrug that he wasn't really into hard partying, especially now.

That's good, Rosemary thinks. He isn't using alcohol or drugs to try to escape. Melinda always fretted that he was a late bloomer, sullen and unfocused, but Rosemary thinks he has good instincts.

She missed Melinda desperately last night, although not, she's sure, half as much as Jeremy did. Somewhat less desperately, she missed Melinda's weekend-before-Christmas party, an interesting mix of library people, church folk, and fellow adoptive parents. Most of all, though, she missed Melinda on Christmas itself, all the more because she also missed Walter so much.

After everyone left, she forced herself to visit him again. She brought him some stollen, which he's always liked, and a fleece jacket because he gets cold so easily. The nursing home was decorated for the holidays, of course, and there were many more visitors than usual, including volunteers singing carols. Some of the residents sat smiling, spruced up in red and green outfits, in their wheelchairs. Others seemed agitated, bewildered by too many strangers.

Walter was asleep, turned toward his window. Rosemary sat with him for a while, remembering all the Christmases they'd spent together, remembering—because she knew he couldn't—his many years as Santa Claus at his firm's holiday party, and his delight in touring the neighborhood Christmas decorations, and how much he always exclaimed at the gifts she gave him.

If he'd woken up, she'd have told him those memories as a story, the way she'd told him about Melinda as a story. That tale had sparked a moment of recognition. Would this have done the same?

But he didn't wake up, and after an hour of listening to his deep, even breathing, her need to be out of the building suddenly rose to an intolerable level. She left the jacket on his bedside table and fled, and she hasn't been back since.

All the ornaments and lights are off now. She folds up the little tree and puts it back in its box. Christmas has been relegated to the garage for another year. The house is empty, too large. Echoing.

Before next Christmas, Rosemary thinks, shivering despite her thick sweater, I have to do something just for myself. Travel, or take a class, or schedule a retreat. Do something I've never done before, something I can't associate with Walter or Melinda. I have to learn how to be by myself, before everyone else is gone and I have no choice.

11

Some readers have always seen in Cosmos's penchant for order and cooperation a dictatorial streak, the clear and present danger of fascism, and even if this is difficult to reconcile with Cosmos's somewhat nebbishy personality and even more nebbishy appearance, with his blue jeans and rumpled button-down shirts and constant worry about, and work on behalf of, Vanessa and Charlie, the theme runs throughout CCcrit. How much order is too much? When does communal effort become coercive, oppressive? What allowances does the CCverse make for rebellion, for individual tangents, for simple dissent?

The CC Four argue convincingly that Cosmos is no dictator. He appears only to newly devastated communities, and goes back home once rebuilding efforts are under way. While some real-world dictators have indeed exploited vulnerable populations, they used times of turmoil to entrench themselves, and were removed—if at all—against their wills. Real-world dictators don't say, as Cosmos is wont to do, "Well, guys, looks like you're getting this under control, so I'll be going home now, okay?" Real-world dictators, if they leave the places they rule, leave them under the thumb of trusted henchmen. Cosmos employs no stormtroopers.

Furthermore, Cosmos simply ignores those who ignore him, who turn their backs on whatever group efforts he's organizing in each issue. He doesn't have lists of enemies, or stables of informers, or secret police. He doesn't throw people who disagree with him into gulags. Indeed, he never meets them. They aren't even on his radar.

And that, according to the naysayers, is another problem. CC doesn't debate his critics. He doesn't engage in constructive dialogue.

The CC Four, and the rest of the CCverse, are sensitive to these issues. And so in issue 72, a small town decimated by a fire found itself, after Cosmos's departure, chafing against the rule of the Misguided Mayor, who had instituted a system of tasks and schedules, fines and curfews, that left his community almost paralyzed. The townspeople of Wishful, Wyoming, despaired. It didn't even make sense to ask CC to come back, since order is his province, and too *much* order was the problem.

The town succumbed to Entropy-worship. Local churches held prayer vigils imploring God for just a little bit of chaos; law-abiding citizens contemplated armed rebellion; a Wiccan group convened a Dissidents' Circle, scattering salt and sage to try to invoke the Emperor.

For once, the Emperor couldn't get in. The town was locked too tightly against him. Disturbed and indignant, EE himself turned to Cosmos for help, appearing in CC's kitchen during an especially frustrating attempt to feed Vanessa, who had lost her appetite over the last three issues and become alarmingly thin. Her doctors were making dire noises about hospitalization, g-tubes, force-feeding. EE showed up just as she had spit the pureed carrots CC was spooning into her mouth all over the kitchen table.

"You!" Cosmos said, not even needing to turn around to recognize his opponent. He feels EE now, a prickle in the skin; they are linked as closely as lovers. "I know you're responsible for this. I know there's no coalition I can mobilize to make her want to eat. I know that—"

"That's not why I'm here," EE said, and gave CC a terse rundown of the MM situation. "He has left no crack for me to enter. His people are paralyzed into productivity. You have to help free them."

"Not my job," CC said, doggedly trying again with the spoon, this time full of bananas. His sister loves bananas. Not these, though. Out they went, a gloopy spray right into CC's face. A tear streaked down his cheek, wending its way past banana chunks. "They have to figure it out for themselves. I've done what I can do there."

"You did too much."

"Nope, old enemy. Sounds like MM did too much. The townspeople need to figure out how to depose him. I can't do everything. I've never said I can do everything. I can't even get my sister to eat her favorite fruit."

He was weeping in earnest now. In the panel, the reader sees him leaning on the kitchen table, spoon abandoned on the wooden surface. His back is to the Emperor, whose expression has softened, and who has reached out a tentative tentacle of darkness, as if in comfort.

In this moment, Comrade Cosmos and the Emperor of Entropy are equally powerless.

Enter Archipelago Osprey.

This is her real name. She insists that it be used in full and spelled properly. She will not tolerate nicknames, abbreviations, or initials. She routinely gets into furious hissing matches with hapless customer-service personnel who mangle Archipelago into Archie or Archibelle or Archangel. She holds popular opinion in contempt and considers decluttering a project for simple-minded automatons. She sneers at rules, laws, and curfews.

She lives in Wishful.

Archipelago has no patience for most of her fellow mortals. She would boast, had she any fellow humans to boast to, that she cares for no one but herself and Erasmus, her pet emperor scorpion, a creature she respects because it has large claws and dislikes being handled, as she herself does. She moved to Wishful because she found a cheap apartment there, and while she paints houses for income when she has to, she has a little bit of money saved, enough to tide her over for a year if she's careful, and she relishes the freedom from other people's expectations. No, that trim's too sloppy. Aren't you going to clean up the drippings on the porch? Why aren't you using dropcloths?

Even Archipelago grudgingly acknowledges some wonder that anyone ever pays her at all.

But they do, and so she's living in Wishful, painting singularly angry and ugly acrylic canvases and feeding Erasmus his crickets and mealworms, carefully dusted with a vitamin/mineral supplement—for all her sneering nihilism, she's a responsible pet owner—when the fire breaks out. Her apartment isn't in any danger, but she can see the action a few blocks away, can hear the high-pitched wailing of screaming and sirens.

Archipelago's exquisitely sensitive to noise, one reason she's such a recluse and why she owns a quiet scorpion instead of a barking pit bull. She doesn't like this din at all, so she puts in her earplugs. She does sit in her window and watch, though. She moves Erasmus's cage onto the windowsill so he can watch, too. This is better than TV.

Naturally, she has nothing to do with the rebuilding efforts when CC shows up. "Fucking do-gooder," she tells Erasmus, dropping another vitamin-enriched cricket into his cage. "Why doesn't he mind his own business and let the town clean up its own mess? Who needs him, anyway? Not us."

Erasmus, waving his pedipalps as he closes in on the cricket, ignores her. Erasmus always ignores her. Erasmus cares only for his crickets, and disdains their source. Archipelago respects this.

Wishful's one grocery store burned down in the fire, but Archipelago maintains a supply of canned food, bottled water, and freeze-dried crickets, insurance against natural disaster, terrorist attack, or the many days when she simply has no desire to go outside. She hunkers down in her apartment while Cosmos organizes the town, and exhales in relief when he finally leaves. She was getting tired of Spam and canned peas, and she was starting to run low on instant crickets, which Erasmus considers vastly inferior to the living variety, no matter how much yummy vitamin dust she dumps on them.

She soon discovers, however, that MM makes CC look like an anarchist.

After a seventy-five-mile round trip to the nearest pet store that stocks live crickets—she tried to trap her own for a while, but found it a tedious and unreliable pursuit—Archipelago roars back into Wishful on her Harley, only to find a police blockade across the main road.

"Ma'am, we can't let you in. It's past curfew."

"Curfew? What curfew?" She would have said "what fucking curfew," but Archipelago isn't stupid, and knows better than to deliberately antagonize police.

"The curfew that's been in the local paper? The one posted on all those signs in town? The one we've been announcing through bullhorns?"

Archipelago eschews newspapers and despises municipal signage. "I don't read much. Sorry."

One of the cops rolls his eyes. "Are you deaf, too? We've been driving around with loudspeaker trucks for the last ten days."

Archipelago has been aware of some din, but put her earplugs in to deal with it. Her earplugs work exceedingly well. "I was listening to music. Sorry."

"Twelve hours a day? That'll damage your hearing, ma'am."

"I'll keep that in mind, officers, thank you. May I go back home now, please?" She pinches the courteous phrases through a clenched jaw, and hopes the cops can't tell.

"No, ma'am. You're past curfew. No one's allowed in by Mayoral decree, not until six tomorrow morning. We can recommend the Motel 6 a few miles up the highway."

"I don't have money to stay in a motel. I have a pet I have to feed. I truly wasn't aware of the curfew, officers. If I promise to come home on time every day from now on, may I please, please *please* return to my apartment?"

Archipelago hates this. She hates begging people who think they can tell her what to do. It reminds her too much of dealing with her clueless parents, a torture she escaped by running away from home when she was thirteen.

The cops frown, ask to see her driver's license—which, blessedly, she just had renewed, so it shows her Wishful address—and confer among themselves. They finally decide that just this once, they'll let her back into town. Not without penalty, though. They have to write her a ticket for disorderly conduct.

Archipelago feels her brain heating up like molten lava. "How much is the ticket?"

"One hundred fifty dollars, ma'am."

Her grip tightens on the handlebars of her Harley. "That's more than the Motel 6."

"Yes, ma'am, but you'll be able to get home tonight and feed your pet."

Erasmus was fed yesterday; he can go another day or two if he has to. He's a desert creature, designed to endure scarcity. "All right," she says, seething, "I'll take the Motel 6."

In the lobby of the Motel 6, waiting to check in, she overhears another guest commenting that the Mayor bought this place last year, which means he has an extremely vested interest in locking out townspeople so they have to stay here instead.

Motherfucker.

Even with her earplugs blocking out unsavory noises from the rooms on either side of her, Archipelago passes a sleepless night. The mattress is too soft. There are bugs. She amuses herself by catching some cockroaches to feed Erasmus—he deserves a special treat after being left alone, even if he probably hasn't noticed and doesn't care—but by the time she finally manages to get back home the next morning, she has a migraine so severe that she has to spend the rest of the day in bed.

Headache finally vanquished, she rises in wrath and heads straight to her ancient computer to do some research. Motherfucking Mayor's going to pay for this shit.

An hour later, she's covered the opening of a shot glass with plastic wrap, picked up Erasmus with a pair of cooking tongs—"Sorry, buddy, but it's for the cause"—and pressed his stinger against the wrap until, indeed, he stings it, leaving drops of venom in the cup. Laboratory professionals use electrical current to excite scorpions into stinging, but this strikes Archipelago as deeply unkind, and is in any case beyond her current technical capabilities.

After she puts Erasmus back in the cage, she gives him a vitamin-dusted cockroach, still alive, to reward him for his labors. He appears to relish it.

She puts the venom in the fridge.

Among the bits of junk Archipelago has hauled around—for no reason other than that they fit into her motorcycle saddlebags and might conceivably come in handy someday—she has a set of steel-tipped bar darts. She takes one of these, cleans the tip with rubbing alcohol to remove any contaminant that might interfere with the scorpion venom, and then coats the tip with the tiny amount of liquid in the shot glass, which she then throws away. She has no idea how stable or persistent scorpion venom is. She doesn't want to take any risks.

Waste of a good shot glass, but if this works, it will be worth it.

She packs the dart carefully into a paper bag, tip up to prevent the venom being rubbed off, packs herself a small picnic lunch to carry in another bag, inserts her earplugs, and sets out for the Mayor's rally.

The Mayor throws himself a rally almost every day. He loves rallies. He loves hearing people cheering for him. Usually the people cheering are people he's paid to cheer. The rallies are poorly attended, and the Mayor hasn't yet figured out how to make attendance compulsory, since the townsfolk who don't come always claim to be working on the Mayor's mandatory rebuilding projects.

Security tends to be lax. The Mayor, in his delusion, believes that everyone loves him, and hasn't yet descended into justified paranoia. So Archipelago has very little trouble strolling behind his podium, gleefully tossing the dart at his back, and then running like hell before anyone even realizes what's happened.

She goes straight home, takes out her earplugs, and turns on her radio. She expects to hear that the Mayor has been stung by a bee, which is how she believes he'll interpret the attack. Instead, she learns that the Mayor has gone into anaphylactic shock and been rushed to the hospital, where he's in critical condition.

Evidently the good Mayor is allergic to scorpion venom.

The radio explains that the Mayor has been poisoned, that doctors are desperately trying to determine the nature of the toxic substance to administer an antidote. Anyone with any information is to call the following number.

Fuck. This is *much* further than Archipelago meant to go. Panicking, she tries to decide what to do. They could trace the landline in her apartment, and maybe her cell phone, too, couldn't they? How long does a trace take? Can she risk it?

E-mail. She can go to the library, create a fictitious Google account, and send an anonymous e-mail. They'll trace it to the library, but lots of people use the library. Although fewer people use the library now than used to, before the fire, and are there security cameras? Archipelago can't remember.

Just as she's resolved to attempt the library anyway, the radio announcer interrupts himself with "devastating news." The Mayor has died.

Also, a bar dart has been found behind the rally grandstand. With fingerprints on it.

Shit. Shit shit *shit*. Why didn't she think of that?

It's the lack of sleep. It's the migraine. It's the fact that for all her sneering bravado, Archipelago has never been an actual criminal, and has no idea how to go about it properly.

She's an actual criminal now, isn't she? Wanted for murder.

Of course the police know that the perpetrator will be trying to get out of town. There will be blockades. She can't run on her Harley; it would be too conspicuous.

Think, Archipelago. Think. It's the beginning of the month. The rent's just been paid. Barring some compulsory roll call, which Archipelago wouldn't put past the current power structure for a second, she has about four weeks before anyone will notice she's gone.

She opens her closet door, extracts a small backpack, puts Erasmus into a large jar with holes in the lid, puts another jar with all her crickets and cockroaches next to it, piles all her cash and coins into a pocket, and sets out on foot, whistling down the stairs as if she hasn't a care in the world, as if she's merely out for a Sunday stroll on this lovely day. She cuts across lawns and through alleys, angling away from any lights or noise that might be police, and in due course finds herself, miraculously, in open country.

Archipelago Osprey is now a fugitive.

12

*D*on't throw that out, please." Anna, wrapped in wool and Gore-Tex against the damp March cold, has just come in from walking the dog. William's standing at the breakfast bar in the kitchen, going through the mail, quickly sorting it into Real and Junk. He's put the latest *CC* issue on the Junk pile.

"What?" He picks up an envelope, waves it: some zero-interest credit card offer. "You need another card?"

"No, William." She unclips Bart's leash; he shakes himself, shedding water, and ambles up to William for a pat. *"Comrade Cosmos."*

"Oh, okay." She's on the living room side of the breakfast bar. He slides the shrink-wrapped issue across to her. "Somewhere in there it should explain how to cancel the subscription. We should have done it ages ago."

"I don't want to cancel it." She tries to keep her voice mild. She usually gets the mail, so he doesn't realize she hasn't been tossing the issues. "I'm reading those."

William looks at her, eyebrows raised. "Really."

"Yes, really."

He frowns now. "Huh. You okay?"

That, she thinks, has to be the stupidest question anyone has ever asked her. "Of course I'm not okay. Neither are you. But that's beside the point."

He shakes his head. "Speak for yourself. I'm fine."

She just looks at him. She doesn't even know how to respond to this, but his head's cocked in the attitude that means he's waiting for an answer. She chooses her words carefully. "You're functioning. We're both functioning. You're back at work. We're paying the bills. We get up every morning and eat breakfast and do what's necessary. But we're not fine. Not individually, not together. Our only son killed himself four months ago after raping and murdering a stranger. If we were fine, something would be very wrong."

William's staring at her as if she's speaking Martian, perhaps because this is the longest set of sentences she's directed at him since Percy died. Then he frowns, almost imperceptibly. "Percy wasn't fine. We are, Anna." Individually, or together? She doesn't dare ask. "We can't blame ourselves."

She feels like she's juggling ten-ton weights. Her eyes ache. "With or without blame, there's still grief." And now she feels like a fortune cookie. Great. "Don't you miss him?"

He's frowning again. "Of course I miss him. Dwelling on it won't do any good. You need to get out of the house more. It really helps."

I was just out of the house, she thinks. I'm the only one who walks the damn dog anymore. "Maybe I do, William. But joining clubs and committees wouldn't fix this, even if they'd have me." He knows Blake kicked her off the board. She hasn't had the courage to attend her knitting group, since the woman who hosts it is another Blake parent. "I'll plan Kip's opening, and I'll probably enjoy it, but that's it. When is the opening, anyway? Has he scheduled it yet?"

"He went to another gallery."

"He *what*?" Anna's genuinely shocked. "How could he do that? You gave him his first show when no one else would, and now he pulls out when the stuff's selling? Oh, Will, I'm so sorry!"

It occurs to her in a dizzy rush that she and William have shared ground again: they've both been rejected by their peers, and maybe that will bring them closer together. But William's staring at her with the baffled expression he wears so often these days. "It's all right. People move on. I always knew he wouldn't stay forever."

Anna blinks away the eerie sense that William's really talking about Percy. She hopes Kip had the decency to fire William in person, at least, and not to write a letter. "When did you find out? Why didn't you tell me?"

"It wasn't important. I didn't want to bother you with it."

Anna closes her eyes. She remembers when William told her everything that happened at the gallery, when he sought her advice and used her as a sounding board. How have they arrived here?

She reaches across the breakfast bar to touch William's hand. It's a calculated gesture. "Will, I wish you'd told me. If you want me to get more involved with life again, you have to talk to me."

He shakes his head. "I don't want to talk about Percy. You don't want to talk about anything else, and you won't talk *to* anyone else, and I can't take that weight, Anna."

She tightens her grip on his hand. "You can't pretend everything's normal. You can't pretend you aren't sick over this, don't miss him, don't wonder why—"

"Stop." He pulls his hand away. "I told you, I don't want to hear it. I wish I did. I wish I was able to. But I can't. Find a therapist, Anna."

She swallows hysteria, takes a gamble. "If I do, will you come with me? Couples counseling—"

"No." He turns away from her. He is, she can tell, poised to leave the room. "That won't change anything."

"It won't change what happened to Percy," she says. It might change the vacuum in the house, the hollow roar where there used to be a marriage, but if she's going to say that, she wants it to be when they're both sitting down, facing each other. Not to his back. "It might change what happens to us." She doesn't know if this is oblique enough or not; in any case, William's walked away from her, down the hall to his study. She doesn't even know if he's heard her. Bart, following him, turns around to look at her inquiringly. "Go on," she tells the dog, and he trots happily after William.

Trembling, she picks up the *CC* issue and turns to walk the other way, to Percy's room, where she's been spending more and more time. The boxes the police brought back are all unpacked, the computer on the desk and the clothing laundered and folded and put in drawers and closet. She knows she should donate the clothing, and she will, but not yet.

As she promised herself in January, she's been going steadily through the *CC* archives, reading from the beginning. She's started to allow herself to read the new weekly issues as they arrive, though, even if sometimes she doesn't quite understand what's happening. That way, she doesn't have the suffocating sense of continuously falling farther behind.

That suffocation, she knows, is the Emperor's work.

She began the series expecting to scoff at it, to be bored and annoyed. Instead, she found herself being pulled deeper into the story, found resonance of it everywhere she turned. Since November, she has been engaged in a struggle with the Emperor of Entropy, with despair and meaninglessness and mortality, with decay. It amazes her that such a huge pop-culture phenomenon can speak so directly to a middle-aged woman.

She wonders how it spoke to Percy. When he first started following the series, he tried to tell her about it a few times, but she could never keep herself from changing the subject out of sheer boredom. Now she aches to go back and redo those conversations.

She wonders, though, what the series has to say to anyone Percy's age, to all those youngsters obsessed with dating and mating and money and jobs and clothing. At that age, she'd simply have found it odd and unfathomable. When she was twenty, twenty-two, twenty-five, her most serious experiences with entropy were traffic jams and dirty laundry.

Anna closes the door to Percy's room. She'd leave it open if she were alone in the house, so Bart wouldn't feel abandoned. She can't stand his whining when he's in the house and lonely, which has been happening more often lately. She's once again begun to entertain fantasies of selling Bart or giving him away or leaving him somewhere or having him put down, but the image of him pulling against his leash as Percy wades into the water always stops her. And, she reminds herself, he's an old dog now. Eight is ancient, for a Wolfhound. She'll lose Bart, too, soon enough. In the meantime, since William's home right now, she can keep the door closed. Bart still prefers William to Anna, which is fine with her.

She really needs to talk to William about the dog-walking issue, even if he won't discuss anything else. If he doesn't want to walk the dog, maybe they can hire someone. Maybe that someone will fall in love with Bart and run off with him.

No. Anna glances at Percy's desk, at the framed photo of him with the puppy. Percy loved this creature. In a way, he's all of Percy they have left, the best of Percy. Maybe that's why William now has so little to do with the dog. In any case, it's why Anna is irrevocably tied to the animal, for better or worse, bad breath and shedding and all, which is more at the moment than she can say for William.

A Stanford 2009–2010 academic calendar hangs over the desk. Percy never wrote on it, but Anna has. She blinks at today's square. Wednesday, March 10: Melinda Soto's birthday.

Her throat constricts. That poor woman. Those poor people. Riding a wave of rage at Percy, she forces herself to stare at the photograph, to remember him as the sweet child who played with his dog.

Melinda Soto had a son. She'd have understood, surely.

When the rest of the world hates your child, with reason or without, you cling to your love for him. You're his mother. Loving him is your job.

Trembling only a little, Anna sits on the bed and opens the plastic wrapping around the issue, taking pains not to tear the cover. Percy was very careful with *CC* as a physical object, and so she is, too. She has a sudden, vivid memory of Percy telling his father—who was marginally more interested in the topic than Anna, or at least willing to pretend he was—about the Comrade Cosmos Club at Stanford. Anna should write them, find out if any of them knew Percy, see if someone might be willing to speak at the memorial service.

This is the first bit of planning she's done for the event. Marjorie, ever efficient, booked the local Unitarian church for that day before she and David flew back home. "July 24 is a Saturday, Anna. We need to grab the building before someone books it for a wedding." No one in the family's religious, but holding memorial services in a church is What's Done. Marjorie has an acute sense of such things, which she's passed down in modified form to William. Anna could care less.

She's avoided even thinking about the service since Marjorie and David left; it's some kind of irony that *Comrade Cosmos* brought her back to it. She starts to ponder a possible guest list, but this quickly becomes painful, another reminder of how isolated they've been. She'll put a notice in the paper, and anyone who wants to be decent can come; surely everyone knows that a funeral isn't the time for privacy.

Anna and William and Marjorie and David will definitely be there. Anna's pretty sure that Karen-who-brought-back-Bart would come, too, if she were invited. Bart should be there, too. Anna wonders if the Unitarians will allow a dog in the sanctuary.

Percy's ashes are currently in a brown cardboard box in Anna's closet. It would be so much easier just to scatter them in the backyard, but that's not What's Done.

Or is it? The memorial service isn't about the disposition of the ashes. If they want to bury Percy in the backyard, they can. If they want to scatter him somewhere, they can do that, too. Where would he want to be scattered?

This suddenly seems like an urgent question. Anna can't believe she hasn't thought of it before. Since William's in the house, for once, maybe she should consult him. She stands up to go find him, but then remembers how he pulled his hand away from hers, how he walked away from her down the hall. He doesn't want to talk about Percy.

She sits down again and picks up the new issue.

On March 10, 2009, Melinda takes the day off work, an annual birthday treat. When Jeremy's in college, she'll be able to sleep in on her birthday, but since he's still in high school, she has to get up early to get him up, fed, and out the door.

She puts on a robe and pads downstairs, rapping on Jeremy's bedroom door on the way. "Jer! Up 'n' at 'em! Time's a wasting!" She thinks she hears a groan in response. If he's not in the kitchen in fifteen minutes, she'll come back up and roust him more forcefully.

Yawning, she starts the coffee, a peppermint chocolate roast she bought as a treat for today. It smells delicious, and she smiles when the odor starts to fill the kitchen.

"God, Mom. How can you *stand* that stuff?"

Jeremy, improbably, is awake and downstairs, standing scowling in his own bathrobe, a ratty blue terrycloth thing he refuses to let her replace.

"Good morning. You don't have to drink it."

"I have to *smell* it."

She decides to change the subject. "You're up early."

"Spanish quiz. Michael and I are supposed to study before school."

"Ah," Melinda says, swallowing past her disappointment. She'd briefly entertained a fantasy that he'd come down to surprise her with a gift, or even just an offer to cook breakfast. He hasn't even said "happy birthday" yet. Has he forgotten? How could he?

There's still a chance that this is an elaborate ruse to surprise her, but the possibility's fading, and the longer she waits to remind him, the more embarrassed he'll be. She thinks. She hopes.

"Jer? You know what today is, right?"

He gives her such a blank look that she knows he's forgotten. Jeremy has no acting ability whatsoever. "Tuesday. It *is* Tuesday, isn't it? Yeah, it has to be, because yesterday was Monday, and—"

"March 10," she says gently, and he blinks at her for a moment before panic blooms across his face.

"Oh, shit. Shit shit shit. Mom, I'm sorry. Happy birthday! I'm sorry." He's blushing. "I didn't—I don't know how I—"

"It's okay, honey." If nothing else, this means he'll be nice to her for the rest of the day. "It's okay. Just sit down and have a nice breakfast so you'll be ready for your Spanish quiz."

"I'll cook!" he says, and he does, and it's good. Jeremy knows his way around an omelette. He throws together cheese, veggies, spices, all of it ordinary enough but in just the right quantities. He even pours Melinda's coffee, although he makes a great show of wrinkling his nose as he carries the mug to the table. He even tries to make conversation about the library. She appreciates the effort.

After he's left for school, she goes back upstairs for another part of her birthday ritual. A framed photograph of her parents sits on her dresser. They're very young in this picture, tan and lean, sitting in a rowboat smiling up at the camera. She doesn't know who took the shot, but her mother told her once that it was taken just after Melinda was conceived.

She carries the photograph downstairs, puts it on the kitchen table—which Jeremy cleared, *mirabile dictu*—and digs around in the cabinets until she finds a candle, which she lights. She sits in front of this makeshift altar and takes a deep breath.

"I miss you guys." This is almost always how she begins these birthday speeches to her dead. Her father died of a heart attack when she was thirty-five, her mother of cancer five years later. Neither of them knew Jeremy, whom Melinda adopted when she was forty-five. "I wish you were here to see your grandson. He's eighteen now, and of course he thinks he's all grown up, but I know better, just like you knew better when I was that age. I wish you were here to give me advice." She swallows. Some years she has a sense of their presence; some years she imagines full conversations with them. This year, they're mute.

She keeps talking for a while, anyway. When it seems clear that nothing's going to happen, she stops. Maybe next year.

When Jeremy was in his *Charlotte's Web* phase, terrified of death, she told him about this ritual, told him that you never really lose the people you love. You just can't see them anymore, and that's hard, but they're still with you. "It's like when we water the plants," she told him. "The water sinks into the soil, and you can't see it, but it's still keeping the plants alive. Whenever we love people or they love us, the love sinks into us and helps us keep going, even when the people aren't here anymore."

She wondered then if Jeremy understood what she meant. She wonders now if she still believes it.

She blows the candle out and carries the photograph back upstairs. The weather's crappy, chilly and unusually gray for Reno, but Melinda spends the day rereading several of the Mitford books, and she enjoys her peppermint chocolate coffee, and when Jeremy comes home, he brings her a card and some supermarket flowers. This weekend, she'll celebrate with Vera, who always drives her out to Gerlach and buys her a gorgeous piece of pottery, and at some point she hopes to celebrate with Rosie, who has her hands full with Walter at the moment. And she's pretty sure that next year, Jeremy will remember.

* * *

*M*elinda's birthday, and it has to fall on the Wednesday before spring break. This is the worst time of the semester. The students are exhausted. Veronique's exhausted. Everyone wants to be on vacation already, although the vacation's all too brief.

The only saving grace is that she knows at least a quarter of the class won't show up. Also, there's a class presentation scheduled for today. Veronique allows students to do these for extra credit; they're usually weak work, but they're much easier to grade than papers. And a presentation means that at least one student other than Amy Castillo will say something today.

Women & Violence has bombed. Veronique thought this topic would engage them, but it hasn't worked very well. They still misread even basic plot points in the books, stare in incomprehension when she tries to introduce anything remotely theoretical, and ignore her efforts to challenge toxic assumptions. Girls who dress slutty deserve to be raped—this from a young woman wearing skintight jeans and a corset—and battered women who don't just walk away from their abusers don't deserve any sympathy, and all lesbians hate men, and all feminists are lesbians.

When Veronique tries to challenge these notions, the students just glare at her mutely. Amy's a delight, but Amy already seems to know everything Veronique's trying to teach, and the problem with having one bright student in the class is that the others are sure to accuse Veronique of favoritism on the end-of-semester teaching evaluations. Amy doesn't need this class, and the others aren't learning anything—except maybe to despise Veronique—and it's Melinda's birthday, and all Veronique wants to do is stay home, or get out of town. Flight, flight. Ten times this morning she's been on the verge of calling in sick, but each time she's remembered this presentation. The presenter probably wouldn't mind a cancelation, but if Veronique cancels today, where will it stop? And anyway, she has other committee work piling up: junior faculty files to read for the tenure committee, a report to write on a new hire's service record.

She could write the service report at home, but no one's allowed to remove the faculty files from the office.

She has to keep making herself go in. It's her job, and this is the last day before vacation.

So she goes to work, even getting there early so she can read the committee files before class. She speeds through them, reading just carefully enough to know which of the cases will prompt the most discussion—at least no one's actually up for tenure this year—but hangs on to the files for an extra forty-five minutes so the secretary will think she pored over them.

Then she hauls herself to class. As she expected, only twelve of her twenty students are here today. The presenter, a twitchy and entirely too thin young woman named Samantha, is setting up the electronic equipment at the front of the room. When she sees Veronique, she scowls and says, "It's not PowerPoint. I'm showing a film clip. And I know the running time doesn't count towards my ten minutes."

"Very good," says Veronique, giving Samantha what she hopes is a sufficiently warm smile. She sits in one of the student seats so she can watch with the rest of them. Evidently this presentation will fill up even more than ten minutes. Excellent.

The one male in the class, a lanky kid named Brent who only wears black and quite clearly has the hots for Samantha, says, "What's the clip from?"

"Sin City."

Brent whistles and sits up a little straighter. *"Sweet!"* He looks like he actually plans to pay attention. Nothing Veronique's done all semester has gotten him to pay attention. He only stopped texting in class when Veronique threatened to confiscate his phone.

Sin City. Veronique frowns, stabbed by a thin sliver of memory. Melinda. Something about Melinda. A shiver runs over the top of her skull. "When did this movie come out?"

"Four years ago," Brent says. "It's *awesome*."

Four years ago. Veronique remembers now: Jeremy wanted to see it, and Melinda said she'd go with him, and the film was so violent it made her almost physically ill. "It was disgusting," she told Veronique. "Women were getting killed and the twenty-something guys sitting in front of me were moaning in pleasure, like they were having orgasms, and afterwards I tried to talk to Jeremy about it and he just rolled his eyes at me. 'It's just a movie, Mom. C'mon, weren't the special effects cool?' He had no emotional response to the carnage *at all*. God, Vera! I always thought he was basically a good kid."

Veronique takes a dizzy breath. "Samantha, you know presentations have to be on work by women. Remind me who made this movie?"

Samantha glares at her. "Well, there are female *characters*. And there were women in the cast and on the crew and everything. Doesn't that count?"

Brent snickers. "Frank Miller, Robert Rodriguez, and Quentin Tarantino." Veronique's impressed; the child actually knows something.

Samantha's chin trembles. "It was a *collaboration*. Are you going to mark me down?"

The presentation checklist couldn't have been any clearer. All right, never mind: it's the Wednesday before break, and surely Samantha can't expect a good grade in the course given her performance to date, anyway. "Let's see it," Veronique says, trying not to snap, trying to be kind. "Can you summarize your presentation for us, though, so we know what we're looking for?"

Samantha shoves a lock of dyed blond hair out of her face, looking slightly relieved. "It's about how there's violence to women at the beginning but then in the middle the guys fight the violence against women and at the end it looks like there's going to be violence again but the movie ends so you don't know." She says this in a rush, in one breath. "So maybe something changed. I'm going to show the beginning, and then I'll talk about the middle, and then I'll show the end."

"What," says Brent, "the first segment? 'The Customer Is Always Right'? Miller said the woman hired the guy to kill her. She had an affair with somebody dangerous who was going to kill her and she hired the Salesman to do it instead."

"It's still *violent*," Samantha says. "I'm just going to show it, all right?"

She shows it. Veronique watches in growing nausea: the man joining the woman on the balcony, their kiss, his shooting her. She imagines Melinda watching this four years ago. She feels herself begin to shake and sits trembling through the rest of Samantha's presentation, which would probably be incoherent even if every other sentence weren't being blocked out by static: flashes of Melinda's face, flashes of the pain she must have suffered as she died, flashes of newspaper images of Percy Clark, that smug young bastard.

After the presentation, Samantha asks if anyone has any questions. None of the other students do, although Veronique notes dimly that Amy's frowning. "I have a question," Veronique says, and she almost doesn't recognize her own voice, as hoarse and cracked as a crow's cry. "That woman who dies. At the beginning. What's her name?"

Samantha blinks. "Well, she's just the Customer, like he's just the Salesman."

"No," Veronique says. "She is *not* just the Customer. If the story means anything at all, she was a person. She had a name. She had a birthday. When was her birthday, Samantha?"

Samantha rolls her eyes. "How should I know?" Some of the other students are laughing. Veronique knows they're laughing at her. She doesn't care.

She's standing now. Somehow she's gotten to the front of the room. "That woman had a name and a birthday and family and friends, but once she's a dead body none of that matters, does it?

Because the violence is the point. But it does matter. How are her family and friends going to deal with her being murdered? What are they going to do on her next birthday? Do any of you even *think* about that?"

"Professor Bellamy?" That's Amy, looking worried. "Are you all right?"

Veronique's not all right. She's crying. She's crying in class, but she's also telling the truth. A great surge of energy pulses through her. She glares at them and says, voice breaking, "*None* of you are thinking about the right story, and probably you can't because you're too young and not enough has happened to you yet, and I guess I have to hope it never does, but what you saw on that screen isn't the real story. It's not even close to the real story. Let me tell you the real story."

*J*eremy's adding whipped cream to a skinny mocha-caramel soy latte when Amy comes up to the counter. He's been working at Emerald City for a month now; it's close to the house, but far enough away from campus that he doesn't see people he knows very often. That's both good and bad. He misses his friends, but he doesn't know what to say to them and they don't know what to say to him, and he can't go back to the time when everything was simpler. He's a different person now than he was at the beginning of November.

The clientele of Emerald City is mostly older people, thirties and forties: parents with little kids, businesspeople on lunch break. Most of the customers tip well, and the café has a decent menu and also does catering. Jeremy's thinking he might like to get involved in that, at some point, but he's trying to make his mark as a barista and waiter first.

It's ironic that he's here making fancy coffee, since he always made fun of Mom for drinking the stuff. She'd laugh at him, if she were still alive.

He was afraid making coffee would be boring, but he enjoys it: the hiss of the espresso machine, the smell of the grinding beans, the ridiculous complexity of the coffee menu. He likes memorizing the favorite coffees of his regular customers, which leads to larger tips. The work's involving enough to get his mind off Mom for at least part of each day—especially important today—and simple enough not to task his limited concentration and patience.

Aunt Rosie says the limited concentration and patience are normal. He hopes she's right.

At any rate, he doesn't miss school, which made him feel both bored and stupid. He doesn't even know if he wants to go back, although he supposes he'll have to, at some point. He can't be a barista his entire life, can he?

Another thing he likes about being a barista is that it doesn't leave him too much time for stressing about his future, or beating himself up for leaving school. Seeing Amy, though, snaps him right back into defensive inadequacy mode. She was absolutely the best thing about his first semester at UNR, the only bright spot in VB's class. She's smart, pretty, and into *CC*, and she's not obnoxious smart, either, not I'm-smarter-than-you'll-ever-be smart, which is VB's brand. She's the kind of smart person who makes everybody around her feel smart, and even though this rather miraculous trick works on Jeremy as well as it does on everybody else, he knows that she's about twenty times too good for him.

She's from Tonopah, middle-of-nowheresville Nevada, and the last he knew, she was living in the dorms, all the way across town. What's she doing here?

"Hey," she says, eyeing the whipped cream. "That looks good."

"I'll make you one, if you want. After this. This one's for someone else."

"Huh. You mean you didn't read my mind while I was walking in the door, and know what I wanted?"

"Nope," he says. "Back in a sec." He carries the drink to Lucy, the lawyer in the corner who orders one of these every lunchtime, and has the belly to prove it. If you met her somewhere else, you might think she got that gut from drinking beer, but Jeremy knows better. The whipped cream, which she always requests specifically even though Jeremy's made this concoction for her a million times, more than cancels out the skinny and the soy.

When he gets back to the counter, Amy's still there, blushing. "Jeremy, I'm sorry. That was stupid."

"Huh?" He starts to wipe down the counter with a damp cloth, one of those chores you do whenever you have a free second in a busy place like this. "What was stupid?"

"Making that dumb joke about the coffee."

"Don't worry about it. How are you, anyway, and what brings you to this fine establishment?"

"I'm fine. I'm here because—well, a couple of things. I wanted to tell you."

He blinks. He thinks this means she's here to see him, which goes beyond slightly miraculous into highly improbable. "How'd you know I even work here?"

"Kevin told me."

Yeah, that's right: he ran into Kevin at Raley's, and they chatted in the checkout line, talked about cars and bands, promised they'd get together sometime, yada yada. Jeremy'd forgotten about it the second he walked out of the store. That was, what, last week, and he was fretting about Mom's birthday today, wondering how he should handle it, if he should call in sick from work and try to do something special, or have Aunt Rosie and VB over for dinner or something. He can't believe he forgot it last year. He thought he'd be able to make up for that this year, do something really nice.

In the end, this year, he decided to do almost nothing. He woke up this morning, lit a candle for Mom, and propped her photo up in front of him while he ate his breakfast, talking to her until he felt silly enough to stop. "Hi, Mom. So, well, I wish you were here. I wish you were alive. I wish Percy were alive, too, so I could kill him, or so you could, although I guess you wouldn't. If you were still alive, you wouldn't have to."

When he was little, Mom told him she did that on her own birthday, talking to a picture of her parents. She said it helped, and now that she's dead, family tradition suddenly seems important instead of stupid. This tradition, though, just seemed empty and awkward, so Jeremy put the picture away. Then he showered, dressed, and came to work as usual, which turned out to be the right thing to do. Today, especially, the job's the perfect combination of busy and mindless.

"So, uh, did you hear about Professor Bellamy? I mean, I don't know how you could have, it only happened an hour ago, but I thought maybe—"

"No," he says, to cut her off. How can girls talk so much? "I haven't heard anything. What are you talking about?"

Amy slides onto one of the bar stools at the counter. "She kinda had a meltdown in class. Because today's your Mom's birthday."

"Meltdown?" Jeremy squints. "What kind of meltdown?"

"Well, she—she ranted for a while, and then she started crying, and then she started yelling at us for being young and not knowing anything, which is when it really got bad. For us. I mean, it must have been bad for her, before, but that was the part she'll get into trouble for, I'm guessing."

Jeremy's stomach knots. He doesn't like VB, but he doesn't want her to get into trouble. She and Mom were real friends. "So somebody reported her?"

"Well, when she started crying, Sandy Askew slipped out and went to get somebody from the English Office, and some other professor—the head of the department, I think—came in right after she started yelling. And he tried to calm her down, and she lost it at him, too, except she kept crying the whole time." Amy shakes her head. "You know, the kind of crying where you can't catch your breath, but she was yelling through it, and I don't think anybody could even understand what she was saying. It was pretty horrible. The other prof wound up calling the campus police."

"The po*lice*? Holy crap! What'd they do, arrest her?"

"I don't know. At that point, the other prof told all of us that class was over and we should leave now, please, and most people couldn't get out of there fast enough. I wanted to stay and talk to her, but the cops asked me to leave. I mean, they were nice about it. One of them took my name and number, said he might be calling me to get my account of what happened."

"Jesus."

"I know." Amy draws a shuddering breath—Jeremy realizes she's on the verge of tears herself—and says, "Anyway, since she was friends with your mom, I thought you'd want to know. And I—it has to be hard for you, too. Your mom's birthday. And I just wanted you to know that if you need to talk, I—"

"That's nice, Amy. I mean, thank you. But I'm okay."

She's looking down at the counter, tracing the wood grain with an index finger. The other hand's clenched so tightly that her knuckles are white, which Jeremy always thought was a total cliché. "I kept meaning to call you after your mother died, I did, I even planned to go to the funeral but then I chickened out at the last minute, but I should have written you a card, anyway, and I'm sorry, and—"

"Amy. Stop." She looks up now; her hand stops moving. "I'm okay. Really. Not all the time, but right now I am. And there were so many people at the funeral I felt like I was suffocating, so just don't worry about it. It was really nice of you to come tell me about Professor Bellamy."

She swallows. She sniffles. "You're welcome."

"You want a coffee? On the house?"

Amy shakes her head. "I don't think I need caffeine right now."

"Herbal tea, then? We've got some fancy stuff that comes in funky little cardboard pyramids. Peppermint. Green with lemongrass. Chamomile." Does green tea have caffeine? Yes. Not as much as coffee, or even black tea, but he shouldn't have offered it to her.

She doesn't seem to have noticed. "Sure. Thanks. Mint, please."

So he makes the tea, which takes about ten seconds, and as he gives it to her he says, "What are you going to do? About Prof Bellamy? Are you going to do anything?"

He doesn't know what to do, and then he does. "Yeah. I'm going to call my Aunt Rosie. She and Bellamy and my mom go way back." Even if she and VB don't exactly get along. "She'll know what to do." He laughs, which makes Amy look at him as if maybe he's having a meltdown, too, and says, "I can't believe you took another class with Bellamy."

"I like her. I know most people don't, but she's really smart and she cares about this stuff, and so do I, and she just gets frustrated because most of her students could care less. So do I. I get it."

"You wouldn't have a meltdown, though."

Amy shudders. "Well, no. Except I might if my best friend had been murdered and it was her birthday and nobody remembered or cared, which is what she was ranting about."

Jeremy blinks. Crap. Did VB think nobody else had remembered? How could she have thought that? Did Mom tell her what happened last year? Yeah, she must have. But how could VB have thought he'd forget this year, too?

Should he have planned something after all? But he wouldn't have known what to do. That's Aunt Rosie's territory, all that ritual stuff with Martha Stewart place cards.

He'll call her. She'll fix this.

As if on cue, Amy says, "Aren't you going to call your aunt?"

*r*osemary stands in the ER, wearing her badge and maroon volunteer vest—pink pinstripes went out in the 1950s—and staring in disbelief at a sobbing Veronique, who's being escorted past the nursing station by two policemen.

"Room thirty-eight," says the charge nurse, and Rosemary shakes her head, almost protests aloud. That's a psych room. Veronique doesn't belong there. Veronique may belong in a room for neurotic, prickly people short on tact, but she doesn't belong in a psych room. Not in the "we won't let you leave until you're evaluated by a psychologist" room, the room where the suicidal and homicidal patients go. The room where everything's taken away from you, all clothing and belongings, and you're kept under constant observation until someone decides if they can let you go or need to send you to an actual psych hospital for seventy-two hours of observation.

What in God's green earth is going on?

She hears Veronique howling now, something about insurance. "My insurance won't work here, I'm only supposed to go to Fortunata, I can't be here, you have to take me there—"

"Professor," one of the policemen says, "we called Fortunata. They're full up. This is where we had to bring you. Your insurance will understand that."

His voice is calm, soothing. He's had practice at this. Rosemary sidles closer—Veronique still hasn't noticed her—and sees that he's a UNR cop.

The bottom of her stomach drops out. She's picturing some version of Columbine, Virginia Tech, but Veronique doesn't seem to be injured, and were there other victims? She hasn't heard a Code Triage, which alerts hospital staff to a mass casualty, and the nurses at the charge desk seem as bored as always, without the slightly manic energy they display when they're expecting something really bad, and if Veronique were the victim of a shooting, how could she walk in under her own power, and why would she be taken to a psych room?

Rosemary turns to a nurse at the desk, someone she knows a little bit and who may be willing to answer questions. "What can you tell me about the patient who just came in? Thirty-eight?" She isn't going to say she knows Vera, because that may send the nurse into I-can't-tell-you-squat HIPAA paralysis.

"Hmmm?" The nurse looks up, blinks, says, "just a sec," and performs a complicated tacking maneuver with paper and computer keyboard. "Huh. UNR prof. Had some kind of breakdown in class. They're bringing her here for evaluation."

Rosemary's heart pounds against her ribcage. Oh, God. Did Veronique snap and kill a student? "Was anyone hurt?"

"Don't think so. Don't really know. Sorry."

"Thank you." She still isn't going to let on that she knows Veronique. She wonders if Veronique will be willing to talk to her. One of the sacred laws of chaplaincy is that if the patient tells you to go away, you go; chaplains are the only hospital workers patients can dismiss, and patients need all the power they can get. Strictly speaking, Rosemary isn't even supposed to signal that she recognizes Veronique unless Veronique acknowledges her first, but this is a bit of legalism Rosie's never been able to maintain. When she runs into acquaintances in the hospital, she always says hi; they always say hi back. They always seem glad to see her.

But none of them have been in psych rooms.

She can still hear Veronique's voice, tearful, rising and falling. A nurse is in the room now. "Okay now, sweetheart, try to calm down. Just breathe for me. Can you do that?"

"Another nutcase," a passing tech mutters under his breath, and Rosemary has to force herself not to dress him down. *That's no nutcase: that's my friend!* Most of the ER staff don't like psych patients, who rarely present clear-cut medical symptoms and all too often offer behavioral challenges. Rosemary sympathizes with the staff's frustration, but she sympathizes more with the patients, who are usually even less happy about the situation than their caregivers are.

Most of the time, she's not so crazy about Vera herself. Here, she's completely on Vera's side. But she can't be Vera's chaplain. You aren't supposed to minister to people with whom you're emotionally entangled.

Should she call Hen? But then Hen would feel compelled to come here. But that's her job, isn't it?

Rosemary pulls her phone out of her pocket. She has voice mail. From Jeremy.

Oh, God. But no: Jeremy's not in Veronique's class this semester. He's not in any classes this semester. He's working at the coffeehouse today, isn't he? He can't even know about this; he must be calling about something else.

A registration clerk's in with Veronique now; Rosemary won't be able to do anything for a few minutes. She ducks out the ER entrance to use her phone, and listens to Jeremy's message. Evidently a friend gave him a blow-by-blow of the classroom crisis. "Aunt Rosie, I don't know where she is now. I hope she's okay. Anyway, I thought you'd want to know. Please call me back if you hear anything."

She calls him. He answers right away. "Jeremy, I'm at the hospital. She's here. I'm working this afternoon, and two UNR cops just brought her in for psych observation. She doesn't know I'm here yet."

"Psych observation? Are they going to lock her up?"

"I don't know. I hope not. Listen, do you have any idea what triggered this?"

"Yeah. Amy said she was upset because it's Mom's birthday. She thought we all forgot about it."

Rosemary's hand goes to her mouth. Later, she'll realize that she's absorbed Walter's gesture, made it her own. Of course she knows it's Melinda's birthday. She decided to work her shift as usual to distract herself. She'd been planning to call Jeremy and Veronique afterward to see how they were doing, but she should have done it this morning. "Of course I didn't forget. I just, I didn't—"

"I know," Jeremy says. "I didn't forget either, but I decided not to do anything special. I guess that was stupid."

"You did what you needed to do," Rosemary says. She's facing the double glass ER doors, and she sees the registration clerk walk past them. "I'm going to try to talk to her now, okay? I'll call you later."

*t*he first Cosmos knows of Archipelago is a news item on the radio. He's spooning bananas, once again, into Vanessa's mouth—her appetite has picked up a little, to his immense relief—when he hears something about the death of the Misguided Mayor of Wishful. "Authorities are seeking a person of interest," the announcer says, and Cosmos puts down his spoon to turn up the volume. He could look this up on Google News later, of course, but it's here now, and anyway, he might forget.

The mess in Wishful has been eating at him. "It's not your fault," Roger keeps telling him, as they sip their Guinness in the semidarkness of the deserted library. "You did the best you could. You did what you always do."

"But if I'd stayed longer—"

"C'mon, Cos. You couldn't have stayed longer. Vanessa was wasting away to nothing, and you had to take care of that insurance mess for your dad, remember? What happened in that town is the town's problem and the town's responsibility."

Cosmos knows Roger's right, but the police state in Wishful still bothers him. That's never happened before, although if he thinks about it, he concedes that it was probably just a matter of time before someplace he'd helped out took a wrong turn after he left. He doesn't know what he could have done to prevent it, anyway.

The radio drones. "Behind the bandstand where the Mayor collapsed, police found a throwing dart with traces of scorpion venom on the point. An extensive sweep of the town's population has discovered that a woman named Archipelago Osprey purchased *The Care and Feeding of Your Pet Scorpion* on Amazon. com five years ago, before she moved to Wishful. She is not in her apartment and neither is the scorpion, although a terrarium suitable for such an animal suggests that the creature is still alive. Police believe she took the scorpion with her when she fled."

Archipelago Osprey? Cosmos shakes his head. Good lord. With a name like that, how could she not get into some kind of trouble?

He shrugs, glad he's not the one who has to find her. He's tired. He's getting too old for this stuff. If he had a sidekick, he'd be handing over the reins right now. Actually, he has thousands of sidekicks, but they only seem to stay sidekicks for the duration of whatever crisis he's coaching them through.

"Next time," he tells Vanessa, picking up the spoon again, "I'm naming a successor. Wherever I go next, anybody who's really on the ball's going to get tapped. Tag, you're it."

Vanessa doesn't answer. She has never answered, never will. She is the job Cosmos cannot put aside or delegate for more than a week or two. But he wouldn't want to. He loves his sister. "Banananananananana," he tells Vanessa, and she opens her mouth, and he believes that inside, wherever it counts, she's smiling.

Archipelago, meanwhile, isn't smiling. Archipelago is hiding in a field behind a drugstore in some other little bumfuck Wyoming town. She's fed Erasmus, who doesn't seem to have reacted to his change of habitat, and she's so hungry herself that she'd seriously consider munching down on his few remaining crickets, if it weren't for the fact that she's not sure where to get more. The crickets are Erasmus's food. He didn't ask for any of this. She has to keep his life as normal as possible.

The crumpled newspaper in the trash, when she smoothed it out, informed her that the murder—*manslaughter*, Archipelago tells herself with rising panic, *manslaughter, it wasn't intentional*—has indeed been pinned on her. Her driver's license mug shot is on the front page. Fortunately, it's such a bad likeness that no one who sees her in person is likely to connect the two, but if she goes into a pet store to buy crickets, she could be in trouble. She needs to hoard her small remaining wad of cash, anyway. She withdrew the daily maximum from the ATM on her way out of Wishful. She doesn't dare use her ATM card again: they'll trace that in two seconds.

Maybe she should turn herself in, explain that it was manslaughter, that she didn't know the Mayor was allergic to scorpions, that she wouldn't have done it if she did. She wasn't trying to kill the guy, much as she loathed him. She just wanted him to have even a fraction as bad a day as he'd visited on her.

If she tells them that—

No. Manslaughter's still a prison sentence, and she can't afford a lawyer and wouldn't want a state-appointed yahoo, and she has a feeling that assault with scorpion venom probably carries some kind of penalty, too. And what would happen to Erasmus if she turned herself in? The authorities would kill him, probably.

All right, then. She has to stay free, both for her own sake and Erasmus's. And she needs to try to find free sources of food for both of them. She could trap crickets for Erasmus, but the fields around here were being sprayed as she walked into town. Erasmus is used to yummy vitamin powder. She doesn't want to risk feeding him insecticide instead.

And she's so hungry that she can't think clearly. She has to think clearly right now. She needs food and a safe place to sleep, and a shower would be nice, too, because she reeks to high heaven.

Food first. Once she's eaten, she can tackle the other problems, beginning with food for Erasmus.

The easiest way to get food is to steal it, although she's going to look suspicious wherever she goes: a scraggly smelly person lugging a backpack. No ordering at a fine restaurant and dodging the bill in this getup. They'd kick her out the second she walked in. So would Burger King, probably.

Pizza.

She once worked in a pizza joint. Pies that were ordered but not picked up got tossed at the end of the night, still in their boxes, often still warm. So: find a pizza place, and then find the nearest Dumpster. She checks her watch. It's ten P.M. The pizza parlors should be closing right about now. Every town has a pizza parlor. Even Bumfuck, Wyoming.

The trick's to find it without looking too conspicuous. Scraggly smelly person lugging a backpack, casually strolling around downtown Bumfuck after hours. Right. Eateries are usually in whatever passes for downtown, near banks and city halls and parks. Police stations are there, too. And Bumfuck does not, from the looks of it, exactly have a swinging night life.

If she were by herself, she'd stash her backpack behind a bush and stroll around on foot, which would be marginally less suspicious as long as no one smelled her. But she can't abide the idea of abandoning Erasmus—what would happen if someone stole the backpack and found him?—and the only place she can put him is the backpack.

She should have brought a coat. But it's summer, and aside from the hassle of carrying a coat, it would have made her even more conspicuous, both here and on the way out of Wishful.

Tomorrow, maybe, she can find an army/navy surplus place and buy a—

No, she can't. She's in Bumfuck, Wyoming, which she's pretty sure has no army/navy surplus place—although there may be a thrift store—and she can't spend money on a coat, and she'd stink up any store she walked into, anyway. And she's a fugitive. She doesn't dare call attention to herself. This is craziness, Archipelago. You need to eat. Your brain needs food. Your stomach needs food. Hear it, growling?

Bumfuck doesn't have a swinging night life. So maybe no one will be out and about to be suspicious of her. It doesn't matter; she has to eat, and her mind's fastened onto the possibility of pizza like a piranha onto a tourist's leg. She doesn't let herself think about the toppings she wants. Any toppings will be fine. Any toppings will be wonderful. If the pizza place—this mythical restaurant she isn't even positive exists—discards a jalapeño pepper pizza with anchovies and pepperoni, she'll devour it. It will be the best thing she's ever tasted.

She'll wait until eleven, just to be safe.

She waits until eleven, and then, as casually as possible, strolls in the direction that feels like downtown. In no time, she's in a town-squareish area. Bank. Post Office. Salon. And there—yes, thank you, universe—there, between the insurance office and the medical building, is a pizza parlor.

As heavy as her backpack's become, Archipelago almost skips across the street. She wants to sing.

Here she is, in front of the pizza parlor, and here she is, turning aside to stroll down the alley behind it—imagine! an actual alley in this podunk town!—and here is the Dumpster she knew would have to be here, and here she is, opening the lid of the Dumpster, and here, yes, is a pile of three pizza boxes, delicious aromas wafting up from them along with less delicious aromas from the other contents of the Dumpster, and here is Archipelago, lifting out the three boxes of steaming pizza, her eyes watering with unaccustomed gratitude.

She puts the boxes on the ground and opens them. Extra cheese, this first one. Meatballs on the second. The third is one of those hideous Hawaiian things with ham and pineapple, two items Archipelago believes should never come near one another, much less meet on pizza, but this once, she doesn't care. These are good pizzas, edible pizzas, not a jalapeño or anchovy in sight.

She decides to start with the extra cheese. She sits down with her back against the alley wall, and has just lifted the first slice reverently to her mouth when a figure appears at the mouth of the alley. "Miss? Would you like a Pepsi to go with your pizza?"

What the hell? Archipelago squints at the figure trudging toward her, which resolves itself into an overweight cop solemnly holding out a bottle of pop. "Here. I bought it for lunch and never opened it, and I'm going home now, and pizza tastes better with a drink. I'm sorry it's not beer, though you're probably better off sober out here, and I'm sorry it's warm."

She gapes up at him, too afraid to move. He smiles. "I think I know who you are, but I don't care and I'm not going to report you. That prick had it coming. My cousin lives in Wishful, and she needs dialysis treatments and they wouldn't let her back into town when she got back late from one of them. She had to go to the Motel 6. Is it true he owned that place?"

It wasn't deliberate, Archipelago wants to say. *I didn't mean it.* But she can't say that, because it would be an admission. She doesn't trust this guy as far as she could throw him. He's playing the nice cop routine, thinking she'll fall for it because she's tired and hungry and has nowhere to sleep, but she's not stupid and she knows never, ever to trust a cop. Ever. He can't be telling her he's going to blink at a murder charge. He can't. Arresting her is his job. Why isn't he doing it?

She doesn't say anything, doesn't dare say anything: just pulls her knees to her chest and glares. The cop bends and puts the Pepsi down next to her. "Here you go. In case you get thirsty. I'm sorry I don't have anything for your bug, if he's with you."

Arachnid, Archipelago thinks. He's an arachnid. That's much more dignified than calling him a bug. Bug sounds cute. Erasmus isn't cute.

But the cop's trying to trick her again. She won't let him. She's too smart for him. She sets her chin and keeps glaring.

The cop tips his hat. "You take care, now, you and your bug. You want to get out of town before ten tomorrow. That's when one of my colleagues starts working, and he's not as nice as I am."

Archipelago forces herself to nod. She hates this man, hates his blithe disregard for his job and his willingness to break rules and his clueless attempts at kindness, as if she needs Pepsi to rot her teeth. All of that, except the kindness, is supposed to be her baili-wick, not his. She didn't mean to kill the Misguided Mayor; it was manslaughter, not murder, but the cop can't know that. What's he doing, letting her walk? What's wrong with him?

He tips his hat again and turns to waddle away. Archipelago considers throwing the bottle of Pepsi at him, but knows that would be madness, sheer suicide.

This whole mess is her fault. She shouldn't have come to a town in the first place. She should have stayed in the fields. In haystacks, if those exist anymore. She should have hitched a ride on a freight train. Are there still hobos?

Archipelago has no idea how to stay alive out here.

She almost begins to weep, but starts to eat her pizza instead. Who knows when she'll see pizza again? It's amazing she actually found it. But she *did* find it; she had that much of an idea of how to stay alive, in the middle of this sodden mess her life has be-come, this heap of chaos.

As she thinks that, she hears a buzzing in the alley, a vast whooshing sound, and feels the hair on her neck lift. She turns to find herself facing a towering pillar of darkness filled with swirling stars, two ruby eyes the only recognizable features. "Daughter," the voice booms. "Minion! You are of my camp!"

"Oh, sod off!" Archipelago spits. "Goddamnit, I'm just trying to eat a slice of pizza! What is this, Grand Central Station? Go away!"

"You are my follower! You are my child! You are—"

"I'm my own woman!" Archipelago's standing now, screaming at the whirlwind. "I'm not your follower! I'm not a Minion any more than I'm a Comrade! I'm *myself,* you thermodynamic asshole!"

Weak as she is, she wishes she could hit the Emperor, get into a fistfight with him. Weak as she is, she thinks she'd win, because she's so angry. And then she realizes that she's not really angry at the Emperor.

She's angry at Cosmos.

She's angry at that do-gooder, bleeding-heart, muddle-headed meddler, that clueless crusader, that fucking idiot.

She knows where he lives. Everybody knows where he lives.

Get out of town, the cop said, and she wondered where she could possibly go. Now she knows. Now she has a destination.

First, though, she's going to stuff herself so full of pizza that she can barely move.

14

*S*o you would have been happier if your friend hadn't been at the hospital that night?" Unctuously concerned, pen poised above paper, the therapist watches Veronique. The therapist's name is Brandy, which Veronique finds hilarious, although she'd never share this with the good psychologist. Brandy wears her blond hair pulled back in a bun so she'll look like a professional, not like a cheerleader, although Veronique knows there are professional cheerleaders, too. Brandy wears tailored suits and lots of tasteful gold jewelry. Brandy wears her pseudo-empathy like an expensive perfume.

Mortification. That's the only word for this.

"I would *not* have been happier," Veronique says. She's determined to maintain her intellectual integrity, to remain precise and rigorous. "At that moment, nothing would have made me one iota less miserable. But seeing Rosemary there made it worse. Made me more miserable."

Brandy smiles brightly, as if she's just scored a point in a tennis match. "Because you were ashamed."

"Of course. Have you ever been in an ER as a psych patient? It isn't an empowering experience."

Brandy looks sober now. "No. I know it isn't." Veronique notices how neatly she's sidestepped the question. All therapists are crazy themselves, aren't they? But if this fashionable twit hasn't done ER time herself, she's seen her patients do it. She frowns down at her notes and says, "But Rosemary's the person you stayed with after you left the ER, correct?"

"Yes."

"And yet you still—"

"I still would have preferred to leave the ER, take a cab to her house, and ask to stay there for a few days, instead of having her see me in a paper gown under police guard. Correct."

Brandy's frowning again. "And how have you been doing on the meds? Any new side effects? Last week you said, let's see—" She flips back a page in her notes. "—you had some dry mouth, a little dizziness?"

"Those, still. Nothing new, no." In fact, Veronique has no side effects, because she hasn't been taking her antidepressants. Every day she ceremoniously flushes that day's dose down the toilet. She's done enough Internet research to know what the likely side effects of this drug are, so she pretends to have them.

"And how are you feeling? Mood-wise?"

Peachy keen, sister. My best friend was raped and murdered six months ago, and I'm on medical leave from my job with orders to seek psychological help, and the only reason I wasn't locked up in a loony bin for at least three days was because someone I know and don't even especially like was there to witness me raving in my paper gown and swore to various and sundry authorities that she'd keep me safe at her house, after I'd sworn to the same authorities that I wasn't planning to kill myself or anyone else. But I'm on happy pills now, so all's well with the world.

"I think I'm doing better," Veronique says. "I think I'm on a more even keel." But Brandy's frowning again, which can't mean anything good.

She shakes her head. "Veronique, I have to say, your affect seems a little flat to me. I wonder if you need a higher dosage, or a different medication altogether."

Oh, hell. Veronique doesn't want to go through the hassle of switching meds she isn't even taking. She's only pretending to take them out of fear that noncompliance will endanger her medical leave.

Mollify the good shrinkette. Act like you're on board with the program. "Maybe you're right, but I think I'm just tired. I didn't sleep well last night, and after all, I am still grieving Melinda."

"Insomnia?" Brandy's frown has deepened. "How many hours of sleep do you think you got? We can give you a sleeping aid—"

Veronique laughs, trying not to sound hysterical. "No, really, I think it's just that I had some iced tea late in the day. Black tea, with caffeine. I won't make that mistake again." In fact, she's been sleeping like the dead every night, and would sleep much later in the morning if Rosemary weren't stopping by every day, often before noon, to check up on her. Rosemary's one of those people who showers and gets dressed almost before she's opened her eyes in the morning, and who believes that physical illness is the only legitimate reason to stay in your PJs past seven A.M. Given her druthers, Veronique would lounge in her bathrobe, drinking coffee and reading, until at least lunchtime, but raids from the Rosie Police have made that untenable. Veronique's unexpected vacation is, accordingly, much less pleasant than it would have been otherwise. "Can we see how I'm doing next week, and change the dosage then if we need to?"

"Of course. But you'll call me if you feel significantly worse? And you'll keep checking in with Rosemary?"

"Yes, I will. Thank you." Actually, Rosie's the one doing the checking in, but Brandy doesn't need to know that. Veronique stands up and shakes Brandy's hand, remembering to smile and make eye contact. Mollify the shrink. Observe proper mammalian protocol.

She leaves the office with a sigh of relief. Outside, daffodils and irises and apple blossoms droop on stems and branches, blasted by the late-spring snowstorms that always seem to hit Reno in May. It's not snowing, but looks like it might start again any moment. As usual, everyone's complaining about the weather—this is a seasonal tradition in Reno—but Veronique rather likes it. It mirrors the state of the world: uncaring forces cutting down the vulnerable and the beautiful in full bloom. Sunshine would be a lie.

Her own lies don't bother her. They're civil disobedience. They're self-defense.

Psychiatry functions at least in part to enforce conformity, to keep outliers within the range of normal behavior. Brandy and Rosie and the UNR cabal are so anxious for Veronique to take her meds less because they care about *her* discomfort than because her behavior has made *them* uncomfortable. They want her to take psychotropic drugs so they'll feel better when they're around her.

Veronique has, of course, pretended to agree with the prevailing opinion. Yes, she's been suffering from depression for years, compounded by Sarabeth's desertion and her growing professional discontent. Yes, Melinda's death triggered a breakdown, but actually—hallelujah!—the breakdown was a *blessing,* because it alerted everyone to how much pain she was in, and now, yes, she needs to take the nice happy pills that will rewire her brain so she won't hurt anymore.

She's researched the happy pills. She knows they don't immediately alter mood—they aren't uppers in the conventional sense—knows they aren't addictive, knows they won't impair her intellect. She understands that depression is a medical, biochemical illness, and knows that these drugs have saved many lives. Many people need them.

She doesn't.

She's not crazy, and she's not depressed. She's grieving and she's angry, but in her situation, she'd be crazy if she *weren't* grieving and angry. Her breakdown in class was indeed unprofessional and inexcusable—even if it was also the most alive she's felt in years, even if she still believes everything she said during her tirade—and she's rather surprised that UNR hasn't just fired her. She supposes she has tenure to thank for that. But however unseemly, the crisis doesn't mean that she needs to take happy pills.

It means that she needs to get out of her job. She needs to retire, whether she can afford to or not. But until she can see her way clear, she needs to play along with the prevailing opinion. She's trying to be strategic about this, milking the medical leave while she explores options. She has an extra bedroom; she can take in a boarder, some nice studious grad student. She can't quite figure out how to make the budget work, but she'll get there. She has to. She can't possibly step back into a classroom. She couldn't do that even if she wanted to, even if she missed teaching. Just thinking about setting foot in the English Department again—although she knows she'll have to, if only to sign papers and clear out her office—makes her want to sink through the ground.

She's pretty sure the classroom fiasco only confirmed everyone's worst opinions of her. She tries not to think about the gossip, from both students and colleagues, that must be circulating around the department. If they care enough to talk about her at all, that is.

Her chair's called a few times to ask how she is. Since part of her tirade was directed at him, she can't decide if the calls are unusually generous of him or an attempt to rub salt in her wounds; either way, those conversations are damned uncomfortable. But otherwise, there's been resounding silence. No cards, no e-mails. Her world has narrowed to Brandy and Rosie, who treat her like she's two.

She feels a buzzing in her pocket: her phone. She pulls it out and looks at the caller ID. Rosie, of course.

She's exceedingly tired of this leash.

She doesn't answer.

For good measure, she turns off the phone.

Sighing, Veronique gets into her car. She knows she should go home, check mail, and go over the damn finances again, but she's bored. She wants to do something else, go somewhere else: a place where she can be normal, where no one expects her head to start swiveling three hundred and sixty degrees.

But where? Reno's a small town. Anywhere she goes—cafés, libraries, stores, the art museum—she's likely to see someone she knows, who'll either look at her with pity or avoid her altogether.

She sits in the car, pondering, and then smiles, suddenly cheered. Every year, Veronique bought Melinda a birthday gift from Planet X, the pottery studio in Gerlach, two hours northeast of Reno. The ritual of driving out there is one of the things she missed most about Melinda's birthday. But why not go just for herself? Why not buy herself a present? Something beautiful and extravagant: something she'd ordinarily never buy, and finances be damned, for once. A retirement gift. A you're-sane-even-if-no-one-else-knows-it gift.

Melinda urged Veronique to spend money on herself, the last time they drove to Gerlach together. This would be a fitting moment to honor Melinda's wish.

It's noon now. She can drive out there, have an hour or two to shop, and still make it back by dark. She has a full tank of gas, and the winter tires are still on the car—she doesn't have them switched out until June, in deference to Reno weather—so she'll be fine even if she hits snow, which she really thinks she might, since the clouds are even darker now than they were a few minutes ago.

She knows she should call Rosie to let her know. To report in. Screw that, as the students would say. Veronique starts the car and heads toward I-80. She's doing this to get away from her parole officer for a few hours, and she'll be back before Rosie knows she was ever gone.

She drives east on 80, past craggy red-rock cliffs. The road parallels the Truckee River. She feels ten pounds lighter each mile she drives from Reno; soon she'll be weightless. And indeed, she feels like she's floating by the time she takes Exit 83 to Wadsworth, and from there turns onto Route 447, the road that leads past Pyramid Lake to the Black Rock Desert.

As often as she's made this drive, Veronique always forgets how beautiful it is, how calming she finds this journey into the desert, into the white of salt flats and green of sagebrush, all of it cradled in the bowl of brown mountains and blue sky. From emptiness into emptiness: the drive will sweep the cobwebs out of her mind and the ache out of her heart, and leave her refreshed and tranquil. This was the right thing to do.

Despite the clouds and the snow still clinging to the mountaintops and lying in patches on the ground, wildflowers bloom along the side of the road. Veronique cracks her window to let the smell of sagebrush flood the car. As vulnerable and exposed as she's felt lately on campus, she feels safe in the desert.

Melinda always loved this trip. Veronique can almost hear her, commenting on the shape of clouds and shadows. She can feel Melinda in the car, in the passenger's seat. She knows that if she turns her head, the illusion will vanish, so she only looks ahead, at the road and the desert, so demanding and austere.

In a few more miles she reaches Nixon, one of the tiny towns on the Paiute reservation around the lake. She decides to get gas, despite her nearly full tank; this is remote country, and you can't be too careful. When she came out here with Melinda, they always bought snacks from the convenience store, too. Melinda usually ate sensibly, fruit and vegetables and whole grains, but on road trips she gleefully indulged in junk food: potato chips, Hostess cupcakes, sickly-sweet orange soda that fizzed going down the throat and left an aftertaste of aluminum scrapings.

In Melinda's honor, Veronique will buy junk food.

Inside the store, a Paiute guy in a Tribal Police uniform chats amiably with the woman behind the counter. They look up as Veronique walks in, then look away. An Anglo tourist. Nothing to see here: Veronique is a transient who'll buy her junk food and soon be gone, no one with whom they need to concern themselves.

After her most recent encounter with police, Veronique revels in this anonymity.

She uses the restroom, finds her chips and cupcakes—the chocolate ones with the white squiggles on top—and, at the last minute, substitutes root beer for orange soda. The sugar content is just as high, without the aluminum scrapings.

The clerk, bored, takes Veronique's money, efficiently counting out change without breaking the rhythm of her conversation with the cop. The car waits outside, gleaming a dull gray. Seventy-some miles to Gerlach, nine miles farther to Planet X. *How many miles by candlelight?*

Once Veronique has her loot in the car, she discovers that she can't bear the thought of eating any of it. Never mind: it will keep. "This stuff has a shelf life measured in geological epochs," Melinda told her once. "That's why it's junk food." Stomach soured, Veronique sets out, driving into the growing dimness of the desert. The clouds have become so thick that she turns on her headlights.

The road's a ribbon. You can see for miles here, towns visible hours before you reach them, because towns plant trees and have lights. Hands steady now on the steering wheel, Veronique gazes into the distance, squinting. That small group of trees, still visible in the gloaming, is Empire, which she'll reach in an hour or so. Beyond Empire the road curls left, toward the mountains and a larger oasis: Gerlach.

Neither place much deserves to be called a town. Empire's a few houses and many trucks huddled around a gypsum mine; Veronique's car travels through and past it in an eyeblink. Gerlach—a restaurant, a hotel, several bars, and a scattering of houses, made famous by Burning Man—takes two blinks, three if you slow down to the twenty-five miles posted on the signs. Veronique cruises through town at forty. Nobody's out here, and there are no other cars on the road.

A few minutes later, she takes a left onto the washboard road leading to the pottery studio. The trees here are tall, rustling, with clouds caught in their branches. Veronique parks the car and gets out, inhaling the tang of sagebrush. Somewhere a bird sings, its voice bright liquid.

She seems to be the only customer. Is the place closed? Will she have to leave? But she sees the potter standing on the porch of his workshop; perhaps the sound of her car has called him outside. He waves; she waves back, and meanders, relaxing, into the closest of the three gallery buildings, groping for a light switch as she enters. She won't ask permission. Let him come find her if he wants her to leave.

Clean lines, beautiful forms: everything here is both lovely and useful. Peace settles over Veronique like a blanket. Her knee doesn't even hurt. What pill could possibly work this well? She gazes at plates and bowls, mugs and vases, sets of plain dishes and one-of-a-kind pieces, shaped like fantastical sea creatures here where water falls so rarely. In the track lighting, the pieces gleam as if wet with surf.

The Great Basin was an ocean once. Melinda talked about that all the time, about ichthyosaurs and the delicate whorls of marine shells etched in desert rock. Veronique picks up a small round pot, ridged like a sea urchin. Cool and heavy in her hands, it could be the fossil of a creature that actually lived here, millennia ago. She turns it, admiring how old it looks, how organic, reveling in the feel of the ridges against her skin.

The pot doesn't want to go back on the display table. It wants to come home with her. She looks at the price tag and feels a slight pang. It's pricy, yes, but not quite the extravagance she'd planned driving out here. And she's not ready to leave.

She wants to stay, wants to let the oceanic expanse of the desert dissolve her heart to sand. She wants to stay here and breathe. She even has an excuse for dallying: outside, a few white flakes swirl past the dark trees. The cats would be furious at her if she missed their evening feeding time, but they have a clean litter box and enough water and dry food for several days. They'd be fine, if indignant.

Cradling the sea-urchin pot against her chest, she turns and finds herself facing a display of business cards. Planet X Guest House. Veronique smiles, and takes one, and goes to find the potter.

Melinda guzzles her Nixon-bought orange soda and lets out a huge belch. Veronique, hands on the wheel, snorts. "That stuff'll dissolve your stomach, you know."

"I doubt it. You're thinking of Coke. Anyway, it's my birthday. This is the one day a year I consciously court carcinogens, remember?"

Veronique laughs. "What did the carcinogens cost? I should pay for them, since it's your birthday."

"Don't be silly. You're going to buy me a piece of expensive pottery; I'll buy my own Ring-Dings." Melinda pauses, watching her friend's profile, and then says, "It's lovely of you to do this, Veronique."

"You always say that. I enjoy it, you know."

Melinda pushes a wisp of hair behind one ear. "This time, you should buy yourself something. You never do."

"I did, actually. Years ago. Sarabeth and I drove out here, and we agonized for what seemed like hours, and we picked out a gorgeous pot. And when we got it home, well, it was still gorgeous, but the magic was gone. For me, the Planet X stuff is more beautiful at Planet X. Those pieces need to be with their kind. For me, it's more of a museum than a store." She glances at Melinda. "They look great at your house. They wouldn't at mine."

Melinda doesn't believe this. Veronique's decorating scheme is spare and Southwestern; the pots would fit beautifully. Melinda's interior design is, to put it kindly, eclectic. The pots Veronique's bought her are hardly visible in all the clutter, but Melinda loves them anyway. She knows they're there, even if no one else would without an archeological excavation.

"What happened to it?" she asks Veronique. "The pot? I've never seen it, have I?"

Veronique waves a hand, as if to shoo away a mosquito. "Sarabeth took it. She always liked it better than I did, anyway."

"Well, you should get yourself something. To replace that vase Nepotuk broke. You have a place ready-made for it."

Veronique smiles vaguely, but waves her hand again, and Melinda decides that sometime this year, she'll drive Veronique out here and treat her to a pot. She can tell that Veronique won't buy one for herself. For that matter, Melinda—lover of large jewelry and chunky handknits and art glass and artists' cooperatives—has never seen Veronique buy anything impractical for herself, never seen her invest in beauty for its own sake. As far as Melinda knows, Veronique hasn't even dated anyone since Sarabeth left.

At least she has only two cats, and not several dozen, although Melinda can't imagine Veronique hoarding anything. The woman's an emotional anorexic; she might be healthier if she did have several dozen cats. Sometimes Melinda wonders if Veronique was different when Sarabeth was around—Melinda met Vera after the breakup—but she suspects it's just how Veronique's wired. And maybe it's why Sarabeth left, for that matter.

Yes, Melinda thinks, I definitely need to treat her to something. Something more lasting than a meal out. She knows that Veronique will protest, will try to dodge any gift. Melinda will just have to find some way around her formidable defenses.

*a*nna sits outside, on the deck, in sunshine. It's May, and at last the sun's out. The weather hasn't turned very warm yet, but no matter. All over the city, people are sitting outside, faces like flowers turned up to the sky. This is an annual ritual, the day when the residents of Seattle emerge from hibernation.

Bart sits next to her. They went for a nice long walk earlier, and he's tuckered out. He lies on the sunny teak of the deck, basking, his tail giving an occasional thump.

Anna doesn't know where William is. At one of his support-group meetings, maybe.

She's come out here with her laptop, her knitting, the latest issue of *CC,* and a stack of notecards. The job she needs to do today—much easier in sunshine and fresh air—is to write a set of invitations to Percy's service in two months. It's a small list, and she's almost afraid to send the invites, because it will hurt more if no one comes after getting a handwritten note. But she's Percy's mother, and she owes him the effort of trying to gather people who liked him once, who found good in him. She's also sending invitations to her own circle, people she once considered friends. It's almost a test, to see if they'll come and offer any kind of support.

Marjorie and David are of course already coming. They don't need an invite. Marjorie offered to pay for engraved invitations, but Anna said, "This isn't a wedding. I'll write the notes myself. It will be good for me." She's not exactly sure how it will be good for her, but she supposes that it represents a kind of reaching out, which is what William and his parents keep telling her she needs to do.

And so she sends a note to her knitting group ("I just wanted to let you know"), to the Stanford CC Club ("In case any of you knew Percy"), to Percy's college roommates and high school friends ("Please pass this along to anyone else who might want to attend"), and, in a kind of desperation, to his pediatrician ("Because you took care of Percy for so many years, I thought you might want to know . . ."). It all feels like shamefaced begging. None of these people want to know anything about Percy, or about her and William. None of them have bothered to express sympathy, and Anna finds that she no longer views this as a tactful protection of privacy. Writing the notes, she finds herself growing increasingly angry. She knows it's an impossible situation. She can all too easily imagine that if the positions were reversed, if someone she knew had lost a child to suicide after that child had committed an unspeakable crime, she'd sidestep the issue. She wouldn't know what to say. She'd tell herself the family needed space. She'd tell herself she didn't know them well enough to intrude, that surely they were surrounded by loving family and friends. She would, yes, probably blame them, wonder what they'd done to create a child who would do such a thing.

But even if she avoided face-to-face contact, she'd do *something*, even if it was only to send a plant.

Anna is trying very hard not to feel as if something's wrong with her because she isn't surrounded by loving family and friends. She wonders if people are afraid of her now, if they think that she, too, will commit some atrocity.

And so it is a relief, after so many empty words, to write the last two notes, the ones to people who've offered kindness. The first is to Karen, who brought Bart back home. The second is to someone Anna has never met.

Dear Rev. Alphonse-Smith:

In November, you were kind enough to send a few words of sympathy about my son, Percy. I find it ironic that you, who knew and loved the woman my child so terribly and inexplicably murdered, are one of the very few people who reached out to us after his death. My husband and I thank you for that, and we would like to let you know that Percy's long-delayed memorial service will be held on July 24, on what would have been his twenty-third birthday, at the East Shore Unitarian Universalist Church in Bellevue. Please don't think I'm informing you of this so you'll send us a tree! Rather, I ask for your prayers on that day, which will be very difficult for us. William and I are not religious; I myself do not know how to pray, and I do not even know if I believe in prayer. But I know that it will be a comfort to me to know that you are thinking good thoughts on our behalf.

I hope this note is neither offensive nor overly forward, and I hope that everyone who loved Melinda is finding some way to heal.

Very truly yours,
Anna Clark

After all the forced notes, the polite phrases squeezed through simmering rage, this one flows easily, and so Anna is not surprised to find herself weeping as she signs her name. She sees that a tear has fallen on the card, has smudged a few words. Never mind: they're still readable. She'll send the card as is. She's not sure if she'd be able to bear rewriting it.

She seals the note, addresses it, stamps it. There: the chore is done. She'd planned to reward herself by knitting a few rows of her long-neglected shawl, and then by reading the new *CC* issue. She wants to know what will happen to Archipelago. She's startled, and a little disturbed, that the CC Four are treating her so sympathetically. After all, Archipelago killed someone. Archipelago is hardly Percy, but her isolation—and desperation—speak to Anna's own, and Anna has found this story arc compulsively compelling.

She's started to explore the online discussion forums, too, and had thought she might do some of that this afternoon. She initially logged on to see if she could find any posts by Percy, but since she doesn't know what his username was, she quickly abandoned that project. Right now, she's trying to suss out how other readers feel about Archipelago.

But suddenly she's exhausted, too tired to knit or even to read. It's the kind of fatigue that feels like being pulled under anesthesia: entropy exhaustion. Anna glances at the dog, who's stopped wagging his tail, and sees that he's fallen asleep, too. He moans and twitches, jerking his head, and Anna wonders if he's dreaming about the beach. Poor dumb brute. She bends down to stroke the top of his head, grateful that Percy never wanted a pet scorpion. Bart murmurs and mutters with little huffing breaths, but doesn't wake.

*D*id she say anything about her plans this afternoon?" Rosemary asks. She's sitting at Veronique's kitchen table with one cat in her lap and another winding itself around her feet. Veronique gave her a key a long time ago, "just in case," but this is the first time Rosie's used it. After three hours of not being able to reach Vera, she panicked and let herself into the house, afraid of what she'd find. She didn't find anything. "I'd feel really silly if I called out the cavalry and it turned out she was just stocking up on tofu at Trader Joe's."

"I understand that," Brandy says, "and I'm sure you know that I can't talk about anything Veronique discussed in session. But if someone I cared about hadn't been answering her phone for five hours, I'd be concerned. I urge you to call the police."

I hate this, Rosemary thinks. I hate babysitting Vera. It feels like taking care of Walter all over again. I hate talking to this shrink, because I can't tell if she's just playing the CYA game or if "I urge you" is HIPAA code for "Yes, you should be worried and take action."

It occurs to her that there may be a workaround. "Can you try to reach her? And call the police if you believe there's cause? I think you'd have more credibility."

After a pause so long that Rosemary fears the connection's been broken, Brandy clears her throat. "Under the terms of my therapeutic relationship with Veronique, it wouldn't be appropriate for me to try to call her without a prior indication from her that I should. Do you understand?"

"You can return her calls, but you don't just call your clients out of the blue."

"Exactly. But why don't we do this: try her again, and call me again if you still can't reach her, and then I'll call the police. I'm about to leave the office, but I'll give you my cell phone number."

"Thank you," Rosemary says. "That's above and beyond the call of duty."

"You're welcome. And if you do reach her, please call me anyway, to let me know."

"Yes, of course. Thank you so much."

Oh, hell, Rosemary thinks as she hits the end button. The shrink must be really worried. They never give out their personal numbers.

She calls Veronique's cell again: straight to voice mail. The phone's off, then. It's been off since that first call Rosemary made at noon, the one Veronique neither answered nor returned.

But Veronique's clumsy and forgetful with her phone, and could easily have turned it off by accident. She's never entirely gotten used to the technology. Rosemary doesn't know if she even knows how to access her voice mail; the outgoing message is still the computer-generated one that comes with new phones.

Rosemary looks at her watch: 5:30. Veronique feeds her cats at six on the dot. She's often joked that she can't have her own dinner before she gives them theirs, because they'll give her no peace. They're already radiating anxiety, fastening themselves to Rosemary as if at least eight of their nine lives depend on how thoroughly they can ingratiate themselves with her.

All right, then. She'll give it another half hour. If Veronique isn't home by six and still isn't answering her cell, Rosemary will call Brandy and let Brandy call the cavalry. In the meantime, she'll feed the cats. She can allay some of their fears, at least.

*J*eremy's lying on the couch in the living room, his laptop on his chest. He woke up today feeling crappy—although he's pretty sure his funk's more emotional than physical—and decided to call in sick to work. He's never done that before. He still likes the job, but he just can't deal with coffee grounds and milk cartons today.

He's been trying to figure out why he feels so lousy, what about today in particular has made his mood plummet. Probably part of it's the weather. May is when Jeremy always gets tired of waiting for spring, and wants warmth *now*. And May's when school gets out. Everybody he knows has another year finished, and he doesn't. He still doesn't want to be back in school, but he doesn't want to feel left behind, either.

The effort of staying in step just feels like too much work, though. This is Emperor territory, so Jeremy's been idly scrolling through the WISS thread on the CC message board. He never got around to writing his own essay, but reading other people's makes him feel a little less alone, even though he's seen most of the reasons before.

I switched sides when I got fired because of the economy.
I switched sides when the girl I loved dumped me for my
    best friend.
I switched sides when my brother was killed in Iraq.

That's the closest to Jeremy's, although no one's written, "I switched sides when my mother was raped and murdered by someone who claimed to be a CC fan." He doesn't think he wants to write that; it would be too much of a giveaway to anyone who's been following the news at all, despite his anonymous handle of "Kid Coherence."

He's been thinking about Guatemala again, though, mainly because he feels like he *should* want to go back there and learn more about his birth parents. That's what Mom would want him to want, but it's not what he wants. Not yet, anyway. Maybe it will be, someday. Yeah, he wants to be somewhere else, but not there.

Right now, being here is semi-okay. He's been reading Mom's old journals, trying to learn more about her. She started keeping the journals after college, and seems to have stopped the year she adopted him; he can't find any more recent than that, anyway. The entries are mainly about various boyfriends. What a bunch of jerks! They make Jeremy glad, for once, that she adopted as a single parent. She dated a guy who nagged her about being neater. She dated a guy who dumped her because he thought librarians were boring. She dated a guy who collected his lovers' pubic hair. Ewwwwww.

Losers. Aside from how completely bizarre it is to imagine his mother having a love life, reading this stuff makes Jeremy want to track these guys down and scream at them. "My mother was amazing, you moron. My mother was worth ten of you. My mother's left pinky was more interesting than anything you've ever done."

When she was alive, all he did was criticize her, chafe against her. Regret burns his throat.

Sighing, he scrolls through another few WISS posts. Okay, how about this? "I'm supposed to be a Comrade because my mother adopted me from a war-torn country after my birth parents were killed, which is the kind of thing that should make you believe in noble do-gooderism, but instead my adoptive mom was killed, too, and my godfather, who's sort of the closest thing I have to a father, developed Swiss-cheese brain from Alzheimer's, and how can I still be a Comrade after losing all of them?"

No. Just thinking about writing this makes Jeremy feel like his skull's filled with lead.

He scrolls listlessly through a few more WISS threads—car accidents, broken legs, house fires—until he's brought up short by a thread title. "Request from Anna Clark."

Anna Clark? Percy's mother Anna Clark? Fucking Christmas tree Anna Clark?

The post's dated today. Like, two hours ago. Holy shit. She just wrote it. Jeremy pulls himself into a sitting position, so he'll have a better viewing angle, and clicks on the post title.

Dear Comrades and Minions:

My son, Percy, was a CC fan and collector. As some of you are probably aware from the news, he also committed a terrible murder and then killed himself. I truly cannot find any hints or reasons in his history that would have made him kill an innocent stranger, and I am struggling to make any sense of this that I can. I know that I cannot blame his actions on a comic book—and I've now begun reading CC myself, working my way through Percy's collection, and to my surprise am enjoying it—but so much of the series is about facing pain and chaos, and so many of you have also faced pain and chaos, that I thought it might be helpful to talk to some of you. The Emperor claimed Percy. I am trying to remain on the side of meaning. I know there's nothing any of you, or anyone really, can say to comfort me, but if you are willing to respond to this, I would welcome your thoughts. Sincerely, Anna Clark. P.S. Does it bother anyone else that Archipelago's getting away with murder?

Jeremy blinks. Holy shit. Percy's *mother* is looking for CC pen pals?

And is she *nuts*? Posting in a public forum like this could pull the media down on her like fruit flies on a rotting banana.

Well, sure, she's nuts. Her son certainly was, and these things run in families, don't they?

Shaking his head, Jeremy hits A on his cell phone—he has Amy on speed-dial now, a small triumph that would have meant a lot more before Mom died—but it goes to voice mail. Amy's probably studying for finals or working on a paper or otherwise being productive. She's much better at being productive than Jeremy is, and he's still a little in awe that she even speaks to him. "Hey, A, so here's some crazy gossip. Check out the WISS boards on CCnet.

Percy Clark's mother just posted there. I swear I'm not making this up. Catch you later."

He's pretty sure she'll call back the second she gets that. It really is juicy. Percy's mom has given Amy a reason to call him: there's a sweet irony.

Feeling much more energetic than he did a few minutes ago, he sits up straighter on the couch and eyes Anna's post. It has three replies; there was only one the first time he read it. He scrolls through them.

So sorry. Wish there were some way to make sense of this, but not even Cosmos could do that. You have our sympathies. And I'm betting Archipelago gets hers.

Ms. Clark, if you've read CC, you know that it isn't about murder. The Emperor doesn't kill people, at least not directly. He isn't a murderer. He's a force for chaos and disorganization, but murder requires planning and intent—just really negative planning and intent. So I think you're looking in the wrong place. Good luck finding peace. By the way, I agree with you about Archipelago.

Comics don't kill people, people kill people, and you and your son must both be morons not to know that, and he deserves to be dead. So does Archipelago. I'm betting her own bug kills her. Anyway, nobody feels sorry for you, lady. We feel sorry for your garbage son's victim and her family. Suck it up.

Oh, man, Jeremy thinks. That's hella mean. But it's also exactly what she should have expected from posting here; Jeremy's amazed that the first two responses were as kind as they were. This woman's really clueless.

Mom's last postcard is upstairs in Jeremy's room, stuck into a corner of his mirror. He looks at the turtles every day. He doesn't have to look at the back anymore, because he has it memorized. *Just met guy your age, Percy, who likes CC too.*

Everyone has told him that if Percy hadn't struck up a conversation about that, it would have been about something else. Everyone has told him that Percy must have already targeted her, or that maybe he didn't, but the content of the conversation didn't matter. Jeremy's devotion to CC, he has been repeatedly assured, is not responsible for his mother's murder.

Percy Clark was responsible for his mother's murder.

Mom told him that Percy said his own mother wouldn't go near CC. More irony.

Should he respond to the post? But what would he say, if he did? Does Anna Clark know that Mom and Percy talked about CC? How could she know? Should he tell her? No, that would only make things worse. Wouldn't it? But there's no way to make things better.

He remembers VB asking him what CC would do.

He remembers Amy telling him about VB's nervous breakdown. Nobody talks about how you get through the rest of your life after the murder's solved. Yeah, no kidding. Percy's mom has to be going through that, too, right?

Jeremy's never thanked her for the fucking Christmas tree. Sending it was clueless, but at least she tried. He ponders, composes sentences in his head, and decides that all of them sound completely lame. Amy's a good writer. When she calls back, he'll ask her to help him compose a reply.

His cell phone rings. He smiles. This will be Amy. He answers without even looking at the caller ID. "Hey, A!"

"Jeremy." The voice is distorted; he can hear frantic breathing. "Jeremy, it's Veronique Bellamy, and I'm really sorry to bother you, but you need to call your Aunt Rosie and tell her to leave me alone, because she won't listen to me, and calling the cops on me was as completely inappropriate as anything I've done since your mother died, including this phone call, and I'm truly sorry for that, but Rosemary won't listen to me because she thinks I'm insane but she may listen to you, and—"

"What?" The cops, again? VB's accumulating quite a rap sheet, unless she's still talking about what happened in March. "Prof Bellamy, what are you talking about? Where are you?"

"I'm in Gerlach. I'm staying at the Planet X Guest House as a little treat for myself, and I'm absolutely *fine,* but Rosemary called the police because she thought—I don't know what she thought, but she's demanding that I come home, and I *won't.* I'm fine. The cops told her I'm fine! I'm not two years old. You just tell her that."

The line goes dead. Jeremy blinks at his phone and then hits R. Aunt Rosie's on speed dial, too.

VB isn't. He didn't even know she had his cell number.

Aunt Rosie's furious. "She should *not* have dragged you into this. That's completely inappropriate."

"She knows that." This would be funny, if they weren't both so upset. "That's what she said, too."

"Well then, she shouldn't have done it! I'm going out there. I'm going to bring her home. I know I shouldn't drag you into this either, but she already has, so do you want to come with me?"

"Um," says Jeremy. The couch is pretty comfortable, and he isn't sure he feels like moving. On the other hand, VB and Rosie sound furious at each other, and if he's there, maybe he can keep the peace a little. On the third hand, he should stay out of it. On the fourth hand, what would Mom want him to do? And what would CC do?

And if VB refuses to budge, which is what Jeremy would do in her position, because Rosie really is treating her like she's a little kid who's run away from home, well then, Rosie's going to be really upset. And Jeremy loves Rosie, and if that happens, she'll need company driving home. And the first clue that Uncle Walter had Alzheimer's was when he drove off across Nevada without telling anybody, and that must be making Rosie even more upset, and doesn't VB remember that?

"Okay," Jeremy says, resigned. "Can you give me half an hour to take care of some stuff here?"

"Of course. I'll pick you up in thirty minutes."

He has to eat something, shower, get dressed. And Amy still hasn't called back. Jeremy looks unhappily at Anna's post. There are two more responses.

Your son needed serious psych help and maybe you do, too. We aren't therapists. Why are you even posting here? Why are you wasting your time even thinking about Archipelago? She's not real.

When my brother killed hisself we found drugs in his room and u should look for drugs too cause no 1 just does this.

Jeremy shakes his head. He doesn't envy her having to read this crap. He clicks on "respond to post" and types,

No answers for any of us. Sorry some people here are being assholes. Brave of you to post, but pretty stupid, too. You should just delete this whole thread. Never thanked you for the tree. Thanks.

He doesn't sign the post, not even with his CC handle. She'll know who it is, and he really doesn't want her searching for every post from Kid Coherence. The last thing Jeremy needs is Percy Clark's mother stalking him.

PART THREE

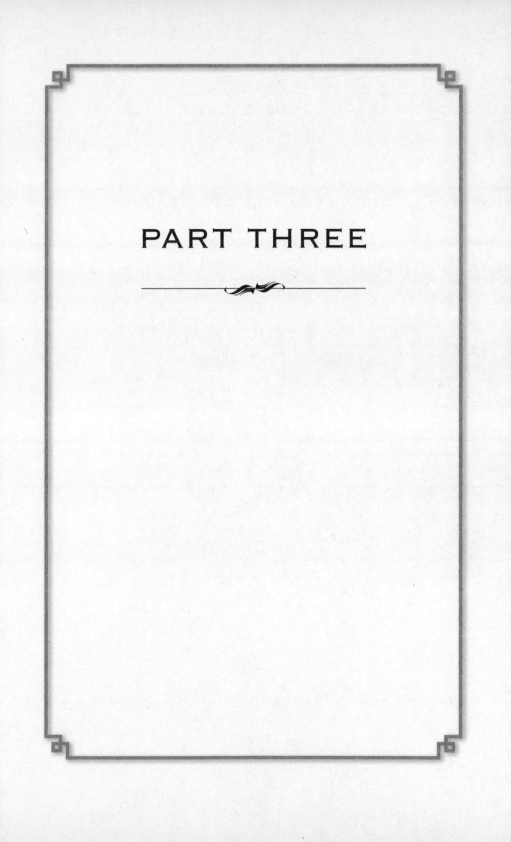

15

*a*nna sits on her living room floor, surrounded by photo albums: large ones, small ones, fancy ones with satin covers, homely handmade ones fashioned from cardboard and tinfoil. There are envelopes of Polaroids, printouts of Facebook albums, photographs liberated from drawers and closets and the corners of mirrors. She didn't know there were so many pictures of Percy in the house. How can a life be so well documented and remain so completely opaque?

It's July 1; in a month, Percy's memorial service will be over, and she'll be able to move on to whatever comes next, a future she can't even imagine. Right now, though, she still needs to plan the service.

She's determined to do this right, as if it's a normal funeral. At normal funerals, there are display tables with photographs and memorabilia, so Percy's service will have one, too. The framed picture on Percy's desk, the one of him and Bart, will definitely be included, but she also wants to use some baby pictures. Percy was a beautiful baby, calm and sunny. She's determined that anyone who comes—and she still isn't sure who that will be—will see him as he was then: blond, laughing, chubby-cheeked, as curious and quick to learn as any child.

Once again her mind falls into the familiar litany. Percy slept through the night sooner than most babies, never had colic, and didn't even come down with any of the major childhood illnesses. He didn't bully other kids and wasn't bullied by them. He sailed through school easily. Was Mexico some horrible price for all his blessing? What went wrong?

Always the same questions. They loop through her brain, Ouroboros-like. William and his parents dismiss them briskly: "No, of course not. You did nothing wrong. We did nothing wrong. It's his responsibility."

But the world blames the parents. Anna knows that. She doesn't blame herself, not exactly—and it amazes her that she doesn't—but she hungers fiercely for explanation, something she can hand to the people she knows must hold her responsible. Part of her knows this desire is cowardice, the yearning to deflect blame. But she truly doesn't believe she deserves blame.

She can't imagine the crime itself. Her gorge rises at the very thought of it, and she is heartsick and enraged for Melinda—for all women who have suffered this or who have even feared it, who cannot trust their moats to protect them, as indeed Anna's has in some sense not protected her—but she can't even begin to put Percy in this picture. She's tried. Her brain stalls, freezes, careens off-road.

She supposes some mothers would have tried to dwell in denial, to insist that their child hadn't done this, couldn't have, no no, it must have been someone else. Anna hasn't. She gives herself some small credit for facing the facts, the evidence. Is that a sign that somewhere deep down, she believed Percy capable of such a thing?

If the suspicion ever existed, she cannot drag it into the daylight.

As many times as she's scrutinized the history, she always comes back to the same answer. Whatever sent Percy swerving off the edge of sanity and civilization, she truly doesn't think it was anything within her or William's control, anything they could have seen or prevented. They didn't, heaven knows, beat Percy or insult him or commit any other kind of abuse. He rarely fought with them even as a teenager. He wasn't a wild partier. He wasn't the product of a problem pregnancy, and Anna hasn't been able to find any family history of crime or psychosis.

Everything about Percy was completely normal, until suddenly it wasn't.

She looks down at the album in her lap. Percy as a newborn, Percy sitting up for the first time, Percy's first birthday party. All the sweet, trite, predictable pictures taken by first-time parents.

She thinks about Melinda Soto, about Melinda's adopted son. She thinks Melinda was very brave, to bring home a baby from another country. Look how badly things can turn out even when the genes are known quantities. Look how kids can break your heart even when they're homegrown.

Her own heart breaks for Jeremy.

Jeremy has lost a mother and Anna has lost a son; she's smart enough to see the pattern, smart enough, too, to know not to go there, not to succumb to the temptation to try to fix this by forcing a relationship. It isn't possible. It's deeply wrong of her even to be tempted.

She was shocked to find Jeremy's post on the CC boards, although she supposes she shouldn't have been; given the popularity of the series, half the world must be on the CC boards at any given time. She sent him a cautious private note: "I grieve with and for you, and hope you are finding your way." He didn't answer. She can't blame him. She can't imagine his rage. She thinks that Jeremy Soto must be even angrier at Percy's death than she is, because there is now no living outlet for his fury.

Sometimes—but only sometimes—she finds herself relieved

that Percy didn't go through the hell of arrest, extradition, trial, life in a Mexican prison. Other times, she berates him for walking into the water, for walking away from consequences and responsibility and the possibility of answers. She doesn't understand, will never understand, why Percy killed Melinda, but she understands completely why he killed himself.

She looks down at the photo album. Here is Percy on his first day of kindergarten. She carefully removes the photo and turns the page. Percy on a summer vacation they took in Maine. Percy at high school graduation. Percy in his freshman dorm room at Stanford. Percy with his father, with his grandparents, with various friends who have not bothered to respond to her invitation to the service.

And here, at last, is Percy with her. She is not in many of these pictures, because she's usually the one taking them. But last summer the three of them, with Bart, went on a day hike in the Cascades. They hit a rough patch of trail, and Percy helped her around a clump of protruding tree roots, and William, ahead of them on the trail, turned and snapped the photo.

Anna, knuckles against her teeth, lifts the photo with her free hand. Percy, hair shining like a halo, holding her hand, his other arm strong and reassuring around her back. She remembers how patiently he led her around obstacles. "Here, Mom, step here where it's level." She can hear his voice, kind and courtly, as clearly as if he's in the room with her. She can't see his face, or her own: they're both looking down at the ground. What would she see in his eyes if she could?

*D*ammit," Melinda says, "I could have slapped him! He's known all his life what's right. I've taught him that. You help people; you leave whatever place you're in better than it was when you got there. That's the core of every genuine faith on the planet, and Jeremy's always gotten it, but this time he didn't."

The three women sit on Rosemary's deck, sipping iced tea and watching Walter mow the lawn. After a brutally hot summer's day, the temperature has at last cooled enough, with the last glimmers of light, for them to sit out here comfortably. A breeze moves the trees in the neighbor's yard, creating a gentle whooshing sound. "He's thirteen," says Veronique. "He's an adolescent. His job right now is to rebel."

"There were other thirteen-year-olds there, and they were doing fine! They were pitching right in and doing the work, not sulking and playing hooky! And they're his friends! I thought he'd have fun!"

"Were their parents on the trip, too?" Rosemary asks. "He might have felt self-conscious having you around."

"Some of their parents were there, yes, of course."

Veronique makes a sympathetic clucking noise. "They were probably fighting with their folks, too, where you couldn't see. Mel, kids get impossible at that age. Girls, too. It's the damn hormones."

And you would know this how? Melinda thinks furiously. In your childless state?

She hates this. Being angry at Jeremy, being angry at her friends. Being angry at herself.

"Did he originally want to go?" That's Rosemary. "Or did you tell him he had to?"

Melinda looks over Rosemary's fence, out at the distant mountains, velvet blue against the darker blue of the sky. "I—well, I told him we were going."

"Melinda!" That's both of them: Vera and Rosie, who so rarely agree on anything.

"His friend Richard went last year and had a great time! Jeremy wanted to go, then!"

"Then," Rosemary says gently, "Richard's white."

Melinda squints at her. Dammit! Does everything have to be political? She's political herself, but can't they all give it a rest for once? And since when does Rosie talk about race? She'd have expected that from Vera, but Vera doesn't know the kids at church. "Yes? So?"

"So white Richard goes with his mostly white youth group—that was before Tony Nguyen went off to college—to help build a rec center for poor brown kids. White Richard comes home feeling ennobled; we don't know what Tony made of it. This year, the mostly white youth group, in which Jeremy's currently the only brown kid, goes to help build a school on a Native reservation, alongside Native kids their own age. Furthermore, the white kids in the youth group know that Jeremy was adopted from Guatemala, because he made a nice little speech about it in church. You see where I'm going with this?"

Melinda swallows. "No." Rosemary's being a self-righteous pain in the ass, something else that would be more in character from Veronique. "No, I don't. Give me some help here, please?"

Veronique studies her cuticles, and then fiddles with a loose thread on her chair cushion. Rosie gets up to pour everyone more iced tea, but keeps talking, looking at the glass and pitcher instead of at Melinda. "The church kids look at Jeremy and maybe think, *He came from a place like this.* The Native kids look at Jeremy, who looks more like them than the white kids do, and maybe think, *How'd he wind up with them?* And Jeremy maybe feels torn down the middle."

"I think you're overanalyzing," Melinda says. "They're just kids. Jeremy's friends with the kids in youth group; they know him. They don't think about skin color."

"The hell they don't," Veronique says, looking up from the chair cushion. "They're teenagers, which means they're acutely self-conscious about every aspect of physical appearance. I'm not saying they're racist. I'm saying that if they were color-blind, they'd never know when to cross the street. Color-blindness is a lovely ideal, but it doesn't exist."

Melinda shakes her head. "That's cynical even for you, Vera."

"It's not cynical. It's realistic. I'm sure they're all lovely children who'd never dream of being mean to anyone based on ethnicity, but that doesn't mean they don't notice it. And they'd never admit to any of this, especially in church. Kids learn what not to say."

"I still think you're overanalyzing, and I really don't want to talk about this anymore."

Now both of their eyebrows rise. "Mel?" Rosemary says. "What happened?"

"Oh, for Pete's sake! I brought up the subject so I could vent, not to be subjected to group therapy! Can we talk about something else?"

Rosemary laughs. "How about another game of Scrabble? I'm determined to beat *one* of you, at least once."

She brings out her board, and they play while the moon, huge and orange, rises over the mountains to the east.

Veronique wins easily, as usual. Melinda comes in dead last, which isn't usual, but Rosemary seems more concerned than pleased. After the game, Vera goes home, pleading fatigue, and Rosemary and Melinda clean up.

"We shouldn't have gone to Arizona," Melinda says, putting another glass in the dishwasher. "I shouldn't have made him go. He wanted to go camping with the Clemonsons, but I told him he could do that later in the summer—they go camping almost every weekend—and that it was important to go on the youth group trip."

"Hmmm," Rosemary says, and then, "He's thirteen. You brought him home when he was a toddler. If he hasn't learned what you've tried to teach him by now, he never will."

"I know."

Rosemary laughs and touches her shoulder. "He'll forgive you, Mel. Don't look so miserable."

"We had a fight," Melinda says quietly. She's glad they're by themselves. Vera will hear about this eventually, maybe even from her, but she isn't here now, and Melinda's in no mood for more lecturing. "A horrible, horrible fight. I said awful things, Rose. Unforgivable things."

"That's not like you. What triggered it? Do you know?"

"The heat, maybe. And—when we got home I was going to tell him the truth. About his parents."

"That they were killed in that mess in Guatemala. The war."

"The civil war. The genocide. Yes. I thought he was old enough to know that. I was worrying about how to say it. But now I can't. Not after what else I said."

"All right, Mel. Shoot: what was the worst thing you said?"

Melinda stares out the window over the sink so she won't have to look at Rosemary. She watches the moon, smaller now and whiter, lovely and diminishing. "I asked him," she says, "how he could refuse to help these kids after I'd snatched him out of a hellhole in Guatemala. I asked him where he'd be if I'd refused to help him. I called him an ungrateful little shit."

"Ouch," Rosemary says. "Yeah, that's pretty bad."

"But it wasn't just the words, Rosie. It was the tone! I said it—I screamed it—hatefully. I shamed him. I wasn't just guilting him for not working, which would have been bad enough. I shamed him about who he was, where he'd come from. I put myself above him, and not just as his mother."

Rosemary grunts. "What did he say?"

"He said, 'I'll go back there if I'm not good enough for you.'" Her voice only breaks a little, repeating the words that have stung her every moment for the past week. "And then he started to cry, and glared at me, and ran outside. And he wouldn't speak to me the rest of the trip, Rose. He barely speaks to me now."

"Mel," Rosemary says, and gives her a hug. "It's bad, but you'll work through it. All parents lose their tempers. You're human."

She means to be comforting, Melinda knows, but nothing can comfort her right now. If only she'd thought before speaking. If only she'd never uttered the judgment she can now never unsay.

They finish the dishes, and Melinda goes home. And eventually

Melinda's irritation with Vera fades, and she tells her the story, too, and Veronique says, "Well, if I said that, I'd get fired, even with tenure, but mothers have more job security than professors do. He'll be fine. You'll be fine. There'd be bumps in the road right now even if he weren't adopted. It's going to be all right."

Wincing, Jeremy wipes down the counter at Emerald City. He burned himself on some steamed milk this morning, and even though he iced the spot right away, it still hurts. The pain's making him irritable. He doesn't want to chat with customers the way he usually does. He finds the roar of the espresso machine as unbearable as screeching brakes.

He doesn't want to be here. He doesn't know where else to go, though. He's come to a standstill at home: halfway through Mom's study, the sheer volume of her stuff defeated him, and he gave up. He did unwrap his Christmas presents, in June, and he's cooked a few of the dishes from *The Tra Vigne Cookbook*, but he feels like he's living in a museum instead of a house. Or in one of those cemetery houses, what are they called, mausoleums.

And it *is* a mausoleum, because Mom's urn is sitting in the living room. Some of the ashes are at church now, in the columbarium. Jeremy still plans to scatter some in the desert, the scoured landscape his mother loved. He still really wants some in the garden, too—he thinks they belong there—but if he puts them there, he feels like he won't be able to leave the house, even if he also keeps some for himself. And all of this feels like scattering Mom in too many places, anyway.

Between yearning to be somewhere else and not knowing where he can go, or how, he can't sit still right now. It's like his own skin hurts him even without burns, a coat of nettles he yearns to shed.

That's probably why, when Hen called to tell him about Percy's funeral, he only thought, or didn't think, for about twenty seconds before saying yeah, sure, he'd go. A road trip! Seattle's one of the cities he's wanted to check out anyway, and there's a science fiction museum there, with a CC exhibit. Amy's coming, too. She says it's for moral support, but he thinks it's really for the museum. He doesn't dare believe that it might be for him.

And here she is, grinning as she walks through the door of the coffeeshop, waving the latest *CC* issue. She's taken to stopping by at the end of every shift, and sometimes they go out for a bite afterward. It's not dating, exactly. They haven't even held hands yet. Jeremy still feels shy around her, because he doesn't know how much of this is pity. A lot of the time, he's not fit to be around anybody, anyway.

Grouchy bear. That's what Mom always called him, when he was in a bad mood. He hasn't been in a bad mood with Amy yet, hasn't let himself be, but sometimes it's a lot of work, and he doesn't have the energy to sign up for more of that by becoming even a provisional couple.

But she's here, smiling at him. "Read this yet?"

"Nope. I should, I take it?"

"Yep. It's fantastic. Here." She hands it to him.

Well, all right. He's still at work, but the place is slow right now. He can take a few minutes to flip through the issue. He checks to make sure the counter's dry; Amy's not one of those human-hands-must-not-touch-my-issue collectors, but he still doesn't want to get coffeehouse spill on the thing.

Oh, man. Is this ever dumb. The Midwest Regional Tourney of the World Rock, Paper, Scissors Society is in turmoil. A maverick judge has declared the rules null and void and is rewarding players who invent new throws. The flick of a Bic previously concealed in a palm—Fire—burns paper, melts scissors, turns rock to molten lava. "That's some fire," Jeremy says. "What, a Bic's the flames of Mount Doom?" *CC*'s usually more realistic than this, although he knows there's been some controversy about how it's gotten too serious and real-worldy and needs to be more fun, to return to its pulp roots.

"Just go on," Amy says. She's taken a seat at the counter, resting both elbows on it and leaning toward him.

In another match, someone uses a shaking hand to signal Earthquake, which shatters rock and buries both paper and scissors. Elsewhere, a gyrating index finger, Tornado, again trumps all the other throws, which it spins and scatters in its wake.

"Okay," says Jeremy. "I get it. Obviously the mad judge is EE."

"Yes, of course." Her laughter's a breeze against his cheek. "But you aren't finished. Go on."

"I dunno, Amy. Does this have a good ending?" He flips to the back of the issue. Water. Water everywhere, flooding the convention hall, players desperately trying to swim to safety, as the Emperor of Entropy, unveiled, hangs cackling from the ceiling. "Water destroys all!" he chortles. "Flood banishes order! Entropy always wins!"

That's the last frame, with a *To Be Continued* panel underneath. Jeremy blinks at it. "Okay. I know you're smarter than I am, but I don't get it. How is this fantastic?"

"To be continued!" Amy says. "They've never done that before."

"Yeah? So? It's always continued; come on, you know that. Saying so explicitly is just a marketing gimmick. They're trying to pump up interest in the tree-zine because everything's online now. Scissors cut paper: the scissors are the economy."

"Paper covers rock," Amy says. "The rock is the bottom line. Bedrock. But, look, anyway, that's not the point. The point is, the game's circular. It never stops. In Rock Paper Scissors, each element beats another but is beaten by the third. Rock beats Scissors but is beaten by Paper; Paper's beaten by Scissors but wins over Rock; Scissors are defeated by Rock but cut Paper. None of them can be the absolute winner. Are you following me?"

"I think so," he says, although he's not sure. "I mean, okay. But what about the wildcards? Fire and Water and Earthquake?"

"They replace circularity with dispersion. Typical EE move! Fire's extinguished by water but spreads in earthquakes; think about San Francisco in 1906. That looks like the start of a circular set. But earthquakes—and that's the one of the three that scares us most, because we can't control it at all—doesn't defeat either of the others. It *empowers* them. It spreads fire and makes water more powerful and destructive: dam breaks and tsunamis, yeah?"

"Destructive," he says, stacking some mugs while he talks to her. He doesn't have enough energy for this conversation. Mom probably would have loved it: all the geology stuff. "Entropy wins either way. That's what EE *wants*. That's why he wins."

"He *thinks* he wins. But look, earthquakes uncover things, too. Old cities and whatnot. They let us know where our infrastructures are weak and need to be reinforced. And when people are hurt in them, other people gather to help. So they become occasions for knowledge and compassion. And they help build the world; they make mountain ranges."

Mom definitely would have loved this conversation. Oh, God. Does he have a crush on a girl who's like his mother? "I dunno, Amy. That's a pretty big stretch. And what about water? Water really does trump everything, right? It wears away rock and blunts scissors and dissolves paper. So it's the ultimate winner, like EE said. I mean, I know the people are swimming, so they'll be okay, at least some of them, but—"

"*Right*. Exactly! And rock can also divert water even as the water's wearing it away, and metal and paper can float on it even as it's slowly making them dissolve, and paper can be used for sails or wings or kites to carry things over or along it. *And,* Jeremy, it's the ultimate source of life! We came out of the ocean, and we live in amniotic fluid before we're born, and our bodies are mostly water. So when EE points at all that destruction, he's pointing at creation, too, and he doesn't even know it!"

Amniotic fluid. Jeremy remembers the Mayan women who had their bellies cut open. All that fluid, all that life escaping. All that life escaping from Mom, because of Percy's knife.

He's stopped stacking mugs. He shakes his head to clear it. He refuses to cry. Mom.

Mom. Last Christmas. She was telling him about some TV show, one of those Planet Earth things. Something about volcanoes. He blinks. "Water. My mother told me once that without volcanoes, water would wash all the land into the ocean. She said we need volcanoes and earthquakes so we'll still have continents. She saw it on TV."

Amy hops from foot to foot, the happy dance he finds impossibly endearing even though it's completely dorky. "Right! There you go! Even when EE thinks he's wrecking things, he's also building them. He can't win. He can *never* win, not ultimately. Because his destruction is always an occasion for renewal, for rebirth."

"Huh." That sounds suspiciously like something Hen would say. But in another dizzy, narrow flash of memory, Jeremy sees the buzzard, the Bird that Cleaned the World, circling above the receding floodwaters, looking for carrion. He hears his mother reading him the story. His throat aches. "But the new life will always die, too."

"And be replaced by still more new life! See? Circular."

"Okay, so EE can't win. But neither can CC."

"Right. *Right.* They need each other. It's all about *balance.*"

Jeremy's head hurts. If this were anyone else, he'd cut the conversation short, but it's Amy. "Yeah, I guess. But that's a seesaw, not a circle. I mean, Rock Paper Scissors has three elements. CC and EE are only two. What's the third? Archipelago? How? We've been following her for what, a year now? I think she's only there to break up the CC stories, though, make 'em more interesting."

Amy laughs, softly. "To be continued. The third element could be Archipelago, sure, although I don't see how either. It could be time. It could be us, the observers. It could be God."

Jeremy shakes his head. "Trinity crap? I'm not going there. Hen can't even figure that stuff out. Okay, so look, here's my question.

Here's why I've been reading *CC* all these years, I think. What do you do when you feel like Entropy's won? What—"

But he remembers the answer, or an answer. That program. Mom said it talked about mass extinctions on Earth. There've been at least two of them, she said, cataclysms that killed ninety percent of everything alive. But that desolation made room for new forms of life: for complex organisms after the first cataclysm, and for mammals after the second.

"Are you okay?" Amy's peering at him, looking concerned. "Jer? You just stopped talking."

"Fine. I'm fine." But he doesn't think he is. All right, so new life develops, but it takes millions of years. Even if he lives to be older than Mom was when she died, he doesn't have that long.

You're doing *what*?" Veronique says. She knows she's being rude. She doesn't care.

"We're going to Percy Clark's memorial service."

"We?" Rosemary showed up unannounced at the house five minutes ago. The spot checks have gotten worse since the Planet X expedition, even though the police easily found Veronique at the guesthouse and called Rosemary to say she was all right.

She hadn't disappeared. She hadn't even tried to leap across ice floes; no one had needed bloodhounds to find her. She'd left a paper trail a mile wide: credit-card receipts at the Nixon convenience store, at Bruno's—the famous Gerlach diner where she treated herself to dinner—at the guesthouse itself. She wasn't even *trying* to disappear. She was just getting away. The only thing she'd done wrong was not returning Rosie's call, and then turning off her cell phone. Well, all right: two things.

But now Rosemary's become even more intrusive than she was before. It would serve her right if Veronique did disappear. "We who? You and Walter? Is he fit to travel?"

"No, of course not. I meant you and me, and Hen and Tom, and Jeremy. Oh, and Jeremy's girlfriend. Amy."

"Amy?" Veronique squints. "Amy Castillo?"

"I don't know her last name. Tiny, redhead. Cute. She's into that comic book he loves. You know her?"

"She was one of my students last semester. They met in my class." She was one of my students this semester, and saw me fall apart. And she's twenty times smarter than Jeremy is.

Veronique knows better than to say any of this. She wonders what Amy's doing with Jeremy. Pity, maybe. Should she tell Rosemary that Amy saw the incident? No. Too embarrassing, and it would just make Veronique look vulnerable again, which would defeat the entire project of getting Rosemary to treat her like a grown-up.

They're sitting at the kitchen table, where Veronique keeps the Planet X sea-urchin pot as a centerpiece. She picks it up now, cradling it in her lap. It's her reminder that she is in fact an adult who can make her own decisions. "Rosemary, I don't want to go to Seattle. I don't know why in the world Jeremy would want to go either, but that's his business. I'm not an infant, and I'm not in any danger. I wasn't in danger in May, either."

"I think," Rosie said briskly, "that it's important for all of us to go. Percy's family reached out to us. We should reach back."

"Fine. We'll send them a tree."

Rosemary sighs and looks away, out the window. "Will you come to support Jeremy, at least? Or to support me? Vera, *please*."

Vera was Melinda's nickname for her. That's a low blow, but Veronique finds herself responding anyway. She tries to imagine a long car ride with Amy Castillo, and finds herself awash in dread. Dread and mortification. Amy saw her disintegrate into a sodden, shrieking mess. She never wants to see Amy again. What can she say to get out of this?

"If I go," she says, clutching the pot so tightly that later she'll find the pattern of the ceramic pressed into her palms, "I will curse that monster aloud and spit in his coffin. Is that what you want?"

"Hen's spoken to his mother. He's been cremated, so no coffin, only an urn. And Hen has a free place for all of us to stay. Some priest friend of hers up there has a huge house."

Rosie's deliberately misunderstanding her. "I'll curse his parents," Veronique continues, desperate and implacable. "I'll tell them that they must be monsters, to have raised such a child. I'll stand up and scream in the church."

"Hen says that Anna says no one will talk to them. They've been shunned. She might even welcome screaming."

Veronique shakes her head. "I don't care. Percy's parents are not my problem, and I don't want to go." She wouldn't want to go even if Amy were staying here.

Rosie turns back to face her now. Veronique sees that her face is wet with tears, that her hands are clenched as tightly around each other on her lap as Veronique's are clenched on the Planet X pot. When she speaks, though, her voice is still steady. "I'm not treating you like an infant. I'm the infant. Vera, I've lost my husband and one of my best friends, and I can't lose you, too. I know we wouldn't even know each other if it weren't for Melinda, and I know we'll never be as close to each other as either of us was to her, but you're the only other person I know who remembers her the way I do. I know you hate me right now, but will you please, please come to Seattle? For me?"

Veronique blinks. The universe spins, revolves, resettles itself with an almost audible thump. Rosie hasn't been stalking her because she thinks Veronique's needy. It's Rosie who's the needy one. She's just admitted as much.

Vera opens her mouth and then closes it again, riding a sudden rush of feeling. She's so used to people pulling away from her— her students, her colleagues, Sarabeth—that she feels as if she's been given a gift.

Hell of a gift, she thinks. There have to be less annoying ways to be needed. Ways that don't involve student witnesses.

Still.

She eyes Rosemary, noting almost clinically that Rosie's hands are still clenched, while Vera's own have relaxed somewhat. "I'll think about it. I'll let you know in a few days. But only if you promise, from now on, that you'll give me some warning before you show up at the house."

Rosemary is mortified. She's always secretly considered herself saner and stronger than Veronique. Until the scene in Vera's kitchen today, she didn't even know that her own motives were so—childish? Selfish? She doesn't even know what word to use.

Until today, she honestly believed that she was hounding Vera for Vera's own good. She believed that the situation had been created by Vera's weakness, not her own.

No, not weakness. She catches herself; this is a bias she corrects often enough in her ER patients, too many of whom believe that needing anyone else is a personal failing. We all need other people. We're designed to need other people. We're healthiest and happiest around other people.

This isn't just theology. It's science, neurotransmitters and psychology labs. Orphaned monkey babies, given a choice between two kinds of surrogate-mother doll, will pick the one covered in soft terrycloth every time, even when their food's dispensed by the cold wire mother-mannequin.

Mammals need connection. We don't live by monkey chow alone. Rosemary knows that. Shame wraps around her like a shawl anyway.

And she thinks, once again, of Walter. She's been visiting him every week in the nursing home; she's managed to distance the beloved body who lives there from the beloved person who no longer seems to be inside, or who, at any rate, no longer knows her.

Sometimes Walter remembers that she's visited before. Once, gently, he patted her hand and said, "My dear, it's kind of you to come see me, but I don't know if my wife would like it."

Her breath had snagged in her throat. "Does it bother you, that your wife isn't here?"

He'd frowned, and then his features had smoothed again, as if he'd found peace. "No. It's better for her not to come. It would hurt her too much to see me like this. She's too tenderhearted. I never told her, but I think she'd have been happier if she'd been able to hold back more of her heart."

Rosemary had blinked at him, vision swimming. What else hadn't he told her? She briefly entertained the notion of asking him this, but quickly recognized it as both unethical and dangerous. What would she do if she learned something devastating, that he'd had an affair or considered divorce or even simply loathed some piece of her?

No. Let him keep his secrets.

She wonders now, though, if he's ashamed of needing help, of needing the care of the people—women, almost always women— who tend to him every day, and who are strangers almost every time they enter the room.

She'll say good-bye to him before they leave for Seattle. She'll tell him that she won't be there that week, but that she'll be coming back. And she'll hope that, even for a little while, he'll remember that promise.

16

*f*or a year now, Archipelago Osprey has been stalking Comrade
Cosmos, and for a year, he has eluded her. Her initial journey to
Keyhole was delayed by weather, illness—a bout of dysentery from
Dumpster diving—and transportation problems. When she realized that Keyhole was her destination, she ducked into a public
library and used Google Maps to get walking directions from
Wyoming to Kansas. According to Google Maps, the journey should
have taken eight days and eleven hours, although it wasn't clear to
her if this figure included time to sleep, to eat, and to trap crickets.
In any case, it seemed reasonable to expect that she could cover
the distance in a month.

She had no intention of hitchhiking. She wanted to stay alive,
and she wasn't sure that even the intimidating sight of an empire
scorpion would dissuade the kind of creeps who drive around in
trucks looking for female hitchhikers.

From Bumfuck, she walked in what she believed was a south-
easterly direction until she reached the nearest largish town,

where she not only found an army/navy store but managed to shoplift a compass, a Swiss Army knife, a USA road atlas, several rolls of duct tape, and a sturdy pair of boots in her size. Although this remarkable theft was greatly aided by the fact that the store's proprietor was asleep at the time, snoozing behind his counter, Archipelago was still pleased with herself. Her pride lasted about fifteen minutes, until she realized, after scrutinizing the maps and the compass, that she'd been walking northwest, not southeast. She'd actually *increased* the distance between herself and Cosmos. She'd thought she was navigating by the sun. How had she gotten so turned around?

Setting out in the proper direction from Boottown, she skirted around Bumfuck and was making decent progress until the dysentery felled her. In some other horrid little town, she wound up in a small women's homeless shelter, sleeping on a cot and attending mandatory prayer meetings, which seemed a small enough price to pay for clean laundry, showers, and food. She healed and left the shelter, lifting some bottled water, canned meat, and baby wipes on her way out of town.

After that she walked for three days, cheerfully, until horrible blisters developed from the new boots. At that point, Archipelago liberated a girl's bicycle from the front yard of a moderately large home—at night, when everyone was asleep—telling herself that anybody who left a bike lying in the grass deserved to have it stolen.

The bike was only a little small for her. The larger problem was that it had a purple seat, sparkly fringe on the handlebars, and a pink aluminum frame. Either it had been ridden by a teenager who wanted to return to her carefree youth, or a five-year-old with a growth disorder. In any case, the bike would have been too identifiable even had it been Archipelago's style.

She hid out in a small clump of woods and spent a day covering the bike frame and seat with black duct tape. By now, she was adept at cadging food from stores and fast-food places, and almost equally adept at trapping crickets.

Pedaling was easier than walking, except when she had to go uphill, since the bike had no gears. But she was making better time than she had on foot, and developing buns and calves of steel in the meantime, and honing her hatred of Cosmos, who'd ruined her life.

Weirdly, given her odd conveyance and constant petty theft, she managed to steer clear of police. She began to consider herself a gypsy, a vagabond, the last of the hobos, even if she was on a bike and not stealing free rides on boxcars. She almost started to enjoy herself.

The night she crossed the Kansas border, she celebrated with a chocolate bar she'd stolen miles back and saved for just this occasion. Erasmus got the last of the mineral powder on a free-range cricket she'd snagged for him at dusk. "Soon," she told him. "Soon we'll find our enemy, and you'll get to sting him, and we'll see if *he's* allergic. Erasmus, I think my hatred of the Mayor is really what ramped up that sting, which means that if you sting Cosmos, he should drop dead instantly. Or not. But anyway, that's the plan, and, uh, after that happens, I'll paint houses again, and get another apartment, and you can have more mineral powder."

Truth to tell, she hadn't given much thought to what would happen after she found Cosmos. The epic journey to find him was her end-all and be-all. Cosmos was her white whale.

It was cloudy and windy, threatening rain. She hid the bike in some bushes and scouted for a dry space nearby, rolling herself up in a tarp she'd acquired along the way. She woke, some hours later, to the sound of a freight train.

Train? She hadn't seen tracks near here. She staggered to her feet, noting sluggishly that it was dawn, or would have been without so many clouds. The air was thick and green, diseased. She peered in the direction of the train sound, and saw swirling against the darkness a darker funnel.

Oh, *fuck.* "Erasmus, we're in fucking Kansas," she snarled aloud.

"Shit." What was she going to do? Weren't you supposed to find a bomb shelter or hide under a bed or something in a tornado? But she was outside. Could she dig a hole to hide in?

Not in the time she had, no. Panicking, she threw herself into a ditch, hugging the backpack with Erasmus in it to her chest. She squeezed her eyes shut and curled into a fetal position. If she died, who'd feed Erasmus? If Erasmus died, how would she get her revenge on Cosmos?

Neither of them died, but the tornado passed within yards of them, and when Archipelago emerged wild-eyed and shaking from the ditch, she saw only dirt where she'd hidden the bike. There'd been bushes there. Now there was nothing. The spot had been scoured. Her bike had either been transported to Oz or was scattered in shiny duct-taped bits all over the county.

Archipelago took a deep breath. All right. She'd walked before; she could walk again. Her feet were a lot tougher now. And, she realized, Cosmos would surely be at the scene of the storm destruction. Her heart lifted. As terrifying as the tornado had been, it might make her job simpler. She smiled, and began to follow the path of wreckage the storm had left.

For the next nine issues, though, wherever she showed up, Cosmos had just left. He'd already arrived at the town she found wrecked by the tornado, and he'd also already departed to go back home. When she found her way to Keyhole and knocked on his door, the aide hired to care for Charlie and Vanessa told her that Mr. Cosmos had just left to fly to California, where there'd been some mighty bad wildfires. Would she care to leave a message?

She wouldn't. She couldn't get to California, either. She hunkered down in the countryside outside Keyhole, waiting for Cosmos to come home, but every time she thought she was ready to pounce, something happened. Her pack, with Erasmus in it, was stolen by a biker gang, and she had to stage a hair-raising rescue operation, and when she had her friend back, Cosmos was gone again. She sprained her ankle running after a cricket, and had to spend a week in her increasingly cozy woodland camp with her foot elevated. She had Cosmos in her crosshairs in the parking lot of a supermarket and was ready to stroll up behind him with her venom-tipped dart when a woman with a cart full of potato chips and children got between them for just long enough for Cosmos, clueless, to attain the safety of his car.

Archipelago didn't allow herself to become discouraged, but she did begin entertaining conspiracy theories. "Fucking Entropy's *helping* him," she told Erasmus. "Gotta be. Every time I get close, some little piece of chaos interferes. The bad guy has his back. How twisted is *that*?"

Maybe she should have been nicer to EE back in the alley in Bumfuck. She'd flipped him the bird, metaphorically speaking, and he was showing her who was boss.

And of course, the moment she thought this, he appeared: darkness visible, galaxies streaming into space, depth, and vastness. The tornado had been a lot scarier. Once, she would have said as much, but if her conspiracy theory was right, she couldn't afford to piss the thing off.

"Oh, all *right*," she said, glowering up at him. "You win. You da man. I'm in your camp, yessirree bob. You can have my soul or my heart or my firstborn child or any other damn thing, except Erasmus, okay? What'll it be?"

His voice was a distant booming, thunder and theatrics and the threat of bombs. "All I require, daughter, is your acceptance of my sovereignty."

"Yeah, fine. Is that all? You got it. So listen, can I get a little *help* here?"

In answer, a wind swept through Archipelago's camp, a breeze stiff enough to blow dirt into her face and force her to close her eyes to protect them from debris. She felt something blow against her skin, flattening itself against her neck. When the wind died down enough for her to open her eyes, she peeled the thing away and discovered that it was a photocopied flyer.

Rock, Paper, Scissors Tourney, the paper read. It was in the next county over, not far at all. Next month, which would give her time to get there. And the toastmaster was none other than Comrade Cosmos.

17

*t*he last time Rosemary was in Seattle, it was to board the cruise ship headed for Alaska. As far as she knows, that's the last time Veronique was in Seattle, too.

They were there with Melinda. And Walter. The four of them flew up, back in the days when flying was still fun, when you didn't have to get to the airport two hours early and take your shoes off in front of strangers, back when planes had leg room and airlines served real food. Rosemary seems to remember that there was free wine, even, but perhaps her nostalgia's casting an overly rosy glow over the memories. And flying didn't cost a fortune back then, either; there were inexpensive commuter tickets even at the last minute, and no charges for luggage.

Rosemary and Walter often reminisced about that trip, when he could still remember anything. She wonders what Melinda told Jeremy about it.

She's pretty sure that Jeremy's never been to Seattle. He and Amy are poring over a guidebook in the backseat of the van. It's a shiny rental van reeking of New Car, a scent Rosemary has never liked, but one she hears the rental agencies dispense from spray cans into the innards of every vehicle, old or new. Hen's driving, with Tom riding shotgun.

"I'm so psyched about the science-fiction museum!" Amy says happily. The child speaks exclusively in exclamation marks; just listening to her makes Rosemary feel old and tired. "Can we go twice? Once for the CC exhibit and once to see everything else?"

"I dunno, Amy." Jeremy sounds as sick of this drive as Rosemary feels. Flying to Seattle is so much easier. "We're going there for a funeral. We have to see what happens."

"Yeah, sure, I'm sorry." Although Amy's sitting behind Rosemary, Rosemary can hear the blush in her voice. "I didn't mean to be insensitive. It was awfully nice of Mrs. Clark to say we could come."

Rosemary's curious to meet this woman, so trusting of strangers who have every reason to hate her dead son. "No reporters," Hen said. "That was her only stipulation. She doesn't want this to turn into a media circus." If Vera had her way, Rosemary knows, they'd show up with a full press corps and a mob of strangers hurling eggs, tomatoes, and curses at Percy's urn, if not at Percy's parents.

The funeral's on Saturday, but they won't drive back until Monday. Jeremy's taken a week's vacation from the café, and Hen's arranged for an associate priest to preach and celebrate the Eucharist on Sunday. When Veronique fretted about paying a professional pet-sitter to feed her cats, Rosemary got one of the youth group kids to do it. She's paying him, although she hasn't told Vera that.

Airfare for all of them would have been prohibitive even with plenty of notice, so Hen, Tom, and Rosemary chipped in to rent the minivan. Veronique refused. "I only agreed to this damn fool trip because you insisted, Rosemary. If you can't afford to pay my way, I'm not going." Rosemary's chosen not to tell anyone else about that.

Veronique did pay for their first gas stop, though; maybe it's her way of apologizing.

Hen limited everyone to one suitcase and a small personal item. "Like airline carry-on," she told them. Well, Rosemary thought, at least we don't have to go through an X-ray machine and take our shoes off to get into the van.

Amy responded to the limitation with typical exuberance. "Cool! It's like *Survivor*! We only get one luxury item!" Her luxury item is her laptop, although Hen could have allowed her two: improbably, given her age and gender, her other piece of luggage is a small rucksack.

Driving's less expensive than flying, but only marginally more comfortable, and it takes a lot longer. They've been on the road for four and a half hours, passing up and down darkly furred slopes bordered with wildflowers. The van's flickered through sunlight and shade, an alternation that should be pleasant, but instead has given Rosemary a headache. They've just stopped in Klamath Falls for lunch, piling with groans out of the van. Rosemary's amazed she managed to hold her bladder for that long, although everyone else in the van makes a beeline for the restrooms, too.

Rosemary hates highway rest stops. Like airports, they're all alike: bright lighting and shiny tile, anonymous and depressing despite cheerful displays of artwork or tourist information. The people there always seem distracted, their minds already on wherever they're going next. Time on the road is lost time, a waste of a commodity already infinitely precious. Whoever said that the point was the journey and not the destination wasn't taking planes or driving on highways.

They have eight more hours to go. After they all pee, Tom will replace Hen in the driver's seat. In another four hours, roughly, she'll take it back again, and finish the trip. They'll stop overnight in Portland if they have to, but Hen wants to do the trip in one day, both to save money and to give them more time in Seattle itself.

Greg, Hen's seminary buddy in Seattle, has invited all of them to stay at his house. He has in-law quarters originally built for a recently deceased mother-in-law, three extra bedrooms—two belonging to children away at college, one a dedicated guest room—a living room and family room, both with sleeper couches, and a finished basement. Hen, Tom, Jeremy, and Amy have brought sleeping bags. "Oh, we'll work it out," Hen said cheerfully of the sleeping arrangements.

Rosemary wonders how a priest can afford a house that size in Seattle. It's like those TV shows where New York City editorial assistants live in Park Avenue penthouse apartments. Well, maybe he inherited money, or married it.

Dibs on the in-law quarters, Rosemary thinks. She hasn't said it yet. She knows that Vera probably wants them, too. Maybe she and Vera can share them, although at this point, Vera would rebel against that. Once it might have seemed like a slumber party; now, even after Rosemary's confession, Vera's likely to believe that she's under surveillance.

Jeremy hates riding in backseats; they make him claustrophobic. He knows the others would let him sit in front if he asked, and maybe he will at the next stop, but back here, at least he can sit with Amy, who wouldn't be making the trip if it weren't for him. And right now, he couldn't move if he wanted to. Amy's dozing, her head pillowed against his shoulder, which has gone to sleep in apparent sympathy. He likes Amy a lot, but this isn't helping his claustrophobia any.

"Jeremy," VB says, "you doing okay back there?"

"Sure." She's been extra solicitous the whole trip, as if she's trying to take care of him. He doesn't even know why she's here. She's told everybody often enough that she has no sympathy for Percy or his family. There's a weird vibe between her and Aunt Rosie, and he wonders if Rosie somehow made VB come to keep tabs on her. He can't imagine VB doing anything she doesn't want to, though, and he doesn't know how Rosie could force her.

He still doesn't like VB, but he has to hand it to her for pulling off that Planet X caper. The potter told Jeremy about that when he and Rosie showed up to check on her: how when the police arrived at the guesthouse, VB came to the door wrapped in a blanket and informed them regally that she was fine, thank you, and that Rosemary Watkins should mind her own damn business. VB sent the two of them away, too, just as Jeremy had predicted. Good for her.

This new VB, the one who speaks her mind even when other people don't like it, is a lot more interesting than the old one, who just sat and glared at you like she had a stick up her ass. The old VB always made Jeremy feel like he'd done something wrong that she wasn't going to tell him about, just to make him feel stupid for not already knowing it. Now she lets people know what's bothering her. She shouldn't have lost it in class like that, but Jeremy still respects her a lot more than he used to.

"All right," she says. "But listen, Jeremy, if you decide you don't want to go to the funeral, you don't have to. I'm not going, that's for sure. We can sit it out together."

"If I change my mind, I'll let you know. I don't think I will." He wants to go. He needs some sense of Percy beyond what they've all seen in the papers: the handsome, smiling photos, the popular and privileged honors student who somehow stumbled sideways into insanity. Jeremy thinks he'd go crazy if he didn't know who killed Mom, because he'd keep imagining different people, keep wondering if anyone he passed on the street could be the murderer. Having a name is a relief. Now he wants more than that. He wants—

He doesn't know what he wants, exactly, except that he's pretty sure it isn't revenge, which wouldn't work anyway, because Percy's already dead. He isn't glad that Percy's dead, exactly, not that he's sorry either. He doesn't know what he feels. Everything about

Percy evokes a numb horror in him, and the numbness is threatening to spread out and infect the rest of his life, as if EE has injected some mad-scientist virus into his bloodstream. He wants to go to the funeral to meet people who aren't numb about Percy. He wants to plug Percy into some earth-normal context: family, friends.

He doesn't know if this is the right thing to do. He can't be sure he won't start screaming halfway through the service, although he's made a promise to himself that he'll leave instead of making a scene. He doesn't need to pull a VB.

Looking down, he realizes that he has a more immediate problem. Amy's begun to snore softly, and a shining slug's trail of saliva descends from her lower lip onto his T-shirt. If he wakes her up to tell her she's drooling, she'll be embarrassed. If he doesn't wake her up, she'll be more embarrassed when she finally wakes up on her own, and he'll be wetter. He shifts to get more comfortable, hoping the movement will waken her. It doesn't.

Stuck, Jeremy thinks, and for the first time in weeks feels an overpowering urge to cry. Crazy, he thinks, blinking back a tsunami. After everything else, why should this trigger tears?

And then he remembers. When he was still very small, five or six maybe, his mother took him to a small zoo north of Reno, a place that nursed injured wildlife back to health and kept the animals if they weren't fit or strong enough to be released back into the wild. There were coyotes there, and once a month in warm weather, the zoo welcomed guests after dark for a coyote howl. When the coyotes howled, the humans howled along with them. Melinda brought Jeremy, bundled in a fleece jacket against the chill of the desert evening, cool even in summer. For once, he was alone with Mom: neither of the auntie-grannies came. He'd been anticipating the event for what felt like forever, although she'd probably only told him about it the day before. Being alone with his mom made him feel like a big boy.

Howling was fun for a little while, but then he fell asleep. When he woke up, his mother was carrying him back to the car, and his face was stuck to her shirt in a puddle of drool. He can still feel the ripping sensation against his skin as he lifted his head.

"Want to howl more," he said.

"I'm sorry, sweetie. It's over. No more howling tonight."

"But they're still howling!" Behind him, the wavering song of the coyotes was already fading, mournful and haunting.

"Yes, they are, but they're howling by themselves now. The people, like us, have to go home and go to bed."

"They sound lonely, Mommy."

"They aren't lonely, Jer. They have each other. They're singing together."

"They sound sad. They sound like they're crying. Maybe they miss their mommies." The naturalist who led the howl had explained that these coyotes had been taken in as pups after someone killed their mother.

"They have a safe home," Melinda said firmly, giving Jeremy a squeeze, "and I'm right here." Had her voice truly caught, or is he just inventing that now, knowing what he knows now that he's older? His birthmother, the one in Guatemala who's dead, whom he'll never be able to remember. Had Mom been thinking about her? How could she not have been?

"I want to help them howl."

"We'll come back sometime, I promise. I didn't know you were so tired!"

They never went back. The promised expedition was put off in favor of other outings—movies, trips to Lake Tahoe, swimming lessons—and finally forgotten altogether. Jeremy hasn't thought about the incident in years, hadn't even known he remembered it. His cheeks are slick. He lifts his free arm to dry his face, and Amy stirs.

"Are we there yet?"

"Nope. Hours to go. I was just shifting. Go back to sleep."

"Unh." She lifts her head—does he hear a faint ripping sound?—and says, "Oh, God, Jeremy, I drooled all over you! Crap!"

"It's okay."

He hears a sigh and sees VB bend in front of them, hears her rummaging through the overstuffed Lands' End canvas tote she brought as her luxury item. After a minute, she passes back a pale, moist rectangle. Amy takes it.

"Baby wipe," VB says briskly. "I figured they might come in handy. There you go, kids. Don't say I never gave you anything."

Jeremy hoots. "Like Archipelago with her baby wipes!" Come to think of it, Archipelago and VB have somewhat similar personalities, although VB has cats, not a scorpion.

VB gives him a blank look, but he knows Amy will understand the reference. She doesn't say anything, though. She's scrubbing at his shirt. The wipe smells like baby powder, a scent Jeremy has always found nauseating; he feels his nose wrinkling. "Aim, it's okay. You can leave it, really."

"Jeremy?" VB says. "What's wrong?"

He closes his eyes, willing them to stop leaking. The walk to the car, coyotes mourning behind them, the faintly shining slug-trail of Jeremy's spit on his mother's shirt. Small as he was, he tried to wipe it with his hand, and Mom laughed. "It's okay, Jer. I'll put it in the laundry when we get home. But that's nice of you, to try to clean it for me."

He was so upset. He started crying again. Melinda thought he was tired, but Jeremy, remembering the story after so many years, thinks that was only part of it. He was grieving for and with the motherless coyotes, and he was grieving because he'd wasted in sleep some of this precious time alone with his mother, away from the other women with their constant chatter.

He's the only person in the car who remembers the coyotes. He understands for the first time that the auntie-grannies are a memory bank: so much of his life has happened with one or more of them there. He's always resented that, but now it means that some of Melinda is preserved outside of him, that other people can bear the burden of memory for him. The coyotes, though, are his alone.

What would it be like not to be able to remember? What would it be like to be Walter?

He squints, blinks. "Memory," he said, and nudges Amy with his elbow. "Hey, Amy, that's the third element! In the game. Order. Entropy. Memory."

She frowns, chewing her lower lip in a way he's come to see as charming. "Yeah? I'm not sure I follow."

"I'm not sure I do, either, exactly. Okay: Order trumps Entropy and Entropy destroys Order—"

"That's your seesaw."

"Yeah. That's the seesaw. But Memory: that's what lets us rebuild." He blinks, his lashes still wet, sticky now, like his face against his mother's clothing or Amy's against his own. "It feels right. I can't explain it yet, but I think it's right."

Amy squirms and brings her knees up onto the seat so she can hug them. It's her thinking position. VB and Rosie both half-turn, now. Rosie says, "What's this, kids?"

"Um," Jeremy says, balking. It seems too complicated to explain to the auntie-grannies. But when Amy gives them a quick summary, both Rosie and VB seem to understand what they're talking about. Well, sure. VB's a professor, isn't she? And Rosie's probably thought about memory a lot, because of what's happened to Uncle Walter.

Trees whoosh past outside. The two women are quiet for a moment, thinking. VB has the furrow between her eyes she gets during class when she's trying to teach something difficult, which means at least she's taking this seriously. "Memory tips the seesaw," she says after a second, and Rosie gives a soft grunt of approval.

"Right. That's it, Vera."

Amy's nodding now, although Jeremy hasn't gotten it yet. "What?"

Amy laughs. "Order trumps Entropy and Entropy destroys Order. That's the seesaw, evenly balanced. But memory's what people use to restore order, because they remember how things are supposed to be. So memory's CC's secret weapon."

"Memory and hope," Rosie says, "because sometimes people build things that haven't existed before. Memory, hope, imagination. Your CC has a lot of secret weapons."

"Entropy's outgunned," Amy says, sounding almost giddy. "EE's *toast*, J."

He looks out the window, at the passing trees. What he remembers most clearly now, what he'll never be able to forget, is that his mother is dead, murdered. "Memory fuels revenge, too," he says.

"Anything can be misused," Aunt Rosie tells him. She reaches across the top of the seat between them to squeeze his hand. Her fingers are cool and very soft. "And entropy—time—it softens memory and makes it easier to bear. Maybe only a little bit, but still. We find out we can still breathe. That's something."

On the Alaska cruise, Melinda is restless, distracted. She's just started the process of trying to adopt, and every time she sees a child on board, she stares: smitten or alarmed, the others can't quite tell, but anyway fascinated.

"Mel," Rosemary says over dinner one evening, when Melinda keeps craning her head to peer at two twin toddler girls—who brings kids that small on cruises, anyway?—"you have to stop ogling kids. You're going to scare their parents."

"Sorry." Melinda reddens and turns to face the others again. "I'm being goofy, I know."

"You're being creepy," Veronique says, and Melinda rolls her eyes.

"None of us has kids. Doesn't that seem weird to you?"

"No," says Veronique. "Lots of people don't have kids. It's something we have in common, that's all."

Melinda bites into her roll. "But why? Did all of you want to be childless? I mean, okay, I know it's none of my business, and I guess I'm turning into one of those horrible people who act like anyone who doesn't have kids is a mutant who deserves to be interrogated about it in public, but—"

"Mel," Walter says mildly. "We're friends. It's okay." He glances at Rosemary, who shrugs.

"I don't mind talking about it. We tried. It didn't work. We didn't feel strongly enough about it to adopt. A kid would have made our lives too complicated." She shakes her head. "Our parents were upset. They wanted grandchildren. My mother gave me a lecture about how selfish I was being, only living for myself. On the other hand, my mother's most of the reason I spent twenty years in therapy, so I took anything she said with a grain of salt."

"And we'll all help you," Walter says, smiling. "So, see? We're all having a kid after all."

Veronique snorts. "Well, fine. But I don't like children. Oh, don't stare at me like that! I'm sure I'll like yours, Mel. I like the idea of them well enough, and I know they're important, but in practice they're loud and annoying. I wouldn't have patience with a child."

Melinda squints. "Vera, you *teach*."

"College students. Who technically aren't kids anymore, although sometimes I wonder, but even when they act like children, they're children who can dress and feed and bathe themselves. I'm not responsible for their welfare. I'm just responsible for trying to teach them to think, which Lord knows is difficult enough."

Someone at the next table yells, pointing out the window. "Whale! Whale! I just saw a breach!" Everyone in the dining room leaps from their seats, abandoning tableware and cutlery in a loud clanking rush to press against the windows, even though—as the ship's naturalist explained to cruisers gawking on the deck that afternoon—breaching means that the whale has dived, and might not resurface for a long time.

While everyone else peers through the window, pointing

hopefully at any splash or ripple on the water, Melinda sneaks a furtive glance at the twin girls, sitting piggyback on their parents' shoulders so they can see over the crowd. One child gazes out the window with everyone else, asking in a piercing whine, "Where whale?" The other, oblivious, happily plays with her mother's barrette. She isn't loud or annoying at all.

*t*he in-law quarters are small, but they have their own bathroom and even a tiny kitchenette. The most important factor, though, is a door. Veronique closes it to block out the din from the others. Too much chatter. Since the meltdown, she's lost whatever tolerance for strangers she had. She knows it's lovely of this priest—Greg, that's his name, Hen's friend—to put them all up, but her head's still buzzing from the road. All she wants to do is nap.

They got here an hour ago. It's a large, airy house, and Greg and his wife Linda had dinner waiting for them, a buffet with salad, lasagna in a warming pan, mixed vegetables, garlic bread, cookies. Iced tea, lemonade, soda. Veronique thought that eating real food in a stationary chair would make her feel better, ground her again, but it didn't work. Hen and Rosie promptly got into church gossip with Greg and Linda while Jeremy and Amy chattered about the museum they want to see.

Veronique couldn't follow any of the conversations, but they weren't meant to include her, anyway. She sat and ate her lasagna, feeling like the kid without friends in the junior high cafeteria. Then she got up and started browsing the bookshelves, which contain a pretty respectable selection of literary fiction and chewy theological tomes. The others were still eating, still chattering. Although she knew it was childish, she found herself wishing they'd notice her absence and call her back to the table. They didn't, of course.

So she excused herself, pleading headache. She'd ruthlessly claimed the in-law quarters the moment they got there, although she could tell Rosie wanted them. Tough. Rosie dragged her along on this ridiculous expedition. Veronique's the one who doesn't want to be here, which in her mind entitles her to extra consideration. Rosie can have the guest bedroom, even if it means she'll have to share a bathroom.

Veronique opens her suitcase—Tom carried it in her for her—and extracts a light sweater. She's chilly, even though it's summer. She misses her Planet X pot, its weight and solidity, the fierceness of its uncompromising ridges against her skin. She wishes she'd brought it as her one luxury item. She could have packed it in a box with foam peanuts, or just held it unprotected on her lap. She suspects it's stronger than she is right now, and it's a link to home, to Melinda.

The luxury item she did bring was her own pillow, now on the bed with the suitcase. It has cat hair on it. Everything in Veronique's house has cat hair on it. Greg's in-law quarters will now have cat hair, too. She supposes she should warn him, in case anyone else likely to stay here is allergic, but she'll do that later, or tomorrow, or before she leaves. She's too tired now. And, anyway, the entire house is immaculate, which means that Greg and his wife either clean like crazy or, more likely, pay someone else to do it. The cat hair will be history.

Veronique drags her suitcase off the bed—light as it is, it hits the carpet with an audible thump—and lies down, hugging her pillow. The bed's comfortable, a really good mattress, not one of those saggy sofa cushion things. She feels herself relaxing for the first time since leaving Reno.

Tomorrow the others will do their sightseeing, since they've arrived a day earlier than Hen thought they might. Veronique doesn't know what she'll do. Maybe she'll go shopping and try to find another pot. Right now, though, she needs to sleep.

*Y*ou need to get some rest," William says.

"After the service." Anna just blew up at the caterers over the price of salmon canapés. She knows she's being unreasonable. She doesn't care. She's been using this company for years; they always cater the gallery openings. The last time Anna worked with them, the salmon canapés were reasonable. Now they're outrageous, and Anna suspects the caterers don't want to be associated with Percy's memorial service. She thinks they're trying to get fired. She thinks they could at least have been nicer about the price of the canapés. This is her son's funeral.

Is she being paranoid? She doesn't care about that, either.

Standing in the kitchen, looking out at the deck, she rubs her forehead irritably. A few months ago, she craved sunlight. Now it's making her eyes hurt, and she yearns for clouds.

"If you act like that at the service, no one will stay." William's voice is bland, but kind enough; she gives him a sharp look anyway. He's been completely silent on the subject of the memorial, giving her total creative control, and this is the first hint she's gotten that he may share her anxiety about the social aspects of the event, about the importance of the service as a way to restore or maintain their reputation in the community. This is, Anna knows, a completely selfish motivation, but right now she feels entitled to behave selfishly.

It's not like it matters. Nobody's going to come, except immediate family and the people from Reno. Anna's anxious to meet them, but they can't help with the local situation, and they can't eat more than a bit of the food she's ordered. Most of the salmon canapés will go uneaten. The flowers will wilt and die. The family reputation will remain ruined.

Entropy will conquer all.

"Take an Ambien," William says. Some small part of her brain knows he's right; she hasn't slept for two days.

"I'm afraid of Ambien." She's begun to have obsessive dreams about Clarke Beach, dreams in which she's the one wading into the water, Bart straining against his lead to try to save her. "People sleepwalk on that stuff. They open the fridge and eat everything inside, and then get into the car and drive to the supermarket and buy every pint of ice cream in the place."

William lets out a long, dramatic sigh. He's mocking her. "Okay, so take a Valium. Drink some scotch. Jesus, Anna! This thing was your idea, and it's too late to cancel now."

"I don't want to cancel."

"Then try to hold it together, all right?"

She walks to the kitchen table and sits down. She knows she needs to sleep, but she isn't tired. She's never felt less sleepy in her life. There's too much to do. This is too important.

"What are we going to do with Percy's ashes? Afterwards? We haven't talked about that."

"I have no idea. Let's talk about it then."

"Do you have any ideas? I thought maybe the Cascades—"

"I said let's talk about it then." William's voice has gone quiet with warning. "After the memorial, all right? One thing at a time."

She swallows bile. "He's your son."

"Do you think I don't know that?"

Anna puts her hands flat on the table and presses, as if this will keep her voice from rising to a shriek. "Don't you care?"

"About his ashes?" William's standing in the kitchen doorway, his face a mask of controlled fury. "No. I don't care about his ashes. His ashes are dirt. They aren't him. They don't mean anything. I cared about him when he was alive. If he were still alive, in prison, I'd be doing everything I could to help him, whatever horrors he committed. He was my son. But he's not alive. He's gone. The ashes don't matter."

She swallows again. "Do you care about the memorial?"

"It's the right thing to do."

Which doesn't answer the question. She closes her eyes and sees Percy with Bart, sees Percy helping her over the tree roots. Images from photos. It occurs to her that of all the photos she's looked at, she's found none of the three of them together. William doesn't approve of family portraits. He thinks they're tacky. She believes his parents may have, must have, some photos of all three of them, but they haven't given her copies.

Marjorie and David will be arriving at Sea-Tac in a few hours. If Anna had thought of this earlier, she'd have called and asked. It's too late now. What they've brought with them is fixed now, unalterable, unless a neighbor could FedEx—

No. Too complicated. And maybe not important.

The last time she was at the airport was to pick up Percy. When he came home from Mexico.

Anna takes a breath, feels a shiver of premonition down her back. When she speaks, she hears her voice break. "William. Do you care about me?"

If this were a movie, a book, a graphic novel, even, he'd come and knead the knotted muscles in her neck, speak loving words of reassurance, promise her that together, they'll get through this. But they're in real life, in uncharted territory.

"Anna, please." His own voice is frayed now. "I'm almost as tired as you are. Can't we talk about all this after the service?"

He doesn't wait for her answer. He turns, whistling for the dog, the old escape route. She hears the rattle of the leash, hears the front door open and close. He could so easily have said, "Of course I do," even if he didn't mean it, even if she wouldn't have believed it. How hard would it have been for him to mouth any of the conventional phrases, to say the Right Things? How hard would it have been for him to throw her the smallest of bones?

Too hard, apparently. She can't imagine what all of this is like for him: can't even begin to, because he hasn't told her, hasn't let her in. She realizes with a sliding sensation in her bones that her marriage is over, another casualty of Percy's violence. It's been over for months, maybe even since before Melinda Soto died, but that brutality broke it irrevocably, and made the wreckage visible.

For a moment rage sweeps through her. If only Percy hadn't

gone to the bar that evening. If only he hadn't met Melinda Soto. If only he hadn't lost his mind. If if if.

But he did.

July 24 will be his twenty-third birthday. That morning, she decides, she'll get up and have a private birthday moment, before the fiasco of the memorial service. She'll take her coffee and a bran muffin out onto the deck, and she'll put a candle in the bran muffin, and she'll sing "Happy Birthday." Not to the killer, no. To the sweet child she knew before that, the sweet child Percy would somehow still have been, or could have become again, if he were still alive now.

The rage is gone, and for the first time in days, she feels bone-heavy fatigue, aches with it. William's right; she needs sleep. She doesn't think she'll have to take drugs to achieve it.

18

the Rock, Paper, Scissors Tourney is being held in a large, pseudo-elegant Hyatt where Archipelago feels as out of place as she would in Buckingham Palace. The place is clean and shiny. She's neither. She assiduously and regularly washes herself with baby wipes; for this occasion, she even sneaked into a gas-station bathroom to apply some shoplifted sample-size shampoo to her hair. She's wearing her least grungy jeans, a new-to-her black pair she lifted from a thrift store a few months ago. Even with all that, she can't pass here. She tries, ambling through the lobby to the conference registration area, until she notices two things at once: a matron to her left moving away from her, nose wrinkled, and a security guard to her right moving toward her, jaw set.

She skedaddles. This is too important. She has to do it right, and she can't afford to risk getting eighty-sixed from the place before she's even seen Cosmos. "Don't do this to me," she mutters aloud to the Emperor. "You're supposed to be helping me now, remember?"

But the mess that's complicating her position is hers, not the Emperor's or anyone else's. She acknowledges the justice of the situation—of *course* the Hyatt doesn't want the Wild Woman of the Midwest dropping dirt all over its carpets—even as she manages to snag, from a table in the lobby, a conference schedule someone left there.

Then she's outside, plotting her next move. Her best chance of getting close to Cosmos is probably the banquet, and that's to-morrow night. The ticket's a whopping fifty bucks, which would ordinarily seem preposterous since she has only one hundred left. On the other hand, this is a special occasion. She grits her teeth and resolves to spend the money. But first she has to get presentable, which means somehow finding something appropriate to wear to a banquet. She strongly suspects this won't be Buckingham Palace territory—she's in geekland, not high society—but she still needs to move a step or ten up from her usual attire.

She's brought everything important with her: the money, Erasmus, a few crickets. She calculates. She has to wash up, or no place will have her. Down the road from the fancy Hyatt, she finds a no-tell motel where twenty dollars gets her a room for an hour. The clerk wrinkles his nose at her, but doesn't otherwise comment. She doesn't have to sign anything. She doesn't need to proffer a credit card. Thank God for the underworld.

The room, entirely too reminiscent of the Motel 6 that started all this, is small and smelly and dark, beset by disquieting noises from either side. Archipelago runs hot water to kill the cock-roaches in the tub—she should catch them for Erasmus, but she's short on time—and then starts up the shower. Killing the cock-roaches seems to have killed the hot water, too, so Archipelago shivers and shakes through an icy shower. Refreshing, she tells herself, teeth chattering. It's refreshing. She scrubs her hair with the remaining shampoo, applies a dollop of stolen conditioner, and rakes at her skin with a tiny bar of hotel soap she acquired some-where or other.

Afterward, she actually feels better. She dresses, leaves, and finds a thrift store. Inside, she walks up to the counter—none of her usual scuttling through back aisles—and pulls out another twenty dollars as the sales clerk squints at her. "This is what I have to spend. I need some new clothing. Something, well, something a little nice. I have a job interview next week. Can you help me?"

The clerk's face softens. "Bless you, honey. Let's see what we can do." She's old enough to be somebody's grandmother, although not Archipelago's. "A job interview: that's a big deal. What kind of job?"

"Office," Archipelago says, the lie catching in her throat despite all the dishonesties she's been committing for months now. "Filing." She's praying the woman won't ask her where. "I haven't worked in a long time."

"Lot of people in that position, but you got an interview. Good for you. I'm Lucy."

"Ethel," Archipelago says, because she doesn't dare use her real name, and then she thinks, *oh, shit, she'll think I'm making fun of her, fuck.* Archipelago only knows about *I Love Lucy* from a class in pop culture she took in her one semester at community college, but Lucy's old enough to have watched the show. Fuck.

But Lucy just laughs. "Ethel? Really?

Archipelago's spine goes limp with relief. "Ethel Rose. Really."

"That's pretty. Okay, Ethel Rose, let's see what we've got. You're a tiny little thing. That's good: more in the small sizes." Lucy herself isn't small, but she flips efficiently through the racks, picking out items, and then shepherds Archipelago through the process of trying everything on.

Lucy initially chose an armful of skirts, but when she sees Archipelago's bare legs, as densely furred as any lumberjack's, she purses her lips. "Y'know, I don't enjoy shaving myself, and it shouldn't make a difference, but in a job interview you don't want to take any risks. Why don't we try some slacks?"

"Fine with me," Archipelago says weakly. She stays in the dressing room while Lucy, rummaging through another rack, shoots out questions. Does Ethel Rose have a real purse, or only that knapsack? How's she set for shoes? How does she feel about some simple jewelry, or maybe a scarf?

Only the knapsack, alas, and only boots, and Ethel Rose will trust Lucy on the accessories, but are there any biggish purses? Because, uh, well, a little clutch wouldn't look too professional, would it?

"I have just the thing!" Lucy crows. She reappears in the dressing room with a pair of pinstripe slacks, a tasteful white blouse— "If I wore that, honey, tomato sauce would travel from other states to land on the collar, but I think you can carry it off"—a vinyl briefcase that might pass for leather at five hundred feet, and a pair of black pumps. "I'm worried about the shoes. I think the rest of this will fit you, though."

"All I have is twenty bucks," Archipelago says.

"I know. Don't worry. You just try all that on. Ooops, forgot the scarf!"

Archipelago tries on the outfit, which, for a wonder, fits perfectly. The shoes are a little big, but she can stuff toilet paper into the toes or something, and Erasmus's jar will fit into the tacky briefcase. She steps out of the dressing room, and Lucy beams approval. "That's great! You look terrific! Here, just one more thing." She waves a burgundy scarf and fastens it with a shiny silver-plated scarf pin around Archipelago's neck. "*Very* nice!"

"Thank you," Archipelago says. "But how much—"

"Twenty dollars for the lot," Lucy says. "Don't give me that look. You go out and get that job, Ethel Rose."

Archipelago changes back into her grungies while Lucy packs the new outfit into a shopping bag. Then it's outside again. Time to plan next steps.

Archipelago scopes out a place to camp tonight, a grassy abandoned lot with a disintegrating shed that will at least partially shield her from prying eyes. Sitting cross-legged in this rickety shelter, she scans the schedule. The banquet's at seven tomorrow, with a cocktail hour at six. All right. She'll get there at six forty-five, when banquet seating has already started but when she should have enough time to get a sense of the room. Unless, of course, Cosmos attends the cocktail hour. In that case she'll be able to sting him right then.

She hopes the banquet tickets won't be sold out, but she can't risk showing up at the hotel too many times and being IDed by those pesky security guards. *Entropy, help me,* she thinks, and hears a rush of wind somewhere far off in response. Okay, then.

This is, she knows, a suicide mission. She won't be able to get out of the hotel the way she got away from the grandstand. She'll be arrested. As she thinks this, she realizes that it's a relief. She's tired of hiding, tired of stealing, tired of living out in the weather. After she buys her banquet ticket, she'll only have ten dollars left. Jail won't be fun, but it will be dry, and there will be food there.

But what about Erasmus? He hasn't consented to be used as a weapon, and they won't let her keep him in jail.

Is there a zoo in these parts? Or even a good pet store? She could milk Erasmus for his venom and then leave him with a note and some crickets on the threshold of someplace where he'll be cared for. Like a baby in a basket. She feels a tear rolling down her cheek. Does she even trust anyone else to take care of him? But she has to. And he deserves a better life than she's been giving him lately. Emperor scorpions live eight years; she's had him seven. He's an old man, not a baby at all. Let him retire in comfort.

A little wobbly in the knees—that's hunger, she tells herself fiercely, not sentiment—she stands up and hefts her backpack. She'll leave the Lucy-stuff here. She passed a library, and they'll have computers. She can Google places that might take in Erasmus. A Humane Society, even? But they're connected to Animal Control, which means law enforcement, and she doesn't want Erasmus punished for being an accessory to involuntary manslaughter.

On her way to the library, she hears sirens. Spooked—did Lucy recognize her and turn her in?—she ducks into an alleyway. But the sirens speed past. Cop cars, fire engines, ambulances. What in the world could be happening in this tiny town to warrant all that?

And then she sees a plume of smoke in the distance. From the direction of the Hyatt. She ventures out onto the street again—all right, the sirens evidently weren't for her—and dodges around a clump of concerned citizens who've gathered to share news.

"Hyatt," says one.

"Chaos," says another.

"Fire and flood," says the third.

Oh, no. Not again. Oh no you don't, Entropy. You said you were *helping* me, you motherfucker!

If the Hyatt's become a disaster area, the banquet will be canceled.

On the other hand, if the Hyatt's a disaster area, Cosmos will be sure to be there directing relief efforts. He'll be wandering around without the shielding of a podium. Archipelago may be able to get in there, use Erasmus to sting him directly, and take advantage of the craziness to get out again, scorpion still safely in her possession. Her new plan doesn't fix the ten-remaining-dollars-and-nowhere-to-live-with-winter-coming-on issue, but she'll deal with that later. She's done it before.

She'll have to slip under a lot of police radar to do this, but the cops are going to be distracted, and they won't be expecting anyone to be trying to get *into* the scene of a disaster. The site will be cordoned off, but she's on foot and used to slinking. She's been evading cops for months now. She'll get in somehow.

Alrighty, then. Heart lighter, Archipelago takes one of her zigzagging, surreptitious routes back to the hotel, which is surrounded by flashing emergency vehicles. The fire's out, doused with water from the water tower next door. People on stretchers are being wheeled out of the hotel. Archipelago hopes to all that's unholy that Cosmos isn't one of them: not because she wouldn't like to see him hurt, but because she wants to do it herself, and if he's in an ambulance, she won't have access to him.

She watches the cops, waits for a convenient distraction while one takes what sounds like a personal phone call and the other four go into a huddle about something—thank you, Entropy—and ducks under a barricade. Assorted dodging maneuvers get her into the lobby. She overhears snatches of information.

"Sprinkler system jammed."

"Fire."

"Right during a really critical match." Archipelago snorts.

She's inside, wading through inches of water from the fire hoses. Hiding behind a bedraggled potted plant to avoid a clump of paramedics, she scans the lobby. Yes! There's Cosmos! Thank you, Entropy!

She wiggles out of her backpack and uses her treasured pair of extra-long tweezers, tips padded with felt, to pull Erasmus out of his jar before donning the backpack again. She'll move in, sting Cosmos, get away somewhere safe, put Erasmus back in the jar, and make her getaway as quickly as she can. This is hardly a foolproof plan, especially since it will probably be more difficult to get out of the building than to get in—the first responders are alert to exiting survivors—but it's all she's got.

She waits for the latest clump of uniforms to leave and then sneaks up behind Cosmos, who's bending over a stretcher, blocking Archipelago's view of its occupant. "I'm so sorry this happened," he's saying. He sounds forlorn. "I promise we'll get you help."

"But I don't have insurance!"

The voice, a woman's, sounds familiar, but Archipelago doesn't have time to worry about this. She thrusts the squirming Erasmus at Cosmos's back, praying that the emperor's stinger will be able to penetrate the fabric of Cosmos's T-shirt.

It works. "Ow!" says Cosmos, and whirls to see what happened. In the process, he reveals the face of the woman on the stretcher.

Oh, fuck. It's Lucy, wearing a competitor's badge, her face bloody. *Lucy* plays Rock, Paper, Scissors?

"Ethel Rose?" says Lucy in astonishment.

"Archipelago Osprey?" says Comrade Cosmos. He sounds equally astonished.

"Oh, shit," says Archipelago, and gets ready to run while Cosmos is still gaping, too much in shock to do anything. But then she hears a roaring noise, and from somewhere—where? how?—a wave of water thunders down on them, and all three cry out as Erasmus is swept out of Archipelago's grasp.

19

*J*eremy doesn't consider himself religious anymore, if he ever really was. Sunday school was something he did because Mom said he had to. When he was fifteen, she gave him the choice of opting out, and out he opted.

Still, he grew up in St. Phil's, with its stained glass and organ and rich wooden pews. As Episcopal churches go, it's not a very fancy one, but he doesn't realize until he walks into the Unitarian church in Seattle how much it shaped his idea of what churches should look like. This place doesn't look or feel or smell like a church. It's too colorless, too sterile, all clean lines and clear glass. Danish modern. It feels like a fancy hotel conference center.

The Reno contingent—all except VB, who opted out—enters in a tight clump. Greg's already arrived; he and Hen hug as if they didn't have breakfast together two hours ago, and chat in subdued voices. There are a few other people here: a group of dark-clad folks in the front few rows who must be family, a few kids Jeremy's age who must have been Percy's friends, scattered adults. Not many.

It's nothing like Mom's funeral. Jeremy knows it's mean for him to be happy about that. He doesn't care.

In the front of the church, on a pedestal surrounded by flowers, sits a simple wooden box, smooth and polished. Behind it, on easels, are three photographs of Percy. One is the one they've all already seen: Percy blond and grinning in a Stanford lacrosse uniform, stick swung casually over his shoulder as he lopes across a sunny field. In the second, he's helping some older woman—his mother?—along a wooded path. In the third he's younger, hugging a very large puppy. "Oh, great," Jeremy hears himself saying, as if from a distance. "He loved dogs."

The minute he says it, he wants to clap his hand over his mouth. He didn't come here to be snarky: not out loud, anyway. He can be snarky later. But Amy squeezes his hand, and Aunt Rosie touches his shoulder. "If this is too much, you can leave," she whispers. "Don't worry about us, Jeremy, and don't worry about Percy's family. Take care of yourself."

"Thank you so much for coming," someone says, and they all turn to face the voice. It belongs to a haggard woman—blond hair trimmed in a perfect chin-length bob, elegant black suit, tasteful gold jewelry—who has appeared in front of them. Behind her stands a tall man, gray-haired, handsome once, you can tell, but eyes sunken and face lined now. "You must be—Melinda's friends. I'm Anna Clark." She holds out her hand. "Thank you so much for coming," she says again, more forcefully, and Jeremy flashes back again to Mom's funeral, to the misery of the receiving line at the end. Thank you for coming thank you for coming thank you for coming. He repeated the syllables so often they became nonsense, meaningless noise. But Anna Clark sounds like she means them.

Amy squeezes his hand again. Jeremy wonders if she'll ever hold his hand when they aren't at a funeral. "You're welcome," Hen says.

"I'm so glad you're here." Anna's a broken record; her husband's a mute mannequin who stares past them, his eyes somewhere else.

"I invited everyone I could, but so few people—because—I just wanted to share good memories. There were. Good memories."

"Oh," says Rosemary, and moves in a rush to hug the woman. "I'm so sorry. We're so sorry."

Anna lets herself be hugged, but her face over Aunt Rosie's shoulder stays tense, distracted, the eyes roaming until they fix on Jeremy. "You're Melinda's son, aren't you?"

"Yes." Suddenly his good suit feels like a straitjacket.

"I—I can't imagine. I—" Rosie finishes hugging her and steps backward, murmuring. Anna takes a visible breath and forces out clearer sentences. "I meant to try to meet you before. I meant to invite all of you to dinner last night. Things have been getting away from me."

"It's okay," Jeremy says. He's afraid the woman will shatter in front of him. Her husband still hasn't made a sound. Amy's grip on his hand is cutting off his circulation. "I mean, that would have been nice, it was nice of you even to think of it, but—"

"We're all doing the best we can," Aunt Rosie says, "and it's extraordinarily generous of you to allow us to be here."

Anna blinks, makes a groping motion in the air in front of her. "Allow? I'm honored. I—you're the ones who are generous, and I should—"

"No shoulds," Rosemary says gently. "There are no rule books for this. Anna, we're very sorry for your loss."

Anna breaks, then, and turns to muffle her sobs against her husband's chest. Eyes distant and unseeing, he clumsily pats her shoulder. Rosemary whispers to Jeremy, "Let's step away for a moment, shall we?"

"Yeah. I need a drink of water, anyway." Sandwiched between Aunt Rosie and Amy, he makes his way to the water fountain in the foyer.

"We don't have to stay," Rosemary tells him when he's finished slurping. "If it's too much—"

"I wish people would stop saying that. I'm staying." He turns, shaking off the two women, and returns to the sanctuary.

He sees the table now, along the right-hand wall, the display of more photos, trophies and awards, memorabilia. He remembers the table at Mom's funeral, the snapshots and favorite books and favorite rocks. Jeremy wills himself to walk over to this one, to look at the pictures. Percy as a chubby baby in his mother's arms; toddler Percy riding a tricycle; tan and buff Percy, laughing, in a Stanford sweatshirt. Here's an album with more: birthday parties, Christmas, family vacations. Percy grinning, arm-in-arm with his father, Mount Rushmore in the background. Percy on a beach somewhere. Mexico? Jeremy's stomach spasms, and he swallows bile. It can't be Mexico. They wouldn't have put that out here, would they?

Don't look at that picture. Look at the other things on the table. A lacrosse stick. A yearbook. A pair of bronzed baby shoes. And—Jeremy sees now, and how did he miss it before?—a stack of slipcased print issues of *CC*.

Just met guy your age, Percy, who likes CC too. The postcard's still at home. He thought about bringing it, but it's stuck in his mirror frame and doesn't want to budge. He was afraid he'd tear it if he tugged. He feels his fists clenching. If he walked up to Anna Clark and said, "One of my mother's last conversations was with your son, about *Comrade Cosmos*," would she remove the issues, out of common decency?

He watches a hand reach to touch the plastic covers. "Oh, man," Amy says, her voice thick, her fingers resting lightly on the plastic. "He was really a collector, wasn't he? Mint condition. These must be worth money."

Jeremy's chest tightens. It hurts to breathe. "I'm going to look at the urn now," he says. "Don't follow me, please." Amy turns to him with a frown, but he moves away from the table, up the side aisle, around the first pews—people there watching him, but he can't read their expressions—toward the pedestal. Golden wood, with the golden boy inside.

Jeremy expected to feel rage, thought he'd have to fight the urge to knock the urn to the floor, to scatter the sick fuck's ashes through the sanctuary. But he feels nothing. The fury he felt even a moment ago, looking at the *CC* issues, has evaporated. This isn't Percy, any more than Mom's ashes are Mom.

He feels something on the back of his thigh. A sharp voice says, "Bart!" and Jeremy turns to find an improbably huge dog gazing at him with somber, sorrowful eyes, while Mr. Clark frowns and tugs at the leash. "I'm sorry, Jeremy. Anna insisted that he be here. He usually behaves around strangers."

So you can talk, Jeremy thinks, and then, I'm not exactly a stranger. He holds out a hand, tentatively. The great beast nuzzles it. The tail beats, once. Then the dog returns to Mr. Clark and sits obediently on command.

"He's the puppy in the photo," Anna says, and Jeremy turns to find her standing next to the urn. She gives a wan smile. "Older now, of course. He—well, he was the last of us to see Percy alive. I thought he deserved to be here. I guess that sounds crazy, but Percy really loved this animal. He—I keep thinking he must still be alive somewhere. My Percy. The person who died wasn't my Percy. The person who did that to. To your mother. Wasn't my Percy."

"The woman who died," Jeremy hears himself saying, "was my mother."

Anna Clark sags, lets out a breath, reaches out to lean on the pedestal for support. "Thank you, Jeremy. That's the first honest thing anyone's said to me."

*i*t's inexpressibly horrible, a charade. Anna sits in her pew, William an unbending poker next to her, Marjorie and David letting out sighs and sniffles on her other side. Several times, Marjorie reaches for her hand. Anna shakes it away. This was a mistake. She shouldn't have done this. What was she thinking?

There's some music, a pleasant piano piece, an arrangement of "Here Comes the Sun." Anna chose it because Percy liked that song and often hummed or whistled it in the house, but now it sounds entirely wrong. Awash in humiliation, she listens to the Unitarian minister's bland, sincere homily. The minister's a short-haired, owlish young woman who goes on a few minutes too long about the Tragedy of Suicide and What We Don't Understand and the Agony of Percy's Inexplicable Behavior, and then—as Anna instructed her—invites people up to the podium to share good memories of Percy, Because We Are Here to Support the Family in Their Grief, and We Also Wish to Acknowledge and Honor the Family and Friends of Melinda Soto, Who Have Graciously Joined Us Today. Heads throughout the sanctuary whip around. Where, where? Jeremy nods, half raises a hand, gives a small bow in his seat. Anna bites back a laugh, which she knows would sound too shrill and hysterical.

No one else moves. Then Marjorie clears her throat, stands, and marches the short distance to the microphone. "I'm Marjorie Clark, Percy's grandmother. I couldn't believe it when I heard what had happened—none of us could—and I suppose I never will"—oh, get on with it, thinks Anna, the minister already said all this—"and I'm sure I'll never understand it, but I can tell you that the Percy I knew was a sweet boy." She goes on to tell a story about taking Percy grocery shopping when he was three, how he stopped stock-still in front of a display of lettuce and said, "That's the biggest salad in the *world*!" A few people laugh, politely. Anna doesn't. It's completely irrelevant.

Marjorie's saying something about the Reno people now, thanking them. Turning to gesture at the urn, she wishes Percy a sentimental good-bye, and then sits down.

Someone else has gotten up. Toby Tobin. At least his mother

isn't here. Anna would have banned him, too, if she'd been able to, but that's Poor Form.

Wait, didn't the bitch say Toby wouldn't be able to come? Because they'd be away? Something about Europe? Whatever happened to keep Toby home? Maybe he doesn't like his mother any better than Anna does? No: more likely it's something else. And he's talking; Anna should listen.

"Percy and I played lacrosse together," he says, gripping the sides of the podium so hard Anna can see his pale knuckles. "I've known him since kindergarten, because we both went to Blake, and—well, we weren't always friends. We competed a lot. But I couldn't have told you anything bad about him, and like everybody else, I'll never understand this. It would be a lot easier if I could point to something and say, 'Oh, yeah, he was clearly off,' but I can't find anything like that. And I think we're all going to spend the rest of our own lives looking, and it's really scary because I'll never be able to take anyone at face value again, but maybe that's a gift, too." He stops, swallows. "I'm talking too long. Anyway, I just—I feel awful for everybody. I wish I could do something to change it, any of it."

He leaves the podium, giving Anna an abashed half nod as he passes. She nods back. He said the same thing Marjorie said, but he said it much better. His words were honest, heartfelt, and noncloying, which is worth a lot right now. It's worth even more that he even came. Anna concedes, only a little grudgingly, that Toby seems to have grown into a fine human being. *And Percy didn't.* Of course, if she weren't terminally irritated with William's mother, alert for self-congratulation in every syllable of her speech, maybe she'd have liked Marjorie's comments, too.

Anna glances around the sanctuary. No one else has stood up. The minister clears her throat and moves forward, but Anna stands abruptly, feeling as brittle as a burned-out lightbulb, and makes her way to the mike. The few feet seem like miles, but this fiasco was her idea. If you want something done right, do it yourself.

She looks out over the tiny, scattered audience. "I've thanked all of you for coming," she says, "but I'm thanking you again. The fact that so few people are here shows just how brave and caring all of you had to be to show up. That means the world to me, and to Percy's father." She's pretty sure it means precisely nothing to William, but that part's formula. She takes a deep breath. "Twenty-three years ago today, my only child was born, and I held him in my arms and I imagined a bright, happy future for him. I never imagined that I'd outlive him, and certainly not under these circumstances. I'm sure many people, and maybe even people here, are happy he's dead, consider it right and fitting. Other people are probably angry he's dead, because it means they can't kill him, or because it means he won't suffer for decades in prison. I understand both of those positions. I do."

She pauses. They wait, watching her. "I don't have any answers. His father and I knew something was wrong as soon as he came home from Mexico, but he wouldn't talk to us about it. He didn't leave a note. I believe he felt so horrible about what he'd done that he couldn't live with it. Maybe that's not true. Maybe he didn't feel horrible about what he did to Melinda. Maybe he was only terrified of the consequences. I don't know. Whatever answers he might have been able to offer, he carried them into the water. So of the stories that might be true, I tell the one that comforts me the most: that he felt remorse. I'm his mother. Please grant me that."

Her voice wavers, just a little, and is answered by rustling from the pews. William has looked away, and Marjorie's frowning. Anna doesn't care. She takes another breath. "But this I do know. When Percy killed Melinda, he also destroyed himself. He did that the second he began to hurt her." Her voice breaks on the word "hurt"; she can't bring herself to say "rape." "He did that even before he walked into the water. The Percy I knew was a nice kid, a fun and decent kid, not a genius but smart enough. He loved his dog. I believe he loved us, his parents. He was loyal to his friends." Damn few of whom have shown up today, but she's already said that. "All of that's banal, I know, and it makes Percy sound utterly ordinary, and the Percy I knew was, except that he was mine. That Percy died in Mexico. That's the Percy I'm mourning, the one no one else even seems to want to hear about or to remember, because the other Percy—the one who did such horrible things to Melinda— has taken center stage."

Everyone's staring at her now, even Marjorie and William. Well, at least she has their attention. She supposes she's being unkind— Marjorie and Toby have both remembered that Percy, or tried to— but she doesn't care. The minister comes up behind her, clears her throat again, says gently, "Anna," but Anna shoos her away.

She's not done talking. It's her party. She paid for the damn salmon canapés. She'll talk as long as she needs to.

She feels dizzy. Breathe, Anna. "Twenty-three years ago today, my only child surfaced from the waters of my womb." That sounds pretentious as hell, but so what. This is her only son's funeral. "Eight months, two weeks and four days ago, he walked into the waters of Lake Washington." Pause. Breathe. "Many of you know that Percy was a *Comrade Cosmos* fan. Some of you are, too." She sees Jeremy Soto wince, watches his shoulders hunch. She keeps going even though he's glaring at her. She deserves that glare, maybe—Percy deserved it—but she needs to say her piece. "After Percy died, I started reading *CC* from the first issue. Not because I thought it would give me answers, but because Percy loved it, and I'd never bothered to try and share that with him when he was still alive. I didn't expect to get pulled into it, but I did."

Jeremy's wiping his face now, a series of fierce swipes. The girl sitting next to him grips his shoulder. "If you follow *CC*, you know that this month's issue opens with a flood. Cosmos and Archipelago are caught in that flood, and Archipelago's pet scorpion has been swept away, and she's grieving terribly, even though most people wouldn't mourn a scorpion. She's grieving because Erasmus the scorpion was hers, and she loved him."

She takes another breath, feeling stronger now. "I don't want to push this too far. Percy wasn't a scorpion. Not literally, anyway." William scowls, but there's a ripple of laughter from the others. Good. "But when I saw that flood, I thought about my own womb, and I thought about Lake Washington, and I thought, We all come from the water, and we're all swept away in floods sometimes, and sometimes the people we have to work with to find safety are the last ones we expected. Sometimes the only way to survive is to work with people we thought we hated. Sometimes those are the people who wind up saving us, just like Cosmos, I'm pretty sure, will save Archipelago."

The minister's hovering again. Anna turns to her and snaps, "I'm almost done," and the woman retreats. "I'm not asking any of you to save me. I'm not claiming I can save you. But we're in a flood, and when the waters recede, everything will look different. Our task now is to save what we can." She swallows. "I ask that you try to save at least one memory of the Percy who died in Mexico, the one I loved. Thank you."

She steps away from the podium. Her legs are rubbery. William stands and helps her back to her seat; Marjorie takes her hand—she permits that, now—and David reaches around Marjorie to squeeze her shoulder, hard. For a moment, this moment, they're almost a family. It won't last.

The minister's talking again. Anna doesn't even try to listen. She closes her eyes and breathes.

*t*he day before Melinda leaves for Mexico, she listens to Science Friday on NPR. They're talking about the moon. There's water on the moon, it turns out, quite a bit of water. Several dozen buckets of water, trapped in the moon's icy poles.

She reads more about the story when she gets home. Scientists are excited: this could open the door for a lunar space station, since there's now a water source, although it doesn't seem to Melinda that several dozen bucketfuls would go very far. Other commenters are more interested in how the water got there. One of the leading theories is that it was carried on asteroids that smashed into the moon. Some people believe that studying the moon's ice will provide invaluable information about the history of the entire solar system.

As she packs her suitcase—the aqua swimsuit, or the red one that's less slimming but more comfortable? okay, both—Melinda muses over the story. She thinks the moon is a little like Nevada: even a trickle of water transforms a wasteland into a potential windfall that sets speculators panting. She likes the asteroid theory, though. The moon is still scarred, but the objects that wounded it also brought potential life. What hurt the moon also has the capacity to mend it.

She laughs to herself. The church reading group just finished Henri Nouwen's *The Wounded Healer*, and this would fit right in. She'll have to tell her own Hen about it when she gets home.

*t*he rain's started again. Yes, of course it has: this is Seattle, after all, even if they're here in July, during the dry season. Standing at a window in the church fellowship hall, clutching a glass of punch and a plate dotted with salmon canapés, Rosemary stares out at the falling water and wonders what Walter's doing.

Everything aches. She's stiff from the long car ride, from the strange bed, from the tension of sitting through this dreadful funeral. Yesterday she went to Pike Place Market and did a little shopping, but that seems like a century ago.

The funeral was hideous: soothing platitudes from the minister—who clearly hadn't known Percy—the tone-deaf offering from the grandmother, that jagged and heartbreaking speech from Anna Clark. Percy's school friend was the most credible speaker, and certainly the briefest.

As awful as Melinda's funeral was, it was better than this.

Under these circumstances, what would a good funeral look like? Rosemary has no idea. But once again, she's grateful to be

Episcopalian. The Episcopal Church gives good funeral. There's a well-defined liturgy. There's a shape to the thing, a shape created both to express and to contain grief, a shape that points to hope.

The Unitarians have no Eucharist. She expected that, but there wasn't even any Scripture. The minister quoted Plato's maxim about always being kind, because everyone you see is fighting a terrible battle. True enough, but completely inadequate.

And what would have been adequate?

How would Hen have handled this service? Rosemary will have to ask her, later.

In the meantime, she aches for Anna Clark. The Reno contingent was at least a quarter of the audience. Don't the Clarks have friends? But it would be too easy to blame social isolation for what Percy turned into, and clearly he hadn't always been socially isolated. Clearly the Clarks are upper crust.

"Excuse me," says a voice behind her, and she turns to find Anna standing there, twisting a napkin into shreds. "I just wanted to see if you needed anything. You look lonely over here."

Rosemary blinks. She's not the person who's lonely. Or rather, she supposes that she *is* lonely, but her loneliness is nothing compared to Anna's.

And suffering isn't a competition. How often has she said that to hospital patients who insist that they're "fine," because the person in the next bed is so much worse off?

"Just processing," Rosemary says. She's a chaplain. She ought to be able to talk to this woman.

"It was nice of you to hug me before," Anna says, her voice fraying, and Rosemary finds her bearings. Anna's being a hostess, doing what she knows. It's not a bad strategy.

"You're exhausted," she says, taking Anna's elbow and guiding her to a table. "Please, sit down. Let me get you something. Some punch? Some cake? Have you been able to eat?"

"Eat?" Anna makes a face.

"When's the last time you ate?"

Anna laughs, incongruously. "I had breakfast. Cereal. But that was hours ago, wasn't it? Would you mind bringing me some cheese? And crackers? Maybe some of the canapés? That would be very kind of you."

"Yes, of course." Rosemary hurries to fix the plate, hoping Anna won't have wandered away when she gets back. Primary mourners at a funeral are usually as difficult to speak to alone as the bride or groom at a wedding. But when she returns to the table, Anna's still there, frowning down at her hands clasped on the table in front of her.

Rosemary stays still a minute to make sure she isn't interrupting a prayer, but Anna looks up at her. "Are you—will you sit down? Will you sit with me?"

"Of course." Rosemary sits. "I thought maybe you were praying. I didn't want to disturb you if you were."

"No." Anna looks down at her hands again, and then unfolds them and reaches out for the plate Rosemary's put in front of her. "I don't—I'm not religious. We just had the funeral here because, well. Funerals. Churches. You know?"

Rosemary nods, and feels herself softening toward the Unitarians. The poor minister. What a service to get stuck with.

"I don't know how to pray," Anna says. "Maybe if we were religious—"

"No," Rosemary says. It would be much, much too easy—and false—to blame Percy's pathology on godlessness. People who do believe in God are perfectly capable of committing horrors, anyway. "Anna, this isn't your fault. Not yours, not your husband's."

Anna gives her a long, level look now, and says very gently, "That wasn't what I was going to say."

"Oh." Rosemary feels herself reddening.

"I was going to say—" Anna offers a small, crooked smile. "—that if we were religious, maybe I'd have answers."

"No." Rosemary shakes her head. "It's not that easy, believe me. I'm religious, and I don't have answers. Only questions."

"Do you believe there are answers?"

"Well sure, of course, I mean there have to be, but I don't know if I'll ever learn them, or if they'll make sense if I do." She shakes her head again; this is too abstract. Chaplain mode, Rosie. "When you spoke, you talked about wanting to hang on to your good memories of Percy. Tell me your best memory. Tell me what you loved most about him."

Anna Clark smiles, a fleeting expression that vanishes almost as soon as it appears. "Well, there was that day in the woods. When we were hiking, and he helped me. That's one of the photographs in the chapel. It's a very precious memory. But this morning, I remembered—I don't know why it came to me now." She frowns and pushes a strand of hair out of her face. "No, I do know, because we've gotten all these flowers. I invited a lot of people and they didn't come, but some of them sent flowers. Anyway, when Percy was a little boy, he used to pick dandelions for me. We had a garden, you know, lots of flowers, and I worked hard to keep dandelions off our property"—she laughs now—"but he liked dandelions. They were soft and furry, he said. Even when they were still yellow, even before they went to seed. Anyway, so he'd go off to school, and he'd come home with mashed dandelions in his pockets. It was so sweet. I couldn't bear to tell him they were weeds. He asked me if we could have some in our yard, and I told him that dandelions were happier living in wild places." She looks down; her hands are clasped again. "He was seven or eight then. He only brought them to me for a little while, but he was so proud of himself. Pockets full of mashed dandelions."

"Extra detergent in the laundry," Rosemary says, and Anna grimaces.

"Yes. Did you—did you know Melinda?"

"Very well." Rosemary speaks as gently as she can. "She was one of my best friends. My husband helped her bring Jeremy back from Guatemala."

"Oh!" Anna's eyes overflow. She looks away—Rosemary can

tell from watching the side of her face that she's working to compose herself—and then says, "Is your husband here, too? I don't remember seeing him."

"No, he's not here. He has Alzheimer's. He's in a nursing home."

Anna looks back at her now, face blanched. "I'm so sorry. That's terrible. Watching someone disappear like that—"

"Yes." Because she wants to be generous, because Anna's been so open with her and was so brave during the service, Rosemary goes on. "All those shared memories you count on with a spouse, being able to say, 'Remember when we went on that trip' or 'Remember when we got our first house,' that stuff. That's no longer there, even though the person's body is."

"My husband and I—" Anna breaks off, bringing her hand to her mouth. "We don't. We don't share memories. He's not sick, but it seems we remember everything differently. Sometimes I wonder if we lived the same lives."

Rosemary tries not to wince. The situation's completely predictable—any death of a child, let alone this one, is hell on a marriage—but that doesn't make it any less hideous. "That's hard."

"Yes."

"It must be even harder now."

"Well, I only noticed it—after Percy. I suppose it must have been true before that, but there hadn't been anything important to handle. We just lived in our routines." She shoves away the stray strand again. "And I suggested couples counseling, but he—won't." She draws in a deep, ragged breath. "I don't think we'll still be married this time next year."

Rosemary's chest tightens. "That's very, very hard." She remembers how Anna kept repeating herself, before the service. Now Rosemary's the one doing it.

"Oh, God." Anna gives a strangled half laugh. "You're not a reporter, are you? You promise you won't tell anyone that? I shouldn't even have said it. I didn't mean to say it."

"I'm a chaplain," Rosemary says. "A lay chaplain, in a hospital. So I'm used to hearing stories. No, I won't tell anyone. When you said it, did you believe it?"

"Yes." Anna looks up. From across the room, the tall husband moves toward them. He sees his wife and nods, gesturing. "He needs me. I have to go. Thank you. For the cheese, too."

She stands up and moves away, leaving Rosemary breathing through a new pain she doesn't understand, a jagged tearing in the throat. So much loss: of course she feels for this woman. But there's something else, something more. What?

Walter: yes, of course, something about Walter. But what?

That he isn't here.

That he no longer remembers Melinda, will probably never remember Melinda.

Yes. But all of that's old. What's the new pain?

And then she realizes. Talking to Anna felt at least a little like talking to Melinda: frank conversation with another woman, with someone she likes and whose company she enjoys. Rosemary always loved how honest Melinda was, how free of bullshit. Maybe Anna isn't always like that, but Rosemary thinks she'd like Anna, if they met in a book group. They could be friends. Rosemary can't talk like that to Vera—not yet, anyway, although they may be inching toward it—or even Hen.

Suddenly Rosemary feels terribly alone. She wants to be back in the van, even though the drive up here was interminable. She wants to go home, to be in places she knows, even if too many of the other people who used to be there too are gone.

*a*lmost dozing on the rocking ferry, Veronique sips her licorice tea and stares out the rain-streaked window. She can't see much, of course: grayness receding into mist, the blurry reflections of the other passengers, most of them in shorts and sports sandals, who read or doze or listen, feet tapping, to their headphones. No two seem to be sitting together. Everyone's scattered, isolated. Veronique guesses that most of them are residents of Bainbridge Island, heading back home after errands in the city. She's surprised not to see more tourists like her, but maybe the rain's driven them inside.

This morning, she was proud of herself for not going to the funeral. She was proud of herself for figuring out bus schedules and planning a fun day, the kind of day Melinda would have loved. The Art Museum, Pike Place Market—Veronique didn't find another pot she liked, but she did buy some delicious chocolate, and even virtuously saved some for the others—a boat ride.

She enjoyed herself, in a rather forced and determined way. She thinks even Brandy would have approved. But now she's tired, and the rain's reminding her of the rain the day Melinda died, not to mention making her knee throb, and she's teetering on the verge of tears. She tells herself that her blood sugar's wonky. She ate too much chocolate. The snack bar's just over there, and even if it's as overpriced as these things always are, she should go buy some protein. A hot dog. A hot dog with mustard. That would taste good right now.

She doesn't move, though. She feels glued to the seat. As desperate as she was to be alone when she was surrounded by the others and their chatter, now she'd give anything to have someone with her. Even annoying Amy. Even nagging Rosemary.

She wants to take a nap. But she knows that if she went back to Greg's house and no one else was home yet, she'd just feel more bereft.

What happened? Today started out being fun, just like the trip to Planet X did. That stayed fun. This one's gone downhill. So what's the difference? Veronique, you analyze narrative for a living. This is narrative. Analyze it.

She stares out at the rain. Bad weather, but it wasn't great on the trip to Gerlach, either.

She misses Melinda now, but she missed Melinda then, too.

This trip is new. She's never been here before. She's been to Gerlach a lot.

Is that it? It sounds like it could be, but it doesn't *feel* like it is. She definitely needs protein to work this out. She hauls herself out of her seat and buys an overpriced, alarmingly gray hot dog from the snack bar. She eyes the thing—if she dies of botulism on the ferry, it will take a long time for the others to find out about it, since no one knows where she is—and considers calling Rosemary. "I'm about to eat a hot dog on the Bainbridge Ferry. I just wanted to let you know, so if I keel over from food poisoning, you'll know where to look for me."

She lets out a guffaw, and some other passengers give her strange looks. She'd actually love to interrupt Percy's funeral by calling Rosemary with that message. It would serve Rosie right. But, Veronique reluctantly concedes, it's probably not worth the ill will it would create. The drive home will be very long: she doesn't need to be lectured the whole time. And anyway, from the state of the trash bins, it looks like other people on the ferry have been eating hot dogs, and Veronique hasn't seen any corpses.

All right. Live dangerously. She wrestles open a tiny plastic squeeze bag of mustard, squirts it onto the hot dog—getting some on her shirt and some on her seat in the process—and eats. The hot dog tastes fine. Actually, it tastes good.

She finishes the hot dog, lets out a small and dignified belch, and returns to staring out the window. They're nearing Bainbridge Island, a dark dimness in the rain, and the other passengers are stirring, getting ready to disembark. Veronique will just sit here and ride back to Seattle.

All right. Where were you, Veronique?

This trip is new, whereas she's been to Gerlach a lot. But that still doesn't feel right. Why not?

She ponders, absently wiping a drop of mustard off her arm as the ferry docks with a small thump. Gerlach was new in a lot of ways: because she was making the trip without Melinda, because she was disobeying expectations. Of course, she's doing that here, too, by not going to Percy's funeral, but everyone knew she wouldn't. She announced it beforehand, instead of just striking out on her own on a daring adventure. It's not like Rosie's going to become frantic wondering where she is, not unless she rides the ferry back and forth all night.

Rosie.

Oh, hell. That's it.

When Veronique took off for Gerlach, she *knew* Rosie would worry. She wanted Rosie to worry. Half the fun was yanking Rosie's chain.

She wanted Rosemary to come after her, as much as she protested at the time. She wanted to prove that someone would care if she disappeared.

Veronique makes a face at the backs of the departing passengers. The Gerlach trip wouldn't have been nearly as fun without that adolescent, I'm-running-away-from-home rebellion. Without that, it might just have felt lonely, the way she feels now.

With a sigh, she gets up and moves to another seat, so that she'll be facing Seattle as they approach it, and pulls out her bus schedules. She'll go back to Greg's house. She'll take her nap. When the others get home, she'll be nice to them, and she'll ask how the funeral was, and she may even care about the answer.

Two hours later, damp but triumphant at having navigated the bus system again, Veronique walks up the hill to Greg's house and sees cars in his driveway: the rental van, his battered Toyota, another car—a Lexus, of all things—she doesn't recognize.

The front door's open. She walks in and calls out, "Hi, everybody. I'm home." She hears voices from the living room, and follows them, and blinks. Jeremy and Amy and a frail blond woman are poring over a table of comic books while Rosie and Hen chat in the background. They look up when she enters the room; they must not have heard her before.

"Did you have a nice day?" Hen asks. Rosie looks worried, almost panicked.

"I did," Veronique says, "thank you."

"This is Anna," Rosie says. "Percy's mother." She gives Veronique a fierce look: *don't make any trouble.* "Anna, this is our friend Veronique."

The blonde looks up from the table, turns to Veronique, extends her hand. She looks very tired. "Hello. I'm glad to meet you."

"She's a CC fan," Amy pipes in. "She has some cool ideas about stories. You should talk to her, Professor Bellamy."

Shaking Anna Clark's hand, Veronique feels her eyes filling with tears. For herself, not for Percy: not even for Melinda. *I don't want to be in this story. I don't want to have to think about this story.* But the others expect her to behave. "Hello." She knows it sounds cold, but it's the best she can do, because her old rage has come swirling back, a blizzard in July. She shouldn't even have to meet this woman.

"Professor Bellamy," Amy says, her voice both gentle and urgent, "today would have been Percy's birthday."

Amy's the only person here who witnessed the March meltdown. Veronique shudders, and to her horror feels herself blushing. Then she takes a deep breath—she's a grown-up, and she can do this— and holds out the paper bag from Pike Place Market. "Anna, I'm sorry. Would you like some chocolate?"

20

*t*he water tumbles Archipelago, Cosmos, and Lucy through the hotel lobby. Archipelago's never been a strong swimmer. She swallows water, chokes, thinks furiously, *How could all this be coming from the hotel pipes?*—later she'll learn that the water tower next door burst apart, but she doesn't know that yet—and paddles frantically in her ridiculous outfit. The shoes have come off, which is no great loss, but the rest of the wet clothing clings to her, and the water's cold, and she's freezing and terrified, and she's scared that she'll hit something, or something will hit her. She sees a large, tacky painting of a tropical beach scene bobbing like a raft on the water—the lobby furniture doesn't float, since it's all metal and glass and leather—and grabs it. She even manages to haul herself onto it. The frame's thick, and the canvas seems to be pretty strong. Waterproof, even, since it's reasonably dry up here: sealed by the paint, no doubt.

She lies on her stomach on the painting, as if it's a surfboard, and paddles with her hands. "Hey!" she hears nearby. "Hey!

Glug!" Somebody's sputtering, kicking and sinking. Archipelago reaches out, grabs a wrist, and pulls.

It's Cosmos, of all people. He hauls himself up on the picture next to her. His teeth are chattering. He looks even less prepossessing soaking wet than he does the rest of the time. Archipelago snorts. Some superhero.

"Thanks," he says.

"Fuck," she answers, and thinks about pushing him off the picture, but she's in enough trouble right now, ringed around by 911 types. There's no way she's getting out of this undetected. Well, all right. There's food, in jail, and the problem of Erasmus has been solved, although not in any way she could have wished. Her throat aches. She knows she'll never see him again.

"Where's Lucy?" Cosmos says, craning around to peer at the stuff bobbing on the water. "Do you see her?"

Who the fuck's Lucy? Archipelago wants to say that, but she can't. She knows who Lucy is. Lucy was much nicer than Archipelago had any right to expect.

Shit.

"Don't know. If we go that way, do you think we can get out?"

"I don't want to get out. I want to find Lucy. Archipelago, c'mon. Help me, would you?"

She wants to find Lucy, too. She helps Cosmos paddle, turning the makeshift raft in a circle so they can scan the water for any sign of Lucy. Fuck. She's helping Cosmos. Does that make her a Comrade?

No. She's not helping Cosmos. She's helping Lucy, who helped her, even though Lucy was helping her try to hurt Cosmos. Cosmos has nothing to do with her helping Lucy. Cosmos just happens to be here, and this mess is his fault, anyway. If he weren't here, EE wouldn't be pulling out the big guns. Of course, if Cosmos weren't here, Archipelago wouldn't be, either.

But this is too much alternate history to ponder while paddling a raft in a flood, and anyway, they have company. There, sure enough, is the Emperor of Entropy, visible now that Archipelago's thought has summoned him, towering above the lobby's massive, tacky central staircase. Lucy's stretcher has lodged on a step just above the water. She sees them and waves, weakly.

"Oh, thank God," says Cosmos, and paddles toward the stairs. Archipelago helps him, because she doesn't know what else to do.

"Didn't know you were religious," she tells him.

"It's a figure of speech."

They reach the stairs—not a moment too soon, since the tacky painting's starting to buckle and disintegrate—and climb to higher, drier ground, pulling Lucy with them. Lucy's not light: it takes all of Archipelago and Cosmos's combined strength to haul the stretcher to safety. When they're done, Archipelago realizes in a dizzying rush that she's glad she's here. She's glad she helped Lucy. She enjoyed working with someone else, although she still wishes the someone weren't Cosmos. Even so, she's relieved that he isn't allergic to scorpion venom.

They sit on the steps, shivering, waiting for rescue personnel. Lucy, improbably, is asleep, smiling while she snores. "I didn't mean to kill the Mayor," Archipelago tells Cosmos. "You won't turn me in, will you? The cop in Bumfuck didn't."

He gives her a blank look. "In where?"

"Some little town in Wyoming. He knew who I was. He didn't turn me in. He let me go."

Cosmos sighs and rubs his nose. "He shouldn't have done that."

"Well, I *know*. I thought so, too. But he did. Will you?"

"Can't," Cosmos says glumly. "You don't want me to, not really, do you? Look: the Mayor's family needs closure. The cops need to know what really happened. You need to get someplace where you can eat more. You're scary skinny, you know."

"Fuck," Archipelago says, and her voice breaks. "I came here to hurt you, too, and now Erasmus is dead and I'll never even be able to find his body in all this muck, and you're going to lecture me about how it's my fault, right? I've been stung by my own sins? Because if I hadn't taken Erasmus out of his jar to sting you, he'd still be alive—"

"We don't know that," Cosmos says. He sounds very tired. "He might have been safer out of the jar than in it. Can scorpions swim? Do they float? I have no idea, but if he were trapped in a bottle it might have smashed and, I don't know, cut him or something. I mean, I don't know that it would make that much difference. Why did you want to hurt me?"

"Because if you hadn't meddled, the Mayor never would have turned into such a goon!"

"That's another thing you don't know."

"Of course I do! You showed up, and then he—"

"No. Logical fallacy, Archipelago. You're confusing chronology with causation. It's a pretty safe bet that without the Emperor—hey there, old buddy—the Mayor never would have turned into such a goon, but I don't know how much I had to do with it, except that without me, there would have been even more chaos, and maybe he would have been *more* of a goon. You know?"

"It's all your fault," Archipelago says, but to her great humiliation it comes out as a wail, and she's crying—it's the cold, it has to be, she never cries—and Cosmos puts both of his arms around her and rocks, trying to soothe her. It's how he'd soothe Vanessa.

"There, there. There, there now. You've been through a lot. I know you have."

She wants to tell him to let go. She wants to tell him not to touch her, but it feels good. Because she's cold, she tells herself fiercely, because she's on the verge of fucking hypothermia, and she damn well doesn't need a fucking man to make her happy, *especially* not this one. She'd rather—she'd rather—

"Archipelago," Cosmos says, sounding startled. "Can scorpions swim? Look. What's that?"

She peers in the dimness, sees a flicker of darkness in a familiar shape. "Erasmus!"

Her tweezers are in her pocket. She pulls them out, executes a deft grab, and pins Erasmus neatly around his middle. He wiggles and writhes. He's having a bad day. "Erasmus," she says, and she's weeping with joy this time. "Erasmus, are you okay?"

CC readers will send up howls of protest over this happy ending. Erasmus should be dead. It's too corny for Erasmus not to be dead; it's too neat. Even if—as both fans and Archipelago will discover via Internet research—scorpions are tough critters who can live underwater for startling amounts of time, it's simply too convenient for Erasmus to have washed up precisely where Cosmos, Archipelago, and Lucy have also found refuge. Corny. *CC* usually relies on a particular brand of gritty realism: this issue completely violates that aesthetic. It's bad writing. This issue is badly written.

And even Archipelago, sobbing for joy at having recovered her pet, will suddenly stop blubbering and say, in something more like her normal voice, "Oh, *fuck*."

"What?" asks Cosmos, who's inched away from her and Erasmus on the stairs.

"If he's alive, I have to keep taking care of him. And how can I do that if I'm in jail?"

"It'll work out," he tells her.

And so, in future issues, it will. Emergency workers will rescue Cosmos, Lucy, and Archipelago. One of the medics, who has snakes and lizards at home and sympathizes with the plight of unpopular pets, even finds a specimen cup to keep Erasmus in, and obligingly pokes holes in it with an IV needle. The three humans are treated for exposure at the local hospital. Archipelago finds herself under armed guard, and then under arrest. To her intense misery, Cosmos becomes her biggest champion. He tells everyone that she didn't mean to kill the Mayor, that it was just an immature hijink, that she's sorry. He tells everyone how she saved him in the flood, how she nobly helped him save Lucy. Lucy tells everyone that she sure is disappointed that Archipelago lied to her like that, but the child's good deeds have made up for it, and everyone deserves a second chance.

Good deeds. Archipelago's been saved from the water only to die of shame.

Rallied by Cosmos, hundreds of people she's never met chip in small change to make her bail. The judge gives her five years' probation with a hefty list of community-service commitments, including painting parks buildings and teaching schoolchildren about arachnids. To her astonishment, she's hired as a docent at a local nature reserve. She gets another apartment, two blocks from Cosmos's house, and he's over sharing pizza and a Guinness with her—Roger being out of town at the ALA—the evening she discovers that Erasmus is really dead, has died peacefully of old age after a long life of many crickets. And Archipelago breaks down and bawls like a child, and Cosmos comforts her, and one thing leads to another, and assorted critics excoriate the CC Four for reinscribing heteronormativity where it was neither needed nor wanted. Why the hell couldn't Archipelago just start her own outlaw lesbian biker gang and ride off into the sunset, huh? Are the CC Four being pressured by corporate interests? Why have they gone soft?

At this point, many fans abandon CC, moving on in disgust to edgier pop-culture phenomena. A significant percentage of the fans who remain, meanwhile, will have begun to critique Cosmos's American isolationism. When Charlie dies, Archipelago remains in Keyhole to care tenderly for Vanessa—who reminds her of herself, a less lucky version of her, messy hair and all—while Cosmos goes to Haiti. After Vanessa dies of pneumonia one miserable winter, Archipelago accompanies Cosmos to Africa. And, as always, the Emperor is everywhere, howling and cackling, smiling down at Cosmos and Archipelago when he thinks no one's looking.

But all of that's in the future. We will leave Cosmos and Archipelago here, on the sodden stairs, awaiting rescue as they stare in wonder at Erasmus. We will leave the critics to argue about whether Erasmus's return is a blatant allusion to resurrection, or just *really* bad writing, or whether resurrection itself is just really bad writing. We will leave our heroes cold and shivering but newly hopeful, facing a future they cannot know and can only dimly imagine.

For now, for them, it is enough to know that there *is* a future. Their story is not over. Even in the midst of decay and dissolution, of entropy and endings, they will keep breathing and working. They will light candles and love without logic. They will make the best of what they have for as long as they have it.

21

Jeremy points through a high doorway. "There he is." Behind them, huge cardboard figures of Cosmos, Roger, and Archipelago tower over the museum patrons. They're together; EE's isolated in his own room, the walls painted black with spinning stars, a booming cackle cleverly audible in this space, although you couldn't hear it back among the Good Guys.

"Doesn't that violate the premise?" asks Anna Clark. "I mean, the whole idea is that he shows up whenever you think of him. He's always in the room. So why did they put him in a different room?"

"Yeah," says Amy. "And why's Archipelago in the Good Guy room instead of the Bad Guy room? And where's Erasmus?"

"She doesn't belong in the Bad Guy room either," Anna says. "She keeps saying she's not a Minion. Remember Bumfuck, and the pizza in the alley?"

Jeremy shakes his head. Anna's perfectly groomed from the top of her blond head to the tips of her Gucci pumps. She may be wearing tastefully faded blue jeans, but she has a Coach bag slung over her shoulder and flawlessly lacquered fingernails. Even hearing her say the word "Bumfuck" is some heavy cognitive dissonance.

She just doesn't look like a CC fan, even as broad-based as the fandom is. She looks like somebody's mom. She *is* somebody's mom.

Was.

"She joined forces with EE last month," Jeremy says. "Remember? So he'd help her get to Cosmos? But now she's helped Cosmos, so I guess she's on his side after all."

"The museum installation went in months ago," Amy says. "Do you think they knew what would happen? Got inside info from the CC Four somehow?"

"Maybe they moved her, Aim. Anyway, I'm hungry. Anybody else want lunch?"

"I do!" VB's been trailing grumpily behind them. Amy and Anna invited her to come to the SF museum so maybe she'd start understanding CC better, but Jeremy doesn't think she's been trying very hard. She seems oppressed by Seattle, overwhelmed, like a plant ripped out of its natural ground. She's clearly desperate to get back home to Reno. He wonders how much of that is her breakdown, and how much she's always been like that. Limited. Needing what she knows.

He still doesn't like her, but he feels a lot sorrier for her than he did before Mom died.

On the other hand, he really likes Seattle: all the coffee shops and buses that will actually take you places—Reno has a bus system, but it's crappy—and the energy of the streets, and the fact that he doesn't feel like a sore thumb here. There are a lot more non-whites here than in Reno. Reno's better now than when he was little, but it's still not as no-big-deal mixed as Seattle. Or San Francisco, yeah. He went there with Mom a few times, but he didn't know anyone. He was just there with Mom, which always made him feel a little self-conscious no matter what the population around him was like.

He feels guilty even thinking this way.

He loves Mom. He's grateful to Mom. He wishes more than anything that she were alive. But he'd also, more than ever, really like to get out of Reno for a while, and he's starting to feel like maybe he's actually ready to think about a move.

If Mom were still here, he thinks she'd approve.

He's fallen behind the others—VB's in the lead now, heading to the snack bar—and Amy turns to check on him. "You okay?"

"Yeah. Just thinking."

But he stops thinking about cities to think about lunch. The snack bar's pretty crappy, the usual hot dogs and chips, and VB groans. "I had a hot dog yesterday. I don't know if I can handle another so soon."

Anna laughs. "There's a little restaurant not far from here. Excellent chef. Let's go there. My treat."

The three Reno-ites, Gore-Tex-clad ducklings, follow her outside. It's still raining, but there's intermittent sun. Anna leads them a few blocks to a French bistro, a fashionably distressed hole-in-the-wall, all heavy wooden farm tables and butcher-block paper placemats, where the staff clearly knows her. They're the only people there. Amy sits down and looks around, blinking. VB picks up a menu as if it might bite her, and peers at it. When she speaks, she sounds strangled. "This is—a bit much. There must be something between this and hot dogs."

"We're here," Anna says, "and I love this place. Let me be generous. I'm not trying to atone for anything. I'm just buying lunch. Sometimes lunch is only lunch."

Jeremy picks up his menu. Anna, deftly, covers the price column with her napkin. "Don't look at that. Just look at the food."

"Okay." He does. It looks delicious: consommés and pâtés and reductions and truffle oil and artisanal cheeses. His mouth waters. "This reminds me of Fourth Street Bistro. In Reno. Mom took me there for my birthday."

Anna winces. "And that's a good memory, I hope? Jeremy, I'm not trying to be your mother—"

"Of course not. You didn't know. And even if you had. Like you said. It's just lunch. And yeah. It's a good memory."

The waiter arrives with water and warm, aromatic bread, and soft herbed butter, and cunning little bowls of yuppie olives. The four of them smooth over the social awkwardness by eating. Jeremy wishes Aunt Rosie was here, because he feels more comfortable with her than with any of the others, even Amy, but she had no interest in the museum. She went to church with Hen and Tom and Greg instead. Yesterday, when the plans were being made, Anna offered to pick up the others and bring them here.

He wonders how Mom and Anna would have gotten along, if they'd ever met. But he thinks he knows. He can just see Anna walking into the library, being polite enough but clearly viewing Mom and the other staff as The Help. He can just see Mom, afterward, rolling her eyes, hear her complaining about the Rich-Lady types. She got them in her book groups often enough. "They're not stupid, but too many of them are wearing blinders made of money, and they don't even know it. And listen to me, with all this 'they' stuff, as if those women aren't just people like the rest of us." She'd laugh and say, "Do as I say, Jer, not as I do."

But Anna *is* different. Nice enough. Generous, certainly. Really pretty smart when she talks about CC. But also from another planet, in ways Jeremy can't quite pin down, and maybe it's just the money, but maybe it's something else. He doesn't know.

He still hasn't told her about the Mom-Percy CC connection. He will tell her, he wants to tell her, but not with the others here. She's working so hard at being nice to them, and he doesn't want to drop any bombs today. They all need a break. The information will keep, like so much else.

They busy themselves with the bread and olives, and then with appetizers. Amy's ordered a chilled fruit soup that clearly delights her, and Jeremy's pretty happy with his crab cakes, although he'd have done the sauce differently. It's a ginger tomato sauce, and he isn't sure those work together. He thinks something else would be better with the ginger. Something tart and sweet. Orange zest, just a hint, maybe, so it wouldn't overpower the crab.

VB's picking at her house salad, looking miserable. Jeremy still feels sorry for her. "Hey, Prof Bellamy, you want some of my crab cake?"

She glares at him. "Would you *please* call me Veronique? Or Vera? It's what your mother called me, and you're not my student anymore."

"Yeah, okay. Sure. Would you like some crab cake?"

"No. Thank you. I'm crabby enough, wouldn't you say?" Amy giggles, and Jeremy blinks. VB tried to make a joke. Oh, Lord. And he knows he should laugh, but her delivery was so flat that he can't. "I'm sorry I'm grouchy," she says. "I want to get home, that's all."

"You all leave tomorrow?" Anna asks.

"Yes. I need to get back to my cats. Amy, have you registered for fall semester?"

She has. She reels off a string of courses which immediately makes Jeremy's ears glaze. He feels Anna's eyes on him. "And what about you, Jeremy? Are you looking forward to getting home?"

He shrugs. "I don't know. I guess. Not really. I have to figure things out. Things I don't really want to think about yet, because they're too much work." They're all looking at him. He sighs and says, "I think maybe, in a few years, or sooner if I can swing it, I want to try living in a real city. Here, or San Francisco." He looks down at the crab cake. "Maybe go to culinary school." He blinks. Actually, he thinks maybe he *does* want to do that, and it's the closest thing he's had to a plan of his own for years. Maybe forever. "But, you know, none of that right away. I have to figure out what to do with the house first. What to do with Mom's ashes. It's stupid to be hung up on that, but I am. Have been."

"Culinary school's a lot pricier than UNR," VB says, frowning.

"Yeah. I know." She thinks he's a shitty student. Well, he *has* been a shitty student.

Anna clears her throat. "When the time comes, talk to me."

VB jerks back and turns bright red. "Oh God, that wasn't what I meant. I wasn't suggesting that you—I wouldn't—I—"

"I know you weren't." Anna's voice is mild, completely matter-of-fact. "Jeremy, you know I have resources. Talk to me if I might be able to help. That's all. I'm not promising anything right now. We'll see what it looks like when we get there."

"Um," he says, but fortunately the main course comes, and they all busy themselves with their food again. Thank God for food. They share little bites of what they're eating, and Amy, teasing, asks Jeremy to critique it, and he does—cautiously, because Anna likes this place and he does, too, and he doesn't want to hurt anyone's feelings, but he does have opinions—and the chef comes over and they chat about local markets and spices and preparations, and, Jeremy has to admit, it's a hell of a lot more fun than talking about *Cranford*.

After the chef's left, Anna claps her hands. "Dessert. I want chocolate, and I'm not going to let the rest of you sit there and watch me eat it. You have to have dessert, too."

Amy nudges Jeremy with her elbow. "You could open your own restaurant. With a CC theme."

"Or Guatemalan," says VB. "If you ever decide to research the culture. That would give you a fun reason to travel there."

"Or only desserts," says Anna. "I'm definitely going for the chocolate decadence. What are the rest of you having?"

Veronique's working her way through a deliciously tangy lemon ice—the least expensive of the dessert options, because she's still appalled that Anna's showering them with charity like this—when Amy asks the question she's been dreading. "What about you, Professor Bellamy? You're going back in the fall, right?"

"Veronique," Vera says. "In this context. Unless you think you won't be able to revert to formality if you ever take one of my classes again." Why is the child even asking about this, in front of Percy Clark's mother?

Raised by wolves.

"Yes, I'm going back in the fall. I'm teaching 101 and a British lit survey." *Not* Women & Lit. She doubts she'll ever be asked to teach that again.

"I thought you wanted to retire?" Jeremy says. "Mom says you did."

Dammit, Melinda! Why did you share that with him?

"I'm working through my retirement options," Veronique says crisply, because she doesn't want to admit to money problems and then have this creepy rich woman throw money at her. Let Anna Clark find other ways to salve her conscience.

Anna frowns. "Were you hit by the downturn?"

Everyone was hit by the downturn, you nosy bitch, not that it's any of your business. Just because I offered you chocolate yesterday, when I didn't even know yet how addicted you are to it, doesn't make you my friend. "Somewhat," Veronique says, trying to sound unconcerned, "and there are also property considerations."

Jeremy, who's been working his way through a massive chunk of bread pudding, stops with his fork halfway to his mouth. "Hey."

"Hey?" Amy laughs.

"Hey yourself," Veronique says, and she's about to start talking about Elizabeth Gaskell to change the subject, but Jeremy cuts her off.

"I should've thought of this before, except I couldn't have, because I hadn't thought seriously about leaving Reno. Okay." He puts down his fork, puts one hand on Amy's shoulder and the other on Veronique's. "You two are friends. Amy and I are friends. Veronique and Mom were friends."

He doesn't consider himself my friend, Veronique thinks. Well, no, of course not. "Yes?"

"Okay. So. I have this house that's paid for, but I don't want to sell it, partly because I grew up there and partly because I want to put Mom's ashes in the garden, which means I don't want it—you know, out of the family. But I don't want to live there right now, either, and I don't want to rent it to anybody who might trash the place." He taps Veronique's shoulder. "*You* want to retire, but you're still paying for your house and you don't think you can sell it right now." He taps Amy's shoulder. "*You've* talked about finding a house to share with friends. *So*"—grinning and expansive, he gestures at both of them —"Amy and her quiet, responsible friends, who are a whole lot like nuns, honest, can move into Veronique's house and pay the mortgage. Veronique can move into Mom's house and not have to pay anything. And I can move *out* of Mom's house and go to San Francisco or wherever without worrying about strangers living in the house, and that way I'll feel comfortable putting Mom in the garden, too."

He sits back, clearly pleased with himself. "Musical houses! What do you think?"

Veronique feels dizzy. "I don't know if I *want* to live in your house. I love your house, Jeremy, but it's not mine, and it would just remind me of your mother—"

"Tell me about it."

"—and I don't want to move. I hate moving."

He waves this away. He's flushed now, excited. "We'll help you. People my age are really good at moving. It's a *free house!*"

Anna raises a finger. "Not quite free, no. Property taxes. Utilities. Insurance."

Jeremy looks taken aback, but then says, "Taxes are low in Reno. Mom always said so. You'd have to pay all those on your own house, too. Or maybe I can pay the property taxes, or the estate can. We'll talk to Tom. Amy? What do you think? V, her friends really are *very quiet*. They hardly party at all. They've never destroyed anything."

Terrific, Veronique thinks. This is worse than any scheme Anna could have suggested, because it's halfway plausible. "I have to think about it."

"Sure. Sure you do." He smiles. "But think about being there and not having to teach. Or grade. And you'll have *some* money, right? I mean, for property taxes and all that other stuff, on whichever house? And food?"

Veronique ignores this. When did her financial profile become an appropriate topic of conversation? "And where would you be living, sir? And how would you be paying for it?"

"Dunno. Haven't figured that part out yet." He picks up the fork again and dives back into the bread pudding. "It needs work, obviously."

"It's cosmic," Amy says, beaming. "Very Comradely of you, Jeremy."

Jeremy puts his fork down again. "And Aunt Rosie's house *is* paid for, I know that much, and I don't know if she could sell it, but maybe the two of you could live in Mom's house. Then she'd be less lonely without Uncle Walter."

Oh, joy. Living with Rosemary would be Veronique's idea of hell. "Jeremy, this isn't a comic book, and we're not chess pieces. I appreciate your concern, but I don't think this is the right time to have this discussion." She glares at Anna, who raises an eyebrow.

"I believe that's my cue to use the powder room. I'll pay the check on my way back. Think about places you might want to go this afternoon."

Home, Veronique thinks. My home. But she shivers. Fall's coming: change, change, and she has to go back to teaching again and has to hold it together, and she suddenly realizes, with an ache of longing, that yes, she'd infinitely rather move into Melinda's house than have to grade one more stack of undergraduate essays.

It can't happen that soon, of course. She has to teach for at least another year. Jeremy has to figure out his culinary school scheme, if indeed he still wants to do it in another six months or even two minutes. It can't happen soon, and probably it can't happen at all. It's too easy, too neat, and it can't be that easy or neat. Life doesn't work that way. She knows that. She has to stay realistic about this. But she's moved that Jeremy even offered. Melinda would be proud of him; this is something Melinda herself would have done. Something of Melinda has survived. And for that reason, if no other, Veronique feels a slight easing in her chest, and allows herself to name it hope.

*a*fter the sterile propriety of the Unitarian service, Rosemary's immensely relieved to be back in an Episcopal church. It's a pretty little place, dark wood and stained glass, with a much more diverse congregation than any in Reno. There are blacks here, Asians, a few same-sex couples of both genders—even not knowing them, you can tell they're together by how they touch each other's shoulders, how they pass the Peace to each other with kisses and long hugs—someone in a wheelchair with something that looks like cerebral palsy, lots of kids. It's a lively, happy place, clearly a healthy congregation.

Rosemary has always loved this set of readings. Abraham bargaining with God to save Sodom and Gomorrah: "For the sake of ten, I will not destroy it." Paul urging the Colossians to faithfulness: "As you have received Christ Jesus the Lord, continue to live your lives in him, rooted and built up in him and established in the faith, just as you were taught, abounding in thanksgiving." And Jesus, in the Gospel, proclaiming the power of persistence: "Ask, and it will be given you; seek, and you will find; knock, and the door will be opened for you."

Greg preaches well, talking about how sometimes it takes a lot of work to perceive God's generosity. Sometimes it feels like you have to haggle, to accept some hard bargains. Sometimes it feels like you're banging at 3 A.M. on the door of a stranger who doesn't want to get up and help you. And it especially feels that way when you're in pain: grieving, struggling with loss, trying to make sense of tragedy.

He looks directly at Hen and Rosemary and Tom as he says that. He tells a funny, bittersweet story about having to propose to his wife three times before she accepted, and notes that as much as he adores his wife, he believes that God's even kinder and more loving. And then he looks at Hen and Rosemary again. "Sometimes we just have to keep trying. The important thing is not to go away, not to lose faith, not to take another offer or try a different doorway, some other place where it costs you less but you'll never get what you need."

It's a good homily. Afterward—after the controlled chaos of coffee hour, with kids darting around adults to grab the best cookies first—Hen and Tom and Rosemary drive to Pike Place Market. Veronique's chocolate is gone. They all want more.

"I needed that sermon today," Rosemary says. "I wish Greg had preached at Percy's funeral."

Tom grunts. "The Clarks wouldn't have known what to do with it. I don't think the Sodom and Gomorrah passage would have been a pastoral inclusion. Anyway, you know funeral texts usually aren't that week's lectionary."

"I know. I didn't say it was a *realistic* wish. I'm glad we got communion today, though, even if it was fish food." Hen laughs, and Rosemary says, "Hen, how would you have handled that funeral yesterday? I've been meaning to ask you."

"Do you even do funerals for people outside the parish?" Tom asks. "I mean, I know you do them for former members nobody's seen for ten years, but total strangers?"

"Nobody's a stranger to God. That's the Episcopal take on it. If the Clarks had come to St. Phil's and asked for a funeral, I'd probably have agreed. I'd have to run it past the vestry first—"

"No," Rosemary says. "*This* funeral. You told me Anna wrote asking your prayers on the day of the service. What if she'd asked you to officiate?"

"I'd have helped her find someone in Seattle."

"What if she lived in Reno, or you lived in Seattle? What if she said she didn't want someone in Seattle? What if she really wanted *you* to do it?"

Hen scrunches up her nose. "Is that a parking space?"

"Hen! Stop changing the subject!"

It is a parking space. Hen backs in with a small crow of triumph, and they all get out and dodge raindrops until they're in the market. Tom peels away to go buy salmon for dinner, leaving Rosemary and Hen to find the chocolate. First, though, they find the craft booths: gleaming silver, skeins of woolen yarn glowing in the dim light, hand-turned wooden bowls. "I think," Hen says, peering at a display of earrings, "that I might have tried to include today's Gospel. I'd have suggested it, anyway. Because that reading doesn't just talk about God keeping promises, the opening doors and so forth. It compares divine love to human parental love. Jesus asks the parents in the crowd, 'If your daughter asks for a fish, would you give her a snake instead? If your son asks for an egg, would you give him a scorpion?' If imperfect human parents work so hard to give good gifts to their children, he says, how much more will God give us? And I'd have talked, I think, about how hard parents—most parents, anyway, and certainly the Clarks—try to love their kids, and how sometimes the kids do hideous things despite the parents' best efforts. And it's not because they did anything wrong. It's because we have free will, and sometimes we misuse it. But God loves and forgives us even when we've done hideous things, and we have to try to forgive our children, and ourselves, when they do hideous things."

Rosemary shakes her head. "So you forgive Percy?"

Hen sighs and picks up a pair of earrings, articulated silver fish with garnet eyes. "I said 'try,' Rosemary. I'm answering your question: I think that's something like what I'd have said. And then I'd have talked about how frustrating it is to knock on doors when no one's answering, and you just have to keep trying until someone does. Anna went through a lot of rejection, planning that service." She holds the fish up to her ears. "You like these?"

"I do. They're lovely."

"You think they're too flashy for church?"

"They're fish. They're fine for church. Anyway, you can wear them when you're not in church."

Hen grins. "Good. I'm buying them. Then we can look for the chocolate." While the merchant's running her credit card, she says, "I'm glad Anna didn't ask me to do the service, though. I felt for that Unitarian minister."

"You'd have done a better job than she did."

Hen shrugs. "She's younger than I am. She's probably been ordained all of ten minutes. And, you know, I'm not sure I could have even thought about doing Percy's service before I'd done Melinda's, and you can't wish having to do a service like Melinda's on anybody."

"True."

Hen decides to wear her new earrings. They find the chocolate, and spend entirely too much money on an assortment of small, heavy bags: truffles and caramels and chocolate-covered pretzels and chocolate-covered orange peel. "For the ride home tomorrow," Hen says happily, and Rosemary snorts.

"You expect there to be any left?"

Hen laughs, the silver fish swinging. They go back outside to wait in the van for Tom, passing the bag of chocolate-covered orange peel back and forth. "So," Hen says, "how did it speak to you? Greg's sermon? What resonated for you?"

Rosemary looks out the window. "What he said. Persistence through grief. Which for me is also persistence in dealing with Walter. I guess, you know, I just have to keep knocking on that door as long as it's still there, and pray that I can catch anyone home, even for five minutes." She rides a long, slow swell of sorrow, and wipes her eyes. "God, I miss Melinda. I'll be a complete mess when Walter dies, because then I'll be missing everybody at the same time. Although I did that when she died, too. But I'd counted on her to get me through losing Walter, and now she can't. Is that selfish of me?"

"Of course not." Hen squeezes her shoulder, and then holds

out a hand for the chocolate. "The rest of us will get you through it. We'll do the best we can."

"I know." Rosemary looks down at her lap. "And I think I'll be better at the hospital now. We get patients who've been staring into the void for so long they don't remember what sunlight looks like. I always felt for them, but I couldn't reach them, not even after Walter's illness. Maybe I'll be able to reach some of them, now." She shivers. "Yeah. Not anything you'd wish on anyone. I asked for fish and God gave me scorpions, or gave me both. The scorpions sure don't taste as good, but they have their own uses." She makes a face. "Give me that chocolate back, would you?"

*M*onday morning, Anna wakes up to a cold, wet nose in her face. She groans, pushes it away, and hears a mournful, muted howl from Bart. What's he doing in the bedroom, anyway?

She swings her legs out of bed, shoves her feet into slippers, puts on a robe, and heads for the kitchen, snapping her fingers for Bart to follow her. William must have left the bedroom door open, which isn't like him.

"William?" she calls. No answer. He's not in the living room or the kitchen. She does a quick tour of the rest of the house and then peers into the garage. His car's gone, but he left the dog here. Weird.

Not that weird, though, not lately. Shrugging, she goes back into the kitchen to see if he made coffee before he left. He didn't. The machine's cold, and there's an envelope leaning against it. A card.

A card?

She very deliberately turns on the coffeemaker, hands shaking only a little, and then reaches for the card. Percy didn't leave a note. Why has William left her a note?

She pulls out the card. It features Monet's water lilies on the front. Inside, William's written in his usual scrawl, *That was a fine and moving speech yesterday. You did a good job on the service. Thank you.*

Nothing else. Her stomach tightens. Oh, God. Is this William's way of telling her that now she'll have to do good job on his service, too? How long should she wait before calling the police? What—

The phone rings, and she jerks toward it, panic fluttering like wingbeats in her lungs, her veins. It's eight on a Monday morning. What—

"Anna, it's Carl. Did I wake you?"

"No," she says. Hearing from her lawyer at this hour's hardly an auspicious sign, but at least she's not hearing from the police. "I'm awake. Are you calling with bad news?"

He sighs. "William just called to let me know he's retained a divorce attorney, and recommends that you do the same. He wants it to be amicable, he says, but he thinks all the communication should go through the lawyers."

Anna laughs aloud. "Communication? What communication? He hasn't talked to me since Percy died."

"Oh, Jesus, Anna, I'm so sorry." Carl sounds more upset than she is. Right now, she's just relieved that William's alive. "And to hit you with this so soon after the funeral—"

"It's okay," she says. "Listen, I need to eat breakfast and take the dog out. I guess I have custody of Bart: William left him here. Can I call you in a few hours, to get some referrals?"

"Of course. Are you all right?"

"I am," she says. "Don't worry." And when she gets off the phone, she discovers, somewhat to her amazement, that she *is* all right. She's been expecting this for months, has been living with the dread of it even before she could consciously recognize what she feared. Now it's happened, and she feels like a boil has been lanced or a fever has broken. She feels better. You aren't supposed to make major decisions for at least a year after a major loss, but if this has to happen—and she can't see any way around it—she'd rather begin.

She knows this slightly giddy peace won't last, knows there will be all kinds of grief to work through, but right now, all she has to do is walk the dog. She gets dressed, gulps down some orange juice, puts a bagel for herself in one pocket and puppy-poop bags in the other, whistles for Bart, and clips him to his lead.

Walking down the driveway, she wonders how they'll split everything. She'd like to keep the house, and she's certainly been spending more time here than William has, but maybe that won't be possible. She'll have to work. Without the house, she could move away from Seattle, move somewhere sunnier. Arizona. Reno. She laughs again. Wouldn't Melinda's crew be surprised?

Jeremy and the others are on the road back home now, she suspects, and she's on a road, too, one long deferred and long intuited. She loves Seattle. She'll stay here if she can, if she can afford it, if she can support herself. William wants it amicable. Is alimony amicable? Does she even want it? She'll need it, for a while, until she can get on her feet, but she doesn't think she needs a moat anymore. Maybe she'll move off the island, into the city. If she can't keep the house.

She walks down the hill, Bart happily lifting his leg to all his usual trees. The sun's out, for a wonder, and it glints on the water, and she thinks as she always does about Percy, about the last time he saw this view. Will William leave her half of Percy's ashes? Will William want any of them?

She shudders, just for a moment, and Bart, heeling as obediently as he always has, looks up at her, concerned. "Okay," she says, and touches his head. "I'm okay." Percy, helping her along the path. There is no one to help her along this new one, this road to another life.

She will, she supposes, find people. Friends, lovers, business associates. She'll have to find them. That's what always happens, after divorces. She's seen enough of them to have faith in the future, even if she can't imagine what it will look like.

Bart does his business, and Anna cleans up after him. She's

chilled, now. She needs to go back, drink coffee, shower. She needs to steel herself for the draining business of calling lawyers.

But she stands by the side of the road, looking through the woods at the water. Another minute, here. Just another minute. There's a faint trail meandering between the trees, made by deer or dogs or kids, and Anna thinks again of that day in the Cascades.

And an image comes to her. She sees herself walking Bart along that trail, sees herself negotiating the difficult places, going carefully, being deliberate. She will go there soon: next weekend, maybe, this week, whenever she can get away from the legal mess. She will drive to that trailhead in the Cascades, and the dog will be with her, and she will bring Percy's ashes. And she will scatter them along the trail wherever she can, but especially in the difficult places, around tree roots and rocks.

Percy helped her over those patches when he was alive. Maybe that was the only good thing he ever did, but he did it for her, and now he will do something else for her. Because she has survived his death, and Melinda Soto's death—because she has survived all the doubts and the questions and the tears—she knows she can survive a divorce, too.

It's a small lesson, the tiniest of gifts, but it's something. Anna breathes, tugs at Bart's leash, and turns. She walks back up the hill, back to the house, back to the ruins of her marriage and the remains of her child.

Melinda lies in her hotel room in a spreading, sticky pool of blood. The blood's warm, but she's cold. The boy who just left the room has beaten and brutalized her, has stabbed her. She tried to reason with him and failed; she tried to fight him and failed. She tried to scream and couldn't, because he'd gagged her with a towel.

It all seems very far away now. As she lies there, she knows she is dying, and she is not afraid. She is only afraid if she remembers what just happened to her: the boy from the pool, the boy who was so polite this morning, grown feral and ferocious, forcing his way into her room, forcing his way into her body with his own flesh and then with bright cold metal. "Don't scream or I'll kill you," and she couldn't, because of the towel, but he did anyway.

When she remembers that, she is terrified.

So she tries to remember other things: her son, her friends, her job. All of that frightens her again, because she knows she'll never again see the people she loves, knows they'll grieve and grasp for meaning. She knows they'll suffer. She doesn't want them to. She can't help them. She knows they will help each other and help Jeremy, but that's not enough. Her inability to comfort her child clenches her hands into fists. Her helplessness hurts more than anything her murderer did to her, because what he did is already over, and this new pain has just begun, is omnipresent.

To escape it, she remembers people who are already dead, who cannot feel pain anymore. Her father, tying fishing flies. Her mother, baking cookies.

Where Melinda lies on the hotel room carpet, the blood a lukewarm lake now, she can see a piece of the sky through the window above her. She sees a glowing whiteness. Melinda sees the moon. It is not full—it is partial, broken—but it is very bright.

And Melinda, at the end of her life, remembers the beginning, remembers the first time she saw the moon. She must have only been a baby then. She remembers how perfect it was, remembers the wonder it awakened in her.

She remembers the moon before it was broken, before she saw its flaws and holes. She knows she has mended it at last, performed the task she has been joking about her whole life, almost. The moon, in memory, is beautiful.

She still remembers the brutal boy, still remembers her friends, her job, her child, but all of that is receding, along with panic and worry and pain. All of that is very far away now, and the moon is very close, so close that she could touch it if only she could lift her hands.

The white light grows, and spreads, and swallows her. Melinda no longer has hands, or a body, or the memory of loss. She dissolves into the brightness, and then there is only the moon shining in the window, onto emptiness.

ACKNOWLEDGMENTS

I wish to thank Tor Books for asking me to write this novel, and Patrick Nielsen Hayden for editing it. As always, I am grateful to Kay McCauley, who is not only my literary agent but a dear friend.

Sharon Walbridge, Jim Winn, and Gary Meyer read and commented on an earlier, very different version of this story. When I decided to rewrite the novel from scratch, Jim Winn—brilliant pianist and composer, one of Entropy's worthiest adversaries—gave me a profoundly helpful pep talk.

Gary Meyer, eagle-eyed editor and beloved husband, has read every word of every version of this book, multiple times.

Christina MacDonald did an excellent job of copyediting.

Danielle Mayabb is the original source of Rosemary's metaphor of Christ as compass.

Todd Renwick of the University of Nevada, Reno Police Services, answered my questions about how the investigation into Melinda's murder would be likely to proceed.

Eric Heidecker briefed me on the availability of junk food in Nixon, Nevada.

Liz Lasater, Sheila Young, Christian Lindke, Melissa Walton, Lucy Larsen, Teresa Poulson, and Nancy Espin—all better traveled than I— confirmed my description of the terrain between Reno and Klamath Falls.

Victor Montejo's *The Bird Who Cleans the World and Other Mayan Fables* is a real book, and was an invaluable resource.

I am indebted to the University of Nevada, Reno, for the boon of a professional development leave from my teaching duties, during which I finished this book.

Thank you all. As always, all errors and infelicities are mine alone.